A CENTURY
OF STORIES
NEW HANOVER COUNTY PUBLIC LIBRARY
1906-2006

TAYLOR SMITH

SLIM TO NONE

MIRA®

ISBN-13: 978-0-7783-2332-7
ISBN-10:   0-7783-2332-3

SLIM TO NONE

www.MIRABooks.com

Printed in U.S.A.

First Printing: September 2006
10 9 8 7 6 5 4 3 2 1

ACKNOWLEDGMENTS

My deepest thanks to Sheriff Lee Baca for free and open access to the resources of the Los Angeles Sheriff's Department. Special thanks also to Homicide Detective Paul Delhauer and Deputy William Moulder for their patient and excellent guidance. Retired Homicide Detective Melinda Hearne was also great about answering my dumb questions. Deepest appreciation also to Linda McFadden (the plot queen), and Orange County Sheriff's Deputy Gary Bale. And where would novelists be without fabulous investigative reporters whose work fuels the background research? I'm particularly indebted to Miles Corwin, P. W. Singer, Anne Garrels and William Langewiesche. Finally, I can't fail to mention Kayla Williams, whose wonderful memoir *Love My Rifle More Than You* taught me so much about being a western woman in Iraq and in the macho culture of the U.S. Army.

Finally, thanks to my agent, Philip Spitzer; Miranda Stecyk, my editor (A.K.A. "Tijuana Mama") and all the great people at MIRA—a joy to work with, one and all. And last but not least, Richard, Kate and Anna, the home team—without you, none of it means a darn thing.

This book is dedicated with love to
Cathy (Couturier) Towle,
who reminds us always why family is so wonderful.

PART ONE

The Rent-an-Army War

*"You cannot have trade without war,
nor war without trade."*

—Jan Coen, Governor General
Dutch East Indies Company (c. 1619)

*"Hiring outsiders to fight your battles
is as old as war itself."*

—P.W. Singer: *Corporate Warriors:
The Rise of the Privatized Military Industry* (2003)

1

Tuesday, August 26, 2003
Hamra Hotel: Baghdad, Iraq

The tinny jangle of the ancient black telephone next to the bed startled Hannah. Jumping to her feet from her crouched position by her duffel bag on the floor, she leapt over her desert camo jacket and bulletproof Kevlar vest and caught the phone on the second bleat.

"Hannah Nicks," she said, wincing at the sharp pinch at her earlobe. It was caught between the receiver and one of the small gold earrings she'd forgotten to take off. Hooking the phone into the crook of her shoulder, she withdrew first the left, then the right stud and dropped them into the toiletry bag on the night table. The hotel room was furnished with battered blond Scandinavian furniture, an oddly modern contrast to the flood-lit palm trees and onion-domed mosque outside her window.

It was after 11:00 p.m. but the temperature inside and out was still hot enough to soften the unlit candles scattered on every available surface of her room. She'd left matches strategically placed next to each one in anticipation of the next inevitable power outage. For now, the electricity was functioning, for all the good it did. The air conditioner was on the fritz and the light situation wasn't much better. Two of the lamps in her room were missing bulbs, while that in the third couldn't be higher than forty watts. Rummaging through her duffel bag, hunting for her good luck charm, Hannah had finally resorted to her high-powered Maglite to see where she'd stashed the tiny velvet drawstring bag that held Gabe's first baby tooth.

She'd already showered—with tepid and slightly brackish water, but she wasn't complaining. The water supply, too, was intermittent, and she'd been lucky to get a chance to clean up at all after the long flight from the States. After the shower, she'd plaited her dark hair into a thick rope that reached almost to her shoulder blades, then dressed in desert camouflage pants, khaki T-shirt and sturdy tan hiking boots.

Losing the little gold earrings was the last vestige of her femininity set aside. In the rent-an-army business that employed her these days, dressing for success took on a whole new meaning. She might enjoy being a girl, as the old song went, but right now, she needed to be in professional mode.

"Ladwell here," the voice on the phone said.

Sean Ladwell was a Brit, ex-Special Air Services, that nation's equivalent of the Green Berets. Pushing forty—a decade older than Hannah and looking twice that, with his ruddy, wind-weathered skin—Ladwell was rumored to have seen private army action in Sudan, Angola, the Congo and Afghanistan since the end of his stint with the SAS. This was apparently Ladwell's third sortie into Iraq on a short-term private security gig.

Currently, he was team leader of a small commando unit assembled by Brandywine International, a private military corporation headquartered in Alexandria, Virginia. The assignment this time out: to extract two family members of a London-based Iraqi intellectual. Washington was courting the exiled academic to help form the new, post-Saddam regime. Rescuing his relatives, who'd become trapped in the war-torn Sunni Triangle, might go a long way to cementing the man's cooperation.

"We head out at midnight," Ladwell said. "Meet up in the armory downstairs at twenty-three hundred hours to collect your ordnance and go over the plan once more."

"Roger," Hannah said. "I'm good to go."

It had taken only twenty-one days for Baghdad and the thugocracy of Saddam Hussein to crumble before the American-led coalition, the latest in a long line of invaders to this region. Once called Mesopotamia, the world's first great civilization, the country had been conquered repeatedly over the centuries—by Persians, Greeks, Arabs, Turks and the British. Saddam's repressive rule was, in the end, nothing but an ugly flash in the historic pan, but building a lasting peace in this country would be a tricky, maybe impossible, venture. This was not an easy region to rule.

Brandywine had several contracts on the go in-country and maintained its own private airline, called Chardonair, to support its operations here and elsewhere. Brandywine's employees were among an estimated twenty thousand private contractors who'd streamed into Iraq over the past few months, looking to reap a share of the riches in this latest corporate El Dorado. The company was running so many protective and assault teams in-country that it had taken over and fortified a large storeroom in the basement of the Hamra Hotel to warehouse a cache of rifles, handguns, fragmentation grenades, rocket launchers, flash-bangs and the other weaponry and supplies needed to keep its resupply lines open. Official U.S. military personnel might be short on bulletproof vests and armor to reinforce their vehicles, but the private contractors lacked for nothing.

"There's a helipad a few blocks from here in the Green Zone," Ladwell said. "That's where we'll rendezvous with the chopper."

"Got it," Hannah said. "I'm just going to take a run up to the roof to use the sat phone, but otherwise I'm ready."

"A satellite call now? Is that necessary?"

"It's just a quick one to my son back in the States," Hannah replied, not that it was any of his business. It was superstition on her part, just like the good luck charm she always carried on these missions. If she died, she wanted one of the last voices she heard to be her eight-year-old son's, and she wanted Gabriel to know she'd been thinking of him at the end. Making that potentially final call was part of her pre-op ritual. If you anticipated disaster, it wouldn't happen—that's what she told herself. In the past, it had been the unexpected nightmares, like losing custody of her child, that had blindsided her. Now, she never doubted the worst was possible, but if she visualized it, maybe she could dodge it.

"You can't mention where you are," Ladwell warned her.

Well, du-uh...

"I know that. This isn't my first time to the prom, you know."

"So they tell me." The team leader's voice betrayed the same skepticism he'd shown from the moment the team was first assembled five days earlier, despite the fact that at twenty-eight, Hannah was neither its youngest nor its least experienced member.

It wasn't personal, she knew. Ladwell, like most of the ex-special forces grunts she worked with, couldn't seem to shake the military mindset that women didn't belong on the front lines of battle. This team and its mission had no official status, however, so the usual rules didn't apply. The whole point of hiring private contractors was to allow governments to distance themselves from unpalatable tasks. The real battle, as far as the Washington political spin doctors were concerned, was the public relations battle. Passing messy jobs to off-the-radar civilian contractors made for handy deniabil-ity later if things turned sticky.

Despite Ladwell's doubts, Hannah was no hothouse flower. She might have dark-eyed, exotic looks and a lithe, athletic figure on which even a T-shirt and cargo pants hung well enough to attract leering glances, but she'd spent six years as a patrol and under-cover cop on the mean streets of Los Angeles, and then the last year and a half doing freelance security work. She didn't need cod-dling and she was more than capable of taking care of herself when things got hairy.

She also knew her way around the Middle East, having spent nearly every summer of her youth in Beirut, Dubai and Amman with her paternal grandparents and other overseas Greek relatives who ran various family businesses in the region, some of which dated back to the turn of the last century.

"We are descendants of Ulysses," Grandpa Demetrious liked to say on those evenings when Hannah would sit with him and her grandmother on their terrace overlooking Beirut's Corniche, a warm Mediterranean breeze stirring the papery red bougainvillea and fragrant white jasmine that draped the balcony trellises. "Our family has always wandered the sea in search of its fortune. Some-times the wind blows us good luck, sometimes not so good, but we sail on nevertheless."

Hannah's personal wind of fortune had blown her back to the Middle East once more when Brandywine management had over-ruled Ladwell's objections to having a woman on the team. Han-nah had done work for them before, she'd handled herself well, and with so much security business opening up these days, resources were stretched thin. And then, there was the clincher: she was the only Arabic speaker in their freelancer database who was available when the call came. Since the contract specs called for at least one member who spoke the language, either she was in or they didn't get the job. End of story.

"I'll be downstairs in twenty minutes," she told Ladwell.

"Don't be late."

Hannah scowled. *Yeah, right.* Like she'd be sitting back, eating bonbons and watching her nail polish dry while the rest of the team got its kit together and headed out.

Dropping the receiver back in the cradle, she grabbed her Global-Sat phone and headed out into the hallway and up the stairs to the hotel's rooftop to make her call to Gabriel.

2

Boston, Massachusetts

Beantown was in the grip of a stifling summer heat wave that crackled with the electric charge of an imminent thunderstorm. Sweaty, lethargic pedestrians dragged themselves through the streets, ignoring blue-black clouds that had shown up like violent bruises on the heavy-laden sky. It was too hot to hurry for shelter, too humid to care about the approaching afternoon tempest.

Patrick Burton Fitzgerald stood high overhead at the windows of his fifty-third-floor offices in the John Hancock Tower, gazing down on Trinity Church, the Charles River and the gracious shops and tree-lined avenues of Boston's Back Bay neighborhood. The Hancock office complex was entirely encased in glass, so that the windows on which he rested his clenched fists ran floor-to-ceiling, wall-to-wall.

Fitzgerald had never considered himself a violent man. At the moment, however, he trembled with the kind of rage that could spark murder. If he got his hands on the bastard who had ordered his daughter's kidnapping, he would cut his throat without hesitation or regret. How dare these people use Amy as a pawn in their power games?

Fitzgerald wasn't naïve. He knew that Americans were less than universally loved in some parts of the world, and he could sometimes even understand why that might be. He wasn't some ugly American who thought that U.S. citizenship gave an automatic right to megalomania. He recognized that other people might interpret facts differently than his compatriots, and that other countries' national interests might not always dovetail with those of the United States. Some conflicts were inevitable.

Unlike many of his business peers, he had grave doubts about the current campaign in Iraq. Although he hadn't joined street marches to protest the war, he had made phone calls to members of Congress and other friends in the administration to express his concern that the legitimate hunt for Osama bin Laden and others responsible for acts of terror against America was being hijacked by an obsessive preoccupation with Saddam Hussein who, for all his brutality, hardly posed the threat to this country that other bad actors out there did.

Fitzgerald was a moderate Republican, economically conservative but not without a sense of *noblesse oblige.* He considered himself cosmopolitan, politically astute and culturally sensitive. In addition to numerous domestic charities, he donated significant sums to international refugee assistance, Third World education and health care for the planet's poorest wretches. Fitzgerald and his wife Katherine had also raised their five children to understand their responsibility to give back to a world that had been uncommonly generous to the Fitzgeralds. In light of the disaster that had befallen them now, however, he found himself rethinking the wisdom of that approach. Had they somehow gone overboard with Amy, their youngest?

A brutal rage seized him once more. If he weren't so wretched with fear, he might be appalled at having been reduced to the same level of animal passion as the terrorists who'd taken his daughter. To hell with civility, however. He wanted them all dead.

Most of all, he wanted Amy home safe.

She was a medical doctor. After completing her studies at Johns Hopkins, Amy had done her residency at a tough inner-city Baltimore E.R. After that, Fitzgerald and his wife had been hoping she'd move on to something a little less risky. Instead, when the International Red Cross put out a call for medical personnel to help rebuild the battered health care system in post-Saddam Iraq, Amy was quick to volunteer her services, signing up before her parents could express their misgivings.

Fitzgerald could almost hear her laughing voice. "Come on, Dad! You know what you've always said—to whom much is given, much is expected. And I've been given a lot, starting with great parents." Her mischievous eyes sparkled, making it impossible for him to remain upset with her for long. "I'll be fine. You worry too much."

Now, she was a prisoner—or worse, Fitzgerald thought, a knot tightening in his gut. There'd been no word from her captors since she'd been taken from a Red Crescent clinic north of Baghdad five days earlier. No ransom demand, none of the usual ranting, cliché-ridden communiqués ordering the withdrawal of American forces. Nor had there been any credible response to the million-dollar reward for her safe return that Fitzgerald had posted two days ago. Of course, the crazies and fraud artists had crawled out of the slime pool in quick enough time, forcing him and his advisors to sift through reams of deceitful, bizarre and mean-spirited messages, looking for the one that might provide a genuine lead or ray of hope. From Amy's captors, however, there'd been nothing but total, bloody silence.

What kind of political cause justified attacking a medical clinic and kidnapping a young doctor whose only reason for being in their country in the first place was to help rebuild it after the long, dark nightmare of Saddam's reign? Amy didn't have to be there. She'd gone in to help the sick, the wounded and the poor. How did that make her a target for terrorists?

Fitzgerald gazed down on the cruciform shape of Trinity Church. If the glass that held him back were suddenly to vanish, he would plummet down and be impaled like an insect on the spire that topped the cathedral's central tower. It couldn't possibly be worse than the agony he was going through now—sheer, gut-wrenching terror. Never in his entire sixty years had he felt so helpless.

He exhaled a shuddering sigh and turned back to his massive, burled walnut desk, willing the phone to ring. It was nearly an hour since he'd put in the latest call to a highly placed source in the administration in Washington. Why hadn't it been returned? They were certainly quick enough off the mark when campaign fundraising time rolled around.

The law offices of Fitzgerald-Revere occupied the entire fifty-third floor of the John Hancock Tower. Softly lit and trimmed out in warm woods and buffed marble, the suite smelled of leather and lemon oil. The deep-carpeted corridors and rich furnishings fairly hummed with the subtle but unmistakable message that behind these heavy doors and silk-papered walls, powerful people carried out important business, defining law and business practices that would guide the nation for decades to come.

To facilitate its extensive commercial and government work, Fitzgerald-Revere had branch offices in New York and Washington, but the firm's headquarters had always been in Boston, since it was here that the founders' family roots had first been set down. Clients could be forgiven for assuming that those roots went back to the

American Revolution, if not the Mayflower itself, given the name "Revere" on the firm's letterhead. Nor did the partners go out of their way to disabuse anyone of the notion that the "Fitzgeralds" in Fitzgerald-Revere were the same ones whose family tree intertwined with that of the Kennedys.

In fact, however, the founding Revere had originally been a Reinhardt who had legally changed his too-German-sounding name about the time that Kaiser Wilhelm's troops began mowing down young American manhood in the trenches of World War I. And if old Ernest Fitzgerald, the other co-founder of the now-venerable firm, had no DNA in common with the man who was later to become President John Fitzgerald Kennedy, neither did he have to answer for the kind of Prohibition-era rum-running shenanigans that underpinned the wealth of that other prominent Boston family. Instead, Ernest Fitzgerald had been an Irish potato famine descendant who'd made his fortune by dint of hard work, a brilliant, precedent-setting legal mind and astute deal-making.

There was no longer a Revere (much less a Reinhardt) in the firm of Fitzgerald-Revere, but Ernest's son, Patrick, was the current senior partner of the firm which had opted to keep its original name, with that convenient if misleading cachet.

Sick of waiting, incapable of turning his attention to anything else, Fitzgerald picked up the phone and punched in his secretary's extension.

She answered immediately. "Yes, sir?"

"Still nothing from Myers?"

Evan Myers, White House deputy chief of staff, had been a junior associate at Fitzgerald-Revere when Patrick Fitzgerald had introduced him to the former governor of Texas, then given him leave of absence with full pay while he ran the northeastern office of the governor's first presidential campaign. Since then, and in short order, Myers had risen to stratospheric heights of power. Up to now, his former boss had never called in the marker. Fitzgerald rarely did, preferring to exercise influence subtly through ongoing access and dialogue rather than the tit-for-tat trading of favors. Now, however, the time for subtlety was over. It was payback time.

"I tried calling Mr. Myers again about ten minutes ago," his secretary said, "but apparently he's still in a meeting."

"Damn."

"His office did promise that he'd get right back to you as soon as it wrapped. Also…" she added, her voice hesitant.

"What?"

"Mrs. Fitzgerald called a while ago."

"Why didn't you put her through?"

"She didn't want to bother you. She just wondered if you'd heard anything."

Fitzgerald sank down in his leather chair and leaned forward on his desk, resting his forehead in his free hand. "I told her I'd be calling Evan this morning."

"Yes, sir, that's what she said. She just wanted to know if you'd spoken to him and if there was any news."

Poor Katherine, Fitzgerald thought. This was even harder on her than it was on him. He at least had the office, where he could go and pretend to be busy.

He didn't bother telling her about the frustrating calls they'd been getting from crackpots and fortune hunters looking to claim that million-dollar reward. Since there was nothing to report from his calls to Washington either, Fitzgerald could do nothing but tippy-toe around his wife, terrified of saying or doing something that would set off the howls of rage and grief they both felt—terrified they might lash out at each other simply because there was no one else to pummel or scream at in their impotent fury.

Katherine would have been sitting at home all morning, unable, like him, to do anything or step away from the phone for fear of missing that one critical call that would bring news about Amy. Reluctant, as well, to ask what else Patrick had done today for fear of sounding critical, as if he didn't care enough to pull out all the stops to bring their daughter home. Fitzgerald himself was afraid to say anything that might get his wife's hopes up, or of saying too little and plunging her even deeper into despair. In the end, he said little or nothing, skulking around with what must seem like stoic reserve at best and, at worst, like cruel indifference.

Behind him, a searing flash of lightning suddenly ripped open the sky and a sharp crack of thunder rattled the windows. Bullet-sized raindrops splattered against the glass.

This wasn't how he'd seen himself spending his golden years, Fitzgerald thought. Now, if anything happened to Amy, there would be no golden years. Only grief and rage to his last pained breath.

3

Baghdad, Iraq

Hannah was in a hurry to make her call and get down to the weapons locker before the team leader started making any cracks about the hazards of working with women, but she opened the hotel's rooftop door cautiously, one hand resting on the gun holstered at her waist. It was her personal weapon, a Beretta nine millimeter semi-automatic, just like the one she'd been trained to use when she became a cop. No matter what equipment her employer made available, she never went out on a job without her own gun, the one she kept cleaned and oiled, the one she knew would never fail in a pinch.

That kind of security was especially critical here. Only a fool walked around Baghdad unarmed. Insurgents and snipers had a habit of popping up at the most inconvenient times. No point in getting shot stupidly.

The graveled rooftop was in darkness, lit only by the ambient light of the surrounding city. She stepped cautiously over the threshold, keeping the door propped open behind her in case she needed to beat a quick retreat, pausing to let her eyes adjust to the dark.

A low murmur sounded from different directions around her, the words indistinguishable but overlapping, the voices clearly engaged in separate conversations. She squinted until she made out four figures scattered around the rooftop, all of them up there for the same reason she was—to get a clear shot at one of the orbiting communications satellites that would bounce their telephone calls to far-flung home bases.

Suddenly, the night air shook with the boom of a mortar round landing somewhere nearby. Conversations paused, then went on as if nothing has happened. Hannah smiled grimly. They were a gutsy bunch, these people who chose to work in the world's hot spots.

The figure closest to her she recognized, their paths having crossed in previous strife-torn locales. The woman worked for National Public Radio, and by the sound of it, she was calling in a story. Spotting Hannah, the reporter gave her a wave.

Hannah nodded back and closed the door to the stairwell, heading for her own isolated patch to place her call. She found an empty corner and set her satellite phone case down on the low wall that ran the perimeter of the rooftop. Then, she paused again as the scents of the city rose to meet her.

There was a particular smell to the Middle East, once as familiar and comforting as her grandmother's cooking. Even now, years since those summer visits, the smell of lemons and oranges, garlic and ginger, or olive groves and the sea instantly sent her back in her mind to a safe, warm place where loving arms had always opened to welcome her.

Here in landlocked Baghdad, however, there were no salty sea breezes to temper the desert heat or damp down the powder-fine, pervasive yellow sand that insinuated itself into ears and noses and every other bodily crevice. And if the smell of spices and cooking fires drifted on the night air as they did in so many other cities of

Hannah's memory, here the scent was tinged with the acrid sting of weapons fire and explosives recently detonated.

Hannah ducked low behind the parapet as she flicked on the sat phone, directing the antenna southwest toward the Indian Ocean regional satellite. Leaning back against the wall, she scanned nearby rooftops for possible snipers as she dialed the Los Angeles number of her ex-husband.

Normally, in the Middle East's hot summers, parents and children gravitated to rooftops and balconies in the evening, dragging out mattresses to make their nighttime beds, eager to catch the slightest breeze. These days, however, sleeping outdoors in Baghdad could prove suicidal. Four months after the capital had fallen to coalition forces and major hostilities had been declared over, the streets were still deserted and dangerous at night. No one ventured out after curfew except military patrols and the insurgents trying to kill them. Even peeking out a taped-up window could invite a bullet or rocket-propelled grenade.

Hannah glanced at her watch. It was late afternoon back in L.A. Gabe had been attending a summer day camp in the Santa Monica mountains, but it had finished a week earlier. Now he was supposed to be enjoying a few lazy days before heading off to third grade at Dahlby Hall, the exclusive private school he attended, where classes were due to resume the Tuesday after Labor Day. As always, Hannah's presence at his first day of school was neither required nor encouraged.

She closed her eyes as a wave of guilt and anger passed over her. It wasn't right that another woman got to see her child over these milestones. For two years now, Cal's wife had been taking Gabe to his dentist appointments, his soccer games, his play dates and his friends' birthday parties. Christie had been the one to read him the Harry Potter stories before tucking him into bed. It was Christie his teachers had called when Gabe had broken his arm in a fall from a schoolyard jungle gym.

When she was back in L.A., Hannah had her son on weekends, for two weeks in the summer and for alternate holidays, but how much longer would even that unsatisfying schedule last? Already she felt pressured to relinquish her visitation days on those occasions when Gabe was pulled between her and a chance at doing something special with his friends. It was no use making him feel guilty about it. That way lay only resentment. What was going to happen when he hit his teens and had a girlfriend or played team sports? How eager then would he be to pack up his bag and move for the weekend to his mother's little condo across the city?

On the other side of the world, she heard the phone ring in Cal and Christie's Mulholland Drive mansion. It picked up on the third ring and a Spanish-accented voice said, "Hello, Nicks residence."

The satellite connection was as clear as if Hannah were calling from next door. She pictured Cal and Christie's housekeeper standing by the phone in their massive granite and travertine kitchen. It overlooked a sprawling hillside garden with an infinity swimming pool that seemed to drop off the edge of the earth.

"Hello, Maria. This is Hannah, Gabe's mother. Is he there?"

"Oh, hello, Miss Hannah. No, he's not, I'm sorry," the housekeeper said. "He just left with Mrs. Nicks to get some new shoes and his school uniforms."

Even now, three years after Cal's remarriage, it still grated to hear someone else besides his mother called "Mrs. Nicks." It wasn't that Hannah had an emotional attachment to her ex-husband's name. She'd seriously considered going back to Demetrious after the divorce, but in the end, had decided against it. It wasn't just the paperwork hassle. Sharing a name with her son seemed more important than severing that link to the man who'd cheated on her and then dumped her. God knew, she shared little enough with Gabe, the way things had worked out.

"They should be back in a couple of hours," the housekeeper said. "Would you like Gabriel to call you when he gets in?"

Damn, damn, damn.

"No, I'm out of town on business and I'm going to be out of touch for a while. I'll have to call back. Could you tell him I called and said I love him?"

"Yes, of course. I am sorry you missed him," the housekeeper said.

"How's he doing?"

"Oh, very good. He had some friends here for a sleepover last night. They put up the tent in the backyard and slept out there." Maria laughed. "Mookie wanted to sleep with them, but the boys put her out. She had gone into the pool with them earlier and she was getting their sleeping bags all wet. And she smelled, Gabriel said."

"Ah, yes, the ripe odor of wet border collie," Hannah said, smiling. The puppy had been Cal and Christie's gift on Gabe's sixth birthday two years ago—a bribe, maybe, or a consolation prize. Lose your mom, gain a dog. A fair trade, right?

Whatever it was—the dog, the fabulous house, the new school and many friends—the strategy had obviously worked. Although Gabe had originally been unhappy with the changed custody arrangements, crying to move back with his mother, he clearly considered the Mulholland Drive mansion his home now and no longer even mentioned going back to living full-time with Hannah. Though he assured her he understood why the change had been necessary, she couldn't help feeling she'd let him down—and that once more Cal, damn him, had ended up looking like the hero.

Hannah had met Calvin Nicks during her freshman year at UCLA. Barely eighteen years old when she arrived in Los Angeles from her parents' home outside Chicago, she'd been swept off her feet by the handsome pre-law senior who lived down the hall from her dorm room. Being young and on her own for the first time was no excuse for her incredible stupidity about practical matters like birth control when she'd fallen in love with Cal. She might have come from a sheltered background in an immigrant family, but she'd grown up in the freewheeling 1980s, for crying out loud, not ancient Greece. What a dope.

When she'd discovered she was pregnant, Cal had been no more eager than she to consider the possibility of a termination. Whatever happened later, he had loved her then, she was pretty sure. To marry her and provide for their child, he'd been ready to give up his dream of law school and becoming a criminal prosecutor, but Hannah couldn't let him do that. Instead, she'd dropped out and taken a job as a dispatcher with the Los Angeles Sheriff's Department, working right up to her delivery date, then going back to night shifts three months later while Cal stayed home to study and take care of Gabriel.

Maybe the drift had started then, with the two of them coming and going from their little apartment on completely opposite schedules. Or maybe it was when she decided to take up an offer to enter the police academy. Thanks to her cosmopolitan family, she spoke three languages in addition to English—Greek, Arabic and passable high-school Spanish. That made her too valuable an asset to waste on the dispatch desk, the sheriff's department personnel management decided.

Had she loved police work too much and Cal not enough? Did he resent the excitement of a career that put her on the street and then into undercover work in record time? Despite the claims he made later during the custody hearing, she'd been conscientious about being there for Gabe and juggling her schedule as much as possible to meet his needs. At the end of the day, though, maybe too many of her husband's needs had gone unmet. Maybe she had to take some of the blame when he drifted into a series of affairs, first with a fellow student, then some miscellaneous women he met in his first job at the district attorney's office, and finally with Christie Day, the local television news anchor who became his second wife. But even if Hannah accepted some of the blame for the end of the marriage, that didn't mean that Cal had had the right to jump at the first opportunity to steal her son.

If only the courts had agreed.

It was an undercover job, a major drug, arms and money laundering sting carried out in cooperation with the FBI, DEA and ATF, that had done her in, putting the final nail in the coffin. She and Cal had been divorced for nearly two years by then, and he'd left his job at the district attorney's office and gone over to the dark side, working for a high-end defense firm with a stable of bad-boy clients. She'd been working long and irregular hours. With no family around to provide backup care and less than flexible babysitting arrangements, she hadn't been in a position to turn down Cal and Christie's offer to keep Gabe full-time for the few summer weeks the sting operation was expected to last. Christie had even rearranged her schedule at the TV station, taking the crack-of-dawn news shift in order to be home by 9:00 a.m. to care for Gabe while Cal was at work. In retrospect, Hannah realized, it had all been part of Cal's master plan, but at the time, she'd been absurdly grateful.

It didn't help that a few weeks had turned into four months as the sting operation dragged on and on. By the time it ended and the case went to trial, Gabe had already been enrolled at Dahlby Hall, made friends and begun to settle into a new routine with no need for the kind of outside caretakers that Hannah had to rely on. Yet even then, Hannah thought, with Cal determined to petition the court to reverse their original custody arrangements and having the money and the legal connections to press the matter until he got his way, she might have kept her son.

The bomb had ended her hopes. Planted by one of the defendants in the sting, who'd somehow discovered the identity of the undercover cop set to testify against him, the explosive had blown up more than her little house in Los Feliz. It had also destroyed any chance of convincing the courts she was the better parent to provide a secure and stable environment for a child. Even Hannah, shaken to the core by the assassin's near-miss of her and Gabe, had conceded that, barring a lottery win, there was no way she could afford the kind of advantages Cal and Christie could offer her son.

Most people thought it was the events of September 11, 2001 that had pushed Hannah out of the sheriff's department and into the freelance security game, but the truth was, it was sheer financial need. She made nearly five times her police salary doing the kind of work she was doing now. She was on track with a plan that would allow her, if she were very careful, to take several years off and devote herself full-time to her son's needs without having to worry about where the grocery money would come from. She had a real shot at petitioning for a review of her case, she thought—if only she could survive long enough to see her game plan to fruition....

4

Washington, D.C.

Evan Myers felt his cell phone vibrate inside the breast pocket of his subtly pinstriped, two-thousand-dollar navy-blue suit. He silently cursed both the interruption and the twitch of anxiety it set off in his gut.

He was perched on one of Richard Stern's low, armless visitors' chairs, forced—by design, he was certain—to gaze up at the older man who occupied the massive leather chair on the business side of a broad oak desk. As Myers pulled out his phone and flipped it open, he couldn't fail to notice the irritation that flickered across Stern's lined face. Myers hoped his own expression didn't reveal how that made him feel—like a misbehaving schoolboy caught passing notes.

Not even his Armani suit could quite overcome the youthful impression cast by Myers's slight, five-foot-eight stature, his thick mop of red hair and his rosy, puckish face. He'd just passed his thirty-sixth birthday, had graduated *summa cum laude* from Yale Law School, and had fast-tracked with the prestigious Boston firm of Fitzgerald-Revere. Now, as White House deputy chief of staff, his carrot-topped head could often be spotted in close proximity to the president during press scrums and state visits. Yet in spite of all that, Myers still found himself being carded by clueless bouncers at trendy Washington watering holes. It was unbelievably irritating.

As for Richard Stern, the man on the other side of the desk, his demeanor was as humorless as his name. With a shock of steel-gray hair and flint-colored eyes behind rimless glasses, the assistant national security advisor had a reputation for ruthlessness and a background as sketchy as his current mandate seemed to be. Stern was portly in girth and close to sixty years of age, yet there was nothing avuncular about him. Having spent most of his adult life swimming in the murky back channels of covert operations, he had a sharklike slipperiness and a corresponding cold disdain for any poor sap whose blood he scented.

Stern and his small gang of handpicked associates occupied a suite of first-floor offices at the northeast corner of the Old Executive Office Building at 17th Street and Pennsylvania Avenue, adjacent to the White House. A five-story, white, Empire-style monstrosity that Mark Twain had deemed the ugliest building in America, the OEOB had been the site of numerous watershed events in U.S. history, as well as some notable scandals—cursed, perhaps, by the ghost of its architect, who committed suicide over his much-maligned creation. Built in the late 1800s and originally called the State, War and Navy Building, the OEOB's ornate rooms had been at the center of all of the country's early international dealings. Here, in 1898, America declared war on Spain and then, two months later, signed a treaty of peace. More than a thousand other international treaties had been signed on behalf of America in its ornate halls, including the Treaty of Versailles, which ended World War I, and the 1942 United Nations Declaration.

In recent decades, with White House office space at a premium and much in demand by politicos hovering at the hub of power like flies at a sugar bowl, the neighboring building had been housing administration overflow as well as a few power brokers who deliberately sought to maintain a lower profile. In the late 1980s, Colonel Oliver North had secretly orchestrated the Iran-Contra affair out of Room 392 of the OEOB. In a failed bid to keep her boss from going to jail over his criminal dealings, Colonel North's secretary had shredded incriminating documents in a basement cubbyhole of the same building—documents detailing illegal sales of U.S. arms to Iran and the equally illegal diversion of those proceeds to President Ronald Reagan's favorite "freedom fighters," the antigovernment Contras of Nicaragua.

With so much tradition, both grandiose and disreputable, behind it, it was little wonder that a figure such as Richard Stern would have chosen to establish his lair in the OEOB.

The entire White House office complex was surrounded by blastproof concrete barriers, high wrought-iron fences, armed guard posts and countless security scanners and cameras. In spite of that already elevated level of vigilance, entering Dick Stern's personal domain took things one step further, requiring even an official as highly placed as Evan Myers to pass through yet another security barrage and—the ultimate insult—to be accompanied at all times by an authorized escort. Myers had never fully grasped the precise nature of Stern's mandate, nor understood the reason for these obsessive security arrangements. Although he chafed at having been summoned like some junior flunky to this meeting on Stern's turf, however, he was damned if he was going to let the man intimidate him as he did most everyone else.

When his phone vibrated again, Myers flipped it open and glanced at the text message on the screen.

"*Again,* Evan?" Stern asked peevishly.

"Nature of the beast, Dick," Myers said, reading the third communication his assistant had sent in the past forty minutes. "We're at the president's beck and call over there."

This latest message, however, did not concern demands of the Oval Office. Apparently Patrick Fitzgerald had called yet again. Myers had never seen his former boss and mentor so rattled, but considering the kidnapping of Fitzgerald's daughter, it wasn't surprising.

"Anyway," Myers added, tucking the phone away, "that's why I wanted to meet in my office."

Stern grunted. "Not possible." He almost never entered the White House. Myers wondered whether the president even knew the man, much less what he was up to over here.

Hundreds of characters circled around any administration, drawing power and authority from it. Much as they needed and wanted that presidential imprimatur, however, some of those people made a point of flying beneath the radar of Congress, the media and the public, their activities largely invisible even within the administration's inner circle. Dick Stern was a case in point. The man seemed to answer to no one, yet when problems of a certain sensitive nature arose, he was inevitably tagged as the go-to guy.

"Patrick Fitzgerald has called again," Myers said. "We can't keep putting him off. God knows, the State Department isn't giving him any joy. If I don't get back to him with an update on his daughter, the next call he'll make will be to the Oval Office. And you know he'll get through, too, Dick. Fitzgerald is too big a fish to ignore if the party has any hope of making inroads in New England next year. And when he does make that call, the president's going to be calling us both in for a sit rep."

"You can't let that happen."

"Explain to me why not. A young American woman's been kidnapped from under the noses of our own forces in Iraq. The press is saying she's being held by some fundamentalist warlord. The State Department, like I said, is clueless. Meantime, both the CIA and the Pentagon claim to have no idea where she is or what this Salahuddin character wants. For the life of me, I can't figure why we haven't already launched a rescue mission. Are we in control or not over there?"

"It's not that simple. That part of the county is still in flux."

"Are we at least talking to this Sheikh Salahuddin who's supposed to have taken her? I mean, is *somebody* who speaks for us talking to him, since Langley's spooks and the military don't seem to be in the loop?"

"I can't say."

"Can't or won't?"

"Both."

"Because if we *are* in negotiations over Amy Fitzgerald's release, Langley claims to know nothing about it. The director was asked about it point-blank at this morning's security briefing. Are you saying the DCI lied to the president's face?"

"I didn't say that."

Myers made a forward rolling motion with his hand. "So what *are* you saying?"

"I'm saying you need to get back to Fitzgerald and tell him to sit tight. We're doing everything we can."

"Are we?"

"Of course, but we need to move cautiously. There's more at stake than a girl stumbling into a place she had no business being."

Myers threw up his hands. "For God's sake, Dick! It's not like she was some stoner blithely hitchhiking her way through Katmandu or Goa! She's a doctor who was working in a frigging Red Crescent medical clinic, taking care of Iraqi women and children. Some of whom, may I remind you, are injured because they got caught in our own crossfire. I'd say that kind of dedication goes some way to winning hearts and minds, wouldn't you?"

"As I recall," Stern countered, "the International Committee of the Red Cross was warned that we couldn't guarantee the safety of their personnel if they went into the Sunni Triangle before it was fully secured."

"Small comfort to Patrick and Katherine Fitzgerald. And not really good enough when it comes to the media, either. She's still one of ours. This makes us look really ineffectual."

"Screw the media."

"And the Fitzgeralds?"

"I feel their pain."

Somehow, Myers doubted it. The man had ice water in his veins and no family that Myers knew of—thank God. Scary characters like this shouldn't be allowed to reproduce. "So? What can I tell the Fitzgeralds?"

"The situation is very sensitive."

"And...?"

Stern exhaled heavily. "Tell them we're making inquiries. Look, Evan, you're a big enough boy to realize that there are much bigger issues at play here. Issues of major strategic consequence."

"Such as?"

"America's role in the region and in the world. Our ability to continue to be the only global power worth a damn. The last superpower."

"And what's that got to do with Amy Fitzgerald's kidnapping?"

Stern drummed his stubby fingers on the desk, scrutinizing the younger man across from him. Once again, perched on his low armless chair, elbows akimbo, Myers felt like the not-very-bright truant in the principal's office. He decided to demonstrate that he wasn't as clueless as he apparently seemed.

"You're afraid of alienating fundamentalists like this sheikh for fear we'll lose access to Iraqi oil," he said.

"It's a little more complicated than that, but yes. As long as soccer moms and NASCAR dads want to exercise their God-given right to drive gas-guzzling SUVs, that is one consideration." Stern shook his head. "Look, the Saudi regime is getting ready to implode. The House of Saud is being pressured to distance itself from us. U.S. oil companies have been losing contracts left and right in that country, and guess who they're losing them to? None other than Lukoil."

"Lukoil?"

"The Russian state oil company."

"The Russians? A threat to us? Get real. They're no superpower, not anymore—if they ever were. And Muslim fundamentalists hate the Russians, too. Look at what happened in Afghanistan."

"Old news, young Evan. Conservative Saudis had no use for godless communists, it's true, but these days, Moscow's run by a conservative Orthodox Catholic. The Camel and the Bear are getting pretty damn cozy, thank you very much. The Saudis say Lukoil's lower cost structure is the reason they're getting all the contracts to develop new fields over there, but it's never been about the money. Even if it were, the Russians are keeping their offers ridiculously low just to ingratiate themselves with the Saudis."

"To undermine us?"

"Partly. The Russians want to pull the rug out from under Chechen rebels giving them so much grief. Those Chechens are being financed by Saudi fundamentalists."

"As I understand it," Myers said, "our oil companies started backing away from Saudi projects anyway in the wake of 9/11. I'm not surprised the Saudis are looking to deal with anyone but Americans at this point."

"Yeah, they're in a major snit, all right—which plays right into the hands of the Russians."

"I still don't see what this has to do with Amy Fitzgerald's kidnapping in Iraq."

Stern sighed heavily, as if it should be self-evident to anyone but a moron. "The Russians have domestic oil reserves nearly equal to the Saudis'. About the only other country with that much oil still in the ground is Iraq."

"There's Iran, too."

"Yes, but the Iranians haven't learned how to play nicely with others, have they? Until they do, they're a total write-off."

"Okay, so you've got Russia, Iraq and the Saudis…"

"Right. The Russians and Saudis were already moving closer to Baghdad before we went in and toppled Saddam. Think of it—the three largest oil patches in the world, strategically linked and controlled by people who certainly haven't got us in their bedtime prayers. If Moscow and Riyadh controlled Baghdad, they'd have us by the short and curlies, now, wouldn't they?"

"And you think that's their game plan."

"There you go. We put it on hold when we invaded Iraq, but the question is, can we keep it together?" Stern kicked back in his chair and folded his hands over his ample sternum. "Think about it, Evan. Who has a bigger interest in promoting instability over there? If the anti-American forces in Iraq build up enough steam and we buckle and walk away, who's left to come in and bring that country's oil industry back online? Why, none other than the Russians, of course."

Myers sat back in his own chair and stared at the older man. "Are you serious?"

"Dead serious."

"But—well, forgive me, Dick, but that sounds like old-school paranoia. You don't think maybe you're just a little jaded by your Cold War past? Seeing commies in the woods again?"

Stern scowled. "Need I remind you that the president of Russia was a senior KGB officer, raised on the sour milk of anti-Americanism? If you don't think this is a big problem, then you're in the wrong business, son."

Myers shook his head. "In the meantime, what am I supposed to tell the Fitzgeralds about their daughter?"

"Tell them we're doing our best. But do not," Stern added, "do *not*, young Evan, promise them anything." He drummed his blunt-tipped fingers on the brown leather desk pad once more. "And while you're at it, encourage Patrick Fitzgerald to keep his own counsel, for God's sake."

"In other words, don't go to the media."

Stern's hands rose, palm up, as if it should be self-evident. "Although it's rather a case of shutting the barn door after the horses have already escaped."

"What do you mean?"

"That damn reward. The jungle drums are already beating out the news of that bit of folly."

"Well, can you blame them? It's what I'd do if my daughter were kidnapped and I had the money."

Stern shook his steel-gray head irritably. Shards of light flickered off his rimless glasses. "If Fitzgerald thinks he's made things easier by offering a million-dollar reward, he's sadly mistaken. He needs to lie low. Tell him that, for God's sake."

"And if he does? What are the odds of them getting their daughter back safe and sound?"

Stern shrugged. "One hopes for the best and prepares for the worst. Wars have casualties. You know that. I know that. Amy Fitzgerald should have known that before she blundered into the

Sunni Triangle." Before Myers could protest, Stern added, "Stay on top of the Pentagon and Langley. Meantime, I'll see if I can find out anything on my end. That's the best we can do."

A few minutes later, once Myers had been escorted out of his office and out of the building, Stern wheeled in his chair and reached for a phone on the credenza behind his desk. He punched a series of numbers on the base, then listened while the system bounced the call across several international satellite links. The line picked up quickly at the other end, but the voice sounded groggy. It wasn't just the scrambler encoding their communication, Stern realized, glancing at his watch. It was after midnight over there.

He didn't bother to identify himself. "Kenner, look sharp!"

"I'm here. What's up?"

Stern's trained ear picked up the faint hint of an almost untraceable accent, although he knew that not one in a million other listeners would hear it. The man he called Kenner had American pronunciation and syntax down perfectly, and he used American colloquialisms with ease. It was only one of the reasons Stern found the man so useful.

"The Fitzgerald problem is looking to get out of hand," he said.

"How so?"

"Patrick Fitzgerald has posted a million-dollar reward for his daughter's safe return. He's also calling in markers to pressure the administration to take action. What were you thinking of, standing by while they kidnapped the American woman?"

"They needed a doctor and the local clinic had just gone through a personnel shift."

"And nobody knew it was an American there? A girl, for chrissake?"

"What can I say? The intelligence was faulty."

"Nonexistent, is more like it. Enough is enough. It's time to get this situation back under control. Got it?"

Stern barely waited to hear the assent from the other end before hanging up. He didn't need to. Orders were meant to be followed. He had no doubt that his would be.

5

Wednesday, August 27, 2003
Iraq, the heart of the Sunni Triangle

The Brandywine team came out of the hills just after 1:00 a.m. There were four commandos with the forward unit that set out from the landing zone. They'd left the pilot and a base guard on backup at the LZ with the understanding that the chopper would pull back to a safer distance if there was any sign of enemy activity in the area. They had no desire to draw undue attention to their effort to extract the two Iraqi civilians from the insurgent-held town of Al Zawra.

Hannah was the lone woman in the advance group that headed down into the valley. Sean Ladwell, the team leader, was on point. Hannah and Marcus Wilcox were in the two and three positions, while Oz Nuñez was on rear guard. Nuñez, a former marine sniper, carried an M40A1 rifle, while the others had M-16s. In addition, each team member carried a 9 mm semiautomatic pistol with sixteen rounds, half a dozen spare clips, plus a personalized assortment of backup guns, knives, fragmentation grenades and smoke bombs. Wilcox, a former

NFL linebacker who'd quit pro ball on September 12, 2001, also had an M203 grenade launcher slung around his Kevlar'd torso. They were armed for bear but hoped to need none of it, slipping back to the LZ before sunup with their rescue targets in tow.

Four pairs of tan leather boots negotiated barren, rock-strewn terrain as they crept stealthily toward the target: the small market town of Al Zawra, population eight thousand, some fifty miles north of Baghdad. Four heads took constant, 360-degree readings of the terrain as they crept forward. Four pairs of eyes were fixed on the green-tinted shadows in their night-vision goggles, searching for any movement that would betray opposition forces. Hunting, too, for seemingly innocuous bumps in the terrain that could conceal improvised explosive devices.

The air, hot and arid, was laden with powder-fine grit. It was all Hannah could do not to sneeze inside the itching balaclava pulled over her head, nose and mouth, but she dared not make a sound that might announce their approach.

The caution was well warranted. They were coming in from the back side of the town that pressed up against the hills rather than via the main road off the Baghdad-to-Tikrit highway. Advance intel suggested that this flank was the most lightly guarded. The half-mile stretch of open ground between the foothills and their objective had also been aerial-surveyed with ground penetrating radar looking for land mines. Still, it paid to be ready for surprises. It could mean the difference between success and failure, life and death—or worse, capture. The gruesome images of recent hostage beheadings, flashed round the world via the Internet, were graphic reminders of the fate that could await them if they screwed up.

Hannah held her M-16 rifle clutched close to her body. Upon arrival at the first mission briefing at Brandywine International headquarters in Virginia a week earlier, she'd been greeted by wolf whistles and a few dubious propositions. Even though she'd been careful to show up wearing an old police academy sweatshirt, faded jeans and scuffed boots, her dark hair knotted behind her head and her makeup nonexistent, it had taken only a nanosecond for these clowns to jump to the conclusion that she was there to offer coffee, maps and maybe a hot-blooded romp to brave boys willing to risk their necks for a cause deemed worthy enough for a lucrative payday.

The kibitzing had faded fast, replaced by raised eyebrows and skeptical muttering when she was introduced and her role in the mission outlined. The grumbling hadn't altogether died down since. They'd be happy to bed her, the grunts made clear, they just didn't want to babysit her out here when their lives would be on the line.

Hannah informed them she didn't need babysitting from anyone, thanks all the same. In any case, there was nothing they could do about her inclusion. It was a management call, and management had decided: she was in. She liked to think it wasn't just because she spoke Arabic, but realistically, with even the team leader reluctant to have her along, she knew it probably was the tipping point. This mission—*any* mission in Iraq, these days—was risky enough. Without someone who spoke the local language, it could be impossible to pull off and maybe suicidal to boot.

Now, as they crept out of the hills, there was no distinguishing Hannah from the men, rigged out as she was in full paramilitary camouflage gear. She was on the tall side for a woman, five-eight in her bare feet, an inch more in her hiking boots. At least one of the men in the group was shorter, although Oz Nuñez was built like a Humvee, low, wide and solid. Hannah's Kevlar body armor concealed a slender frame under her dark outerwear, while the balaclava and night-vision goggles obscured her long hair and deceptively delicate features.

Hannah's fingerless leather gloves clutched the barrel and stock of her rifle. The gun was set to burst pattern, ready for any threat, but she projected outward calm as they crept toward their target. Only she knew that her heart was pounding against the khaki cotton T-shirt under her body armor, beating out the universal anthem of fatalists everywhere: *When you've got nothin', you've got nothin' to lose.*

That about summed it up, she thought, as an itchy bead of sweat ran the rim of her goggles, then soaked into the lower part of the balaclava covering her nose and mouth. It was way too hot to be wearing complete covering, but they were going for anonymity and the intimidation factor here. Nothing said wet-your-pants scary like the Ninja warrior look.

The market town they were about to enter was under the thumb of Sheikh Ali Mokhtar Salahuddin, a militant anti-western Sunni warlord who'd managed to survive Saddam Hussein's brutal reign of terror through sheer, Machiavellian bloody-mindedness, plus a close alliance with the dictator's sadistic monster sons. Uday and Qusay Hussein had been killed in a shoot-out with U.S. forces the previous month. Saddam himself was on the run and his former soldiers had thrown away their uniforms, but all that meant was that there was no telling the players without a scorecard—and the scorecard kept getting rewritten. No matter how many times the administration back in Washington crowed "mission accomplished," Iraq was descending into anarchy, with allegiances shifting daily.

Meantime, the ruthless Sheikh Salahuddin clung to control of his personal fiefdom. He was a force that would have to be reckoned with or eliminated, sooner or later, Hannah imagined, but as much trouble as the warlord was proving to be to coalition forces, the Brandywine team hadn't been sent to bring him down. Rather, its mission was to extract an old woman and her granddaughter living at the western edge of the town. It seemed like a lot of firepower for some granny and a kid, Hannah thought, but who was she to question orders?

Dawn was still a few hours off, but a searing wind stirred the fine sand that seemed to blanket the landscape. Hannah's clenched jaws scraped grit over tooth enamel, while underneath the balaclava, the sweat on her cheeks and brow congealed into a gluey, sandpapery mud pack. *Great. A dermabrasion facial,* the repressed girlie-girl in her thought ruefully.

The group moved ahead stealthily, pausing now and again when Ladwell raised his hand. They pivoted, taking in every nuance of their surroundings. Even with night-vision goggles, it was a tough call to distinguish anything. The boulder-strewn, scrub-covered terrain was an abstract painter's canvas of green, splotchy shadows. Whirlwinds of dust obscured the stars and the crescent moon overhead. That wasn't necessarily a bad thing, though. The lack of light and definition, combined with their dusky camos and matte black weapons, would also render the team virtually invisible to any adversary. In theory, anyway.

If captured, they were hosed. No rescue would be mounted to save their sorry hides. Officially, they weren't even here. They would not be counted among the dead, wounded and captured in this dirty little war where the enemy could be anyone from a Saddam *fedayeen* to an adolescent holy-martyr-wannabe body wrapped in Semtex.

Despite the high risk, Hannah hadn't hesitated to sign on for the mission. After all, if she bought it here, who would mourn? What family she had didn't need her. Gabe would be the beneficiary of the hefty insurance policy that came with these contract jobs, so that if one day he wanted to escape the clutches of his father and the woman who was now his mom in all but name, he'd have the means to do it. As for Hannah's police career, that had self-destructed, too, along with the rest of her once reasonably happy life.

Behind her were nothing but burned bridges. And when you've got nothin', you've got nothin' to lose.

6

Al Zawra, Central Iraq

Zaynab Um Ahmed awoke with a start, the ripe smell of leather filling her nostrils. A gloved hand was clamped onto her mouth. She struggled and tried to cry out, but her captor was relentless. Another hand bore down on her collarbones, exerting more than enough force on those frail bones to keep her pinned to the mattress.

Her first thought was for Yasmin, her twelve-year-old granddaughter, who'd been sleeping in the twin bed next to hers, but she could neither move nor see if the child was safe. No sound came from the other bed. Zaynab struggled and moaned, but the man holding her down was unyielding.

She turned her attention to the ghostly, nearly featureless head looming over her. The room should have been pitch-black, and yet was not. In a dim, reddish glow, she made out a pair of dark eyes, intently fixed on her. When Zaynab whimpered, the head gave a sharp, warning shake, and a whispered command sounded from that awful lipless face. "Shhh, grandmother! Be still."

The old woman went limp, her terrified gaze darting left and right in that red spectral glow. There'd been no electricity in town for weeks now, ever since Salahuddin's men had seized control of the area, taking advantage of the power vacuum left after the American invasion. No one knew whether Salahuddin had cut the power lines and telephone communications or whether the foreign forces had done it. All anyone knew was that the country was sliding into anarchy. This was what some people had feared would follow if Saddam were ever overthrown. No one loved the dictator, but in a nation rife with ugly ethnic divisions, the devil one knew was perhaps preferable to whatever supposed savior might follow—for some, anyway. Zaynab had known too much grief in her sixty-two years to believe in anyone anymore.

People said Salahuddin was the spiritual "younger brother" of Osama bin Laden, but Zaynab had her own take on the opportunist who was now terrorizing her town. After all, she'd known the little monster all his life. He was about the same age as her own children, but unlike Mumtaz and Ahmed, Salahuddin had dropped out of school at sixteen, becoming a drunk and a thug who was suspected of several sexual assaults. He had wormed his way into the inner circle of Qusay Hussein, but inevitably fell afoul of the dictator's family and landed in jail. Some people said it was during his time in prison that he adopted the *jihadist* cause. Whatever the case, after he was released, Salahuddin disappeared—to Afghanistan, some said, to fight the Soviet invaders of that country.

He'd shown up back in Al Zawra only a few months earlier, calling himself "Sheikh" Salahuddin. Whether or not he was a follower of bin Laden, Zaynab thought, he certainly didn't need the blessings of Al Qaeda to launch a so-called holy war. He had always had delusions of grandeur and been given to spouting the worst kind of hateful nonsense. Since he'd taken over the town, nothing had been working.

Zaynab tried to make out where this dim red glow in the room was coming from. Out of frugality and fear of fire, she was always careful to extinguish candles and oil lamps before she and Yasmin went to bed. Even on bright, moonlit nights, she kept the curtains drawn close against the dangers that lurked outside. But now, the room was a patchwork of black shadow and crimson light. The armed invaders—from her pinioned position on the bed, she could make out at least two others dressed in full military camouflage—were carrying shielded torches.

As Zaynab turned her gaze back to the soldier holding her down, a sense of weary inevitability and terrible sadness overcame her resistance. Of course these men had been sent to kill her and her granddaughter. Why not? Everything else had already been taken from her. Now, why not her precious granddaughter and her own useless life?

The soldier took away the hand on her shoulder, lifting one finger in warning. Zaynab felt too beaten down to move as he reached up, yanking off the balaclava that had obscured all features but those dark eyes.

Zaynab squinted, then blinked through her tears. This was not one of Salahuddin's hooligans. In fact, it was no man at all. It was a young woman with the dark eyes of the forty-two virgins who were said to welcome devout men into paradise. Was she dead, then? And did the *houris* come to faithful women, too? How was it possible that the angels of paradise were dressed like soldiers, in camouflage shirts and trousers? Had things gotten so bad that even heaven was beleaguered by battling forces?

The dark-eyed soldier-angel leaned close and whispered urgently in the old woman's ear. "Shhh, grandmother! Don't be afraid. Mumtaz has sent me."

Mumtaz? Zaynab puzzled. *But…how? She is far off in London.*

It had been ten long years since Zaynab had last seen her daughter. Mumtaz's husband had been a professor of mathematics at the University of Baghdad. Zamir was not a political creature, never had been. He might never have fled the country had Saddam not turned his murderous gaze in the direction of Iraq's intellectuals. Mathematics, Zamir always said, did not concern itself with the shifting winds of human ambition, but with the unassailable logic of formulas that could be tested and proven. But then, as one after another of his colleagues fled or was imprisoned or killed for daring to express any opinion at all that distinguished him from a dumb rock, Zamir, too, found himself challenged. Perhaps he had some warning or premonition of danger. Whatever the case, Zamir defected while attending a mathematicians' conference in Paris, taking Mumtaz with him.

When they didn't return, Saddam's soldiers came to Al Zawra, questioning Zaynab and her son for days about what they knew. In the end, the soldiers must have been convinced by their protestations of innocence, for they'd finally gone away and left the family alone. Mumtaz and Zamir had ended up in London, Zaynab had heard through intermediaries. Now, apparently, there were two young grandsons she had never laid eyes on. It broke her heart to think of them growing up among strangers, far from the land of their people, but at least they were safe there. Perhaps they were the lucky ones.

Was it possible Mumtaz had now sent a message through this dark-eyed warrior *houri* who spoke strangely accented Arabic?

As if reading her mind, the woman-in-man's-clothing nodded. "Yes, Mumtaz, your daughter," she murmured.

She was not an Iraqi, certainly, nor was her Arabic the Cairo dialect heard in movies and on imported television programs.

"Mumtaz heard about what happened to her brother," the warrior-woman said. "To your son, Ahmed, and his wife, Fatima."

Zaynab's son and daughter-in-law had been killed two months ago in a shoot-out at their café near the central marketplace. A newly appointed official named by the American civil administrator had arrived from Baghdad and began taking afternoon coffee breaks at the café, talking to merchants and other local people, listening to their concerns about the uneasy security situation. He'd seemed like a good enough man, but Salahuddin, sensing a challenge to his authority, had issued a *fatwa* against what he called the "agent of the infidels." In addition to the official and his bodyguard, Salahuddin's men had gunned down six civilians in the café that day, including Zaynab's son and daughter-in-law—Yasmin's parents. Then, they had burned the café to the ground.

With her son dead, Zaynab had needed to find a way to support herself and Yasmin. Their family had once been prosperous, but it had fallen on hard times in recent years. During the time of international sanctions when goods grew increasingly scarce, they had sold off jewelry and anything else of value in order to purchase goods on the black market. By the time the café was destroyed, drying up even that modest source of income, there was nothing of value left to trade away and no one with money left to buy it in any case. In the end, Zaynab had taken to selling tea from a trolley in the marketplace.

And still, she worried. Hiding behind a scrim of false piety to justify his ambition, greed and brutality, Salahuddin had been issuing one restrictive command after another, and his bearded enforcers beat or arrested anyone who did not obey. If the rumors were true and he decided to forbid women to go out in public at all unless accompanied by a male relative, she and her poor granddaughter would starve to death. They no longer had any living male relative except her son-in-law in far-off London.

The old woman glanced over at the next bed. Yasmin was sitting up but she was restrained by a stocky, dark-haired soldier. The child's eyes were huge and frightened. The soldier held her firmly but his expression seemed apologetic. Zaynab spotted two other burly, camouflage-clad soldiers in the room, guarding the door and peering around the edges of paisley window curtains that had grown tattered and thin. Their fingers were poised on the triggers of terrible-looking rifles. None of them looked like Iraqis. They were too well-fed.

How could they have entered so silently? Of course, Zaynab's ears were getting old and feeble, but surely Yasmin would have heard something? Or the chickens they kept in the courtyard? How had these soldiers gotten by without the hens raising a squawk? Not to mention Salahuddin's men, who were said to patrol the town all night long? Ostensibly there to guard against infidel invaders, as often as not Salahuddin's men, most of whom were not even from Al Zawra, just strutted around, lording it over everyone, stealing whatever they pleased, and harassing farmers and shopkeepers who were up to nothing more nefarious than trying to provide for their families.

Even in the time of Saddam, may his name be cursed forever, the town had not lost so many innocents to senseless, ugly violence. These foreigners had good reason to be nervous, Zaynab thought. If Salahuddin's men found them, they would be dead before sunup.

She studied the strange warrior-woman and her comrades, and they in turn studied her, all of them weighing their risks. Finally, Zaynab nodded. Only then did she realize that the warrior-woman had been holding her breath. She exhaled heavily now and released her grip on Zaynab's shoulder, allowing her to sit up. The soldier holding Yasmin released her, too, and as soon as he did, the girl leapt across the space between the two beds. Grandmother and granddaughter wrapped themselves in each others' arms, then looked back at the warrior-woman, who seemed to be the speaker for the others.

"My name is Hannah," she said. She had a rifle slung over her chest, but she shrugged out of it, set it aside, then settled herself at the foot of Zaynab's mattress. Her hair was very dark, most of it caught up in a plait except for wisps that clung to the damp skin of her forehead, cheeks and neck.

"Are you American soldiers?" Zaynab asked.

"My commander here is British," the woman named Hannah said, nodding at the wiry man guarding the door. "The rest of us are American. We're not soldiers, though."

"You look like soldiers."

"Think of us as protectors."

"Protectors of whom?"

"At the moment, you and Yasmin."

"I don't understand. How can that be?"

"I told you, it was your daughter Mumtaz who asked that we come here."

The warrior-woman unbuttoned a pocket on the leg of her pants and withdrew a folded piece of paper, then unclipped a small flashlight from her belt and turned it on. Like the men's, it had a red shield around the lens, narrowing its beam. "This is from your daughter," she said.

Being careful to keep the light aimed low and away from the window, she handed the paper to the old woman, holding the light on it. Zaynab took the paper.

"Is it really from Auntie Mumtaz?" Yasmin asked.

Hands trembling, Zaynab unfolded the note. She peered at the writing, and gasped. "Yes! I recognize her handwriting!"

"Shhh," Hannah murmured, touching her arm. "Whisper. Tell your granddaughter what it says."

Zaynab read:

Mama,

Please, you must do what these people say. They are friends and will keep you safe. Go with them. We have arranged visas for you and Yasmin to come and live in London with Zamir and me and the boys. Yasmin, you will go to school here and we will love you as our own daughter. Neither of you need ever be afraid again. It is for the best, I promise you. Come away from that terrible place.

We send you love and a thousand kisses.

Mumtaz

The old woman's eyes misted as she clutched the note to her broken heart. Then, she looked up at the soldier-woman and nodded. "Tell us what we are to do."

7

Al Zawra: Compound of Sheikh Ali Mokhtar Salahuddin

The man known as George Kenner had gone by many names in his lifetime, taking on and casting off identities as easily as most people switched hats. At the moment, as far as the sheikh and his followers knew, Kenner was a Canadian-born ex-paratrooper-turned-private-military-contractor who had converted to Islam twenty years earlier while helping Afghan freedom fighters expel Russian invaders from their country.

It did no good for Kenner to try to pass as an Arab, not with his startling, pale blue eyes, fair skin and white-blond hair. Brown contact lenses and a dye job might have camouflaged his eye and hair color temporarily, but those solutions were unsuited to the kind of open-ended operation on which he was currently engaged.

In any case, the language would have given him away as soon as he opened his mouth. There were myriad accents and dialects throughout the Arabic-speaking world, but none of these came naturally to Kenner. As gifted a linguist as he was, having been trained from youth to blend like a native into certain foreign milieus, he would never speak better than kitchen Arabic. He'd come too recently to the language. Better to adopt the identity of a sympathetic former infidel from a country deemed relatively benign and then get on with the job of infiltrating Salahuddin's inner circle.

Kenner had come to Salahuddin on the recommendation of a *mujaheddin* chief in Kabul, who'd praised his foreign-born brother for his piety, his ruthless devotion to the cause and his superior tactical skills. Inside the *jihadist* movement, the Kabul contact reported to Salahuddin, Kenner was called "Juma Kamal," but his brethren accepted that his Muslim identity should remain secret to all but a select few. Kenner was of more use to them traveling incognito under his infidel name and that useful Canadian passport, which rarely received more than a cursory glance from border guards.

That Kenner's Canadian background was fiction, his religious conversion a farce and his Kabul sponsor long since turned by U.S. intelligence remained a secret to all but a tiny handful of individuals back in the American capital. Washington had a miserable track record for running humint—human intelligence—sources, inside the nearly impenetrable fundamentalist Islamic warrior movement. The only reason Kenner's cover had remained intact thus far was that the existence of the double agent was known to so few.

Here in the so-called Sunni Triangle, the self-styled Sheikh Salahuddin had seized on the opportunity offered by the current confusion to return to his hometown, wrest control of it and then extend that control over the region. If his campaign went as planned, he would be a major force to be reckoned with, playing a key role in the formation of the new national government.

Salahuddin claimed to hate the traitor Saddam Hussein, a fellow Sunni who paid lip service to Islam when it suited his aims but who, together with his corrupt sons, lived like the worst of infidels. If Salahuddin had once enjoyed a decadent life himself, his time in prison had allegedly convinced him there was more glory to be found in being a holy war leader. Now that Saddam had been overthrown, he had no wish to see the Americans' tame Shia lapdogs take over the country, divvying it up between themselves and Kurdish riffraff. While a power vacuum existed, Salahuddin told his followers, the time was ripe to exert the moral authority of the Prophet's true way—and there was no shortage of potential followers among the country's Sunni minority, which was terrified at the prospect of rule by Shias and Kurds, gunning for bear after Saddam's long, dark reign.

Kenner had been infiltrated into Salahuddin's camp ostensibly to help organize and train the sheikh's warriors, but really to keep track of his plans and try to turn them in a direction favorable to Washington's interests in the oil-rich region. Either that, or, if Salahuddin couldn't be co-opted, eliminate the threat. If the sheikh had known where the mercenary's true loyalties lay, he would have been far more careful about welcoming him into his proverbial tent.

Sitting on the edge of his cot, Kenner frowned at the sound of dead air in his cell phone. His caller had hung up on him. Typical.

He'd known Dick Stern over a decade now, since long before the ex-CIA deputy had arrived at his current exalted status in the White House inner sanctum as assistant national security advisor. He'd met Stern back in the days when he was running covert operations into Soviet-controlled Afghanistan. Since then, Kenner had carried out several deniable assignments at the CIA operative's behest, including at least one assassination of a foreign opposition leader—a totally illegal operation that remained to this day unknown to anyone else in the American capital, least of all the dreaded Congressional intelligence oversight committees.

As far as Kenner was concerned, Stern had always been prone to pomposity—seldom in doubt, never wrong. He demanded absolute, unquestioning obedience from his agents and he got it, because to cross him was suicide, professionally and sometimes literally. On the other hand, the man did have a talent for landing on the winning side of domestic bureaucratic skirmishes, which made him a reliable source of lucrative contract dollars to a free agent like Kenner.

Kenner had been asleep when Stern called from Washington. His room in the sheikh's compound was a private one, closet-sized but infinitely preferable to the overcrowded barracks that the bulk of Salahuddin's fighters occupied. When his razor-thin cell phone had vibrated in an inner pocket of his shirt, he'd come instantly awake. Salahuddin was paranoid about cell phones, forbidding their use in the compound for fear of overhead satellites that fished through the ether, listening for suspect conversations and using the signal to zero in on enemy targets. Kenner was careful to keep his link to his handlers well hidden from view at all times, and was trusted enough at this point never to be subjected to a body search.

After the short conversation with Stern, Kenner tucked the phone away once more, then sat on the edge of the cot, thinking about the best way to deal with the problem of the American doctor. On the one hand, her capture had inflated Salahuddin's reputation in this campaign where image was everything. The foreign press was already coming to name him as a power to be reckoned with, which helped attract followers to the sheikh's camp.

From an American perspective, this kidnapping could be played a number of ways. In a worst-case scenario, if anything were to happen to the doctor, it would cement Salahuddin's reputation as a power to be feared. If nothing else, it provided a convenient high-profile villain to shore up the American public's support for the invasion of the country, now that it was becoming clear that the weapons of mass destruction play had been a bluff. On the other hand, if the public outcry over the doctor's kidnapping became too clamorous, the American military might be tempted to launch a strike against Salahuddin. Kenner couldn't let that happen. Salahuddin was too useful to him. He'd spent too long working this plan to stand back and see his protégé eliminated.

The rich tapestry of the prayer mat lying in one corner of the room, prearranged so that it was facing toward Mecca, caught his eye, and he scowled. Five times daily, when the muezzin called the pious to prayer, those who could get to the mosque did so in order to pray shoulder-to-shoulder as tradition demanded with their fellow believers. The sheikh accepted that Kenner's responsibilities often prevented him from praying at the mosque, but he believed the convert made use of the prayer mat. Kenner, however, barely gave the rug a glance.

Reaching over the side of the cot, he grabbed his boots, pulled them on and laced them up, then got to his feet. Approaching his midforties, his short-cropped hair rapidly going from white-blond to pure white, Kenner's body retained the lean, hungry appearance of an Arctic wolf, with cold blue eyes to match. He strapped on his gun belt and slipped the knife he always carried into the sheath at the small of his back. Then, he stepped outside onto the low veranda surrounding the compound's open central courtyard.

A mosque stood at one end of the compound. Behind it, a series of rooms ran off a rectangular inner square, open to the sky above. In times of peace, the rooms were used for meetings and for Koranic instruction of the village children. These days, they held an armory and barracks, as well as the makeshift infirmary that Salahuddin had ordered set up after the last shoot-out with American soldiers, in which several of his followers had been wounded.

It wasn't that Salahuddin spared all that much compassion for the injured, Kenner knew. If they couldn't fight another day, they would have served the cause better by dying in battle. The sheikh had no problem sending young men out to blow themselves up on suicide bombing missions, especially the less talented among them. It was a win-win situation. They had the reward of paradise, with its forty-two *houris,* and Salahuddin had holy martyrs to bring in more recruits for the cause. But instead, these men wounded by the Americans were brought back to the compound moaning and groaning about their injuries, and that was just bad for morale. The sheikh had needed a doctor to take care of them and shut them up, and the American girl had turned out to be what he got.

Kenner moved around the edge of the veranda towards the sheikh's quarters. A wide-branching fig tree stood in the center of the courtyard, silhouetted by the light of a small fire that burned in a brazier at the far end of the yard. The scent of smoke drifted on the warm night air. Except for the occasional spit and crackle of the flames, the compound was silent and dark. Kenner looked up. A twinkling swath of stars blanketed the pitch black sky.

As the sound of a low murmur reached his ears, Kenner turned back to the brazier and noted that two   no, three   of the men who were supposed to be on night guard were instead lolling around the fire on molded plastic chairs. They obviously hadn't noticed him.

Stepping deeper into the shadows of the overhanging roof, Kenner crept ahead. Silently withdrawing his knife from the leather sheath at his back, he hugged the wall as he padded toward them, silent as a panther. The gleam of the fire danced on their glistening skin. One of the guards, sitting with his back to the veranda, was old enough to sport a thick, black beard and mustache, but the other two were barefaced youths. The younger men's eyes glittered as they watched the dance of the fire in the brazier. All three were mesmerized by the flames—and blinded by them, Kenner thought contemptuously.

He stole up behind the bearded one, then sprang like a coiled snake, grabbing him by the hair and pulling the head back so that the blade of his matte black knife had clear access to the soft, vulnerable skin beneath the wiry beard. The man's white plastic chair tipped back on two legs, and he stared up, terrified, into those pale Arctic eyes. The two youths sprang to their feet, tipping over their chairs as well as the Kalashnikov rifles that they'd carelessly propped against the armrests.

"You're dead," Kenner growled, as his knife etched a superficial but memorable line in the man's neck.

Too surprised to remember to reach for their sidearms, the youths stared, open-mouthed, while their bearded comrade whimpered for his life.

"And the two of you," Kenner added, glancing up at them, "would be just as dead if this were a real enemy infiltration. Did you see or hear me approach?"

"N-no."

"Of course not, idiots. Your eyes were blinded by the light and your ears were filled with the sound of your own yammering. Why are you not patrolling the grounds?"

"We were," one of them protested.

"We only just stopped for a moment to take a little tea."

"And if this were the moment that the enemy chose to strike?" Kenner asked. "What good are you if you cannot see him coming? If you cannot kill him before he kills you? If you cannot at least sound a warning to your brethren asleep in the barracks? If we relied on your vigilance, we could all be dead now."

"It was a mistake. We meant no harm," the bearded one said breathlessly, petrified to move lest the knife at his throat cut any deeper.

Kenner gave him a disgusted look and yanked his head back another inch or two. Finally passing equilibrium, the chair tipped over backwards. As the man tumbled to the ground, Kenner re-leased him. Bending down, he wiped his knife blade on the man's grimy shirt, then slid it back into the sheath.

"Return to your posts now," he warned, "and let this be a lesson. If I find you betraying the sheikh with your carelessness once more, my knife will show no pity."

The bearded one scowled but got to his feet as the other two scrambled to retrieve their assault rifles. "Yes, sir. Thank you. May the Prophet bless you," they said breathlessly as they scrambled off to their guard posts.

"And may he keep you alive in spite of yourselves, you morons," Kenner muttered, heading away toward Salahuddin's quarters.

8

Al Zawra: Central Iraq

Hannah pressed the light fob on her black army surplus watch. Nearly 3:00 a.m. The dial went dark again as she released the button—no telltale fluorescent to give away her position in the dark.

Sean Ladwell stood at the window, peering around the edge of the curtain, his M-16 rifle gripped in both hands. Nuñez and Wilcox kept moving from room to room, checking for trouble from alternate vantage points.

Ladwell glanced back at her. "Tell the old woman they need to hurry."

"She knows," Hannah said, watching the grandmother fumble through a drawer, withdrawing underthings that she handed to her granddaughter.

The house fairly hummed with tension, and for good reason. The eastern sky would lighten soon. Roosters would crow in backyard coops. With the electricity down, neighbor women would rise early to start cooking fires to make breakfast for their families. Soon, the whole town would be stirring, including the warlord Salahuddin and his troops in their compound, which advance intel said was behind the mosque, near the town center. If the team was going to head back to the hills for their rendezvous with the chopper without being seen, then they were going to have to leave very soon.

"Why don't you guys wait out in the front room?" Hannah told Ladwell. "These ladies won't want to get dressed in front of men. I'll stay and speed things along."

The team leader glanced at the woman and girl, who were shyly folding clothing on one of the beds. Nuñez arrived in the doorway, back from his circuit of the house. The young ex-marine was short but solidly built. A high school wrestler, Hannah thought. Nuñez had to be at least twenty-one, because that was Brandywine International's minimum age for its contract security forces, but in spite of his flak jacket and armaments, he still looked like a kid playing at soldiering.

"Wait out in the front room," Ladwell told him. Then he turned back to Hannah. "They can't bring much. Tell them that."

"I think they get it that this is no luxury cruise we're offering."

"They should pack only what they can carry themselves. We're going to be moving out at a brisk clip and there's no such thing as chivalry here. No one's going to carry their stuff. We'll be busy enough trying to keep them alive till we get to the LZ."

"I'll make sure they understand."

Ladwell grunted and headed out of the room.

Hannah turned to the woman and girl and switched back to Arabic. "The men will wait in the living room. You should hurry and get dressed now. We have a long walk ahead of us, and we don't want to be running into anyone."

"We are walking to London?" Yasmin said.

"No, just into the hills to the west of here. It's about two kilometers. We'll be picked up there and flown out. I'm sorry," Hannah added to Zaynab. "I wish we didn't have to make you walk, but it was too risky to drive in case of roadblocks."

"No matter. I am strong," the old woman said. "We both are. Come, Yasmin, hurry. Here are your things."

An ornately carved wooden bureau stood between the two narrow beds. Hannah set her flashlight down on top of it, pointing it toward the large oval mirror hanging above to add a dim, red-tinged light for Zaynab and Yasmin to see by. The mirror was gilt-framed and, like the ornate bureau itself, said something about the comfortable and relatively privileged life that this family had once lived. At the same time, the mirror's silver backing was crackled. This, like the peeling blue paint on the walls and the chipped and broken ceramic tiles on the floor, was mute testimony to years of declining family fortunes. In a country where the average annual income wouldn't cover an American family's cable TV service, these people had obviously been among the country's small, educated elite, part of that group who should have helped this ancient and cultured nation move into the future. Such people, however, were just the type to attract the attention of a paranoid dictator.

Yasmin turned her back modestly as she lifted her faded nightdress over her head. Hannah caught a glimpse of birdlike shoulder blades and a pronounced rib cage, the bones jutting too sharply to indicate anything but malnutrition. This child had lived almost her entire lifetime under the sanctions mounted against Saddam's regime after the Gulf War of the early nineties. The dictator and his cronies had kept themselves amply fed, clothed and entertained throughout that time, Hannah thought angrily, but Iraq's children hadn't been so well provided for. Things could only have gotten worse for poor Yasmin after the death of her parents, despite her grandmother's best efforts.

"Here," she murmured to the grandmother, who'd been pulling

clothes from the bureau, "let me fold these while you get yourself ready. You won't be able to take much, I'm afraid."

"We have little enough."

The old woman shut the drawer, then turned to a tall armoire. When she opened it, the scent of cedar wafted through the room. Hannah caught a glimpse of a man's dark suit on a hanger—the dead son's, no doubt—and of two black abayas, or burqas, draped on hooks at the side of the closet.

Zaynab caught her looking at the black shrouds, and she fingered the fabric. "My mother used to dress in full hijab, but in my lifetime, only peasants and uneducated women still did. I never used to wear one of those—my late husband never demanded it, thankfully. I dressed modestly, always wore a kerchief on my head, but I saw no reason to stumble around half-blind. After they killed my son and his wife, though," she added bitterly, "it was the only way to go out safely into the streets. Even Saddam's hooligans and this latest bunch, Salahuddin's men, will not generally harass a woman in hijab. We are invisible. I made Yasmin cover up, too. Not even a child is safe these days."

"I didn't like it. It was hot," Yasmin said.

"You won't need it where you're going," Hannah told her.

Zaynab pushed the robes aside. "Good." She withdrew a long gray skirt and flowered blouse from the armoire, then headed back to her bed to get ready.

Hannah busied herself folding the clothing on the bureau—a few pairs of thin socks and underthings, a child's sweater and T-shirt. Yasmin came over and shyly added her folded nightgown to the pile. Hannah gave her a smile.

The girl had on a white cotton blouse and dark pleated skirt that had seen better days. The blouse was clean, but worn and patched, and a little small for her. The skirt had obviously been let down at least a couple of times, by the look of the fold lines at the hem. Even so, it ended an inch or two above her knee, shorter than girls in this part of the world normally wore. Hannah doubted it was a fashion statement. Yasmin's outfit looked like a school uniform that had been worn long past its serviceable time, after being subjected to all the abuse that children everywhere put their clothes through.

She thought of Gabriel, her son, and the many knees he had taken out of pants, crawling around with his cars when he was little, and later, tumbling off bikes. These days, it was his skateboard that put rips in his clothing and beat down the treads in his sneakers. But Gabe never had to wear pants that had been patched or rehemmed. At eight years old, in fact, his wardrobe cost more than Hannah's, outfitted as he always was in trendy fashions from the upscale children's boutiques of L.A.'s Westside and the Beverly Center. Gabe couldn't care less about style, of course, but it was important to Cal that his son be as much a credit to him as his trophy wife, so Gabe's stepmother kept him turned out in relentlessly preppy fashion.

"Can I take my pictures?" Yasmin asked, pulling a small, leather-bound album from the bureau's top drawer. From the way she clutched it in her thin arms, Hannah could only guess at the memories it contained.

"Absolutely," she said. The girl looked relieved.

Zaynab finished buttoning the cuffs of her long-sleeved blouse. Then, she picked up a brush off the bureau and pulled it gently through her granddaughter's wavy black hair. "We are lucky that Mumtaz sent for us," she said quietly. "Yasmin hasn't been able to go to school this past while."

"You lost your teachers?"

"No, but when Salahuddin took charge, he banned school for girls." She grimaced. "I've known him since he was a boy, you know. I knew his parents. His mother died in childbirth. The father was a brute, and Salahuddin turned out to be a lout just like the old man, drunk and stupid. Then he went to prison and found Allah, they say. Nonsense, I say. Holy warrior—feh! Then he comes back here, calls himself 'sheikh' and starts issuing *fatwas.* I'm surprised he didn't close the school altogether, because even the littlest boys are smarter than he is."

"Ouch, Grandmother!" Yasmin protested. "Too hard!"

"Oh, sorry, little one," Zaynab said, setting aside the brush she'd been wielding like a rake. She kissed the top of the girl's head. Then, she glanced back at Hannah. "Even before he outlawed school for girls, it wasn't safe for Yasmin. People! It wasn't enough that she'd lost her mother and father. At school, the children, even the teachers, some of them…" The old woman shook her head bitterly. "The things they said. The things they did. That's what thirty years of Saddam has turned my countrymen into—cowering pack dogs who tremble before the leaders, then turn around and bare their fangs at the weak and defenseless. We have become a nation of cowards."

"Are we ever coming back here?" Yasmin asked Hannah.

Hannah shrugged. "I don't know. That will depend, I guess. I think everyone hopes things will get better here one day."

The grandmother looked around, as if the finality of what they were about to do had suddenly hit her. "This used to be a beautiful country, you know."

"I know," Hannah said.

"I don't want to die in a foreign land. I want to be here, in my home. I want to be buried near my husband and my son." She sat down on the edge of the mattress. She looked as though she might be changing her mind.

"The future is for the children," Hannah said quietly. "For Yasmin here, and for those two grandsons in London you've never seen. All we can do is what's best for them. What's best for Yasmin now is to get her to a place where she'll be safe, have enough to eat, go to school and become the young woman her parents would have wanted her to be. That's the gift you can give her. And Mumtaz, too. Your daughter must be frantic to have you and Yasmin safe with her."

The old woman's eyes teared up, but she nodded.

"Do you have a small bag we can put your things in?" Hannah asked.

The old woman's forehead creased in thought, and then she turned to her granddaughter. "Your old school satchel will hold everything, I think. It's in the other bedroom. Run and fetch it. It's under the bed, I think. Or...no, on top of the wardrobe."

"I'll help you get it down, Yasmin," Hannah said, grabbing her rifle and flashlight.

"Ready?" Ladwell asked as they emerged from the bedroom.

"Yup," Hannah said. "Just getting a bag to put their stuff in and then we can hit the road."

She followed Yasmin into the bedroom on the other side of the sitting area and reached up to retrieve a blue nylon backpack that was sitting on top of the armoire. The wardrobe stood opposite a double bed covered in a pink chenille bedspread. A ruffled white lampshade topped a pink-striped ginger jar lamp, while a woven jute rug just next to the bed was designed to protect bare feet from the cool, decoratively tiled floor. As in the rest of the house, the impression here was of a middle-class family fallen on hard times. And yet oddly, Hannah thought, this room looked more decorated than the one Yasmin and her grandmother had been using.

By the odd, crumpled look on the child's face, Hannah guessed that this must have been her parents' room. She put a hand on the girl's shoulder. "All set?"

Yasmin pressed her lips together and nodded, starting for the other room. Hannah was right behind her, but stopped short as the beam of her flashlight fell on something behind the door. "Hold up a second, Yasmin."

On a chair hidden by the open door sat an expensive-looking hiker's pack with a North Face embroidered patch on the flap. A bright blue Nalgene hiker's water bottle hung from a carabiner hooked on one of the pack's carrying loops, and a tan, multi-pocketed jacket hung on the back of the chair. When Hannah shone her flashlight on it, she spotted an L.L. Bean label inside the collar.

She frowned. "Where did these things come from?"

The girl's shoulders gave a hesitant shrug. "They're not ours. We're just… I don't know how it got there," she said, suddenly fearful. "We should go now?"

"Hang on." Hannah tucked the flashlight under her left arm and patted down the jacket pockets. Encountering resistance, she fumbled until she found a hidden inside pocket which she unzipped, withdrawing the object she'd felt through the fabric. It was a blue passport with a gold eagle and the words *United States of America* embossed on the cover. She opened it by the light of her flashlight. The young woman's smiling face on the inside photograph seemed vaguely familiar. When Hannah read the name of the passport holder, she understood why.

"Holy smoke."

She hung onto the jacket and passport as she bounded out of the room.

"What the hell…?" Ladwell muttered behind her as she flew across the sitting room and into the bedroom on the other side.

"Zaynab," Hannah said, holding up her discoveries, "how did these get here? And that pack in the other room?"

"I don't…" The old woman hesitated, as if trying to guess what the right answer might be. It was a common response among people who lived in countries where the wrong answer could mean torture or death.

Hannah amped down her excitement. "You know Amy Fitzgerald," she said gently, telegraphing the message that there was no wrong answer here.

The old woman nodded. "She was renting the room of my son and his wife. I didn't like to take money, because really, she is a guest and it was good that she had come here to help the people. But Amy insisted, and it allowed me to buy better food for Yasmin and other things she needed, so in the end, I let her pay me."

"What the hell is going on?" Ladwell asked coming in behind Hannah. "We need to go, Nicks. This is no time for a bloody gabfest."

"I found this in the other room," Hannah said, switching to English. She held up the L.L. Bean jacket and the passport. "You'll never guess who they belong to. Amy Fitzgerald."

"And who's that when she's at home?"

"Daughter of Patrick Fitzgerald, whose family owns half of Boston or something? Amy Fitzgerald's a doctor. She was working in-country for the Red Cross/Red Crescent when she was kidnapped a week or two ago. I read about it on the flight over here."

"And that is significant to me why?"

"Because she's a hostage, and we're here, and there's a million-dollar reward for her return." Before Ladwell could reply, Hannah turned back to Zaynab and asked in Arabic, "Do you know who took her?"

"Salahuddin's men. People said there were wounded men in his compound."

"And they're holding her at this compound?"

"I don't know. Maybe."

"Aha." Hannah turned back to Ladwell and translated. "She says there's a chance Amy's at the compound of Sheikh Salahuddin, here in town."

"I don't give a toss if she is. It's not my concern. We're being paid to get this woman and her granddaughter out safely. Now, get them ready and let's get the hell on the road."

"We can't just walk away and leave, now that we've discovered where she is."

"Allegedly is. She could also be in Syria or upcountry or dead by now." Ladwell passed a finger across his throat. "Beheaded like those other poor sods."

Still, Hannah held back. "Sean, listen, this is worthwhile. Think about it. A million-dollar reward. We could radio the chopper to pick us up at the LZ tonight and take the day to check this out. One day, that's all. I can dress up in one of these burqas in here, scout around and see if I can find out if they're still holding her in the compound in town. If we could get her out…"

"Not a chance. That's not what we were sent in to do. There will be no compromising this mission on my watch."

"Just let's—"

"No. We'll report what we learned after we get these civilians safely out, but that's as far as I'm willing to go. End of discussion. If you want to get paid for your part in this mission, Nicks, you'll put your ass in gear right now, or I swear to God, I will leave you behind and you'll get sweet bloody zip. Now, move it!"

Hannah hesitated, but she knew when she was beaten.

9

Al Zawra, Iraq: Compound of Sheikh Ali Mokhtar Salahuddin

Kenner hung back in the shadows, watching the young American doctor through the window. He had spent most of his life living in the shadows. It was where he felt the most comfortable.

Soft light from a smoky kerosene lamp illuminated the infirmary like an old oil painting of some nineteenth-century battlefield hospital. The room was a classroom of the *madrassah*, the Koranic school behind the town's mosque, used for teaching the young to read and understand the holy texts. Now, rows of straw-filled pallets lined one side of the room. The gray metal supply shelves on the opposite wall held bandages, medicines and other equipment removed from the Red Crescent clinic across town.

The half-dozen *fedayeen* wounded by U.S. forces a few days earlier occupied three of the straw-stuffed mattresses on the floor. Most of them lay still, evidently asleep. They had taken bullets in arms or legs, a relatively minor problem now that the doctor had removed the copper-clad hunks of shrapnel and brought the risk of infection under control with the stolen antibiotics. One of the men had bandaged ribs, cracked against the steering wheel when the Toyota truck he'd been driving had veered into a wall. Time alone would take care of his injuries, but morphine kept him quiet in the meantime.

The injuries of one of the last men were more serious. This man had taken several rounds from an M-16, and the bullets had shattered his right femur into jigsaw puzzle pieces, some of which had been extruding through the skin when his comrades finally managed to get him back to the compound, screaming in pain. That was when the doctor from the nearby Red Crescent clinic had been kidnapped and forced into service.

Amy Fitzgerald was bent over him now, her back to the open window. She had on the same green scrubs, considerably the worse for wear, that she'd been wearing when she was seized from the clinic. Now, however, she also had on a black shawl that covered most of her head and shoulders, concealing her curly blond hair. Salahuddin had been dismayed enough by the surprise of getting himself a female doctor to insist on this exercise in modesty—though not enough to rethink his strategy and release her. That he hadn't known the newly arrived doctor at the local clinic was a woman didn't say much for the so-called sheikh's intelligence apparatus, Kenner thought contemptuously.

The wounded man groaned. Kenner heard the doctor's low, soothing murmur as she prepared an injection. She held the syringe up to the light and watched as a tiny, shimmering stream shot from the tip. When she inserted the needle into the man's arm, he stiffened briefly and then his entire body relaxed.

Dr. Fitzgerald capped the needle, then dropped back onto her heels with a sigh. As she did, the kerchief slipped off her hair and her fair curls caught the lamplight's glow. Watching her patient as his ragged breathing fell into an easier rhythm, she made no attempt to put the head covering back in place.

Finally, she got to her feet with a clanking of the iron shackle and chain that Salahuddin's men had clamped onto one ankle. Bolted to the floor in the center of the room, the chain was just long enough to allow her to move from patient to patient and to the medical supplies. She clumped awkwardly to the shelves, dragging the chain behind her. Her skin was pale with strain, and dark, puffy circles underscored her eyes. She'd lost some weight, but compared to most Iraqi women, Kenner thought, she was in ridiculously good health, with shining hair, flawless skin and the kind of gleaming white teeth that owed as much to expensive dental care as to nature.

Disposing of the needle in a small box, the doctor replaced the cap on a vial of what was probably liquid morphine and replaced the bottle on the shelf. Then, Dr. Fitzgerald walked over to what had been the teacher's table, shoved against the wall underneath the blackboard at the front of the room. Leaning wearily back against the table, she covered her face with her hands. She made no sound, but Kenner thought she might be crying.

A better man than he might have been moved by the sight of a lovely young woman, kidnapped, frightened and alone, but for Kenner, she was merely a problem of logistics and politics—a target for domestic and international attention and a poster child for everything that could backfire in this campaign if things weren't carefully handled. Salahuddin would have to be talked to.

He turned to go, but hesitated as the doctor's hands dropped away from her face. She peered, frowning, in the direction of the window, almost as if she had sensed that she was being observed. Her shackles wouldn't reach as far as the window and Kenner knew he couldn't be seen from where she was, but he dropped back deeper into shadow anyway, backing off stealthily while she stared out into the night, waiting and watching for the next nasty surprise.

She was a very long way from home.

* * *

A soft light also shone in the window of Salahuddin's quarters at the far end of the compound. Insomnia is the trademark of those who would rule the world, Kenner mused. How many plans to conquer were hatched in the dark hours before dawn while innocent souls lay in virtuous sleep?

Salahuddin's personal bodyguard sat on a chair outside his door, massive arms crossed over a barrel chest. A strapping Tikriti named Bashir, the man had once been part of the security entourage of Uday Hussein, Saddam's capricious and sadistic older son. One day, in a fit of pique over some perceived slight, Uday had apparently tossed a pot of boiling water in Bashir's face. Now, puckered and scarred from chin to hairline, the Tikriti's face resembled nothing so much as ground meat. Still, the man had been lucky to escape alive. It had been a fact of life in Saddam's Iraq that those who knew the secrets of his inner circle served without question. If they fell into disapproval, they'd better flee fast and far. If not, they died ugly deaths.

Bashir had fled to Afghanistan, where he had landed in the camp of Salahuddin. The self-styled sheikh, preparing to return to take advantage of the growing confusion in his home country, was glad to offer protection in exchange for intelligence on the ruling family's foibles and security arrangements. At the time, Salahuddin had not yet come out in open opposition to Saddam, but the writing was on the wall. Once, someone that ambitious would have been shot the moment he crossed the border. As the threat of foreign invasion mounted, however, the beleaguered dictator had sought allies wherever he could find them. Salahuddin had returned to Al Zawra and bided his time, consolidating his control on the town as he waited to see which way the wind was blowing in Baghdad. When the Americans overthrew Saddam, he declared himself ruler of this region.

The bodyguard rose to his feet and nodded as Kenner approached. *"Aasalaamu aleikum,"* he grunted. His grotesque face was scarred through to the deepest dermal layers. Incapable of expression, it was all the more unsettling for being unreadable.

"Wa-aleikum aassalaam," Kenner replied. "I need to talk to the sheikh."

The bodyguard's black eyes, like shards of jet set into quivering meat, glanced at the eastern horizon. The sky had not yet begun to lighten, but it wouldn't be long before the first gray-blue glimmer would begin to rise above the nearby hills. "He will be getting ready to make *wud'u*. You should return after the *fajr*."

The *fajr* was the first in the series of five daily prayer times, spaced out from predawn until bedtime. Through repeated prayers in the course of a day, the devout were constantly reminded of God and his blessings and were advised to use the opportunity to seek guidance and forgiveness. *Wud'u* was the ritual washing that preceded prayers—hands, mouth, nose, face, arms, head, ears and feet brought clean to Allah, cleanliness of the body symbolizing the striving for purity of the soul.

"It cannot wait," Kenner said. "I have a matter of importance to discuss with him."

Bashir seemed to scowl, the ripples of his skin creasing deeper as he contemplated this ice-eyed, ghost-haired infidel whom the sheikh had inexplicably admitted to his inner circle. The bodyguard wasn't fooled by Kenner's alleged conversion to Islam. Trust in anyone, let alone strangers, had no place in his experience. Suspicion and paranoia were all that had kept him alive thus far.

He raised one massive hand. "Wait here."

He rapped lightly, then stepped into the sheikh's quarters and shut the door behind him. After a brief rumble of voices, the door opened again and Bashir stepped out, giving Kenner a grudging flick of the wrist that signaled permission to enter.

Inside, Salahuddin sat cross-legged on thick carpets, wearing a long white robe and crocheted skullcap, a wooden lap desk propped across his knees. He was working by the light of a brass oil lamp that hung by a chain from a pole set into the mosaic tiled floor. He gestured for Kenner to settle opposite him.

Despite a long, wiry beard and bushy eyebrows, his face was deceptively benign, his eyes a gentle, doelike brown. Though he had no family outside of the men who followed him, he looked almost fatherly. On the occasions when Kenner had seen him issue an order condemning some poor sod to be flogged or shot, the sheikh's expression left the impression that the ruling pained him more than the condemned man. Salahuddin was a political handler's dream. A man with a face like that could be unstoppable, Kenner knew, having spent a lifetime supporting those whose ambitions meshed with the interests of his own masters.

He had first met Salahuddin in Afghanistan, introduced by none other than Dick Stern, who was at the time working undercover, running anti-Soviet operations with the *mujaheddin* resistance. Salahuddin had showed up in the country for the first time in early 1989, just a few weeks before the Russians finally pulled out of Afghanistan. A young man of twenty-one who'd bought into the *jihadist* movement during a stint in prison, Salahuddin seemed disappointed to have missed out on the fun. Unschooled and largely illiterate, then as now, but intensely ambitious nonetheless, he went on from there to training camps in Syria and Yemen. Like Osama bin Laden, he was a follower of the strict Wahhabi strain of Islam, but there was little evidence that bin Laden had ever accepted Salahuddin as an equal or even a protégé in the struggle against the Zionists and western infidels—which played nicely into Kenner's grand scheme of things. Salahuddin was a man desperate to be taken seriously.

"*Aasalaamu aleikum,*" Salahuddin said, smiling benignly.

Kenner settled cross-legged on the carpet and inclined his head briefly. "*Wa-aleikum aassalaam.*"

"You cannot sleep?"

"My duties prevent it. And you?"

"Just so. I was just going to have some tea. Join me?"

"Thank you."

Salahuddin took a brass pot from a tray at his side and poured out two cups of steaming tea that must have been brought in only moments before. Kenner winced as the sheikh dropped four lumps of sugar into each cup, turning the strong black stuff into syrup that Kenner found almost undrinkable. Many children in the town went without bread, but Salahuddin always had ample food and plenty of black market sugar for his sickly-sweet tea.

"What is it that troubles you, Sheikh?" Kenner asked, glancing at the document spread out on the lap desk. It was a map of central Iraq, he noted.

"The American and British forces are closing in," Salahuddin said, passing a hand over the map. "Up until now, they have been concentrating on the major cities, but now that the larger centers are more or less secured, they are expanding their search for Saddam. I think the encounter with the American forces last week was only the first shot. I fear there will be others."

"They will not attack if they are sure of your cooperation."

"So you say. And yet, they shot my men."

"They could not have known they were your men, Sheikh. And the situation is confused at the moment. The Americans are still trying to sort out who to trust. That's why you should let me speak to them for you."

"I think rather it is I who must decide if *they* can be trusted," Salahuddin replied. "So far, I am not confident. And now, I hear, they have put a reward on my head because I brought the doctor in to care for the men they wounded."

Kenner sat back, confused for a moment until he realized what reward Salahuddin meant. "No, Sheikh, not on your head. The reward is for the safe return of the woman. And it is her family, not the American government that has sponsored it. Her father is a powerful and wealthy man. It may have been a mistake to take her."

"I did not know when I sent for a doctor that it would turn out to be an American woman. There had been an Iraqi doctor at the clinic before."

"Yes, sir, but he was a cousin of Saddam, as you know. He fled after Uday and Qusay were killed, fearing that the Americans would kill every Hussein they could get their hands on. The American girl arrived only a few days before your men took her."

"Nevertheless, I must have a doctor for my men and there is no other. Besides, if the Americans know that I hold a member of one of their wealthy families, they will think twice about sending their bombers and helicopter gun ships against me. And the *jihadist* forces, meanwhile, will know that Sheikh Salahuddin is a serious force to be reckoned with. They are scattered and disorganized. They need leadership. As more and more of them hear of our growing strength here, they will flock to our side."

Kenner sipped his tea and made a show of appearing to ponder the other man's words. "P.T. Barnum," he murmured.

The sheikh frowned. "What?"

"Barnum. He was an American showman of the nineteenth century. He believed that all publicity was good publicity."

Salahuddin raised his cup and nodded. "This Barnum was wise."

"My concern, Sheikh, is that you may not be safe as long as you hold her here. As I say, her father is an influential man. As long as she is in your command compound, someone may come looking for her. She is not worth the trouble."

Salahuddin sat silent for a bit, stroking his beard. "That may be," he said finally, "but unless you can find another doctor for me, she must stay."

Kenner planted his hands on his knees, frowning. "I understand your concern for your men. It is a credit to your humanity and your leadership. However, keeping the infirmary here makes your forces a target and puts you yourself at unacceptable risk."

Salahuddin shrugged. "I will survive, *inshallah.* Or not. I do not fear martyrdom."

"I know that. I might suggest, however, that you not seek it before your time. You are of more use to your people and to Allah alive than dead." He sighed. "At least let me move the infirmary and the doctor away from the center of operations, to the farm we commandeered outside of town. In that way, if the Americans do come looking for her, you and your *fedayeen* are not at risk of getting caught in the crossfire."

And, Kenner thought, the better I can control the situation, deciding whether and when it might suit my purposes to have Amy Fitzgerald show up dead rather than alive.

The sheikh stroked his beard. "Perhaps," he said. "Let me think on it." Then he glanced out the window. "And now, my son, it is time to make *wud'u* and offer up our prayers. Guidance will come to those who believe."

Kenner bowed his head. *"Inshallah."*

10

In the hills west of Al Zawra, in the heart of Iraq's Sunni Triangle

Hannah liked to think it wasn't just the million-dollar reward that motivated her "damn stupidity," as Sean Ladwell put it. After all, she and Amy Fitzgerald were contemporaries—could have been girlfriends, if Hannah weren't the Chicago-raised child of working-class immigrants and Amy the private-school offspring of Boston money and power.

Yeah, right. Girlfriends. That could've happened....

Still, while examining the passport she'd found back at the house in Al Zawra, Hannah had noted that the doctor was twenty-seven, just a few months younger than herself. For all the privileges Amy must have had growing up, she could have turned out to be a ditzy, club-hopping clotheshorse. Instead, according to the profile Hannah had read in the newspapers, she'd studied hard, gotten a medical degree, worked in a tough inner-city E.R., and then made her way to Iraq to try to help out here.

Studying the smiling face and blond, curly hair of the young woman in the passport picture, Hannah had no doubt this woman held the same hopes for a long and happy future that she herself did. But just like Hannah's, Amy's dreams had been disrupted by malicious forces beyond her control. It wasn't fair and it wasn't right. Hannah had spent enough time regretting the nasty surprises in her own life to feel sympathy at any time circumstances played cavalier games with someone's life.

Before the Brandywine team left the house in Al Zawra to head back to the rendezvous with the chopper, Hannah zipped Amy's passport into a pocket of her cargo pants. Even if Ladwell wouldn't buy into a rescue mission, they could at least alert American authorities when they got back to Baghdad's Green Zone that they'd picked up the kidnapped doctor's trail and had a notion where she was being held. Of course, that was no guarantee that a rescue mission would be mounted anytime soon. With every day, the risk grew that Amy's captors would move her—or worse. On the other hand, once they got back to Baghdad, Hannah thought, maybe she could convince someone of the wisdom of putting together a private rescue operation—one in which she herself could play a lead role.

Now, as the Brandywine team crouched in the rocks and scrub surrounding the LZ with Zaynab and her granddaughter, listening to the rotor thrum of the returning helicopter, Hannah felt the passport weighing on her and her frustration mounted. It wasn't all about sisterhood, she had to admit. The more she thought about it, the more she realized that this was as doable right now as it was ever going to be. If Amy was still in Al Zawra, then it might just be possible to spring her, and she herself was the ideal candidate for the job. No one would expect a woman to try anything, so the element of surprise would be on her side. And there was even transport back at the house where they'd found Zaynab and her granddaughter. Looking through the window of a covered shed at the back of the house, Hannah had spotted an old Toyota pickup truck. It had been Yasmin's father's, Zaynab had said. Someone had driven it back to the house the day after he was killed. The keys, presumably, were still in the truck or somewhere in the house. Zaynab would be able to tell her where.

It was about fifty miles from Al Zawra to Baghdad and the comparative safety of the Green Zone, Hannah calculated. An hour's drive. Hazardous, maybe, but she was trained in survival and evasion tactics. She knew the language and the culture. Maybe all her training and experience had been leading up to this very mission. She could do it. There might be no one else who was as uniquely suited as she was to pull it off.

A million bucks. She could do a lot with that kind of money.

In the first place, she could finally afford to hire a decent lawyer to help get her son back. Her ex-husband and his legal buddies had run circles around her bargain basement family law guy during the custody hearings when she'd lost Gabe to Cal and Christie. And if— no, *when*—Hannah went back to court to challenge their current arrangements, she had no doubt that Cal would try to steamroller right over her again. Unless, that is, she had legal guns to match his.

Here, as in many other areas of life, it was a classic case of those who have, get more, while the little guy just keeps falling into deeper and deeper holes. She knew for a fact that colleagues who worked high profile divorce and family law cases had provided their services mostly free of charge to her ex—just lawyer buddies, trading favors. In exchange, as a celebrity defense attorney with a rising profile and several professional sports figures and above-the-title movie stars in his client roster, Cal had Grammy and Academy Award tickets he could trade off, as well as impossible-to-get ringside, rink-side and courtside seats at sporting events. He also had an entrée to the hottest clubs and parties in L.A., all provided by his growing stable of rich clients and their handlers. Hannah would need big bucks to level that playing field.

And that wasn't all. Even the best legal team wouldn't do her much good if she couldn't provide a stable home for Gabe, with opportunities at least somewhat comparable to what Cal and Christie could give him. That meant she had to have enough money to live on for the next five years at least—and ideally, until Gabe finished high school. Living in a tiny condo in Silver Lake, spending nothing on herself and banking most of her security work earnings, she'd started to build up a nice little nest egg. But even with the recent rise in overseas contract security work, the best she could hope to earn in a year was about $250,000, and that was taxable unless she spent at least two hundred days out of the country, which didn't leave much time for being with Gabe.

A million bucks, however, was four years' income in one go. If she could make some kind of arrangement with the Fitzgeralds to dole out the reward in small increments over an extended period, maybe she could even avoid taking too big a tax hit. That meant four years to spend full-time with her young son instead of dodging bullets and sweating it out in one overheated, godforsaken, fly-infested swamp after another.

So maybe it wasn't just the money that started her thinking about going back for Amy Fitzgerald. But the money sure wouldn't hurt.

The sky was still dark, but a navy-blue tinge touched the eastern horizon and the stars overhead were beginning to fade.

Four red flares burned at the corners of the LZ, signaling the team's readiness for pickup. As the chopper dropped, the rescue team and their charges shielded their eyes from the swirling dust. When the skids touched down, the rotors slowed but did not stop. The chopper was slingloading—flying with the side door open, a gunner scanning the area for danger while the bird came in.

"All right, let's move out!" Ladwell said, as the gunner waved them forward. "Wilcox, you go first. Nicks, you're next with the girl. Tell the grandmother to stay close behind with Nuñez. I'll bring up the rear."

Hannah turned to the old woman. "This is our ride," she told her in Arabic. "I'll take Yasmin, and Nuñez here will help you. Take our arms and keep your heads down, both of you. Walk quickly."

Zaynab gave the chopper a dubious look. "I don't know…."

"You'll be fine, I promise," Hannah said. "It's just a short ride to the Baghdad airport. From there, you'll be put on a plane to London. Mumtaz will be at the other end when you and Yasmin arrive."

Still, the grandmother hesitated, her fear apparent. "I have never flown before. I have hardly even been out of Al Zawra. Perhaps…"

Hannah gave her arm a gentle squeeze. "Come on, now, you'll be fine. Hey, you survived invasions, bombs, Saddam and Salahuddin. How hard can anything be after that?"

The old woman tore her eyes away from the roaring machine, looked at Hannah and smiled grimly. "You are right. Yasmin, go with Hannah," she told her granddaughter. "I'll be right behind you."

Wilcox, a refrigerator-sized African-American from Houston, ducked low and led the way, Hannah and the girl hard on his heels. When they reached the chopper, Wilcox and the gunner each reached out one hand and lifted Yasmin into the open doorway as easily as if she were a stuffed toy. When Nuñez and Zaynab came up behind them, Hannah took the bag with their clothes, standing back while Nuñez and Wilcox hoisted her into the bird and the gunner got her strapped in. Hannah tossed the bag in, her mind racing.

Sean Ladwell brought up the rear, crouching low and pivoting with his rifle as he watched for signs of opposition. "Okay, let's go, let's go!" he yelled, his free arm windmilling.

Wilcox turned and offered a hand to Hannah—chivalry dies hard—but she shook her head. "Go ahead," she shouted, standing aside as the big man hoisted himself aboard. She cocked her head at Nuñez. "Go."

He frowned, then shrugged and leapt in behind the others.

Ladwell had his back to the bird, watching their rear, but he glanced over his shoulder. "What the hell are you waiting for, Nicks? Get onboard!"

She hesitated one split second longer, then stepped aside and shook her head. "No, you go."

"Get on the bloody bird, woman!"

"I'm not going."

"What the—? What do you mean, not going?"

"I'm going back for Amy Fitzgerald."

"Are you out of your mind?"

"I'm not leaving her here."

"Yes, you bloody well are."

"Nope."

"This chopper is not waiting for you, this goddamn Fitzgerald woman or anyone. That's not our mission. Now get onboard. That's an order!"

"I've fulfilled my part of the mission," Hannah yelled back. "I was to translate and help you get the woman and her granddaughter out. I did that. They know where they're going and what's happening next. When you turn them over in the Green Zone, there'll be other Arabic speakers on the receiving end. You don't need me anymore."

"You can't do this. Now, get on the goddamn chopper!"

"I'm not going, Ladwell. I mean it."

"You haven't got a hope in hell of finding that doctor and getting her out."

"I think I can. I have an idea."

"Don't be an idiot. A million dollars is no bloody good to you if you're dead, now, is it?"

From the open door of the chopper, Hannah saw Nuñez and Wilcox and the others watching, dumbfounded. "That's my concern, not yours," she told Ladwell.

"You aren't deluded enough to think we're going to wait for you while you try to pull off some harebrained scheme, do you? Or come back? Because it's not going to happen."

"I'll get back to Baghdad. It's only fifty miles."

"It might as well be five hundred. Do you know how many insurgents there could be from here to the capital, even supposing you manage to get out of this town alive?"

"I've got a pretty good idea, but it's a risk I'm willing to take. Now, get going, will you? The sun's going to be up soon. You need to get back to Baghdad and I need to get back to Al Zawra before it gets light."

Ladwell stared at her for a moment, incredulous. "You stupid woman! You can't be serious."

"I'm dead serious. Now, go!"

He looked as if he were going to grab her and toss her physically onto the chopper, but something about Hannah's stance or her grip on the M-16 must have convinced him of the folly of trying. Finally, he shook his head in disgust. "Oh, bloody hell! It's your skin. Stay. But make no mistake about it, Nicks. Even if you get out alive, you'll never work for Brandywine again if I have anything to say about it."

She laughed. "Not a problem. I'll either be dead or rich enough not to care. One way or the other, I won't be looking for any more work in this place."

Ladwell turned away. He reached out to grab the handle alongside the open chopper door, but Hannah grabbed his arm.

"One more thing, Sean."

"What?"

"Don't even think about stiffing me on my fee for this job. I mean it. I get back to the States and the money's not in my account, I am gonna be one bitch on wheels. You don't wanna think about the grief I will cause you and Brandywine both."

He snorted and jumped up into the chopper. "Stupid woman. Let's go!" he shouted to the pilot.

Hannah crouched lower and ducked back and away into the low scrub, waiting for the bird to lift off. The motor revved and the rotors spun faster, drowning out the argument that seemed to be going on inside the chopper. She squinted against the whipping dust as she saw Ladwell gesticulating angrily. It was Nuñez he seemed to be having the most trouble with.

Oh, Lord preserve me. Don't tell me he's pulling some Latino machismo code of honor crap with that bulldog Brit. Not gonna fly, Nuñez. Don't waste your breath.

As if to underscore her point, Ladwell gave one final shake of his head and settled into one of the chopper's jump seats, strapping on his seat belt and waving impatiently at the pilot to take off. The bird began to lift, the rotors whipping a hurricane of sand as the skids left the ground.

Blinded by the grit, Hannah turned her back to the bird and crouched down, covering her head to protect it from stones kicking up around her as the rotors thwapped louder and louder. Finally, the noise level shifted as the chopper reached cruising altitude, shifted directions, and took off in a southerly direction, heading for Baghdad. It took a few seconds for the wind at ground level to settle back to normal.

Great. Another frigging Iraqi dermabrasion facial, Hannah thought ruefully.

She rocked back onto her knees, taking a deep breath and wiping the fresh layer of silt from her face, her hands, and her clothes. "Well, girl," she muttered, "you've gone and done it now."

"That's for sure."

Startled, she leapt to her feet and spun around, rifle at the ready—only to find Nuñez standing in front of her. "What the hell are you doing?" she demanded.

"Stickin' around to watch your back. A person might ask you the same thing."

"I don't need your protection."

"Yeah, I figured that. Those kidnappers don't know how much trouble they're in."

"I mean it."

"I know. I just thought I might be able to help. I'm a hell of a shot, and you know what we old marines are like. *Semper fi.*"

"*Old* marines? Jesus, Nuñez, do you even shave yet?"

"Spent three years in the corps, for your info, lady. Top sniper in my class, matter of fact. Like it or not, you can use my help."

"Yeah, right, and you can use a million bucks, right? What do you think is going to happen here? I get the girl out, then succumb to 'friendly fire,' leaving you to pick up the cash and the glory. That it?"

"Nah, I'll settle for half."

"Oh, no, no, no. Not a chance. This is my gig."

"You seriously think you can pull it off on your own?"

"Maybe, maybe not. But I do know this—I've got a hell of a better shot at it than you."

"You think?"

"Yeah, I do. How's your Arabic, Nuñez?"

"Umm…Ali Baba, *jihad,* Sinbad… Well, okay. Fair enough. But look, Nicks, I don't care how smart you are, you can still take a bullet in the back if there's nobody watchin' it for you."

She frowned, but he had a point. And if she'd simply taken her information back to the Green Zone, she'd have been lucky to collect any part of the reward at all. Even a fifty-fifty split looked good compared to that scenario.

"All right," she said. "You're here now, so I guess I'm stuck with you. But you follow my lead, got it?"

"Check." Nuñez squinted down into the town, where the smoke of the first few morning fires could be seen. "So whaddya say, boss? We should get back to that house before the whole town wakes up, no?"

Hannah stared at him for a moment, then shook her head. "What the hell," she said, turning on her heel and starting down the hill. "Let's go do this."

11

Al Zawra, Iraq

They were back in the kitchen of Zaynab's house as dawn broke and the neighborhood came to life. By the morning light, they could see that the yard, large and surrounded by a five-foot wall, was relatively private, sitting as it did on the corner of two roadways. The closest house, about a hundred yards away, had only one window facing them, opposite the bedroom in which Zaynab and Yasmin had been sleeping. By its small size, Hannah guessed that the window on the house next door was a bathroom window. If they kept quiet and stayed away from the bedroom, there was little chance of neighbors spotting them. As for the roadway, the wall was sufficient to block all but the most determined prying eyes.

"No way I'm sitting back here while you go by yourself," Nuñez said. He leaned back and crossed his arms—not an easy thing to do with a barrel chest covered by a Kevlar-plated flak jacket. "I told you, you can be boss as long as you don't do anything stupid. This is stupid."

"It's not stupid."

"Oh, yeah? So what's the plan?"

"That's the point, Nuñez," Hannah said, opening kitchen cupboards one by one. "There is no plan. Not yet. Not till I figure out the lay of the land."

She walked over to the small refrigerator. It was empty and a little rank-smelling, so she closed it again quickly. With no electricity to keep it running, the grandmother had obviously given up on that modern convenience. She groaned. "God, I'm starving!"

Nuñez ripped open a pocket on his flak vest, pulling out a foil packet. "Beef jerky?"

Hannah glanced back. "I've got some, too, thanks, but you know what? I hate that stuff."

"Pure protein. Keeps you going."

"Yeah, I know, and if I get desperate enough, I'll—aha! Bingo!"

A closet next to the refrigerator turned out to be a pantry stocked with a few canned goods, some fruit and vegetables, and a covered tin that held rounds of flatbread. In a bowl under a damp towel she found something that smelled, when she put her nose to it, remarkably like hummus.

"Hallelujah!" she said, bringing it out to the kitchen table along with some dates. She grabbed one of the flatbread rounds, tore it and handed half to Nuñez. "Pull up a chair."

He walked to the pantry and rummaged around until he found a bottle of some sort of juice—pomegranate, Hannah guessed by the picture on the label. Although she could speak Arabic, she couldn't read it very well, but that sure looked like a fair enough approximation of the pomegranates she used to eat at her grandparents' house in Beirut when she was a kid. Flipping cupboard doors until he found glasses, Nuñez hooked a couple between two fingers and brought them to the table with the juice, dropping his stocky frame onto a stool. His viselike hands wrestled the lid off the bottle. After he'd poured out the juice and slid one glass across the table to Hannah, he sniffed at his own. Apparently deciding that the stuff passed muster, he downed the entire glass in a couple of gulps. Slapping it back on the table, he wiped his mouth with the back of his hand.

"So, where do we start?" he asked.

Hannah shrugged, her mouth full of pita and hummus. "The old woman said she thought Salahuddin was holding Amy Fitzgerald at his compound," she said, after washing it down with a gulp of the sweet-tart juice. "That's by the mosque in town. We saw the layout in the premission briefing, remember? But she could be wrong, or the doctor could have been moved by now. It's nearly a week that they've been holding her. I need to find out if she's still there."

"And how do you plan to do that?"

Hannah popped a date in her mouth. "I have an idea, but I may have to improvise. I won't know until I go into town."

"Fine. We'll go together."

"No, I'll go alone."

"Why should you go alone?"

"Because you'll stand out like a sore thumb, Nuñez, why do you think? You can't just go strolling down the street in the heart of the Sunni Triangle with your M-16 and your Kevlar and figure nobody's going to blink an eye."

"Like you won't stand out? Call me crazy, but I don't think there's too many broads in fatigues walking around this town."

Hannah took another swipe of hummus, then held up one finger as she rose and walked to the bedroom. Once there, she kept to the walls. The paisley curtains were still drawn, but there was no point in risking having her shadow pass across them in case someone was looking out from the house next door. A moment later, she walked back into the kitchen holding up one of the black burqas that had been hanging in the wardrobe.

"Nobody's going to see the camos because I'm going to be wearing this sexy little number," she said. "There's something like eight or ten thousand people in this town. It's not like a small village where everyone knows everyone else. The old woman said Salahuddin ordered women to cover up when they go out in public. Nobody's going to notice one more woman in a burqa, or abaya, or whatever they call these stupid black pup tents in this neck of the desert."

Nuñez snorted and pointed at her feet. "A burqa over combat boots. Yeah, right. That'll work."

Hannah frowned down at her tan leather boots. "You have a point there. Hang on."

She returned to the bedroom and the armoire, rummaging around on the floor until she found a couple of pairs of women's shoes—one pair were black, low-heeled pumps, the other some cheap green Chinese-made sneakers. The pumps would be useless if she had to make a run for it, but the sneakers would be okay—if they fit. Back at the kitchen table, she unlaced her boots, kicking them aside and pulling on the sneakers. They were too tight with her heavy socks, but when she stripped those off, too, the running shoes were only a little snug.

"Not exactly high fashion, but they'll do in a pinch. Literally in a pinch," she added grimly. She turned back to the food on the table. "I can go and nose around, see if I can pick up any sense of what kind of security they have on the compound and whether Amy Fitzgerald's there. I'll scout out access points and try to see if there's any obvious way to do this. It shouldn't take long. I'll get back as fast as I can."

"And what am I supposed to do in the meantime?"

"Lay low, for one thing. If there are neighbors around during the day, we don't need them getting the idea anything unusual's going on over here. Zaynab told me she and her granddaughter kept a tea stand in the central market, so people will expect the house to be quiet during the day. Make sure you don't do anything to draw attention to yourself."

"I don't like this. I didn't sign on for this just to sit back here and twiddle my thumbs."

"Nobody asked you to sign on at all, Nuñez." Hannah frowned. "But as long as you are here, there is one thing you could do."

"What's that?"

"You know anything about cars?"

"Only everything there is to know. Bought an old sixty-eight Mustang when I was fifteen, rebuilt the engine from the ground up."

"Good. That old Toyota truck out in the shed—it belonged to Zaynab's son, the one who was killed by Salahuddin's men. Look around for the keys, then check it out, see if it's in running order. And if there's any gas in the tank. But you should do it quietly, it goes without saying. You can't let anyone spot you out there."

Nuñez looked insulted. "Did I tell you I was the best in my unit at evasion tactics?"

"Well, you are just a bundle of talents, aren't you? Either that or a bundle of BS."

"Lady, you got no idea."

Hannah frowned as she ran a piece of bread slowly through the chickpea dip. "Why are you doing this, Nuñez? You could have been on your way home by now."

"I got my reasons."

"You figured I needed babysitting? This some machismo thing?"

"No."

"Well, what then?"

Nuñez said nothing for a long moment. And then finally, "I got a kid."

"You've got a kid? Exactly how old are you, Nuñez? Twelve?"

"Very funny. I turned twenty-one in April."

"Okay, and so you've got a kid. You married?"

"Uh-huh. Three years."

"Jeez, and I thought I was a child bride."

Nuñez looked up, surprised. "You married?"

"Is that so hard to believe?"

"No. It's just…well, what are you doing this kind of work for? I wouldn't let my wife come to a place like this. No way."

"How chivalrous of you. Fortunately for me, I lost my hero. I was married but I'm not anymore. Got hitched at eighteen, had a kid at nineteen, divorced by twenty-four. Now, I get to do what I want."

"And so? Why you doing this work? You can't type?"

"Typing doesn't pay worth a damn. And for your information, by the way, I used to be a cop."

"No kidding."

"Yeah, go figure. Anyway, I'm probably doing this work now for the same reason you are—the money's good."

"But you got a kid?"

"A son. He's eight."

"And you left him to come here?"

"He lives with my ex and his trophy wife. Needless to say, I'm not too thrilled about that, but up to now, I haven't had much say in the matter."

"I thought the mother always got the kid in a divorce."

"Yeah, well, that's the theory, but it didn't work out that way in my case. Anyway, we were talking about you, not me."

Nuñez sighed. "I got a little girl, Raquel. She's two." He smiled. "Man, she's so cute." He unbuttoned one of his shirt buttons and pulled out a plastic folder, then flipped it open. "That's her with Lara, my wife. They had the picture done for my birthday."

Hannah took the folder and looked down at a very young and

very pretty dark-haired girl holding an adorable toddler on her lap, the baby girl all ribbons and ruffles and smiles. "They're beautiful, both of them," she said, smiling back instinctively at that much domestic bliss. She looked up at the former marine. "So, same question then. What are you doing leaving them at home and coming to this godforsaken place?"

He took the picture back and held it gently in his hands, his thumbs stroking the faces under the plastic cover. "Raquel needs stuff."

"Yeah, kids do, that's a fact. Still…"

"Not like regular kids. She needs a lot of stuff. Equipment and special care and…stuff."

Hannah said nothing, only studied him.

He put the picture away and poured another glass of juice. "Something went wrong when Lara was pregnant," he said finally. "In the womb. The baby's spinal cord wasn't closed off. It's called spina bifida."

"I've heard of that. Oh, man. So, she needs a lot of medical care, then?"

"Yeah. I mean, I've got okay medical coverage, 'cause of having been in the marines and all. But it's not enough. There's some treatment, maybe surgery, that she might need one day. Some of it's still experimental, so our health plan might not cover it. But if there's a chance she could walk one day? And if you couldn't do that for your kid just because it cost too much? I mean, how could you live with yourself?"

Hannah nodded. "Gotcha. Well, okay then, I guess that answers the question. We're both here for our kids." She pushed back from the table and slapped her hands clean on her pants. "So, let's get on with it. Time's a-wasting, and we've got a doctor to rescue."

12

Central Square: Al Zawra, Iraq

Finding Sheikh Salahuddin's compound was a simple enough matter. All Hannah had to do was head for the center of town, about a mile and half from Zaynab's house, then look for the tallest structure around—the minaret topping the onion-domed tower of the mosque from which the *muezzin* made the five-times-daily call to prayer.

There was no doubt great symbolism in the sheikh's choice of the adjoining *madrassah* as his center of operations. It gave a certain pious stamp of approval to his ambitions. Did the mullah who controlled the mosque support the sheikh? Hannah wondered. It was possible. After years of repressive rule by Saddam and his Sunni cronies, the country's Shia and Kurdish populations were gunning for bear now, which made the Sunni minority more than a little nervous. Or maybe Salahuddin had simply made the cleric an offer he couldn't refuse, forcing him to hand over the Koranic teaching center for his own base of operations.

As Hannah turned down a narrow street that led to the central square, squeezing past pedestrians going in the opposite direction, she allowed herself a small smile. Under normal circumstances, it would have been stupid—fatal, even—to indulge in that kind of smugness. She was behind enemy lines, after all, and insurgents had already beheaded a couple of hostages. She was under no illusion they wouldn't do the same to her and Nuñez if they were captured. In this case, however, she knew the smirk would go undetected. Not even the crinkles at the corners of her eyes would give her away, hidden as they were behind the closely woven mesh eye slit of the burqa that covered her from head to toe.

In the stifling heat of midsummer, where the outside temperature had to be pushing the high nineties even now, just a couple of hours after sunup, she was sweating like a horse under the black polyester shroud. She couldn't wait to get out of the stuffy, confining thing, not to mention the green canvas sneakers that had already raised blisters on both feet. For now, though, they served her purpose. As she approached the square with its market and mosque, she knew she looked like just another wife heading for town to bring back a few provisions for her family. A mere woman.

And for all its discomfort, she thought, a burqa hid a multitude of sins. At the moment, it concealed the 9 mm Beretta holstered at the waist of her rolled-up desert camouflage pants. It also covered the serrated hunting knife strapped to her thigh, the wood-handled garroting wire hooked on one carabiner clipped to her belt, and the taser hooked on another. These were her first weapons of choice, silent and swift, if she ran into trouble. In a calculated decision, she'd left her M-16 rifle back at the house with Nuñez, as well as the two-way radio that would have allowed her to communicate with him. No point in pushing her luck. She wanted her hands freer than they would have been if she'd had a rifle to keep still under the burqa, and she couldn't be sure Salahuddin's men weren't monitoring for electronic transmissions. This foray was about advance reconnaissance only. If she could confirm the intel that Amy Fitzgerald was being held in Salahuddin's compound, then she and Nuñez would be back with their full complement of gear and a plan of operations.

The streets near the main square were narrow and dusty, with no sidewalks, so that when the infrequent car or truck passed by, pedestrians had to hug the white limestone walls of the mostly two-story buildings. At least she was in shade here, Hannah thought, feeling a bead of sweat trickle down her spine. Clotheslines were strung between overhead balconies. As she passed under one open window, she heard the sound of children's laughter, answered by the harried snap of a busy mother. Farther along, a group of men dressed in *dishdashas,* the typical Iraqi costume of long tunic and baggy pants, perched on low wooden stools in the open doorway of what looked to be a tailor's shop. They gossiped, drank tea and smoked while two men at the center of the group clacked tiles around a backgammon board. No one, Hannah was relieved to note, gave her so much as a glance as she swept past. She was just another black crow among many out on the street that morning.

As she emerged from the shadows of the side street into the brilliant glare of the central square, the sudden wash of light was blinding, in spite of the mesh over her eyes. The temperature jumped by at least ten degrees. Her body pined for a leap into the cool Pacific Ocean back home, but her head was preoccupied with the problem at hand—how to find the doctor, how to spring her, and then how to get out of town without getting killed.

The market consisted of one long, central building, open on all sides but covered with a corrugated metal roof. The mosque was at the other end. Hannah followed a group of women carrying net bags as they entered the open-air building and walked down the center aisle. The place was crowded and noisy, hundreds of conversations bouncing off the metal ceiling. Merchants selling everything from hemp rope to produce to meat to tools occupied booths on either side of the aisle. Those on the inside were obviously the cream of the town's merchants. Poorer vendors had their goods spread on blankets outside the building. Inside or out, all the goods looked sparse, dusty and slightly seedy.

As she walked past a wooden table bearing half a dozen skinned and fly-covered sheep heads, Hannah could only be thankful for the burqa covering her face. Whatever its discomforts, at least it limited the assault on her sense of smell. Even so, she felt her stomach roil in protest at the sight of those lolling tongues and milky dead eyes.

Emerging from the other end of the run, she found herself face to face with the blue-tiled mosque across the road. On the sidewalk to her left and right, poor farmers hawked a slim output of tomatoes, onions and spices to the crowd of morning market-goers. Spotting an older woman crouched on a blanket, surrounded by a few mismatched dishes and items of clothing and other goods that must have come from her own home, Hannah thought of Zaynab and her granddaughter, living a once-prosperous life but reduced of late to selling tea from a cart in this very market. They should even now be winging their way to a new life in London.

She approached the old woman and hovered nearby, pretending to study her goods but keeping an eye on activity at the mosque and the walled compound beyond.

"Would you like to buy a lovely bracelet? Twenty-four carat. Very nice." The old woman held up a gold bangle.

Hannah crouched and took it, pretending to consider as she continued to watch the activity around the mosque. The bracelet was engraved with a geometric pattern of swirls and dots that managed to look both ancient and very modern. "It is lovely," Hannah agreed, handing it back, "but I wasn't really looking for jewelry."

The old woman had kohl-lined eyes and high cheekbones. She might once have been a great beauty. How old was she? Hannah wondered. Hard to say. Although she was draped like Hannah in a dusty black burqa pinned close under her chin, her face was uncovered. With deeply weathered skin and missing several teeth, she looked seventy-five, but hardship had a way of rapid-aging people, so she could have been fifteen or twenty years younger.

"I have some nice plates here," the old woman said. "They come from the potters of Amman. You sound as if you might be Jordanian yourself, no?"

"I was born there," Hannah said, mentally inventing a personal legend to explain herself and her presence in Al Zawra. The key was to keep it simple yet credible and volunteer as little information as possible. "You have many lovely things, grandmother. Why are you selling them?"

"Ah, well, you know how it is in these times. I am a widow. My husband died in the spring."

"I'm very sorry."

"It was the will of Allah. He had pneumonia."

"There was no medicine for him?"

The old woman shook her head. "He fell ill after the American soldiers came. The doctor ran off and the clinic was abandoned, all the medicines stolen."

"That must have been before the lady doctor came to Al Zawra?"

"Oh, yes, quite a while before that. Although I do not know if my husband would have gone to her. He was old-fashioned, not like the young people."

"Mothers with children," Hannah suggested.

"Just so. The young mothers, they were very happy when she came. Do you have children?"

Hannah nodded. "A son. He's eight years old."

She glanced through her mesh eye covering back at the compound. Depending on how frequently this old woman laid out her blanket here, she might have some idea of what was happening over there. It was an ironic fact of life in the Middle East, even in the most conservative countries, that women were sometimes the best source of information, however much they might be overlooked. Fundamentalists might think them unworthy of consideration as a serious potential security gap, but because of that, women saw and overheard a great deal. Why worry, when these women saw and spoke to no one outside their small family circle? Hannah had once worked a job in Afghanistan, where it was an educated, English-speaking woman in a Taliban-controlled village—veiled and locked away like every other woman there—who provided the critical intelligence on the location of an insurgent leader Hannah's group had been sent in to eliminate.

"I think my son has an ear infection," she told the old woman. "I wish I could get the doctor to look at him."

The old woman grimaced and cocked her head toward the *madrassah*. "Oh, yes, of course, but they won't let her see anyone. It's not right. The clinic is supposed to be for everyone, but now, it's just like before. They've taken the doctor and all the supplies."

"She's still there? Have you seen her?"

"I saw when they first brought her in. And I heard two of the sheikh's men talking yesterday about one of the wounded men she was taking care of, so I am thinking she must still be there."

"Do you think if I brought my son to the *madrassah* to see her they might—"

"You could ask, but I would be very surprised. Buy a lovely bracelet, ladies?" the old woman asked, distracted by three burqa-clad women passing behind Hannah.

Hannah got to her feet, holding her elbows close to her ribs so the metal carabiners on her belt wouldn't clatter. "A good day to you, grandmother," she said.

"And you. Very nice, twenty-four carats," she said to the other women, holding up the sparkling gold bangle.

Hannah stepped back and turned toward the mosque across the road. The courtyard to the side and back of it was surrounded by a high stone wall. To the right of the mosque, a heavy green wooden door was set into the stone wall, hung with elaborate black wrought-iron hinges. Two youths armed with submachine guns stood guard on either side of the door. They looked hot and bored as they watched the passing crowd.

Hannah considered a moment, then decided to cross over and try her luck. Nothing ventured, nothing gained. She paused at the edge of the roadway as a small pickup truck overloaded with bricks roared up, spewing black exhaust, its cargo bed hanging low over the rear tires. Even the black cloth of the burqa was not enough to keep that toxic brume from finding its way into Hannah's nostrils.

The truck passed by and she waited a moment for the air to clear. When it did and she looked across the road again, the green door had opened. Two men emerged from the compound, one bearded, the other not. The two youths on guard outside the door stood up straighter, making a show of vigilance. The two men coming out were dressed in identical tan pants and cotton shirts, Kalashnikov rifles cradled in their arms. Slinging the rifles over their shoulders, they pulled the door shut behind them and crossed the road.

The crowd in the streets parted before them, men and women alike leaping out of their way. One group of chatting women didn't see them fast enough, and the beardless man used the butt of his rifle to shove them aside—as though they were too tainted to be touched with a hand, Hannah thought grimly.

She stepped out of their path and turned her back to the men as they approached her. Once they had passed by, she hesitated only a split second. Then, acting on instinct, she followed them into the market building, her ears tuned in to their conversation.

13

Kilometer 86, Baghdad-to-Tikrit Highway, Iraq

The wounded *fedayeen* groaned as the modified Isuzu panel van hit yet another pothole. Kenner winced. He knew he should have sat up front with the driver, but he would have been crowded in there with at least one other man, and in this heat, that kind of proximity was not a pleasant experience. The back of the truck allowed a little more space, but it wouldn't win any prizes for comfort.

He banged his fist on the window between him and the front seat.

The driver, whose face looked green from the glow of the instrument panel in the nighttime, glanced back over his shoulder. "I am sorry," he yelled through the glass. "There is no way to avoid this unless I take the ditches."

"The ditches are apt to be mined," Kenner yelled back. "Just take it easy."

"I am. I haven't gone above thirty kilometers an hour since we left Al Zawra, but it is impossible to see these holes until we are almost in them."

Kenner glanced ahead down the road. The Isuzu's headlights

had been taped over with black tape in case of enemy aerial sur-veillance, leaving only the lower third open to cast a dim light on the roadway immediately in front of the truck. With a curfew in ef-fect and people as afraid of American planes and gunship helicop-ters as of local insurgents and thieves prowling the roadways, there was not another vehicle to be seen. Now that they had left the town behind, the surrounding countryside was pitch-black under a bril-liantly star-dappled night sky. It was like driving through the void of deep space.

"Just do better or I'll leave you by the side of the road and take the wheel myself," Kenner warned the driver.

Their destination was a small farm about four miles north of Al Zawra, where Salahuddin maintained a second compound used for training his men in weapons and tactics. Normally, it should have been a quick run, but the condition of the road was so bone-jarringly poor that it was impossible to get up any speed. When Saddam had been in power, the highway between the capital and his hometown had been as smooth as any western freeway, but since U.S.-led coalition forces had arrived and begun strafing exit routes used by the dictator's fleeing supporters, there was hardly an undamaged stretch anymore. It wasn't so much a matter of avoiding potholes as of picking which one would be the least likely to break an axle.

The man with the shattered leg groaned as they bounced yet again. Salahuddin's men had spent the day fitting out the back of the van to serve as an ambulance. Crates of medical supplies lined the walls, while the wounded *fedayeen* had been loaded in crosswise on their mattresses. The back was open, covered only by a canvas tarp tied down at the corners, fluttering in the hot night wind. Kenner had his back braced against the supply boxes as the Amer-ican doctor attended to the man with the shattered femur.

"This is stupid," she said. "Why are you moving us?"

"Shut up," Kenner ordered.

"No. This is ridiculous. I can't keep this man's leg stabilized under these conditions. Why did I bother piecing him back together if you were going to put him through this? He has a fever, and it'll be a miracle if he doesn't lose the leg."

"If he loses it, it is the will of Allah."

"And if he dies? The same, I suppose?"

Kenner shrugged.

Suddenly, the truck lurched and the patient groaned again. Dr. Fitzgerald braced herself against the floor and the boxes until they leveled out. "Surely it's Allah's will that you exercise a little common sense?"

"Give him some morphine for the pain."

"I can't. I loaded him up before we left. If I give him any more now, it'll suppress his breathing and he'll die. You won't have to wait for gangrene to set in and kill him."

"Sheikh Salahuddin has ordered you to keep him alive."

"If Sheikh Salahuddin wanted him alive, he wouldn't have ordered him moved."

"It's not safe in Al Zawra anymore."

"So, is the sheikh moving as well?"

"That's not your concern, Dr. Fitzgerald. Your job is to care for his men." Kenner turned back to watch the road through the glass window at the front of the cargo area, but he felt the young woman watching him.

"Why are you here with these people?" she asked. When he didn't answer, she pressed, "Are you American?"

"That, too, is not your concern."

"You said I was needed to take care of these men. Are you planning to let me go once I get them settled? There must be other doctors the sheikh would be more comfortable with. He obviously isn't crazy about having me."

"You will be the sheikh's guest as long as your services are needed."

"Guests come willingly. They don't have to be kidnapped at gunpoint. If the sheikh had asked me to care for his men along with my other patients at the clinic, I would have. But there are people back in Al Zawra who need attention, too. I wasn't brought to Iraq to care exclusively for combatants."

"You should not have come at all, Dr. Fitzgerald. Now that you are here, however, you will do what you're told."

"And if I refuse?"

Kenner drew his gun and leveled it at her head. "Then you will die."

She folded her arms across her chest. "Go ahead, shoot. How will your precious sheikh take care of his men, then?"

He studied her. "Good point." He turned to the patient lying on the mattress closest to him and pressed the gun into his temple. The man's eyes went wide with fear.

"What are you doing?" the doctor cried.

"I am preparing to send a martyr to paradise. Unless, of course, you think you can save him."

"I already have saved him. His condition is stable. He's going to be fine."

"Not if you don't cooperate, Dr. Fitzgerald. If you continue to irritate me, this man's condition is going to take a precipitous turn for the worse."

As the gun barrel pressed deeper into his flesh, the patient whimpered, not understanding the conversation but clearly comprehending that he was in grave danger and that the doctor's response now would mean life or death for him.

"Fine! I'll take care of them, you bastard. Just leave him alone, would you?"

Kenner withdrew the gun from the man's temple and laid it across his lap. "A very wise decision."

If the passengers in the panel truck were having a rough ride, so was Oz Nuñez. He lay spread-eagled on its roof, hanging on to racks that were mounted on either side of it to hold extra jerry cans of petrol. He braced himself each time the dim headlights picked out the shadows of yet another pothole, but there was very little warning before each bounce.

He'd slipped onto the roof as the van passed under a viaduct on the edge of Al Zawra. Now, as the truck lurched and his hipbones slammed into metal once more, it was all Nuñez could do to keep the butt of his rifle, strapped to his back, from smacking noisily against the roof and giving him away.

After dropping him near the viaduct on the edge of town just before sunset, Hannah had taken the Toyota truck ahead down the road. It was while eavesdropping on a conversation between two of Salahuddin's men, whom she'd followed into the marketplace, that she'd learned they'd been sent over to get supplies in anticipation of a move to a location north of town. When one of the men made a joke about finding some pig meat for the infidel woman, Hannah had guessed they were moving the kidnapped American doctor.

Studying the map back at Zaynab's house, she and Nuñez had come to the conclusion that the route they would most likely take was the Baghdad-to-Tikrit highway, since there were no other feasible routes north that they could see. Now, after dropping Nuñez, she was supposed to be scouting out a suitable place for an ambush.

Please, God, let it be soon, Nuñez thought.

As if in answer, his radio earpiece crackled and he heard her voice through the static. "Nuñez, do you read?"

"Ten-four," Nuñez murmured. It sounded like the cop talk he

remembered from TV, so he figured she'd like that. "Where the hell are you?"

"Two-point-five kilometers out of town, by the odometer on the truck. I found a good spot and I'm waiting. Where are you?"

"Damned if I know. En route. It's real slow going. Good thing, too. Any faster and I'd be airborne."

"Hang tough. It won't be long."

"I count a total of four armed men," Nuñez said. Using a telescoping rod with an attached mirror, he'd checked both the cab and the cargo hold of the panel truck. "Three in the front, one in the rear with the doctor and the wounded men. If the guy in back gets wind of what's happening, he could use the doctor as a shield or kill her outright."

"Okay, so we'll have to move fast. I have an idea. Just follow my lead, okay?"

Nuñez winced as the truck bounced again. "Roger."

The driver's watering eyes stared unblinking at the road ahead, gears grinding as he downshifted to avoid something that had fallen in the roadway. It looked like a tool box, although what it would be doing out here in the middle of nowhere was anyone's guess. The other two men in the cab with him cursed as the van lurched.

In spite of the tension, the driver glanced over at them, grinning. "Nice night for a drive, isn't it?"

"Shut up and watch the road," the man in the center grumbled.

"Perhaps we should see what's in that box?"

"Just get going. Next time, I drive."

Still smiling, the driver depressed the clutch, getting ready to shift gears once more.

It was at that moment that an angel of death rose up in front of them, black-winged and faceless. The apparition stood in the center of the dark roadway, silken wings outstretched—Death come calling.

The driver's foot slammed the brake—too late. He screamed as
the specter leapt onto the hood and stared at him through the
windscreen, a giant insect Cyclops with a single mesh eye.

He yanked the wheel to one side, and the tall van went into a tailspin, skidding. Top-heavy and overbalanced, it lifted onto two
wheels as the three men in the cab flailed for purchase. From the
back came screams of pain and the crashing sound of boxes, bottles and bodies spilling and crashing as the top-heavy vehicle rolled
over. Still turning in a slow ballet, it skidded on its side for a few
more meters before it finally came to a dusty stop.

Nuñez had seen the surprise coming and leapt clear just as the
van began to tip.

He whipped his M-16 around and ran to the vehicle now, arriving just as the cab's front passenger door, up in the air now, rose
open with a creak. One hand appeared and then another as a
stunned guard elbowed himself up and out. Another followed.
Down on the ground, they were just patting themselves down to
check for broken bones, when they spotted Nuñez.

One of the men reached for his holstered gun. Nuñez cut him
down where he stood. As the second opened fire, Nuñez rolled
away to the side, firing as he went, and the other, too, went down.

Nuñez got back to his feet. The dim headlights were still illuminated, but did little to light up the scene. He turned around in a
quick circle, watching for another attacker. Seeing no immediate
danger—nor Hannah, either, he realized worriedly—he let the
M-16 drop on the shoulder sling while he unholstered his pistol and
his Maglite. Holding the gun and flashlight cross-fisted in front of
him, he approached the cab cautiously and shone the light in
through the spider-crackled, bloodied front windshield.

His heart leapt. The bearded driver was staring back at him.

Nuñez ducked, but when nothing happened, he lifted his head cautiously once more. The driver was still there, his head wedged sideways against the door. Only on closer inspection did Nuñez spot the hole in the center of his forehead, just below the man's curly black hairline. The guy was dead.

Hannah, Nuñez thought. She must have gotten off a shot while the truck was going over.

He'd seen her from his vantage point on the roof when she first came out of the night and planted herself in the middle of the road. When she'd taken a running leap onto the hood of the truck, arms flapping in that stupid black robe like some bat out of hell, she'd been moving so fast none of those dudes up front had had time to react. In the rush, Nuñez had caught a flash of her khaki trousers and boots, so she must have hiked up the burqa. That girl was *loca.* Crazy. But where the hell was she now?

He hunted alongside the tipped-over van, expecting to see her black-shrouded form lying crushed underneath it. Worried about finding her, he forgot momentarily about the guy in the back of the van. Stupid.

Suddenly, he found himself looking down the barrel of a matte black pistol. The beam of his Maglite rose on a pair of piercing blue eyes and a head of short-cropped white hair.

The man said something to him in Arabic. When he didn't get a response, he switched to English. "Drop your gun!"

Nuñez hesitated for a moment, then lowered his arm.

"Drop it, I said! And the flashlight, too—now!"

Nuñez's gun hit the ground, then the Maglite. It lay on the road-way, under-lighting the scene like a kid's scary campfire trick.

"Who are you?" the white-haired man asked.

"John Wayne?"

"What the hell do you think you're doing here? Who sent you?"

"Nobody."

The movement came so fast, Nuñez didn't have time to duck before the butt of the gun struck his jaw. His back leg buckled briefly, but then he righted himself.

"I said, who sent you?"

"And I told you—nobody." Nuñez braced himself for the next blow, but instead, a blinding light hit him square in the eyes. He winced.

The man, silhouetted now, spun around just as a shot rang out. The silhouette staggered sideways. The light followed him as he stumbled at the dip at the edge of the roadway. He tumbled down the incline and into the ditch alongside.

Nuñez whipped his M-16 around on its sling. "Nicks, that you?" he asked as his eyes adjusted to the dark.

"None other," came the reply. Her flashlight panned over the ditch. "Careful. I'm not sure if I hit him or not."

As if in answer, a shot rang out. Nicks's flashlight splintered, and Nuñez heard her curse as she returned fire. He dropped, letting off several rounds as he ducked for cover behind the tipped-over van. Scrabbling around to the undercarriage, where one of the wheels was still turning in the air, he nearly knocked Hannah over. She was crouched by the back flap.

"Watch where you're going," she hissed.

"Can you see him?"

"No. I don't think he's in the ditch anymore, though. Have you got your flashlight?"

"No, it's still on the other side of the truck. What do you want to do?"

"Shush! Just listen."

They both sat motionless for a moment, but there was no sound in the dusty night air. Then, a moan rose out of the back of the van.

Nuñez peeked around the side of the vehicle but he could see no sign of the man with the gun. With that head of white hair, if anyone was going to be visible, it was that character, but Nuñez could make out nothing in the darkness.

"Cover me," Hannah said. "I want to see if the doctor's okay."

"Gotcha," Nuñez said.

He moved to the corner of the van and peered out into the night. Behind him, Hannah lifted the canvas flap and slipped into the cargo area. He heard her voice calling quietly. "Dr. Fitzgerald? Are you in here?"

Another female voice murmured in response.

"We're here to take you home," Hannah said. "Are you okay?"

There was another reply, but Nuñez couldn't make it out.

"You can't do anything more here," Hannah said. "We have to go. The place they were moving you is just up the road. The sheikh has people waiting at the other end. When the truck doesn't show up in the next few minutes, they'll come looking. We haven't got the manpower to fight off his whole army. We need to get out of here right now."

The doctor must have agreed, because Nuñez heard the rustle of canvas again, and then the sound of feet on the tarmac. The two women came up beside him.

"Can you see him?" Hannah asked.

"Not a damn thing," Nuñez said. "Cover me, I'm going to try to get my flashlight and pistol back."

"No. If he's still out there, you'll just draw his fire. Come on, the Toyota's back over here. The van will give us cover."

Nuñez scanned the horizon once more but saw nothing but blackness and the stars overhead. "I don't like it. Did you see that guy?"

"Only from behind. Was I hearing things, or was he speaking English?"

"You weren't hearing things," Dr. Fitzgerald said. "I don't know who he is, but he's a real son of a bitch. He might be American, but I'm not sure. He had a little bit of an accent, but I couldn't place it. He spoke Arabic, too."

"Well, he's no Iraqi, that's for sure." Nuñez hesitated. "I don't know, Hannah. I got a bad feeling about that guy."

"Yeah, well, I've got a bad feeling about hanging around here, waiting for Salahuddin's thugs to show up," she said. "Let's get out of Dodge, shall we?"

14

Thursday, August 28, 2003
The White House: Washington, D.C.

Evan Myers was in a senior staff meeting when his assistant slipped in and handed him a note. He read it and then whispered, "Did he say what it was about?"

"He just said you should call him back ASAP," she murmured in his ear.

"Something you want to share with us, Evan?" the White House chief of staff inquired.

He'd been in the middle of running down the list of briefing notes that were to be ready by noon so that he could carry them on his run down to the president's Texas ranch. It obviously wasn't a prospect he relished, because the chief had been in a foul mood since the meeting got underway. Myers had visions of his portly boss sweating in his pinstriped suit, riding shotgun in an open Jeep, choking back Texas dust as he tried to bring the president up to speed on the latest national and international developments.

Myers felt his face going warm, and he willed away the self-conscious blush that was the bane of his existence. These days, he could usually keep it under control. As a boy, however, he'd been pathologically shy, prone to stuttering when he found himself the center of attention, his face turning as red as his hair. Avoiding people, he'd turned into an avid reader, starting with tales of Alexander the Great and King Arthur, moving on from there to biographies of more modern leaders. The closer he came to present time in his reading, the more intent he became on being part of something as inspiring as the adventures he read about. After all, he lived in the mightiest nation the planet had ever seen. Why shouldn't he help make the history that would inspire young people of the future?

"I need to step out and return a call," he told the chief of staff. "It's from General Harker over at the Pentagon."

"The Pentagon? Not your usual turf, Evan. What's that all about?"

"It's got to be something about Amy Fitzgerald. Harker's been my contact point over in the E-ring, keeping me in the loop on news out of Baghdad. Maybe there's finally been a communiqué from her kidnappers."

"Or worse," the chief said morosely.

"I hope not," Myers said, getting to his feet.

"Fine, go. But don't forget I need that brief on the oil sands project on my desk by noon."

"You'll have it."

Harker's voice sounded like a gravel mixer. The two-star general had a reputation as a screamer who terrorized his staff. "We just got a message from Baghdad," he said. "She's in the Green Zone and she's safe."

"Amy Fitzgerald? Are you serious?"

"I've got better things to do than make crank calls, Mr. Myers."

"That's great! How did your people manage it?"

"Wish we could take credit, but it wasn't our doing. The details are still sketchy, but apparently a couple of security contractors just rolled into Baghdad in a beat-up old pickup. They had the doctor with them."

"She's okay?"

"Tired, dirty, a little bit banged up from some sort of traffic accident, but nothing more serious than bumps and bruises, I gather."

"This is definitely legit? I can call the family in Boston and give them the news?"

"That's why I'm letting you know. There's a military medevac flight heading out from Baghdad to Frankfurt in a few hours. I'm ordering my people to put the doctor on it, if there's room. I don't think it'll be a problem. I'll have someone pass on further details as soon as we have them."

"Thanks, General. I really appreciate it." After he hung up the phone, Myers scribbled a note on a piece of West Wing stationery. "Suzanne!"

His assistant poked her head around the door. "You bellowed?"

"Take this back into the meeting, give it to the chief of staff," he said, handing her the note.

She read it. "Oh, wow! They got her out?"

Myers looked up. "Yup. I'm going to call her father right now. Jeez Louise, it's going to be nice to be the bearer of good news, for a change."

His assistant grinned as they exchanged high fives. "You da man, Evan!"

Across the street from the White House, Dick Stern was also getting the news from his personal contact in the Green Zone, the CIA's Baghdad chief of station.

Wade Lynch had been Stern's deputy back when the latter was running the CIA station in Cairo. Officially, Lynch's current chain of command ran up through Langley, not the Old Executive Office

Building. Since leaving the Agency, Stern no longer had automatic access to either CIA personnel or information—in theory, at least.

But theory and practice were two different things. Wheels within wheels, overlapping networks, the trading of favors—that was how the real world worked. And the Baghdad station chief was no fool. He was going to want to walk away from the stinking back alleys of the Middle East and from the Agency one day. When he decided to make his move, he could do worse than have a friend like Richard Stern owing him a few favors.

"What do you mean, she escaped?" Stern asked. "How did that happen?"

"A couple of freelancers found out Salahuddin was moving her out of Al Zawra."

"Freelancers?"

"Private security contractors. They ambushed the vehicle, killed a few of Salahuddin's men, apparently, and got away with the doctor. They showed up in the Green Zone about an hour ago."

"Somebody hired mercenaries to go in after her? Who? Her old man? When did that happen?"

"I don't know, Dick. It's all a little murky at the moment."

"What does Kenner say about all this?"

"Nothing," Lynch said. "I haven't been able to raise him."

"Was he there when it happened?"

"I don't know. At the moment, the military guys have got the doctor and the people who sprang her locked down. I haven't been able to get close enough to debrief them yet."

"Who are these security contractors? We know them?"

"I didn't even know they were in-country," Lynch said irritably. "It's like the frickin' Wild West out here, Dick. We got more damn cowboys running around than you can shake a stick at, and no-body's got a handle on half of them. Near as I can figure, these people were with a Brandywine team working a job for the State Department. The rest of the team showed up yesterday with a couple of Iraqi civilians State wanted sprung. Apparently while they were out there, they got word that Dr. Fitzgerald was being held in the area. Two of their people decided to stay behind and try to spring her."

"This is no way to run a war, Wade. Those private cowboys have their uses, but you've got to keep them under tight control."

"Easier said than done. Oh, and by the way, one of the cowboys who rescued Dr. Fitzgerald is a cow*girl.*"

"A woman?"

"Yeah. Go figure. Anyway, I'm trying to hive these two idiots off from the mob here, get 'em alone and see what's what."

"Keep trying to get hold of Kenner, too. I want to know what he knows about this."

"You got it. I'll be back in touch."

15

Hamra Hotel: Baghdad, Iraq

It wasn't like she expected a medal, Hannah thought, taking a long swig of her beer. But neither had she expected them to get the bum's rush they did.

The brew in her hand was wet but not nearly cold enough for her liking, especially given that it was 107 degrees in the shade. She was sitting on the upper deck of the hotel's pool area, waiting for Oz Nuñez to show up, her indignation growing with every passing minute.

After the shoot-out with Salahuddin's men outside Al Zawra, she and Nuñez had made reasonably good time on the drive back to Baghdad, pulling up to the Green Zone, a heavily fortified area at the curve in the Tigris River, a little before six in the morning. There'd been a few moments of tension with the nervous marines manning the checkpoint at the edge of the Zone, but when they realized she and Oz were American and that they had the kidnapped Dr. Fitzgerald with them, safe and sound, they were welcomed with cheers and escorted ceremoniously in to meet the coalition military commander and then the American civil administrator.

After that, though, things had turned suddenly and inexplicably sour. Following an initial group debriefing, Dr. Fitzgerald was whisked off somewhere to contact her family in Boston. Hannah and Oz, meantime, were driven to another area of the Zone where some other American official, obviously irritated, was waiting to ream them out. He wouldn't say exactly what his particular role in the country was, but that in itself spoke volumes.

Whatever his affiliation, the guy obviously had a major bee in his bonnet about their unauthorized action upcountry. Dr. Fitzgerald, he told them, would be flown out of Iraq that very day, but for Nicks and Nuñez, there would be no free ride home. The coalition authority did not look kindly on fortune-hunters and mercenaries—a little disingenuous, Hannah thought, given that government-hire contractors outnumbered official forces in Iraq by about four to one these days.

Had Sean Ladwell, the Brandywine team leader, come back here and queered the pitch for them after she and Oz jumped ship in Al Zawra? Hannah wondered. Why would he do that? It should have been no skin off his nose if they stayed behind to do a little freelance work after the main mission was accomplished.

The bad-tempered U.S. official further informed them that they were lucky not to be tossed into Abu Ghraib prison along with the rest of the miscreants allied forces were rounding up. They were getting a get-out-of-jail-free card this time, but if they were still in Baghdad twenty-four hours from now, he couldn't guarantee their pass wouldn't have expired.

Mystified and more than a little frustrated by this sudden turn, Hannah and Oz had returned to the Hamra Hotel to figure out what the heck had just happened and how they were going to get out of Iraq. The Brandywine team had already departed on the company's Chardonair Challenger jet. With little chance of hitching a ride with an outbound military aircraft and no commercial airline service operating in what was still a war zone, they had themselves a bit of a conundrum. Exhausted and filthy, they'd decided to retire to their respective rooms for showers and a couple of hours of shut-eye, and then meet on the pool deck later that afternoon to consider their options.

Now, Nuñez was late. Hannah glanced at her watch once more. Despite a long shower and a restless nap, she still felt gritty and bone-tired. She wanted to go home. She wanted to hug her kid. She wanted to sleep for a week. Not necessarily in that order.

She took a bite of the chicken wings she'd ordered from the poolside waiter, the first food she'd had since she and Nuñez had raided the pantry of the house back in Al Zawra. She should have been ravenous, but she wasn't. She often forgot to eat when she was on a mission or her brain was otherwise occupied. When that happened, eating became something she needed to remind herself to take care of, another tick mark on her checklist: weapon, ammo, Chap Stick, food… It was nothing new. It used to drive her grandmother crazy, like a personal affront, a rejection of the love that came rolled up in the fragrant output of her traditional Greek kitchen. Hannah had tried to convince her it was her own defect, an inability to think and chew at the same time, but since she was perfect in her grandmother's eyes, that line didn't get her far.

She picked away mechanically at the tabouleh and flat bread that had come with the chicken, knowing she needed to ingest calories or she'd find herself feeling woozy at some inopportune moment, like staring down the barrel of a thief's gun or trying to dodge that tetchy guy from the Green Zone.

She was just glancing at her watch once more, debating whether to call up to Oz's room to see if he'd overslept, when the walls of the sheltered pool deck area reverberated with the *sproing* of the diving board and the splash of yet another cannonball. She glanced over the railing at the water below.

There was something positively surreal about the Hamra Hotel's poolside retreat, a bizarre, beach-blanket-bingo oasis in the middle of the war-torn city. The hotel consisted of two low-rise towers. Between them, and protected by their mass, was a split-level deck with the sparkling swimming pool on the lower level. The hotel was a half mile from the Green Zone across the Tigris River, which was both good news and bad. Since the seat of Saddam's former government now served as the coalition's operational headquarters, the Green Zone was the most protected square mile of land in the entire country. On the other hand, it was also the number one target for opposition mortar fire.

Not that things were quiet outside the Zone. The rest of the city echoed day and night with the periodic crackle of gunfire from insurgents and thieves, who effectively had an untrammeled run of the streets these days. But the few major hotels, fully booked with an army of reporters, aid workers and private contractors, were concrete-barricaded and securely guarded against all but the most heavily-armed assault. With reconstruction projects slow to get off the ground, workers were left twiddling their thumbs, waiting for supplies to arrive. Foreign security personnel also hung out at the hotel during their downtimes. Many news organizations, meantime, forbade their reporters to enter danger zones—meaning most of Baghdad and the countryside—forcing the press to practice what the veterans among them disdainfully called "hotel journalism," reporting rumors from the hotel rooftop with the tension-filled city as a backdrop.

As a result, dozens of expats, male and female, found themselves stuck at the hotel hour after hour, day after boring day. With nothing else to do and nowhere safe to go, they hung out at the Hamra's pool, protected from stray bullets by the placement of its two tow-ers. By now, the place was a round-the-clock party zone, with every-one pretending they hadn't left spouses and loved ones back home—pairing up, shacking up, and generally acting up like col-lege kids on spring break. In their bathing suits and beer-stoked stu-pidity, the only way to tell the security contractors from the aid workers and journalists was that the contractors, mostly ex-mili-tary guys, tended to have shorter hair and bigger muscles.

In the half hour she'd been sitting there, Hannah had already fended off several drunken invitations to don a bikini—or not—and join the fun. She watched a burly blond security contractor hoist him-self out of the pool, water streaming down his broad, tanned back. He turned, and as he stood on the deck, shaking out one leg and then the other, Hannah found herself mesmerized by the snake tattooed on his well-defined chest, its tail circling his left nipple, tongue lap-ping at the tender throat hollow of an otherwise tree-stump neck. Something flipped in the pit of her stomach, but when her gaze rose to his face and she realized he was grinning up at her, she turned hastily away. It had been a dog's age since she'd had a date, much less gotten involved in anything approaching a relationship but at the moment she was hot, grumpy, and in no mood for mating games.

She had just about made up her mind to finish her beer and head up to the roof to try to get a call through to Los Angeles to talk to Gabe, who should be waking up about now, when she spotted Nuñez walking across the lower pool deck in the company of a strapping marine in full desert gear. When Nuñez spotted her on the upper level, he nudged the marine, who tore his eyes away from the poolside pulchritude and followed Nuñez's gaze upward. Han-nah watched the two of them mount the stairs as a lively game of horsy-wrestling got underway in the water—four tipsy women perched on the shoulders of four equally inebriated men, locking wet limbs in an effort to topple one another. It had to be an eye-opener for the local hotel staff.

The marine with Nuñez—a sergeant, she saw by the stripes on his desert camos—looked to be in his early thirties, with a head that seemed too small for his massive body, an unfortunate side effect of the traditional high and tight haircut of the Corps.

"Sorry I'm late," Nuñez said, as they approached her table.

"I was getting ready to call out the marines and launch a search party, but I see they already found you."

Nuñez grinned. "You got that right. This is Gunnery Sergeant Keith Valenti. Gunny, Hannah Nicks, my partner in crime."

Valenti held out a massive hand that swallowed Hannah's whole. "Nice to meet you. You two have had yourselves quite the little adventure."

"You could say that."

"Pull up a seat, Gunny," Nuñez said, straddling one of the molded plastic patio chairs himself. He picked up Hannah's bottle of beer and studied the label. "What're you drinking?"

"Don't know," Hannah said. "Some brand I never heard of, but it's wet. They have food, too, if you want it."

"Nah, I'm okay for now. I had room service." Nuñez waved an arm over the balcony rail, snagging the attention of a waiter who was shooting the breeze with the bartender at the poolside bar, both of them getting an eyeful as a stringer for the Reuters news agency lost her wrestling match and her bikini top. "You want another?" Nuñez asked, glancing back at Hannah.

"No, I'm good."

When the waiter finally tore his gaze away from the shenanigans and glanced up, Nuñez lifted Hannah's bottle with one hand and raised two fingers on his free hand. The waiter nodded and Oz handed back her beer.

Hannah turned her attention to the marine. "So, are you here to arrest us, Sergeant Valenti?"

"Call me Gunny, everyone does."

"Okay, Gunny. Are you here to arrest us?"

"Why would I do that?"

Hannah shrugged. "The way this day's been going, I figured that was the next inevitable step."

"That bad, huh?"

"Oh, yeah."

"Well, I'm not here to arrest you. I'm not even on duty at the moment."

"The gunny's a friend," Nuñez said. "Back when I was in the Corps, he and I were at Camp Pendleton together. I was just on my way down here to meet you when I ran into him in the lobby."

"What a coincidence," Hannah said. She didn't believe in coincidences.

"I heard about you guys showing up in the Zone this morning with that kidnapped doctor," the gunny said. "When they said one of her rescuers was a former marine named Nuñez, I wondered if it might be this idiot here. Sounds like the kind of damn fool stunt he'd try."

Nuñez looked indignant. "No 'try' about it, man. We got her, didn't we?"

The waiter arrived with their beers. Hannah went to sign the chit over to her room bill—putting it on Brandywine's running tab with the hotel—but Valenti took it first, studied it, then dropped a ten-dollar bill on the tray, waving off change.

"Yeah, you did pull it off, at that," he said. He lifted one of the bottles by the neck and held it up. "I guess you guys are in for a big payday. Congratulations."

"*Semper fi*," Nuñez said, taking the other bottle and tapping it against the gunny's before downing a long swallow.

Hannah took a less enthusiastic drink. "I'm not sure about the payday. We have to get out of here in one piece before we can claim it." She studied the sergeant over the top of her beer. "So what else did you hear?"

"What do you mean?"

"About us."

"Not much. Just that you showed up at the Zone in some old beater that was spewing black smoke."

"Oh, man, that truck," Nuñez said. "I didn't think it was going to make it. Ran okay for the first little while, but I don't think the oil had been changed in years. Started kickin' up the last ten miles or so. Practically died on the spot when we pulled up to the checkpoint."

Hannah grimaced. "I thought your motor pool would at least offer a little tune-up before they sent us on our merry way, but no, apparently not. Far from it. The truck was confiscated, matter of fact. 'Spoils of war' or something."

"We're under orders not to let vehicles lie around, even dead ol' beaters," the gunny said. "Too many insurgents looking to turn them into bomb delivery devices."

"When I thought we might be put on that plane back to the States with Amy Fitzgerald, I didn't really care about losing the pickup," Hannah said. "Now, I'm wishing we still had it. As it was, I thought we were going to have to hoof it back to the hotel, but they finally put us in a Humvee and dumped us at the front door."

The marine frowned. "I don't get it."

"*You* don't get it?" Hannah said. "Guess what? Neither do we. You'd have thought *we* kidnapped Amy Fitzgerald, the way they treated us."

"My guys on guard said you were taken in to meet the Administrator. He's the head honcho, you know. I can't believe you'd have gotten in to see him if anyone had a problem with what you'd done."

"Well, no, he was okay about it," Hannah conceded, "but we only saw him for about five minutes. Then we were passed on to other people for debriefing. It was the last guy who really got on his high horse. Gave us bloody hell."

"Who was that?"

"Funny you should mention it," Hannah said. "I've been mulling it over ever since we got back here and you know what? I don't think he ever told us what his name was. What about you, Oz? Do you remember a name?"

"Don't think I picked it up."

"What did he look like?" Valenti asked.

"Somewhere in his forties, maybe," Hannah said. "Five-ten or -eleven, something like. Curly brown hair, going to gray."

Valenti circled a finger over the back of his head. "Bald spot? Wears Docksiders with no socks?"

Nuñez nodded. "That's the guy."

The gunny sat back in his chair and nodded. "Wade Lynch."

"Who's he?"

Valenti arched one eyebrow. "Let's say he's our 'resident intellectual.'"

Hannah smacked a hand on the table and the bottles bounced. "I knew it! Spook, right?"

Valenti shrugged. "You didn't hear it from me."

"So, he's what? CIA?" Nuñez asked.

Hannah looked over at him. "Of course he is. What did I tell you?"

"I still don't get it," Nuñez said. "Why would he be so ticked off at us for rescuing Dr. Fitzgerald?"

"Who knows what those guys are ever thinking?" the gunny said. "I tell my people to give them wide berth. You see one of those clowns coming toward you, cross the street and walk on the other side."

"Yeah, well, I wish we could've," Hannah said. "Now we're stuck here with no ticket out of town and no way to get home and claim that reward. Not exactly my idea of a pat on the back for a good day's work."

The gunny leaned back in his chair and laced his hammy fingers over his surprisingly flat stomach. He looked from Hannah to Nuñez and back, and then a slow smile rose on his face. "How'd you two like to go for a little ride?"

"Where to? Abu Ghraib? No thanks," Hannah said.

"No, someplace not too far from here. I've got something I think you might be interested in seeing. And who knows? Maybe I've got a little proposition to offer as well—a mutually beneficial proposition."

Hannah glanced over at Nuñez. The look he gave her said he trusted the guy, but what did Nuñez know? He'd followed her, hadn't he? Now look where he was. Hannah had a gut feeling they were about to walk into a world of trouble, even worse trouble than they were already in, if that were possible. Normally, she liked to listen to her gut, but in this case, she wasn't sure what other options they had.

She drained the last of her bottle and set it back down on the table. "What the heck? Let's go for a ride. Like the song says, when you've got nothin', you've got nothin' to lose."

16

Hamza Industrial Park: Baghdad, Iraq

Hannah didn't know much about cars, but she knew a museum when she saw one. She'd once taken Gabe to the Peterson Automotive Museum in Los Angeles, where they had dozens of vintage and unique collector cars, like the original movie Batmobile and Al Capone's Duesenberg. This industrial warehouse, grungy though it might be, was for all intents and purposes an automotive museum.

Half a dozen heavily armed Iraqi civilians stood guard around the steel-walled building just north of the Baghdad Central Railway Station. The guards obviously knew Gunnery Sergeant Valenti, because when they spotted him behind the wheel of the Humvee in which he'd driven Nicks and Nuñez over from the hotel, they stood straighter, nodded and waved him through.

Once inside the building, Nuñez wandered down the wide center aisle, mouth open, tongue practically hanging out. The cars were a little dusty on the exterior, as if they hadn't been polished in a few weeks, but otherwise they were in pristine condition. There were about sixteen of them. Several featured polished grill ornaments that resembled an old sixties peace symbol, the Mercedes emblem. Others had leaping silver Jaguars or round BMW logos mounted on the hood. Yet others were European-looking roadsters, models Hannah didn't recognize but which must have been worth a lot, given the reverential way Oz was ogling them.

"This isn't the first treasure trove like this we've come across," Valenti said. "When we entered into Saddam's main palace complex across the river, we found two garages with about sixty luxury and vintage cars. Turns out the old bastard was quite a collector. You should have seen it. There was a 1917 Mercedes. A Packard from the 1930s—a woody, gorgeous. A 1955 Chevy Bel Air, lime green."

Nuñez looked back, wide-eyed. "No way!"

"Way. And a gorgeous Cadillac Fleetwood, seventies vintage. Couple of Rolls-Royces and a Bentley." Valenti chuckled. "Some of my guys thought they'd died and gone to heaven. Only problem was, we weren't the first ones to find them. Turns out the locals had already descended even before we got there. After Saddam fled, people overran the palaces, stealing everything that wasn't nailed down—not to mention a bunch of stuff that was. Gold toilet seats, marble statues, what have you."

"And cars?"

"Yeah, a few of them, we think, by the tire tracks in the dust and the empty bays we found. In some cases, they just grabbed up keys. I had one guy in really ratty clothes show up a few days later, waving keys to a Mercedes. He looked like a street beggar, but he said he was there to pick up his car. We were curious, so we let him in to see if he could pick out which car was supposed to be his. Guy was smarter than he looked. He hit the automatic entry button on the key ring. When the car chirped, he leapt in so fast he sent up dust clouds. Put the key in the ignition, tried to start it up, but the car was out of gas. Didn't stop him, though. He jumped out again, whipped off his shirt, wrapped it around the bumper and tried to drag the thing out of there physically." Valenti shook his head. "Place was a three-ring circus. Pretty comical, actually, except we were wasting so much manpower guarding those damn cars that the brass finally decided enough was enough. They didn't want to run the risk of vehicles falling into the hands of insurgents or being turned into roadside booby traps. Order came down to destroy them."

Nuñez looked at him aghast, like he was talking about deliberately firebombing the Mona Lisa or someone's aged grandmother. "Get outta here."

"Yeah. Broke our hearts. You want to see a red-blooded American boy burst into tears? Order him to destroy a vintage '55 Bel Air. Some of my guys were positively sick when those tanks went to work."

"You ran over them with tanks?" Hannah had been thinking maybe they'd blown them up or something.

The gunny nodded. "You'd be surprised how fast an Abrams can flatten a car. Takes about five seconds. Solved the problem, though. No more gate-crashers. Don't know if you noticed the barricades on the east entrance to the Green Zone? It's partly built out of crushed car bodies. The Bel Air's in that pile. Looks like a chrome and lime sandwich."

"So, what about these ones here?" Hannah asked. "How come they escaped?"

"Ah, well, these we just discovered a few days ago. Don't know how they were overlooked, but this neighborhood's been so hard hit by artillery, even the looters have given it wide berth. It's a miracle this warehouse even survived. Even if the locals knew these cars were here, for the moment, they're too nervous to try to steal them. From what I can figure, these cars belonged to one of Saddam's dead sons—Uday or that other asshole, I'm not sure which."

Hannah glanced back at the Iraqis standing guard outside the open warehouse door. They glanced back periodically, obviously curious but maintaining their posts. "So, how come I'm not seeing any tanks here?" she asked. "Or even other marines?"

The gunny followed the direction of her gaze. "Those are local hires. Like I say, nobody wants to waste American military personnel standing guard over cars. I'm paying these guys out of my own pocket to keep snoops away."

"Out of your own pocket? That's real generous of you," Hannah said wryly, beginning to see what was going on here.

Valenti shrugged. "If the brass knew about these cars, they'd just be turned into steel pancakes, too. Seems like a terrible waste, dontcha think? There's only so much a guy can stomach."

"So, what's the plan?"

Valenti looked from Nicks to Nuñez and back again, weighing them.

Nuñez's brain, meantime, had obviously shifted into overdrive. "You know what these cars are worth?"

"A chunk of change, I would imagine," Hannah said.

"Hundreds of thousands of dollars."

"In a normal market," Hannah said. "This isn't exactly a normal market. As interested as people might be in getting their hands on these wheels, I can't imagine you've got many genuine buyers beating a path to your door."

"That's true," the gunny said finally. "Since Saddam and his cronies skipped town, there's nobody left here with the kind of dough it would take to purchase these babies." A small grin rose on his lips. "Outside the country, though, it's another story."

"You got something in mind?" Nuñez asked.

The gunny nodded. "I know someone at our embassy in Amman. You ever run into a guy named Stewie Glover?"

"Doesn't ring a bell."

"No, I guess it might not. Stewie's State Department, works in admin—material management, that kind of thing. Back in the day when I was a Marine Guard, we were posted together in Africa. Guy's the best scrounger I ever met. Most of those State Department types want nothing more than a cushy posting to London or Paris. Not Stewie. He always asks for the hardship posts where things are sketchiest. The guy's incredible. Drops into a city he's never seen in his life and within a week he's got the black market scoped, knows every fence and luxury goods supplier in town. You need something not available through normal channels or you got something to sell, no questions asked, Stewie Glover's your man."

"And you think this Stewie could find buyers in Jordan for these cars, is that it?" Hannah asked.

"That's the beauty of it. He already has a buyer in mind. He and I kept in touch over the years. When I e-mailed him about those cars of Saddam's that we flattened, he said what a bummer that was, 'cause he knows this rich dude in Jordan who'll pay premium dollar for a rare set of wheels. Apparently this guy's got a collection to die for. Haile Selassie's Rolls-Royce. Idi Amin's personal Land Rover. One of Yasir Arafat's armored Mercedes."

"And a guy like that would love a car that belonged to one of the horrible Husseins to add to his rogues' gallery of wheels," Hannah guessed.

"There you go. I sent Glover an inventory of what we found here. There's one his collector friend's particularly interested in." Valenti started down the center aisle and came to a halt about halfway, next to a low-slung buffed silver number with a toothy grill smile.

"Oh, man," Nuñez breathed. "Is that what I think it is?"

"A 1964 Aston Martin DB5," the gunny said.

"The Bondmobile?"

"Yup. The one Sean Connery drove in *Goldfinger* and *Thunderball*."

Hannah rolled her eyes. "Oh, be still, my heart."

"Oh, no, Hannah, listen," Nuñez said, "you gotta appreciate cars. This is so cool, you have no idea."

"Only about a thousand of these babies ever made," Valenti said. "I know. I researched it online. Not that many of them still around."

Nuñez walked around the Bondmobile, running a hand along its plunging roofline. "It's a collector's item."

"Or will be, until the brass finds out about this place," Hannah said. "Then it's roadkill."

"Unless you guys drive it out of here," Valenti said.

"Drive it?"

"Straight west, overland to Jordan. That highway's still in pretty good shape. I know the army commander at the border crossing into Jordan. I'll give him a heads-up that you're coming through, so there'll be no problem."

"Right. Piece of cake." Hannah consulted a map of Iraq in her mind. "You've got two major cities along that road, Falluja and Ramadi. From what I hear, there's still fighting going on there."

"Just mopping up, at this point. It's a better bet than going south and out through Kuwait. Once you get past Ramadi, there's no hassle in the western sectors."

"There's not a whole lot of anything out that way," Hannah said. "It's empty desert from Ramadi to the Jordanian border. We're talking Lawrence of Arabia country, nothing but sand and scorpions."

"So you know what I'm talkin' about. Five, maybe six hours drive. Clear sailing all the way."

"I took an overland bus on that route with my grandfather when I was sixteen," Hannah said. "I'll never forget that experience. It took us twenty-two hours, including wait time at the border."

Valenti waved it off. "It won't take you that long in this baby. She can do a hundred and forty miles an hour without breaking a sweat.

And when you cross into Jordan, Stewie will meet you, use his diplomatic status to walk you through customs and lead you back to Amman. He'll set you up in top-of-the-line hotel suites and book you first-class tickets home."

"Out of the goodness of his heart," Hannah said.

Valenti shrugged. "You help us, we help you."

Hannah turned to Nuñez. "What do you think this car's worth, Oz?"

"I don't know, but given how rare it is, plus the Bond connection, it's got to be a hundred grand, easy. Like I said, it's a collector's item."

She turned back to Valenti. "There you go. So, you and your friend Stewie stand to split a hundred grand, minimum, and all Nuñez here and I have to do is risk our necks running the insurgent gauntlet from here to the Jordanian border to get the product to market."

"I told you, there's nothing happening out that way. It's a piece of cake."

"Easy for you to say." Hannah tapped Nuñez on the arm. "Come on, Oz. Let's go take our chances begging a ride from one of the charter pilots holed up at the Hamra. Somebody should have a couple of empty seats deadheading out of here."

Nuñez hesitated, gazing at the Aston Martin with an expression of longing that was tragic to behold. Finally, though, he turned to Valenti. "Sorry, Gunny. I got a family. I can't afford to take risks like this on a volunteer basis."

He and Hannah were halfway to the warehouse's big, sliding door before the burly marine broke. "Okay, okay! I'll make it worth your while."

Hannah glanced back over her shoulder. "My while's worth a lot."

"How about ten grand?"

"Each?"

Valenti grimaced. "I was thinking for the both of you. Jeez, Louise! All right, ten each. That's damn good wages for one day's work."

"Twenty for us, but eighty-plus for you and Stewie? And we take all the risk?"

"Hey, I'm taking a risk right now, just holding onto these vehicles. Can you spell 'court-martial'? Not to mention that I've got expenses to cover, starting with those guys on guard out there."

"Who are probably working for ten bucks a day and thrilled to have any job at all," Hannah pointed out. "You've got—what? Fifteen, twenty cars here? Even if each of them is only worth half of what this one is—"

"There's no guarantee I can get buyers for all of them."

"Still…"

"Hey, listen, lady, this is a good deal I'm offering. You get ten grand each and a cool ride out of here. There's no guarantee you'll pick up a seat on one of those charter planes, you know. Of course, if you'd rather hang out at the Hamra's pool playing grab-ass Marco Polo for the rest of the war, then be my guest. It should only last another year or two."

Nicks and Nuñez looked at each other, then Hannah turned back to the gunny. "Fifteen grand each. That's still less than a three-way split. Plus, it goes without saying, you guys also throw in the hotel suites and first-class tickets out of Amman."

Valenti turned to Nuñez. "Man, where did you find this broad?"

"Sorry, Gunny, but she's the boss. That was the deal."

The gunny turned back to her, shaking his head. "Jeez, woman, you are killin' me here."

Hannah shrugged. "Take it or leave it, fella. I got places to go, things to do."

He exhaled heavily. "Oh…what the hell. Okay, you're on. I'll get in touch with Stewie, have him line things up at his end. With luck, you should be able to head out first thing in the morning."

Nuñez grinned and rubbed his hands together, walking back to the

Bondmobile. "That's what I'm talkin' about!" He drooled over the car for a few moments, then turned to the other two with a wide grin. "Come on, let's go back to the hotel, have a couple of beers. On me."

The gunny rolled his eyes. "Big spender."

Baghdad-to-Amman Highway, Iraq

T here was a technique to overland driving in places where danger lurked behind every rock and hillock. Carjackers and bandits
were the least of their worries. No matter how conspicuous a target
the Bondmobile might be, Hannah calculated, carjackers had to
show themselves to get what they wanted, especially if what they
wanted was a snazzy vehicle whose resale value they wouldn't want
to spoil. When they did pop out of the shadows, you waited for the
right moment, got the drop, then took 'em down, end of story. There
was no such thing as peaceful surrender. Even if thieves didn't murder you outright, leaving you in the desert without wheels or water
amounted to the same thing. So, fight or die, that was the strategy.

More troublesome were insurgents. Whatever Sergeant Valenti
said about coalition forces being engaged in nothing more than
mopping-up operations now, four months after the fall of Saddam
Hussein, Hannah suspected that all they'd seen was a temporary lull
in the action, as the local opposition caught its collective breath and
reorganized. Several contractors had already been kidnapped and

killed, and all signs pointed to things heating up. The insurgents were increasingly well-armed, with rocket-propelled grenades and fixed and mobile machine guns. Even the less sophisticated had sniper rifles and crude improvised explosive devices. This wasn't over, not by a long shot.

For the intrepid team of Nicks and Nuñez, the best bet was to be a fast-moving target. They certainly had the power for that, driving a sports car like the Aston Martin, but there were difficulties nonetheless. For one thing, despite its burled walnut and soft leather comforts, the vintage Bondmobile had no air-conditioning. Any time their speed dropped below sixty miles an hour, Hannah insisted the windows go up, since there was always the chance of encountering someone with a good arm and a hand grenade that could be lobbed through an open window. Nuñez griped. In the desert heat, with temperatures routinely hitting triple digits, it didn't take long for the inside of the car to become an oven.

It didn't help that they were wearing Kevlar vests. They'd opted to remove the ceramic plates that provided an extra layer of protection. It was difficult enough to fold themselves into the low-slung sports car with the heavy flak vests on, much less sit for hours on end. But even without the ceramic plates, the things were heavy, hot and cumbersome. Dispensing with them altogether, however, seemed too foolhardy to contemplate. Hannah had no death wish, and despite his grumbling, Nuñez seemed to accept that she knew what she was talking about. Latino machismo notwithstanding, he was an easygoing guy with no obvious axe to grind about female team leaders. Now there was a refreshing change.

Once they got away from the rubble- and tension-filled streets of Baghdad, the first fifty miles of the trip toward the Jordanian border were uneventful. It wasn't until they were approaching the turnoff to Falluja that they encountered their first checkpoint. Hannah was at the wheel, averaging ninety miles an hour when they spotted the barricades up ahead. From this distance, there was no way to know if it was the good guys or the opposition. The guards manning the barrier seemed to be in uniform, but insurgents could easily find uniforms and they loved to play Dressed to Kill.

Nuñez readied his gun and rifle. They'd left their Brandywine-issued M-16s back at the hotel armory, but Sergeant Valenti had found a couple more for them, as well as extra handguns and ammunition. Hannah slowed as the roadblock loomed, ready to leave the highway at the first sign of danger. If she had to, she'd veer right around the barricade and take the car overland into the desert in order to outrun gunfire. But when they got close enough to make out three strapping, corn-fed boys in U.S. Marine uniforms, she and Nuñez glanced at one another and nodded.

She geared down. As they rolled to a stop at the barrier, she murmured to Nuñez, "Just follow my lead. Hiya," she said to the young (weren't they all?) marine who sidled up to her window. His finger was poised on the trigger of his M-16.

A couple of other marines were coming up from the rear on the other side of the car. The barrel of Nuñez's rifle was resting on the windowsill, and it probably wasn't doing much to reassure anyone.

"Hey, guys, stand down," Hannah said, offering what she hoped was a friendly grin. "I think we're all Americans here, so let's not anybody get twitchy, okay?"

"Step out of the car, please," the marine corporal on her side said. The name stenciled over the breast pocket of his camos said his name was Hyter. "And you, there. Lay down that weapon and get out of the car."

"You got it," Nuñez said, lifting his hand off the gun. "I'm just going to reach for the door handle here, okay?"

"Real slow," one of the marines behind him said.

"No problem, bro." Nuñez opened his door. Holding the M-16 by the barrel, he laid it carefully on the roadway beside the car. "I'm stepping out now."

The marine next to him kicked the rifle aside and kept his own trained on Nuñez as he unfolded himself, grunting, from the Aston Martin. Only then did Hannah follow suit on her side.

"You guys got identification?" Corporal Hyter asked. He was apparently the man in charge of the detail.

Oz pulled out his passport and handed it over. Hannah unfastened her flak vest to reach hers, hidden in an inside pocket. Her T-shirt was drenched in sweat, and the slight breeze, however hot, felt wonderful on her body. Wearing the flak jacket was like being wound up in a tent.

"What are you doing out here?" the corporal asked.

"We've been working a contract with Brandywine International," Hannah said.

It was true. They *had* been contractors, even if they weren't now. These guys would have heard of Brandywine and the company's private military units. You couldn't swing a cat without hitting one of the tens of thousands of contractors working in-country these days, mostly under the auspices of Halliburton subsidiary Kellogg-Brown-Root.

"*You're* with Brandywine? A girl?"

"Yeah. Go figure," she said dryly, trying to ignore the fact that all three marines were doing a lousy job of keeping their gazes off her breasts. It wasn't their fault. They were lonely, horny and far from wives and girlfriends back home. Still…

"Yeah, well, those contractors fly first class all the way. I guess somebody's gotta iron their tidy whities," Hyter said. He walked around the Aston Martin. "Nice ride."

One of the other jarheads ducked low to examine the instrument panel, exhaling a whistle. "Sweet! Travelin' in style."

Hannah shrugged. "It's fast, but give me a Humvee anytime. I wouldn't want to pit this thing against a land mine."

"Yeah, well, you hit a mine with one of our Humvees, you're not much better off. They still haven't been up-armored. Brass keeps saying the steel plates are coming, but you know how that goes."

Nuñez nodded. "I hear you, man."

The corporal went back to examining their passports. "And you?" he asked Nuñez. "What's your story? You with Brandywine, too?"

"Am these days, but I've been where you are, dude. I was with the Corps in Kabul after 9/11."

"Yeah? What outfit?"

Nuñez rolled up his sleeve and showed off a tattoo on his right bicep. "Weapons Company, 3rd Battalion, 6th Marine Regiment."

"Don't say."

"Yup. Sniper. *Semper fi.*"

"And now, you're pullin' down the big bucks with Brandywine." The corporal snorted. "Typical."

"Hey man, I'm just doin' a job, is all. Don't knock it. You might find yourself doing the same when your stint's up."

"Money's real good, I hear," one of the younger marines said.

"You couldn't pay me enough," Hyter said. "I get out of this hell-hole, I ain't never comin' back. Where you guys headed?"

"Ramadi," Hannah said quickly. It was just another forty or so miles down the road. There was no point in admitting they were on their way to Jordan. It just begged too many questions.

"What for?"

"We're from head office. They sent us out to look in on some of our teams over there."

"What for?"

"Supply, logistics, that kind of thing," Hannah replied. "Make sure they've got what they need." It was the kind of vague bureaucratic response that normally invited more yawns than follow-up—except not this time.

Hyter smirked and his free hand dropped to his crotch. "Tell you what *I* need, honey. Think you could take care of me?"

Hannah was hot, sweaty, and getting very ripe-smelling in her grimy camos. She knew these guys were desperate, but even so, her inclination was to plant her steel-toed boot in those jewels Hyter was cradling. Fortunately, the ever-chivalrous Nuñez saved her from her own temper and the corporal from a well-placed kick.

"Hey, c'mon man, no need for that kind of trash talk. My partner here is just doin' a job like the rest of us. And you know what? She may not be out of the Corps, but she was a cop. She's paid her dues."

"A cop? Really?"

"Sheriff's deputy in L.A.," Hannah said grudgingly.

"Hollywood cop, huh? Well, la-dee-frickin'-dah. I guess we better let you get on your way, then, Deputy Babe." The corporal handed back their passports. "All the same, you wanna watch your backs. It's pretty dumb, them sending you out here without a convoy. You want my advice, you'll get your butts down the road to Ramadi as fast as you can. Don't stop for nothin' that's not flying the Stars and Stripes. Lot of bad actors out here."

"You got that right," Hannah said, as all three marines gave her boobs one last, lusty perusal.

They were on their way once more, peeling down the highway, the hot desert wind whipping their hair. Hannah was back at the wheel. She would have switched places with Nuñez at the checkpoint, except she couldn't resist the temptation of laying down rubber and leaving Corporal Hyter in a cloud of dust.

"What do we have for food?" she asked irritably. "I'm starving here."

"I'm guessing you don't want beef jerky," Nuñez said.

"Had enough jerks for today, thanks. Jeez, Louise! Hup, hup, *semper fi!*" She snapped a mock salute. "Don't you guys ever get past all that?"

He was settled back into the buttery leather seat. "Nope. No such thing as an ex-marine, only *former* marines."

"Yeah, well, nice club, if you like Neanderthals."

"Don't mind those guys. They're just hard up and bored. I know they act like idiots sometimes, but they don't mean anything by it. You must have dealt with some of that when you were a cop, no?"

She waved a hand at the bag at his feet. It held a stash of food they'd taken from their hotel in Baghdad. "Munchies, please. I'm dyin' here."

He rummaged around the bag. "I've got dates, oranges, some of that flat bread, a tomato—"

"I'll take some dates and a hunk of bread." She took the flat bread he handed her, ripped off a corner with her teeth and laid the rest in her lap. Then she laid a handful of dates on top of that, not so much to keep her pants clean—that was already a lost cause—as to keep the grime off the sticky dates.

"Yeah," she said finally, as she felt her blood sugar starting to climb back into normal range. "I ran into that kind of attitude on the job sometimes."

"I figured. You seem like you can handle yourself."

"Doesn't mean I like it. You can't win. You try to defuse it by being friendly, they decide you're a slut. You push back, you're a bitch. It's exhausting."

"I guess."

"You better believe it."

She kept pedal to the metal for the next few miles as they ate silently and watched the roadway for signs of trouble. There was very little traffic, but she was careful not to get sandwiched between vehicles, speeding ahead of everything they encountered. When she spotted a man with a loaded and tarped donkey cart, she steered the Aston Martin across the center strip, giving him a careful look and wide berth.

"We're going to have to gas up in Ramadi," she said after they'd passed him by.

"You think?" Nuñez leaned across the midline console to check the fuel gauge.

The British-built car was a right-hand drive, which freaked Hannah out just a little when she was behind the wheel, between shifting gears with her left hand and having a limited view of the roadway ahead and behind. As long as they were on a straight run, she was fine, but every time they rounded a curve, she had to resist the urge to cross over to the left side of the road, so strong was her need to be on the outside of the car while she was driving.

"We've still got over half a tank left," Nuñez said.

"Yeah, but it's a couple of hundred miles to the next major town after Ramadi. There might be some small villages, but I don't want to take a chance on them having gas. Better to fill up now. After that, with a full tank and the jerry can Valenti put in the trunk, we should be good all the way to the border."

"Okay, so we look for a gas station."

"There's a little more to it. You've seen the gas station lineups back in Baghdad. If anything, it's going to be worse out here. We find one, I don't want to waste an hour waiting to get to the pumps. More to the point, we get wedged in like that and we're sitting ducks for every Tom, Dick and Ahmed with a gun and grudge. I hate playing the big ol' Yankee bully, but unfortunately, nice people get dead. I heard of three guys getting killed just last week when they got caught in a gas line that suddenly turned ugly."

"So what's the plan?"

Hannah told him.

* * *

About twenty minutes later, they spotted a green road sign, written in Arabic and Roman script, announcing the turnoff for Ramadi six kilometers ahead.

"If we're lucky, we won't have to go into town," she said. "I seem to recall that there was a service station at the forks. If it looks like they've got gas, we'll move in and out fast, so get yourself ready. Get some cash ready, too. The locals are going to be ticked off enough as it is. We don't want anyone thinking we're trying to rob the place. You never know who might be packing fire under his *dishdasha*."

"How much cash, do you think?"

"God only knows. Gas was running sixty cents a gallon before the war. Saddam couldn't export it because of the sanctions, so the stuff was cheaper than water. Now, the refineries are off-line again and supplies are getting scarce, so it's whatever the market will bear. I think if we throw sixty bucks U.S. at the attendant, it should cover it."

"Sixty bucks? For less than half a tank?"

"Hey, it's a bargain at twice the price. No gas, no go." She punched him playfully in the shoulder. "Anyway, you're rich, dude! You're getting fifteen grand for this little run and another cool half mil when we get back to the States and see Patrick Fitzgerald."

"You don't think he'll renege, do you? What if that CIA dude we ran into in Baghdad gets to him ahead of us, gives Fitzgerald some spin about how we don't deserve it?"

"I'm not worried. Amy will be back home by now. She'll tell her father the truth about what happened out there. You heard her. She said her dad was a good guy. He'll do the right thing, Oz, don't sweat it."

He leaned back and grinned. "So, what are you going to do with yours? Buy your kid a pony?"

"Nope, nothing fancy. Gonna bank it, stick close to home for a change and work on getting my son back. I've already lost two years of being his full-time mom. I'm not losing any more." She glanced over at the young ex- (no, *former*) marine. "What about you?"

"I'm gonna build us a new house, a ranch bungalow with ramps and no stairs. When Raquel gets a little bigger, I'll get her a motorized chair so she can go anywhere she wants, all by herself, until some kind of new treatment comes up that'll fix her. I'm going to build it near a school they just put up in Austin. My wife's been looking into it. This place has got programs for special needs kids. When the baby's ready to start school, she'll have the same advantages as every other kid." Nuñez drummed his fingers on his knees. "And I'm going to start a college fund. She's gonna be whatever she wants to be, if I have anything to say about it."

Hannah smiled. He was only twenty-one, but the kid was all grown up just the same. "You're a good father, Oz."

He looked proud.

The first thing they spotted was the green-and-yellow petroleum company sign rising high over the road ahead like a hot-air balloon. As they got closer to the squat and dusty service station, they could see a line of cars, a dozen or more, snaking across the parking lot and out onto the highway, waiting to buy gas. The station had two lanes of old, paint-chipped pumps, two pumps on each island, but the lane between them was blocked off by a rope. A sign was also taped to one of the pumps in the outside row. It appeared that three of the four were out of order. That wouldn't be surprising, Hannah thought, given the sanctions since the last Gulf War and the resulting shortage of spare parts for everything from heavy machinery to toasters.

As they got close to the station, she could see that the unused pumps were half dismantled. One had no hose or nozzle. One had had the meter guts ripped out of it. One was little more than an

empty metal box. The only working pump looked like Franken-
stein's monster, held together with crudely attached after-market
rivets and swatches of duct tape. Obviously the other three pumps
had been cannibalized for parts to keep this one running.

"Okay, timing is everything here," she told Nuñez. "See the
pickup truck at the working pump? We're going to move him out.
I want you to do whatever it takes, short of murder, to get him the
hell away. We need a clear getaway the second we finish gassing up,
so make sure he doesn't hang around to argue. I don't want him or
anyone else blocking our exit."

"Roger," Nuñez said. He checked the ammunition clip on one pistol and tucked it into his waistband alongside the other in his holster.

Hannah took out her own Beretta and laid it in her lap. The tires
on the Bondmobile screeched as she careened wide around the last
car in the queue, then peeled off the highway and into the gravel-
topped lot, kicking up a cloud of dust and stones in her wake. The
driver of the battered Isuzu pickup at the front pump was standing beside his open door, leaning on the roof of the cab, shooting
the breeze with the green jumpsuit-clad attendant, who kept his
hand on the nozzle in the tank while the pump's gauges clicked over
behind him. They barely had time to look up in surprise when
Hannah leaned on the horn.

Nuñez, meantime, had thrown open the passenger side door. He
leapt out of the car, brandishing his M-16, and waved it at the startled pickup driver. "Go! Go! Now!" he screamed.

When the driver hesitated for a split second too long, Nuñez
pointed the rifle at his face, making his meaning dangerously clear.
The man jumped into the truck and fumbled with the keys. The
motor finally turned over, black smoke spewing from the tailpipe.

"Go! Go!" Hannah shouted in Arabic.

The truck lurched and sputtered as the nervous driver gave it gas.

The attendant barely had time to get the nozzle out of the tank. Scraping the truck bed, the nozzle was still dripping gas as the pickup lurched away.

Nuñez pivoted on his heel, his rifle swinging in an arc, issuing a silent but lethal challenge to potential troublemakers. Hannah deftly squealed the Aston Martin into position at the pump, cutting off an old Ford Escort that had been next in line after waiting for God only knew how long to fuel up.

Slamming on the brakes, she pointed her Beretta out the window at the startled attendant. "Fill it!" she commanded.

"You…you should turn off the engine," he blubbered. Despite the stubble on his chin, he was just a kid, younger even than Nuñez. The nozzle in his hand shook, splattering droplets of gas. He looked as if he was going to wet his pants.

"Just fill it!" she ordered. There was no way she was going to kill the motor, not in a situation when every second counted.

As the terrified kid unscrewed the gas cap on the Aston Martin, she took in every nuance of their surroundings, watching ahead of her and behind in the rearview mirrors. Nuñez was pacing back and forth alongside the car, doing his best imitation of a loco gangsta from the 'hood. If they only knew what a cupcake he really was.

As complaints and grumbles rose from other drivers in the long queue, Nuñez suddenly let out a godawful shriek, waving his M-16 around like a maniac. Apparently he'd studied at the Mel Gibson school of overacting, Hannah thought, smiling to herself. It wasn't a bad strategy, under the circumstances. Had she had the luxury of infinite time and resources, she would have preferred three or four guys on backup here, but one apparent lunatic with an automatic rifle was enough to give pause to all but the most foolhardy. There was no sign these people were militants, as far as she could tell. They

were just poor, tired working stiffs trying to keep it together in trying times. She could sympathize. She just couldn't let down her
guard. She was damned if she was going to die in Iraq.

She turned back to the attendant. He was still trying to get the
nozzle in the tank but, in his nervousness, kept missing the opening. "Hurry, hurry, hurry!" Hannah yelled, hoping he wasn't scratch-
ing the car's paint job. Who knew how finicky that collector in
Jordan was? They needed to deliver the product in good condition.

The nozzle finally found its way home and the pump began to
hum, the steady click-click of the turning meter counting out the
gallons. Exhausted as she was, the sound had a lulling effect in the
drowsy heat, but Hannah forced herself to keep her eyes moving,
scanning for signs of danger. Standing still in the middle of a hos-
tile crowd was never a good place to be. Things could go south faster
than a duck in autumn.

Nuñez paced back and forth by the rear bumper, keeping his
watchful gaze pinned on the line of cars behind them and on the
service station building about ten meters off to her right. They had
no idea whether there was anyone inside there. If there was and he
was armed, they could be in a world of trouble.

Just then, she heard a squeal of tires from behind. Nuñez's gaze,
she saw in her mirror, was fixed at that moment on the station
building across the lot. She pivoted and looked over her left shoulder just in time to see a dark blue sedan come shrieking around the
line of cars. The muzzle of a gun was showing out the right passenger window, and the car was coming straight for them.

"Oz! Behind you!"

He swung around, dropping onto one knee but keeping his gun
high. Hannah was already out of the car, leaning on its roof, cupping her Beretta in front of her, taking aim. A shot rang out from
the blue sedan, but the bullet went wide of the mark, pinging off

the metal pole of the tall gas station sign. Hannah's brain registered a ball cap on the shooter but not much more than that.

Before the gunman could get off another shot, she fired. Nuñez also opened up, spraying the sedan with automatic fire. The windshield crackled but held as the car veered left. Its front driver-side wheel caught the edge of a downward incline. The car wobbled, then slid as the driver slammed on the brakes, just narrowly avoiding rolling over into a ditch. The wheels bit gravel once more and the car leveled itself.

Nuñez's M-16 peppered a line of holes in its side and trunk as the car spun around. The shooter was on the far side of the vehicle by now, but he kept shooting out of the window anyway—aiming for rogue migratory birds, Hannah could only imagine. The driver, meantime, looked like he might be thinking about returning for another run at them.

She let off a couple more rounds in an effort to discourage him. One shot took out the driver's side mirror. The next one looked like it passed right in front of his nose and across the front of the car, apparently planting itself in the gunman, Hannah guessed by the sound of his bellow. His pistol fell from his hand, clattering along the roadway. She doubted the guy was mortally wounded, but his pride would probably take a serious drubbing when it registered that he'd been taken down by a woman.

Nuñez glanced back at her, stunned. "Wow! Nice shot. You go, girl!"

She shrugged modestly as the sedan wisely peeled out of the lot and down the highway.

When it disappeared, Oz went back to circling the car, waving his weapon at anyone who made eye contact. There weren't too many to worry about now, since almost everyone who'd been caught in the queue had ducked down in their seats when the fireworks began. The attendant was on his knees beside the Aston Martin, but miraculously, he was still pumping gas.

Behind them, Hannah noticed the driver of the Ford Escort she'd cut off to jump the queue. The man rose cautiously in his seat. He had a round, bearded face with a terrified, deer-in-the-headlight expression. She had spotted a burqa-clad wife and two children in the back seat when she'd first pulled into the lot, but all she could see of them now was the top of a boyish head that occasionally rose above the seat, only to be pushed back down by his mother's panicky hand.

She wasn't proud of humiliating this man in front of his family. There was already way too much of that going on in this country. It was no way to win hearts and minds, but it couldn't be helped. Polite westerners who waited their turns got carjacked and killed. She and Nuñez were particularly vulnerable, since they were on their own, without a protective convoy, and not exactly inconspicuous in that car. Bottom line—they just didn't have time for niceties.

It seemed to take forever, the longest few minutes of Hannah's life and Nuñez's, too, she would bet. Finally, though, the pump stopped. The attendant pulled out the nozzle and recapped the tank. Nuñez backed toward the passenger side door, his rifle still arcing through the air.

"Pay him, Oz."

"Oh, right."

She kept her own gun circling as he fumbled in his breast pocket for the money he'd stuffed there. He threw it across the roof at the attendant, then jumped back in the front seat. His left leg was still outside the door when Hannah put the car in gear and careened out of the lot, tires shrieking. Nuñez maneuvered his rifle alongside his legs in the wheel well and managed to slam the swinging door.

Hannah settled her gun back in her lap. Glancing back in her rearview mirror, she spotted the pump attendant chasing after the flying U.S. twenties. The other drivers were rising back up in their seats now, peering cautiously out their windshields.

A moment later, they were back on the highway and heading for the border. Hannah let out a long, relieved sigh. "Well, we did it." She glanced over at Nuñez. "You okay?"

"Yeah," he said, but he didn't look okay.

"What? You didn't get hit or anything, did you?"

"No."

"Then what's the matter?"

"Did you get a close look at those dudes who were firing on us?"

"Not really. I saw guns and I heard bullets zinging past me. That's about all I needed to figure out they weren't friendlies. Why?"

"I think I saw one of them before."

"Where? Which one?"

"Guy with the baseball cap?"

Hannah nodded. "With the gun. Yeah, I know which one you mean. Where'd you see him before?"

"I'm not sure. I just think I've seen him somewhere, and it's bugging me 'cause I can't remember where."

"Well, keep your eyes peeled in case they decide to take any more potshots at us. It's a pretty open run from here on out, though. We should be able to see anyone coming and I'm not about to forget that blue car."

"They could change cars."

"Yeah, maybe. So, like I say, keep your eyes open." She gave him a grin. "But cheer up, little buddy. The worst is behind us. We're nearly home free."

She wished.

18

Baghdad to Amman Highway, three miles to the Jordanian border

They'd been on the road for over five hours since gassing up in Ramadi. Nuñez had taken over driving when they'd made a brief pit stop near a desert wadi and for the next long, mind-numbing stretch of the drive, Hannah had caught some z's. Now, she was back at the wheel once more. Aside from the occasional American fighter jet roaring past overhead, they'd seen nothing but donkey carts and goat herders for the past couple of hours. The heat and dust and tedium were getting to them both. Not a word had passed between them in an hour or more.

Nuñez started fiddling with the radio, running up and down the dial. A couple of faint signals broke through the static but nothing they could stand to listen to over the roar of the wind in their ears.

"It's gotta be this radio," Hannah said. "It must be on the fritz. Even if all the Iraqi stations are off the air, I can't believe we're not picking up anything this close to the Jordanian border."

Nuñez switched it off in disgust and slumped down in the seat, drumming his fingers on his knees. He was tired and grumpy, like a little kid stuck too long in one place. It reminded Hannah of the trip she'd taken with Gabe when he was six, driving cross-country from Los Angeles to visit her parents in Chicago. Not one of her more brilliant ideas.

It was their first summer vacation together after Gabe had started living full-time with Cal and Christie. They really should have flown back east, but she'd thought she could save money and put in some quality one-on-one time with her little guy. Dumb. It was too long for him to be cooped up, no matter how many points of interest she managed to find along the way and how many motel swimming pools they cooled off in at the end of each day— most of which were pretty pathetic compared to the massive, sparkling saltwater infinity pool at Cal's Mulholland McMansion. While Gabe had had a great time at his grandparents', he'd been antsy for a good chunk of the trip out and back. When they ar-rived back at his father's house in L.A., he bounded out of the car, threw his arms around his joyful pup, Mookie, then trotted off into the house, barely tossing a backward wave at his mother. So much for quality time.

Hannah chewed her lip worriedly as an uncomfortable thought occurred to her. *Maybe the reason I lost him is that I'm just no good at this mothering business.*

Nuñez let out a low groan and swiveled his head first one way, then the other. He looked ready to kick something, just to break up the monotony. Outside the window, the scenery was endlessly dusty and beige. Hannah empathized, but she was damned if she was going to entertain this big doofus with her endless supply of knock-knock jokes or a rousing rendition of "Wheels on the Bus."

"Keep your eyes peeled," she said. "Border should be coming up in another couple of miles. There's a small town on the other side. We can stretch our legs, get a cold drink and maybe something decent to eat before the last leg of the trip into Amman. No shortages of anything over there."

"Good. I'm hot, I'm beat and I'm starving."

She reached under her seat. "There's more fruit here."

The last time they'd pulled over to switch off driving duties, a skinny kid who looked to be no older than Gabe had appeared out of nowhere with baskets of fruit for sale. More out of pity than need, Hannah had bought some paper-wrapped figs and dried apricots, passing up a plump watermelon for fear of dirtying the Bondmobile's soft leather upholstery. As a courier, she was nothing if not mindful of the merchandise.

"Oh, man, no more of that stuff," Nuñez complained. "I feel like a friggin' Fig Newton already. A fat, juicy steak, that's what I want. With fries. And cold beer, lots of it. And a hot shower. I can hardly wait to hand over this baby, get our money, and crash at that first-class hotel suite the gunny promised."

Hannah nodded distractedly, thinking about the handover of the car. There was still enough cop-think hard-wired into her brain to give her qualms about aiding, abetting and profiting from the sale of dubiously acquired goods. Ethical arguments had been tap-dancing in her head ever since Oz's buddy had first taken them to that warehouse in the Hamza industrial park.

A purist could argue that luxury items acquired by Saddam and his monster sons belonged to the Iraqi people, and that only a scoundrel would conspire to steal from a country whose citizens had suffered through such hard times, both during the dictator's rule and since his ouster. On the other hand, Hannah reasoned, the luxury cars were doomed to be crushed and turned into steel flapjacks anyway, if Valenti were to be believed. They were already lost to the new Iraqi treasury, so what she and Nuñez were doing could be interpreted as a cultural rescue mission, preserving a piece of automotive history.

In any case, it was academic. They were too far committed to turn back now. Iraq and the moral ambiguity of what they and everyone else were doing here would soon be well behind her. And good riddance to it, too. They'd hand over the Aston Martin, collect their payment, and then she and Nuñez would be homeward bound, end of story.

She stretched one arm, then the other, working out kinks in her shoulders, watching for signs of the approaching frontier. The last time she'd been this way, twelve years earlier, she'd been on a bus, traveling with her grandfather and several cases of handicraft samples, mostly weavings, bracelets and pots, that he'd purchased from a Baghdad artisans' cooperative. His shop in Beirut had a reputation for stocking interesting, one-of-a-kind goodies from all over the Middle East. With tourism in Lebanon finally rebounding after that country's tragic civil war of the nineteen-eighties, her grandparents' eclectic boutique was once again an essential stop on every savvy traveler's itinerary.

Now there, Hannah thought, smiling, was a road trip to remember. Two years later, her grandfather had died of a sudden heart attack, but she would always treasure the solitary time she got to spend with him that summer, hearing old family stories, visiting artist studios, and helping him select the interesting merchandise his store was known for.

As she remembered it, the border crossing between Iraq and Jordan had consisted of a couple of low buildings on the Iraqi side, manned by a handful of bored guards. The guards had delayed the bus for what seemed like an eternity, searching passengers' bags, desperate, Hannah suspected, to find contraband drugs, currency or historic artifacts in order to break up the tedium of their long, dreary days at the frontier outpost. After a few bribes had changed hands, the bus had finally been released, crossing a few hundred yards of no-man's land between the two checkpoints. Then, the passengers had filed off the bus once more to deal with equally bored customs officials for the other side.

The Jordanian visas, as she recalled, seemed to have no set price but went for whatever the market would bear and the politics of the day demanded. As an American, she'd had to pay something over fifty dollars for hers, a lot more than the obnoxious Parisian academic who'd sat next to her all the way from Ramadi. He'd flatly refused to trade away his window seat on the packed bus so that Hannah's grandfather could sit next to her. Then, to add insult to injury, the Frenchman had proceeded to lecture her on boorish American manners. As a shy sixteen-year-old, she hadn't had the nerve to point out the obvious irony in his position. That was back in the days before she'd learned to push back. She wouldn't be so polite now.

"I sure hope the gunny's friend is there when we get to the border crossing," Nuñez said. "I don't wanna hang around any longer than we have to."

"Me neither." The price of the visa should be a nonissue now, since the infamous Stewie Glover was supposed to be using his diplomatic connections to get them a walk-through. "You know what I want most when we get to Amman?"

"What's that?"

"A good phone line to the States, a hot soak in a really big bathtub and a soft bed."

"There you go. That's what I'm talkin' about. Creature comforts. And those first-class tickets home. I can hardly wait to see Lara and the baby."

"That'll be some reunion. I imagine your wife will be pretty happy when you tell her about that new house."

Nuñez nodded. "She didn't want me to take the contract with

Brandywine, but the money was too good to pass up. There's not too many sniper jobs open back home, if you know what I mean. I was getting real tired of working for minimum wage."

"You haven't got another trade?"

"Not really. Lara's been trying to convince me to go back to school, maybe take up computers or something, but I don't know. I can't see myself working in a cubicle. I'd go stir crazy."

"Ever thought of becoming a cop?"

"Yeah, maybe. You like it?"

"I did, actually. It wasn't anything I'd planned on doing. I just kind of stumbled into it by accident. I went to work as a sheriff's department dispatcher after I dropped out of college, then moved on to the academy after my son was born. It's pretty interesting work. You meet all kinds of strange characters, and every day's different. You go into work, you never know what the shift's going to bring."

"So why'd you quit?"

"I needed money. Why'd you quit the marines?"

"Same reason."

"Well, you got money now, kid."

"Yeah." Nuñez leaned back in his seat, smiling. He was quiet for a moment, his brain obviously turning over. "A cop, hey? You know, that's a thought. Maybe I'll look into that when I get back."

"There you go," Hannah said.

The border crossing came up on them suddenly, an outcropping of the low-slung shacks that Hannah remembered from that trip twelve years ago and a wooden barricade blocking the road. Where there had been Iraqi soldiers manning the post on her last crossing, now she saw only a couple of slouched men in *dishdashas* and crocheted skullcaps. A tattered, wind-whipped Iraqi flag flew from the top of a metal pole that had developed a sideways cant. A wooden barricade like a long sawhorse stood across the roadway. Beyond it was barren no-man's land, and then another steel barricade and a long, gleaming white bunker. A gigantic Jordanian flag flew over its roofline, black, white and green stripes undulating in the wind, a red triangle cutting into the stripes like a bloody gash.

The buildings and the flags were the only way to know where one country ended and another began. All around them, the desert stretched to every horizon. Hannah knew it was another hundred miles or more to the Jordanian capital of Amman, but cutting through the moonscape on that side of the border was wide, smooth, black tarmac bifurcated by a bright yellow line. It was a veritable superhighway compared to the pitted, sand-washed road they'd been traveling for the past six hours.

Hannah spotted a gleaming white Mercedes sedan waiting on the other side of the border. The car carried blue diplomatic license plates and the Stars and Stripes flew from its antenna. There was no way the American ambassador to Jordan would have driven out to meet them. Flying the flag, an honor usually reserved for diplomatic emissaries, could only mean that Stewie Glover suffered from delusions of grandeur. From the way the uniformed driver and the Jordanian border guards were dancing around the man leaning on the car's front bumper, he obviously had them convinced he was a big cheese.

"Looks like Gunny's friend made it," she said. When Nuñez didn't answer, Hannah glanced over at him. His dark eyes were scanning the horizon, and deep creases had appeared on his brow. "What's the matter?"

"Nothing. I'm not sure."

"You're making me nervous, Oz. Spit it out."

"Where is everybody?"

"Everybody who?"

"Our guys. The army. The marines. Shouldn't there be somebody from our side manning the crossing? That's what Valenti said, right?"

She looked back at the Iraqis lounging against the wooden barricade. She'd been so intent on getting across the border and out of this bloody country that she'd momentarily dropped her guard. But now that he mentioned it…

It was no surprise that there was no Iraqi military presence, but Oz was right. Valenti had said that he knew the army commander at this crossing. American forces would be guarding the border against potential incursion from the other side. As a small, weak country jammed in cheek-by-jowl with Israel, Jordan couldn't afford to offend its Arab brethren by kowtowing too obviously to Washington. The Jordanians had supported Saddam in the first Gulf War, and it was no stretch to imagine that the country was harboring a few potential Iraqi insurgents now.

"You think our guys are in those huts?" Nuñez wondered aloud.

"And what? They're napping? And they got here how? Walking? I don't think so." Hannah slowed the car. "No Humvees, no Abrams tanks, no nothin'. No way this checkpoint should be unmanned."

Just then, the two men in *dishdashas* seemed to notice the oncoming sports car. They straightened and positioned themselves on either side of the roadway, which narrowed quickly down to one lane, funneling traffic to a stop before the guard huts and the barricade. Coils of razor wire extending for several yards on either side of the barrier ruled out running around it. Red-bordered danger signs picturing an explosion were posted every few feet at the edge of the roadway, where it stretched out into desert. Hannah had no doubt that where the razor wire ended, land mines began.

"I think we wanna be on our guard here, buddy," Hannah said. *The understatement of the year.* She reached under her seat for her Beretta and tucked it under her right thigh, handy but out of sight.

Nuñez chambered a round in one of his own weapons, tucked it under his armpit, then slipped the safety off the second pistol holstered at his waist.

As they rolled slowly up to the barrier, Hannah spotted a third man standing in the doorway of the guard hut. Unlike the two dark, bearded Iraqis at the barrier, he was dressed in a simple cotton shirt and trousers. He didn't look like a local at all. He was wearing dark sunglasses that made his eyes impossible to see, but his hair was a blond so pale it was white.

"Shee-it!" Nuñez muttered. "That's the guy."

"What guy?"

"The guy from the gas station. The one I asked you if you'd noticed."

"What? The one we thought I shot? Are you sure?"

"Yeah, I think so. And that's not all. I think he was there the night we rescued Amy Fitzgerald. It was dark, but that hair and the build... It looks like him."

They had less than another fifty feet to go before the barrier. It was time to fish or cut bait. "What do you think, Oz? Do we stop and see what his story is, try to talk our way through, or do we make a run for it?"

Just then, the white-haired guy spoke to the men at the barrier. They hustled to pick up automatic rifles that had been leaning until that moment against the hut, and then they snapped to attention, obviously awaiting further orders.

"I would say they've been waiting just for us," Hannah said. "Oh, hell, Oz, look at his arm—the bandage. That *is* the guy I shot. Hang on. We're not stopping!"

As she stomped on the gas pedal, Nuñez raised his gun to the side window. The white-haired man gestured to the two Iraqis, who took up defensive postures and raised their weapons, pointing them at the Aston Martin.

After that, everything speeded up, a swirl of dust and gunfire and tires laying down rubber. With one hand on the gear shift and the other on the wheel, Hannah had no choice but to leave the fighting to Nuñez. She ducked low, peering under the rim of the leather-wrapped steering wheel as she aimed straight for the wooden barricade. One of the Iraqis stood in front of it, his weapon pointed at the windshield, but at the last second, his nerve failed him. He leapt out of the way just as the Aston Martin roared past and through the wooden sawhorse. It splintered like a matchstick toy, pieces flying through the air.

She glanced once to her left as the Iraqi border post flashed past. The white-haired man had thrown off his sunglasses and was crouched, arms extended, his weapon held in a two-handed grip. The muzzle flashed again and again. Nuñez returned fire.

Hannah heard Oz yelling and glass breaking as guns roared around her. Her cheek felt a burn, and then warm liquid was dripping down her neck. She was shot, maybe, but she had no time to think about that. It was probably just a graze anyway, or flying glass. She wasn't dead, and that was all she needed to know. If she intended to keep it that way, she had to make tracks.

Across the open stretch of no-man's land, she could see the man who'd been leaning on the Mercedes gesturing to the Jordanian guards. They threw open the steel barrier, clearing the path for Hannah and Oz to land safely on the other side. If only they could get across in one piece.

And then they were in no-man's land, gunfire still pinging off the car but fading behind them. Hannah kept the gas pedal right to the floor, aiming for Jordanian territory.

Finally, after what seemed like the longest drive of her life, they were on the other side. The Jordanian guards leapt aside as she sailed past, then slammed on the brakes, spinning the steering wheel to the left. The car fishtailed in a dusty, one-eighty arc, finally coming to a stop.

Through the spider-cracked windshield, Hannah saw the white-haired man far on the Iraq side lower his weapon. He stared at them for a moment. Eyes like a cold, blue laser seemed to cut right through her, even from this distance. Then, he bent down and picked up his dark glasses and put them on. He waved disgustedly at the Iraqis before turning away. In the sky off in the distance, Hannah saw the dragonfly outline of an approaching Chinook helicopter.

"Well, that answers the question of how the guy got there ahead of us. He flew in. Bastard! Who the hell do you suppose he is?"

No answer.

"Oz?" She turned. "Oh, Jesus, Oz!"

He was slumped down in his seat. The front of his flak jacket was soaked with blood, but he was alive, breathing heavily.

"I'm okay," he wheezed. His hand was on his neck, and when he took it away for a moment, Hannah saw that his palm was covered in blood.

She cursed and struggled with her door handle. When she finally got the door open, she stumbled out of the low car. One knee hit the ground painfully, but she ignored it, scrambling back to her feet and around the car, pulling open the door on Nuñez's side.

From behind her came the American whine of Sergeant Valenti's friend. "Hey, you guys were supposed to get the car here in one piece. What the hell am I going to tell my buyer?"

"Shut up and help me! My partner's shot!"

Hannah reached in and gently lifted Nuñez's hand off his neck. The bullet had entered just below his ear and behind his jaw. She couldn't see an exit. The wound was bleeding profusely. Hannah put her own hand on the entry hole, pressing firmly to stanch the blood flow as she frantically looked around for something to use as a dressing.

"Have you got a handkerchief?" she asked Glover.

"Yeah, yeah, I do," he said, finally twigging to the fact that there was something more serious going on here than a shot-up car. He handed her a sharply pressed cotton square and Hannah put it on Oz's neck.

"We need to get to a hospital," she said.

Glover turned to his driver. "Juma! Bring the car!"

"Help me get him out," Hannah said. "Hang on, Oz. You're going to be fine."

He smiled weakly but his skin was the color of putty. The Jordanian border guards came over, and together, she and Glover and the two of them managed to lift Nuñez out of the car and into the back seat of the Mercedes that Glover's driver pulled up alongside the Aston Martin.

"There's a town a couple of miles from here," Glover said. He turned to one of the Jordanians. "Is there a hospital there?"

The guard nodded. "A clinic. It is off the main road, on the right as you enter the town. It is not large, but there will be a doctor there. We will call ahead and tell them you are coming."

"Good," Glover said.

"I'll get in back with him," Hannah said. "We need to keep pressure on that wound."

She lifted Nuñez's head off the seat and slipped in under it, settling his head in her lap as she kept one hand on the handkerchief. "Oh, man, it's already soaked through. Have you got something else I can use here?"

Glover had already jumped into the front, his driver beside him at the wheel. He turned and leaned one elbow on the back of his seat, frowning. Then, he held up one finger. "Yeah, here," he said, grunting as he leaned over the center console to a soft-sided cooler on the floor at Hannah's feet. Flipping it open, he took out a wad of paper napkins. "There's water in there, too, if you need it."

"Fine, good," Hannah said, grabbing the napkins and wadding

them into a pad. She threw the bloody handkerchief on the floor and pressed the napkins into Nuñez's neck. "Now, go. Go!"

The driver put the car in gear. Hannah's head whipped back as they careened off down the highway. Her heart was pounding in her ears. She looked down at Nuñez. His eyes were closed.

"Hang on, Oz. You're going to be okay, you hear me? You just think about that house you're going to build for your little girl."

He smiled weakly. "It's gonna be a great house."

"Yeah, you bet it is. Now just shut up and keep thinking about it. We'll have you patched up in no time."

She kept even pressure on the wound, but the blood just kept coming.

"Are you okay?" Glover asked her. "You're bleeding." He pointed at her face.

Hannah used the back of her free hand to wipe her cheekbone. It came away bloody and she had a vague sensation of pain on her face, but it was the least of her worries. "No big deal. Come on, come on! Can we go a little faster, please?"

Glover turned his head to the front. They were coming up fast on a town. "Almost there. The guard said the clinic's on the right," he told his driver.

The driver nodded. "I know it. My mother came from this town."

It was probably only another two or three minutes until the car braked and made a tight right turn into the parking lot of a two-story building, but it was the longest few minutes of Hannah's life. When the car finally came to a stop at a sliding double door marked Emergency in Arabic and English, Hannah looked down at her young partner.

Oz's face was utterly still. He was gone.

PART TWO

The End of Civil Twilight

"Civil twilight is defined to end in the evening when the center of the sun is geometrically 6 degrees below the horizon. This is the limit at which twilight illumination is sufficient, under good weather conditions, for terrestrial objects to be clearly distinguished. Complete darkness begins after the end of evening civil twilight."

—U.S. Naval Observatory, Astronomical Applications Dept.

19

Wednesday, January 26, 2005
Los Angeles, California

The sheriff's department helicopter circled and recircled a six block radius of the south-central neighborhood called Compton. The chopper's rotor blades thrummed a deep, predatory growl. Under the fuselage, the night sun spotlight was at its widest setting, lighting up dark recesses as it panned streets and alleys, hunting for the shooter rumored to be still in the vicinity.

The sun had set at 5:18 p.m. In the half hour that followed, the hardscrabble neighborhood had undergone an eerie transformation. Careworn mothers gossiping over sagging fences started casting worried glances at the descending gloom. Children playing in weedy empty lots were called home and hustled into candy-colored bungalows and boxy, low-rise stucco apartment buildings. The chunky *click-slide* of door locks and dead bolts echoed up and down potholed streets. Across steel-barred windows, curtains, blinds and old bed sheets were yanked into place, concealing occupants from the evil that lurked outside.

Now, it was the end of civil twilight, and the darkness was virtually complete. A chilly marine haze rolled in off the Pacific Ocean, obscuring the stars and throwing a curtain of gauze over the full moon.

This was the hour when the streets turned deadly.

20

The Silver Lake neighborhood of Los Angeles

"Y ou mean they aren't letting you see Gabriel on his birthday?"

Ida Demetrious's voice, faintly accented with the lilt and sibilance of her home village on the island of Cyprus, trembled with the indignation and outrage only a protective mother and grandmother could muster.

"I am seeing him, Ma," Hannah said, walking with the portable phone from the living room into the bedroom of her Silver Lake town house. She'd bought the condo with the insurance money she got after her little house in Los Feliz was blown up four years earlier. B.D. Rashikoff, Russian mobster, wannabe drug czar on the L.A. scene, had been hoping to discourage the court testimony of the young undercover cop who'd built the damning case against him. Apparently that kind of intimidation worked in some places. Didn't work with her. Just the same, Hannah had paid—and continued to pay—a high price for her obstinacy.

Losing that old house was the least of her problems, but Hannah missed the place just the same. It was a prewar bungalow she and Cal had bought, mortgaged to the hilt, when he passed his bar exams and was offered a position in the Los Angeles District Attorney's office. After the tiny, grungy apartment they'd occupied for the first three years of their marriage, shoehorning themselves, their baby and all his paraphernalia into about seven hundred square feet, the oak-lined cottage had felt like a castle. Hannah had always wanted to really tackle the place—strip the years of paint off its beams, built-in cabinets and French doors, bringing it back to its Craftsman roots—but there never seemed to be enough time. Then, in a flash of thunder, smoke and fire, the house was gone.

She and Cal had been so excited when they first bought it. That was when they were still batting for the same team. Hannah was a young cop, he was a prosecutor—one of them catching the bad guys, the other working to put them away. Young, stupid with ideals and ambition, they had heroic visions of personally stamping out crime in this city by the sea. But then, Cal had gone over to the dark side, exchanging his high ideals for the cheesy allure of money and glamour. The media-savvy defense firm he joined after only two years in the D.A.'s office specialized in end-running the system on behalf of celebrity clients who thought the normal rules didn't apply to them. The next step in the makeover of Calvin Nicks had come not long after, when he traded in the Craftsman house and cop wife for a Westside mansion and TV anchor trophy mate better suited to his self-image as a player on L.A.'s celebrity scene.

Still clutching the phone, Hannah dropped to one knee next to her bed. "I'll see Gabe," she told her mother. "I just won't have him to myself. I was hoping he and I could do something special over our standing Wednesday dinner date, but it's not on. I'm a little bummed."

"But it's your night and you haven't seen him in three weeks! Why can't they let him be with you?"

Hannah reached under the bed, flailing through dust bunnies, searching out the long plastic bin in which she stored paper, ribbon, tags and other gift-giving paraphernalia. "Apparently they decided to throw him a surprise party."

"On a school night? Who has birthday parties on a school night? Obviously that woman doesn't know what she's doing when it comes to children."

"I appreciate your loyalty, Ma, but it's not Christie," Hannah said, wondering why she was defending the usurper. "I gather it was Cal's idea. Apparently he's got something special planned."

Her fingers found the edge of the box and she grabbed onto it, tugging it toward her. Overstuffed with years' worth of accumulated wrapping supplies, half of it too wrinkled and mashed to be of any use, the bin caught on the underside of the bed frame and stuck there. When Hannah pulled harder, her grip slipped and she felt the tearing of fingernails already trimmed utilitarian short. "Ow!"

"What?"

"Nothing," she said irritably. "Just tore a nail."

She stuck the ravaged fingers in her mouth for a second, then pulled them out and examined the damage. The index fingernail was ragged. On the longer second finger, a corner of the nail bed had been ripped away and a bright red glistening was already pooling at the cuticle. Even as she studied it, trying to remember if she had any Band-Aids in the house, a drop of blood fell and spread like a tiny chrysanthemum on what she knew for a fact was her only clean blouse, a silk one she kept on hand for those occasions when she knew she was going to be standing next to Cal's wife.

"Damn!"

"Language, Hannah."

"Sorry, Ma, but sometimes 'gosh, darn' just doesn't suffice, you know?"

"So, what's such a big deal that they just had to have this party on your night with Gabriel?"

"I don't know. Knowing how Cal likes to showboat, though, he's probably hired the Radio City Rockettes or something."

"For a ten-year-old?"

"Kidding, Ma. I don't know what the surprise is."

Hannah had moved into the bathroom. Soaking a washcloth, she dabbed cold water on the bloody spot on her blouse, but that only made it bloom larger, a lovely pink blossom in the middle of her chest. She'd have to dig through her closet to try to find a reasonably clean T-shirt she could get away with under the utilitarian black pantsuit she'd opted for, not knowing what kind of celebration Cal had planned. She'd meant to do laundry that morning, but her flight home from Montreal the previous night had been delayed by a snowstorm. She hadn't gotten into LAX until nearly 1:00 a.m., which left her feeling bagged and listless all day. In any case, no matter what she wore, it was a safe bet she'd look dowdy next to Christie Day-Nicks, the apple-fed blond goddess.

"And as it turns out, it's not a school night," she said, shrugging out of the blouse and tossing it into the laundry basket. "Apparently Gabe's got Thursday and Friday off this week. Some kind of teacher development thing."

"Humph! What kind of fancy private school is that, always taking days off? They've only just gone back after Christmas break."

"Don't ask me. I lost the school choice battle long ago. But it's supposed to be a good school."

Should be, she thought, for the exorbitant fees it charged, not that she paid any part of them. That was all Cal's doing. For her ambitious ex, the education offered at Dahlby Hall was more than worth the price of admission. But even more important than any benefits Gabe might reap, she suspected, was the opportunity for

Cal to hobnob with the movie stars and moguls who sent their kids there.

She found a Band-Aid in the medicine cabinet and hooked the phone into the crook of her shoulder while she unwrapped it and put it on her bloody finger. "Look, Ma, I've gotta fly. I'm running late and I give up trying to find a gift bag here. I'll have to stop on the way to pick one up."

"What did you get him?"

Hannah grinned. "Ah! I scored a coup. You know that security detail I was working the last three weeks?"

"Some football player, wasn't it?"

"European football—soccer. And not just some player. David Beckham, the British superstar. Gabe loves him. Never misses a game. He TiVos them all off Cal's satellite dish and watches them over and over. I was part of the security detail guarding Beckham and his wife while they toured North America to promote his new sportswear line."

"Oh, Hannah," her mother said wearily. "I wish you'd take up different work. Running off to all those godforsaken countries the way you do. I'm worried you're going to get hurt."

"I was in *Canada,* Ma. It's a very civilized place, you know. I'm not at much risk of injury in the great white north, unless you count frostbite this time of year. Anyway, never mind that. Listen to this. I got a chance to ask Beckham to autograph a soccer ball. He did, and he even wrote a little birthday note to go with it. I can hardly wait to give it to Gabe." For once, Hannah thought, she could be the parent who came up with the dynamite surprise.

"Oh, he'll love that."

"I think so."

"Are you still going to have him on the weekend?"

"As far as I know. He's got a soccer game Saturday morning, but the plan is for me to pick him up from there. I was going to bring him down to see you after I feed him, if that's okay. I'd wait and take you out to lunch with us, Ma, but he's always starving after his games. I don't think he'll last until we get down to your place."

Hannah's father had passed away the previous year after a long, sad slide into the dark pit of Alzheimer's. After that, her mother had moved out from Chicago to be closer to her two daughters and their children. She now lived near Hannah's older sister in south Orange County, an hour's drive from Hannah's place in Los Angeles. Nora's husband Neal was vice president of a construction engineering firm, and their Turtle Rock home was a suburban showplace. They also owned a couple of town houses near them in Irvine, one of which they'd set up for Ida's use.

"Don't worry about lunch," Hannah's mother said, "but try to get down if you can. I'll make a nice dinner. I haven't seen my little guy since Christmas. I miss him. I've got a birthday present for him here. It's nothing much. I never know what to get the kids anymore. Nora's are almost grown up, and even Gabriel—well, I just can't keep track of all the things they're into, you know? But I have to have something for them on their special day. I can't forget a grandchild's birthday, can I?"

"No, I know, Ma, and they love you for it. Even Nora's kids. Sixteen and nineteen is not too old to want Grandma's fussing. Anyway," she added, "I've really gotta run. I'll call you tomorrow, okay?"

"All right, sweetie. Give Gabriel a big birthday hug from me, all right?"

"Will do."

Hannah hung up and headed to the closet for a clean T-shirt, wondering again about the birthday surprise Cal had planned. She'd been hoping to take Gabe to Moby's on the beach in Malibu. The overpriced restaurant was a stretch on the strict budget she imposed on herself, but his tenth birthday warranted a stretch. The place was his favorite, and with the Beckham security gig running longer than expected, Hannah hadn't seen him in three weeks. So, a splurge then, she'd thought. Hang out on the beach, kick around a ball, watch the sunset, then surf 'n turf at Moby's. Why not? Wasn't that why God invented MasterCard? Only then, Cal had done an end run around her with this surprise party business. She sighed. Murphy's law.

The extended Beckham job had been one of those good news/bad news stories—good news, because she'd banked nearly double her expected fee, but bad because it detracted from her first priority, being a mother to her son. The autographed soccer ball was small compensation for her extended absences from his life, but maybe it was better than nothing.

It wasn't supposed to have gone like this. If her original plan had worked out, she'd have been retired long ago and, assuming the courts cooperated, might have been doing full-time mom duty instead of just snatching time with him between far-flung security gigs. But the Iraq affair two years earlier had knocked her irretrievably off course. Thanks to the influence of the angry CIA station chief in Baghdad, it seemed she'd been blacklisted from government security contracts, at least in that part of the world. Sean Ladwell, her team leader on the Brandywine job, had also been true to his word to have her blackballed when she jumped ship after Al Zawra. Brandywine had apparently struck her from their contractor database, and in the rest of the close-knit private security community, Hannah suspected, her rep was pretty much trashed after word got around that she'd gotten a colleague killed. She wasn't short of work per se, but what she was getting these days wasn't nearly as lucrative as those rent-an-army gigs.

At least she was working again. After Oz Nuñez died in that ambush at the Jordanian border, she'd been a basket case for months, listless, depressed, and bursting into tears at the drop of a sad song. Although they'd only worked together for a few days, they'd bonded in a way Hannah rarely managed. In the end, she'd mourned Oz like the little brother she never had.

As for her brilliant game plan for financial independence and winning back custody of Gabe, that, too, was left in ruins by the fiasco in Iraq. If she'd kept the Fitzgerald reward money she might have had a shot, but there was only one place that money could go—to Oz's widow and their little girl. She and Nuñez had both gone into Iraq with substantial life and disability insurance policies as part of their Brandywine contract package, but when Oz died, the carrier refused to honor the policy, since the assignment had already wound up. At that point, the adjusters ruled, he'd been freelancing on his own time and at his own risk.

It was one of those things she should have foreseen, Hannah thought, had she not been so blinded by the glow of the million-dollar reward for Amy Fitzgerald's safe return. Thanks to her, Oz's widow was left alone to raise a handicapped daughter on nothing but his meager marine pension. Turning over the entire Fitzgerald reward had seemed like the least Hannah could do. She would happily have given Lara Nuñez her share of the delivery fee for the Aston Martin, too, but by the time they blew across the border from Iraq, the vintage beauty was so banged up and bullet-riddled it was barely fit to be cannibalized for spare parts. Stewie Glover had refused to pay up.

Now, two years after the fact, Hannah still felt guilty as hell about how things had gone down. Money, even a million dollars, was a poor substitute for a loving husband and father, but it was the least she could do to honor the friend and ally who'd stuck by her so loyally. If it hadn't been for her, Oz would have made it home to raise the adorable little daughter whose picture he'd so proudly showed off that day in Zaynab's kitchen. Little Raquel would be in preschool now, learning her ABCs, Hannah realized. Oz was missing that, too.

As for her own plans, Gabe was still living full-time with Cal and Christie, and had been for nearly four years. He was well-established in his school and attached to his friends, his dog and the big house off Mulholland Drive. At this point, Hannah thought wearily, the mess she'd made of everything was pretty much unsalvageable.

21

Two L.A. sheriff's deputies were in the bubble of the helicopter circling over Compton. Both were qualified pilots, and they generally alternated manning the controls and operating the surveillance equipment. Tonight, Manny Garcia was handling the night sun floodlight.

Working streetlights in Compton were few and far between, most of the bulbs shot out as fast as city crews could replace them. This was more than idle vandalism. It was survival strategy. In disputed territory where lights made every gangbanger a target for enemies concealed in shadow, it was safer to level the playing field and throw the entire area into a darkness that was only slightly brightened by the overarching glow of L.A.'s urban sprawl.

In this neighborhood, anyone who didn't want trouble stayed indoors after sunset, praying that the danger roaming outside would pass them by. Not just people but houses, too, seemed to disappear into shadow. Only the occasional blue flicker of a television screen escaping through cracks in window blinds hinted at life behind those locked doors.

The helicopter made another pass. The rotating light bucket

under the Bell Jet Ranger had a candlepower of thirty-two million, hot enough to set dry grass ablaze if a pilot were stupid
enough to land with the spot still switched on. Plenty bright,
even at a three-hundred-foot close hover altitude, to pick out a
furtive or running figure clad in the stocking cap, wife-beater undershirt and oversized tan chinos that the suspect was reported
to be wearing.

The first report of shots fired had come in about thirty minutes
earlier. The location was reported to be Palmer Street, near Wilson
Park. The chopper passed over the street and the park. Beyond it,
railroad tracks were sandwiched between the long, dark strip of
North Alameda and the brighter thoroughfare of South Alameda,
the latter a hodgepodge of retread tire shops, check-cashing joints,
taquerias and all-night liquor stores.

The dead sheet call reporting a body down had been logged in
about three minutes after the first shooting report. A patrol car had
arrived on the scene four minutes later, the paramedics six minutes
after the first responders. One look and the EMTs hadn't even both-
ered to unload the gurney from the ambulance. The victim was already
a coroner's case. Male, African-American, name of Damon Shipley.
The kid was nineteen, according to the younger brother who'd been
with him when he was shot. Since the first black-and-white had rolled
in, a couple more sheriff's department units had shown up to help secure the scene for the homicide investigators, but by the time the
chopper arrived overhead, the ambulance was long gone.

The bird circled again, hunting for the suspect the patrol cops said
could be on one of the residential side streets or over on the commercial strip. As they overflew South Alameda, Manny Garcia's spotlight found a group leaning against the graffiti-tagged walls of a
liquor mart, half a dozen young men drinking out of brown-bagged
bottles. Late teens to midtwenties, by the hard-muscled, ropy look

of them. They raised their eyes idly as the chopper hovered overhead, and one of the youths raised a fist, middle finger extended.

Garcia held the night sun on them for a few seconds, then panned the light away. "No shooters there," he said. "Only the innocent would dare look up."

Mike Tillman was at the controls. He snorted. "I doubt there's an innocent in the bunch. What do you wanna bet there's not a few outstanding warrants down there?"

"Yeah, true. But those clowns are cocky. They know nobody's going to hassle them for boozing when we're hunting a shooter."

"Figure they're bulletproof tonight."

"You got that right." Garcia scanned the street. A few cars passed in either direction, but the sidewalks were deserted. "You want to take one more pass over the strip in case our shooter's hiding out on one of those flat rooftops?"

"Nah, he probably wouldn't be that dumb. Most of these guys know it's a trap to get caught up there. One tilt of the rotors and we pepper him with roof gravel so bad he comes down lookin' like Swiss cheese." Tillman leaned into the stick and the chopper wheeled around to the east. "If he's still out there, I'm betting he's ducked down one of those alleyways other side of the tracks. Maybe gone to ground in some backyard."

They circled back over to Palmer, where four black-and-whites sat parked at angles across the intersections, blocking traffic. Yellow tape had gone up, cordoning off the crime scene. The body was still lying in the middle of the road where the paramedics had left it for the homicide team and the coroner's investigators.

The kid had been tall and lanky, by the looks of him—basketball material. Despite the cool weather, he was wearing baggy shorts, and his legs, long and skinny, ended in running shoes like pontoons. The sneakers lay at skewed angles, their fluorescent side strips reflecting the glare of the chopper's searchlight. Dark stains spattered the shoulders of the vic's white sweatshirt, and a glistening dark circle had pooled around the head, running into cracks in the roadway. Compton's streets were pockmarked with too many stains like that. Turning dull brown over time, they were permanent reminders of the violence that afflicted certain parts of the City of Angels. In more affluent neighborhoods to the north and west, shootings went down occasionally, but not with the depressing frequency they did in South Central.

A half-dozen uniforms were guarding the crime scene perimeter. Their job was to hold back looky-loos, but at this hour, there would be no idle passersby. Any gangbangers on the prowl would have scattered at the first wail of sirens, and sure as hell no frightened resident from one of the surrounding houses was going to step out and volunteer information, even if they'd seen the whole thing go down from start to finish. Dozens of gangs vied for control of these streets, but the solve rate for violent crimes was abysmally low. No one wanted to become the bangers' next target.

Except this time, apparently, they did have a witness.

Just outside the yellow tape, next to a chain-link fence surrounding the patchy lawn of a white stucco bungalow, two plainclothes detectives had shown up since the chopper's last pass. They were talking now to a young black teenager dressed in baggy jeans and an oversized L.A. Lakers basketball jersey. In the chill January night air, their breath rose in white wisps.

Tillman hovered the bird over the white stucco house and leaned forward in the bubble, studying the detectives. Then, he pulled back. "Son of a bitch," he muttered.

Garcia looked at him, then down at the group on the ground. "What?"

"Nothin.'"

"Who is that down there?"

The pilot mumbled something in reply, but Garcia didn't make it out. He tapped his headphones and pulled his microphone closer to his lips. "Who did you say?"

"John Russo. And that's the newbie detective he's training, I guess. Chen, I think his name is. Billy Chen."

Garcia peered back down to the ground. "Russo's the one talking to the kid on the fence?"

Tillman nodded.

The newbie was taking Polaroids of the scene and writing in a notebook while Russo grilled the teenager, whose body language spoke volumes about his fear and his reluctance to say anything that could result in his ending up as dead as the blood-pooled body sprawled on the pavement. Nothing new there. That kind of close-mouthedness was par for the course in this neighborhood.

"So, this Russo," Garcia said, "not your favorite homie, huh?"

"You could say that."

The kid below was leaning so far back into the chain-link fence that it was starting to sag inward. He looked in real danger of tipping over it, but still Russo advanced on him, getting right in his face.

"That must be the vic's brother," Garcia said. "Reports said he was there when it went down. Maybe this'll be the one in a million case where an eyewitness actually tells us something."

"Depends how he's handled," Tillman said. "I don't know what this Chen's like, but it don't really matter. Russo's senior man on the scene. He calls the shots."

Just then, they saw Russo step back and stare at the kid for a minute, his fighter's stance telling the officers in the chopper all they needed to know about the level of his irritation. He wheeled, walked over to Chen and grabbed one of the Polaroids out of his hand. Returning to the kid, he shoved the photograph in his face.

The boy cringed visibly. When he tried to turn his head away, Russo grabbed him by the scruff of the neck, keeping the picture right in front of his eyes.

"Jeez, man, it's his *brother*," Tillman said. "Have a heart."

"This Russo—he's a take-no-prisoners type, huh?"

"Total bastard. Take my advice, Manny. Anybody ever suggest you work with him, run fast as you can in the opposite direction." Tillman shook his head. "I wouldn't mind a nice freeway chase right about now so we can get the hell out of here."

Russo finally loosened his grip. When the teenager tried to scuttle away from him, the detective caught him by the sweatshirt and led him to the unmarked sedan he and Chen had arrived in. Once he'd gotten the kid into the back seat, Russo squinted up at the circling chopper. He pulled a radio off his belt. His partner shielded his eyes as he followed the direction of Russo's gaze.

"*Chopper One, this is Detective Russo. You wanna get that light out of my eyes?*"

Garcia panned the night sun away from the crime scene while Tillman flipped his helmet mike over to the ground channel. "Sorry. Just trying to help."

Russo's mouth vented a sharp puff of vapor, but he said nothing for a moment. And then, "*Is that you wasting gas up there, Tillman? Go make yourself useful and find my shooter, would you?*"

"You got any idea where we should be looking? 'Cause we're not seeing much."

"*Stand by.*"

Russo turned back to the kid cowering in the back seat.

"This Russo," Garcia said, "you worked with him before?"

"Not exactly."

"So how do you know him?"

"Let's just say our paths have crossed. Dude's bad news, trust me."

"A hotshot? One of those 'kiss up, kick down' dicks, no time for us peons?"

Tillman only scowled.

Meantime, down on the ground, Russo's head gave a sharp, victorious nod. He stepped away from the car. Lifting his radio once more, he looked up at the helicopter, his free hand pointing east. *"Del Mar Court, Tillman. Look for an orange stucco house with a metal tool shed along the back fence. I'm calling up a SWAT unit and heading over there now. See if you can spot anything, but don't try to flush him out before backup gets here."*

"Roger." Tillman took one last look down. Russo had slammed the back door of the tan Taurus with the kid inside and climbed into the front, behind the wheel. Chen hustled into the front passenger seat. His door was still open when Russo peeled out.

"Lousy luck for the kid," Tillman said, wheeling the bird away. "Killer takes out his brother and then he gets to deal with John Russo. That's more than any human being should have to put up with in one night."

22

Hannah pulled up to the guardhouse outside Mulholland Estates. As her little hybrid came to a silent stop, the brightly colored gift bag on the passenger seat slid forward. She caught it just before it hit the floor.

A handful of show business and sports celebs kept homes in the gated enclave of multimillion-dollar estates perched high over Los Angeles. Some pretty shady characters lived there, as well. It was the perfect place for a pole-climber like her ex, Hannah thought. Once, Cal had prosecuted people who used wealth and connections to rip off the unsuspecting and the innocent. Now, he defended them with glib courtroom skills and sensational press conferences designed to paint moneyed sleazoids, con artists and sociopaths as persecuted pillars of the community. It was enough to make an ex-cop retch.

After driving up the dark, winding curves of Mulholland Drive, she found herself half-blinded by glaring spotlights that turned the roadway in front of the gatehouse from night to brilliant day. A blue-uniformed security guard stepped out carrying a pen and clipboard, another of the underpaid and undertrained rent-a-dicks the paranoid foolishly believed could keep them safe behind their high stone walls. In fact, it was L.A.'s huge freeway system that was the city's real Hadrian's Wall, barricading the city's poorer eastern and southern neighborhoods, holding back the brown and black hordes that these superrich people feared so much.

The guard took one look at Hannah's little car and practically sneered. It was a far cry from the Porsches and Ferraris that normally passed through those gates. "Help you?" he asked, like maybe she was lost and needed directions back to the boonies.

"My name's Hannah Nicks. I should be on your clipboard there. I'm expected."

"Uh-huh." The guy ran a finger down the sheet on his board. "Nicks, you said. Nope, nothing here."

Hannah fumed. Once again, Christie had forgotten to call down to the gatehouse and let them know Gabe's mother was coming. Wasn't it enough they'd taken Hannah's son? Was the humiliation necessary, too? Did they think it would discourage her from coming for him as often as possible? That she'd just fade away into the sunset, out of his life once and for all?

Fat chance.

Well, two could play at this game. Hannah pulled a leather billfold from her pocket and flipped it open. The brown cowhide folder had once held her police ID and shield, and this was one of those occasions when she wished she still carried them. The P.I. license she'd gotten after she left the sheriff's department didn't carry the same power to impress as that gold shield, but it was official-looking all the same.

"I'm here to question people at the Nicks residence on Barn Swallow Drive."

It was half a lie, but it had the desired effect, especially when she saw how quickly the guard's eyes slid over the license. He might have been dyslexic or just semi-literate, because he clearly didn't really register what was written there. He straightened his spine, nodded sharply and reached back for the switch that opened the gate. Maybe he thought she was from Homeland Security or something.

But then, just as the big wrought-iron gate began to swing outward, a delayed flash of insight furrowed his otherwise thought-free brow. He ducked low to peer at her once more. "The Nicks place? And your name is Nicks, too?"

Hannah grimaced and put the Prius in gear. "Coincidence. No relation, believe me." She took off before he had a chance to worry his brain about it anymore. She would have peeled out to show determination to get on with her important work, but peeling was really not an option in her modest but fuel-efficient little car.

Turning into Barn Swallow Drive, she spotted a white stretch limousine—a Hummer, at that—parked at the end of Cal and Christie's red brick driveway. Her heart sank. Laughing boys were clambering all over the gleaming white behemoth, peering through the driver's side window, scrambling in and out of oversized rear doors, poking their heads up through the open sunroof. Whatever surprise Cal had planned, clearly it was more than just a house party.

Every one of the young partygoers was wearing what looked to be an official L.A. Lakers basketball jersey, Hannah noticed, and she suddenly remembered that Cal's client list these days included the Lakers' star center, Keenan Prince. A few weeks earlier, Cal had won dismissal in a criminal case in which the basketball player had been accused of raping the seventeen-year-old daughter of his girlfriend's cleaning lady. When the victim wouldn't be bought off, Cal made her life a living hell both inside the courtroom and out with well-placed innuendos about a mother-daughter team of gold-digging grifters. In the end, both the girl and her mother fled back to the mother's hometown in Mexico. The D.A.'s office, lacking witnesses, reluctantly withdrew all charges.

Hannah grabbed her son's gift bag and climbed out of the car just as Gabe's head emerged through the limo's sunroof. He was dark-haired, his mop a froth of tumbling curls not unlike her own when she let it revert to its natural wild state—except on him, it looked good. Maybe it was the two-hundred-dollar haircuts Christie got him at the Beverly Hills salon she frequented. Or maybe it was just that Gabe was so damn beautiful. Even now, ten years after that morning she'd first held him in her arms, Hannah couldn't believe she'd produced something as wonderful as that young Adonis poking his head out of the Hummer's roof.

"Hey there!" she called. "What's happening, birthday boy?"

He swiveled toward her, his face beaming. He had Cal's gorgeous blue eyes and a wide, wild grin that was all his own. "Mom! Hey! Isn't this cool?"

"Pretty cool," she agreed, tactfully sidestepping the issue of how many kids were being killed or maimed in Iraq in order to safeguard access to fuel for gas guzzlers like that. Ever since Oz Nuñez, she'd been taking every reported casualty over there very personally. "What's up? I thought there was a party or something happening here tonight."

"Party, yeah, but not here. You won't believe it. Keenan Prince invited me and my friends to be his personal guests at tonight's game. He sent over the limo and shirts for everyone. We get to go in the VIP entrance at the Staples Center and down to the Lakers dressing room and everything!" His grin turned mischievous. "Girls gotta wait outside the locker room while we check it out, though. Make sure they don't get butt-flashed or anything."

"That could be embarrassing," Hannah agreed. She tried to peer through the limo's tinted windows. "You've got girls in there?"

"Ew, Mom! Gross! No way."

Hannah grinned. At ten, the prospect would seem pretty yucky, she supposed. Give it a few more years, though…

"I meant girls like you and Christie," Gabe said. "And we've got primo seats for the game. Courtside, right on the floor. All of us! Can you believe it?"

"Yeah!" a couple of his hyper friends chorused. "Can you believe it?"

"Wow," Hannah said. *Why am I not surprised?* But of course, Keenan Prince would be grateful. He'd been looking into the black maw of destruction just a few weeks earlier, the implosion of his career and an income that was reported to be something over thirty million dollars a year when you rolled in all the commercial endorsements. Lucky for him Cal had come along to save his bacon.

"So, you guys are off shortly then?" Hannah asked.

"We're just waiting for Dad. He's inside trying to find his sunglasses."

Sunglasses? The sun had already set. But of course, Hannah thought, all the celebrities at Lakers games wore sunglasses. "Well, do you think I could give you a hug and your birthday present?"

Gabe nodded and ducked down the Hummer's bolt-hole, emerging from the side passenger door and bounding over. Hannah wrapped her arms around him and kissed the top of his head, breathing in his little-boy scent, holding on until she felt him beginning to squirm. She cut it short before he succumbed to terminal embarrassment. His friends, she noticed, were studying her with the kind of frank, pitiful curiosity reserved for homeless street people and divorced absent parents. She was suddenly conscious of her nondescript black pantsuit and red cotton T-shirt. A sad specimen compared to Gabe's glamorous stepmother.

As if sensing her discomfort, Gabe patted her back. "Sorry, Mom. I know you and me were supposed to do something tonight."

She ruffled his baby-soft curls, wondering how it was that his head reached her shoulders all of a sudden. How could he have grown an inch in the three weeks since she'd left on the Beckham job?

Yet another marker missed. How many were there in the four years, five months and six days since she'd lost custody of her little guy?

"This is your birthday, sweetie. It's great you get to spend it with your friends. I just wanted to bring your present. Although," she added, examining the pathetically cheery, tissue-stuffed bag in her hand, "maybe it's kind of lame next to all this." She cocked a thumb at the Hummer and the adventure it represented—not just a scrawled note from some distant sports hero, but a personal connection to an entire team of superstars.

"Thanks, Mom," Gabe said, taking the bag.

"What have you got there?" a musical voice behind him called.

Hannah looked up to see that Christie had emerged from the Tudor-style mansion. She came up behind Gabe, peering over his shoulder at the garish gift bag, her green eyes sparkling. Stunningly beautiful, with the kind of perfectly even features and high cheekbones that television cameras loved, she was tall and slim and—

Oh, God, no! Hannah's gaze riveted on a small mound under Christie's slim pink knit dress. *Oh, no, no, no…*

Her own smile froze as she forced herself to look away from the little bulge that would never, ever be found on Christie Day's stomach in the normal course of events. Hannah ran and worked out with weights to stay in the kind of physical condition that security work demanded. Christie, however, had a personal trainer who came several times a week to the house to supervise her workout routine in the home gym that overlooked the infinity pool and its panoramic views of the city. Her perky breasts, Hannah suspected, owed a small debt to the wonders of silicone, but they were the only part of that figure that wasn't exercised to within an inch of its life. If a mound had appeared on Christie's abdomen now, it could only mean one thing.

And why not? Hannah thought wearily. Christie had given up a

high-profile evening news anchor job to be home during the day
for someone else's child. Getting up at 3:00 a.m. to read the morning news at a local network affiliate had probably lost its attraction
by now, and like Hannah, she was turning thirty this year. Her bi-
ological clock had probably been ticking up a storm.

"Found them!" Cal's voice boomed from inside the cavernous
entry hall. He emerged from the house and bounded down the
semicircular brick steps, waving a pair of Oakley sunglasses. His nut
brown hair was going prematurely gray and yet, disgustingly, it
didn't age him. His vivid blue eyes were as bright as ever, his even-
featured face unlined, his body trim and tight from tennis and the
morning racquetball games he played with one of the senior partners at his firm—good ol' Cal missing no opportunity to brown-
nose. He had on a navy knit golf shirt and tan slacks that shimmered
with that faint sheen that expensive fabrics have.

"Hi, Hannah," he said. "You're late. You nearly missed the boat."

"Sorry. Would have come faster if I'd known you guys were going
out on the town." She cocked a thumb at the limo overrun with yellow and purple jersey-clad boys. "Keenan Prince is really pleased
about beating that criminal beef, I see."

Cal frowned. "The whole thing was a shakedown, way overblown
by the media."

"Yeah, rape has a tendency to get overblown, I find."

"The charges were dismissed."

"The victim fled."

"The accuser, you mean. The way I see it, Keenan was the real
victim here. Anyway, it's hardly the sort of thing to be discussing in
front of the birthday boy, wouldn't you say?"

"Aw, Dad," Gabe said, "I know what happened."

"I know you do. But you also know that a person's innocent
until proven guilty, and that didn't happen here. We don't want to

go around smearing Mr. Prince's name, do we? Especially when he's given you such a great birthday gift?"

"Yeah, it's pretty great," Gabriel agreed, looking back at his friends clambering over the Hummer. The uniformed driver stood by, hands clasped behind his back, a smile of pained forbearance pasted in place.

"So," Christie said, peering over Gabe's shoulder, "what's in that bag?"

"Oh, it's just a little something," Hannah said quickly. "You can open it later, Gabe. You should be with your friends."

"No, that's not right," Christie said. "Your mom came all the way over here with your present, Gabie. You should open it."

Inwardly, Hannah cringed. This was the problem, she thought, not for the first time. Christie was actually a fairly decent person, nicer than anyone that gorgeous had a need to be, and damned if Hannah didn't just hate her for it. She wanted so badly to dislike this woman who'd replaced her, not only as Cal's wife but effectively as Gabe's mother, too. Why did she have to be so bloody gracious? She was certainly a better person than Cal deserved.

"It's just something I had a chance to get during this last job I was on," Hannah told Gabe as he pulled the tissue-wrapped mound out of the bag. "You remember I told you I was going to be meeting David Beckham?"

"Yeah," Gabe said, unwrapping the ball. He studied it for a moment, and then his eyes went wide. "Oh, Mom, wow! Lookit, Dad! Autographed by Beckham himself!"

"Wow," Cal echoed dryly.

"There's a note from him in there, too," Hannah said.

A few of Gabe's friends had gathered around. Excitedly, he showed them the note and where the British soccer star had signed the ball. There was nothing Cal hated more than being up-staged, Hannah knew—although, Cal being Cal, it couldn't last for long. Gabe threw the ball up and tapped it with a header over his buddies. One of them went for the pass, kicking it off toward a third runner.

"Guys, guys!" Cal called. "We need to get on the road. Traffic's going to be heavy. If you want to get to the Staples Center in time to visit the dressing room—"

"Dibs on the back seat!" one of the kids hollered, racing to the limo.

"Me, too!" another cried. The soccer ball rolled into the bushes at the side of the brick driveway.

"Me, three!" Gabe yelled. He started to run after them, but then hesitated, turning back to Hannah. "Mom—"

"It's okay, sweetie. Go and be with your guests. I'll see you on the weekend, okay?"

He looked confused. "But you're coming with us. Right, Dad?"

Hannah shook her head. "It's all right…"

"We have a ticket for you," Christie said.

"We do?" Cal asked.

Christie frowned. "Yes, Calvin, we do. Twelve tickets, right? Gabe plus eight friends, that's nine. You, me, and Hannah. That's twelve."

It was Cal's turn to frown. "I didn't realize—"

Hannah took a step back. "I really don't need to go."

"See? She doesn't want to come," Cal said. "Basketball's not Hannah's thing."

"Of course she has to come. It's Gabie's birthday, for heaven's sake." Christie turned to the boys, smiling. "You guys jump in now, okay? Gabie, your dad will go in the limo with you guys, and your mom and I will come along behind in my car. Here," she added, handing Cal an envelope, "ten tickets for you and the kids. Keenan's business manager had them delivered this morning. I held back two. Hannah and I will meet you on the floor. I think we're more than happy to give the stinky locker room a pass, right, Hannah?"

"I guess," Hannah said. She didn't want to go to the stupid Lakers game. On the other hand, it was fun and more than a little satisfying to see Cal's frustration at having been outgunned. "But I really should take my own car. I have an appointment later this evening."

In fact, she didn't. Business was slow at the moment, which was more than a little worrisome. Had she unknowingly ticked off someone else? Just the same, she had no desire to be a captive member of Cal's traveling circus. Taking her own wheels allowed her to cut out when she'd had enough.

"Got a hot date?" Cal asked, bemused.

It would be so nice to wipe that perpetually superior grin off his face. "No, it's a business thing. I'll probably have to head right off from the game. If that's okay," she added to Christie.

"Of course, whatever you need to do. I'll drive over with you then and come back in the limo with the guys."

Cal waved a hand. "Fine. Let's just hit the road, shall we?" He paused to give Christie a buss on the cheek. "See you over there, little mother." He patted the bulge on her stomach, his eyes flicking back to Hannah. He obviously wanted to make sure she hadn't missed it. Bastard.

The two women stood aside and watched him climb into the Hummer, next to the driver. Then, with a spirited cheer from nine excited boys rising out of the open rooftop, the white beast roared to life and headed off.

Christie waved and watched them go, head shaking. Then, she turned to Hannah. "Sorry about that confusion."

Hannah shrugged. "Not your fault." *Not your fault my ex is a jerk.* "So. When are you due."

Christie had the grace to blush. "May twelfth. I'm sorry about that, too. I thought you knew, but I can see you didn't."

"There's nothing to be sorry for. I'm happy for you."

"Thank you. So, what do you say? I'll just get my bag and sweater, lock the door and we'll get going?"

Hannah nodded. "Sounds like a plan."

While Christie returned to the house, Hannah hurried back to the Prius to clear room on the front passenger seat. She gathered up empty water bottles and old food wrappers, crumpled up map printouts from job interviews long past, and gave the dusty dash a quick swipe with a sweatshirt she found on the back seat. She just had time to jam everything under the seat before Christie climbed into the car, bringing a cashmere cardigan, a soft leather sac purse and the scent of expensive cologne.

Hannah smiled grimly and put the car in gear. The last thing she saw in the rearview mirror before they pulled away was the autographed soccer ball, lying forgotten where it had tumbled away under the hedge.

23

Compton, South Central Los Angeles

It was probably the chopper that started the chain reaction, but the exact sequence of events would be the subject of considerable speculation, investigation and media castigation in the days to come.

Manny Garcia, in the co-pilot's seat, was panning the night sun over Del Mar Court, looking for an orange stucco house with a tool shed out back. "Nothin'. He sure it's the right street?"

"I dunno. Let's ask." Tillman switched over his mike to the ground channel. "Chopper One to Russo."

Detectives Russo and Chen had driven over to Chester Avenue, a block south of Del Mar, followed by a couple of black-and-whites. Russo was just getting out of the driver's seat when Tillman's call went out. Looking down, the men in the chopper saw him raise his handheld radio.

"What's up?"

"We got nothing on Del Mar Court that looks like what you're describing. Your witness sure about the address?"

"Stand by."

Russo opened the rear door of the tan Taurus, motioning for the kid in back to stay put. Leaning one arm on the roof, he dropped his head to talk to him. A moment later, Chen opened the front passenger door and climbed out, scanning the surrounding houses, then peering at the chopper hovering overhead.

Russo straightened and stepped back from the car, lifting his radio once more. *"He says he thought it was Del Mar but maybe not. Check out the surrounding streets."*

"Roger." Tillman switched his mike back to the inside channel before muttering, "Asshole."

Garcia glanced over at him. "What's the deal? You got history with this dude? He jam you up or something?"

The pilot shrugged. "Guy's a jerk."

"What'd he do?"

"Never mind. Let's just see if we can spot this mope, then get the hell out of here."

Garcia panned the night sun over the adjacent streets, looking for orange stucco. There was white, beige, brown, candy-floss pink and powder-blue, and plenty of graffiti to mark the territories of the different black and Latino gangs that jostled for supremacy in the area. No orange stucco, though.

Over on Chester, Detective Chen was leaning against the front of the Taurus, checking his watch.

Tillman and Garcia scanned one yard after another, looking for a metal toolshed. Finally, they spotted one, around the corner from Del Mar on South Pearl behind a low stucco house. The house looked more peach-colored than orange, but maybe it was just the bleaching effect of the night sun. The yard seemed deserted except for two tall, skinny palm trees standing like flea-bitten sentries at the front corners of the lot.

"Try the FLIR," Tillman suggested. "It's chilly out there tonight."

A chilly January night in L.A. meant people actually put on sweaters, although nobody's garden was in danger from frost. "Maybe we'll pick up a heat signature."

Garcia switched off the spotlight and aimed the forward-looking infrared sensor at the corrugated tin shed behind the house. The monitor between the two pilots displayed shades of blue, green and yellow that corresponded to the various cooling rates of the plants and structures below them. But then, as the infrared beam passed over the shed, the monitor picked out an indistinct orange blob against one inside wall. An animal? A large dog, maybe? Or a crouched person, listening for approaching footsteps or peering out an unseen window?

"This is Chopper One," Tillman reported to the cops on the ground. "We may have someone in a shed over on Pearl. We're moving in for a closer look."

"*Negative. Hold your position,*" Russo radioed back.

But the chopper had already dropped closer to the ground, so low that the beating of its rotor blades stirred the fronds of the palm trees like the arrival of a sudden squall. The predatory drone nearly drowned out the ear-splitting sirens approaching from the north-east—nearly, but not quite. At the same moment, both pilots glanced toward Rosecrans Boulevard, where several more cruisers and the SWAT van were racing toward the scene. By the time the men directed their attention downward again, the orange blob was no longer in the toolshed.

The approaching cruisers switched off their sirens for silent running the last couple of blocks but by then the suspect, if that's what the orange shape had been, was on the run and out of range of the slow-moving FLIR. Garcia pushed the infrared aside and grabbed for the spotlight controls once more, switching it back on and panning the ground.

Wearing chinos and a white wife-beater undershirt, the suspect was in full flight now, running across yards and down alleyways. He leapt over a low cinderblock wall, watching his back, the direction from which the sirens had been coming—obviously unaware that he was moving directly toward the homicide team.

Then, with just one house between him and the detectives, he stopped. He hesitated, looking around frantically, back toward Rosecrans and the cop cars he had to know were coming for him, then up at the chopper and its blinding spotlight. Finally, he seemed to come to a decision. Tillman and Garcia watched as he scrambled up an old-fashioned television antenna tower fastened to the side of the flat-roofed white bungalow. On the front side of the same house, the detectives and the uniformed cops who'd accompanied them were spread out like ducks in a shooting gallery.

"Son of a bitch!" Tillman switched on his ground mike. "Suspect on the roof beside you!" His blood ran cold as the runner jumped off the antenna tower and scrambled across the tarred surface of the roof, pulling something from his waistband.

"Gun! Gun! Take cover!" Tillman yelled.

Time slowed, unfurling a lazy ballet stage-lit by the chopper's brilliant night sun. In the street below, Russo was using one hip to slam the Taurus's rear door and lock his witness inside, at the same time reaching to the small of his back for his weapon. His left hand was gesturing wildly to his partner, his mouth wide in a yell.

With another nervous glance up at the helicopter, the suspect tried to find cover, ducking behind a chimney at the front center edge of the roof. He looked as if he'd thought he might leap from there to the ground, but at the last minute, his sneakers skidded on the gritty surface. He slid to a halt right at the edge, obviously startled by the sight of the cops in the street below him.

Tillman dropped the bird even lower and tilted to starboard.

The palm fronds whipped crazily, and stones flew like buckshot off the surface of the asphalt roof. The banger's feet back-shuffled frantically, looking for purchase as the wind of the rotors assaulted him. His arms were wheeling for balance, his gun hand waving erratically.

It was only now, in this slow-mo dance, that Chen finally looked up and realized where the danger lay. Russo was crouch-running toward him, gun in one hand, the other motioning for his partner to get down, but it was all just a split-second too late. Behind them, uniformed officers had fanned out, taking cover behind trees and vehicles, blocking all avenues of escape in case the gangbanger on the roof actually did decide to take a leap off the low roof.

Chen turned away, right elbow rising as his hand reached into his jacket for his shoulder holster. Muzzle fire flashed from the rooftop and then from the barrel of Russo's gun. Chen dropped, falling gracelessly into a heap on the pavement. Several more flashes followed, as Russo, the suspect and the other cops all fired. The gangbanger's gun muzzle was still throwing sparks as he flew off the roof.

A hole appeared in the chopper's tempered glass bubble, and then a spiderweb of cracks spun itself out from the center.

"Shit!" Tillman cried, instinctively pulling the bird back up. "We're hit! Are you—?" He looked over to his partner and a vise clamped onto his gut.

Garcia had his hand on his forehead, and blood was streaming between his fingers. "I'm okay," he said, chuckling nervously. But when he pulled his hand away, the palm was soaked red and blood started running down into his eyes. He slapped his hand over the wound once more, spattering blood on the chopper's glass bubble.

"Oh, Christ, man, hang on!" Tillman cried. "Dispatch! My co-pilot's hit and there's another officer down on Chester Street. I'm pulling out of here."

"*Roger,*" the dispatch operator replied. "*Paramedics are en route to Chester. We're notifying King-Drew to meet you on the roof with a stretcher."*

"No way, not King-Drew!" Tillman shouted. It was the closest E.R. but, plagued by one scandal after another, the hospital had a reputation for incompetence. "I'm taking him to St. Francis." It was a little farther, on the other side of the 105 Freeway, one of the city's major east-west arteries. It was a difference of only seconds for the chopper but it could mean life or death for an E.R. patient.

"Roger, St. Francis Medical Center," dispatch confirmed. *"We'll notify the E.R. over there to meet you on the helipad."*

Tillman took one last look at the scene below. Incredibly, the banger had landed on his feet but then he stumbled backward into the chain-link fence surrounding the yard. He spread-eagled back over it, like laundry hung out to dry, the front of his wife-beater and chinos already sprouting dark stains. His knees buckled. As his arms slipped off the fence, his white muscle shirt snagged on the top spikes. He landed heavily, legs splayed in front, the caught shirt half covering his head. His body tilted, then was still. One of the uniforms approached him warily, kicking the weapon out of his slack hand. Two more ran up and grabbed the shooter's arms, slapping on cuffs, but even from his distance, Tillman could see that the creep's gangsta days were over.

The last thing he noticed before he wheeled the chopper up and away toward St. Francis Medical Center was John Russo, sitting on the pavement by the front bumper of his departmental Taurus, holding the trainee detective's head in his lap.

24

The Staples Center, Los Angeles

She should have known better. Hannah had learned to trust her gut, and right now, her thrumming gut told her something was badly amiss. But then, her head already knew that. Wasn't like it was an earth-shaking news bulletin. She couldn't remember the last time things had been hunky-dory.

So what was bothering her now? The fact that she was forced for the next couple of hours to make nice with her ex-husband and his wife? His gorgeous, *pregnant* wife—the woman who, however she might be trying to make up for it now, had had an affair with Cal when he was still Hannah's husband, then commandeered her place inside the family that Hannah had naïvely believed would be hers for life.

It was doubly irritating inasmuch as Hannah wanted so badly to resent Christie. Frankly, though, she couldn't work up much of a froth of indignation anymore. Grudgingly, she had to admit that Christie was pretty good at this stepmothering gig, if Gabe was anything to go by. He was doing well at school, had nice friends, and was a polite, cheerful kid. No matter how fierce Hannah's own mother-love or undying her resentment that she'd been shoved aside as the central figure in her son's life, Hannah was no longer sure that she could do the job any better than Christie was—no more certain about that than she was about anything else.

How was it, Hannah wondered, that at not yet thirty, she was already so ground down?

Cal, meantime, was basking in the glow of excitement rising off the birthday boy and his school friends. They were so pumped about sitting next to the Lakers team bench that somebody was going to burst a gasket. Cal also looked pretty smug about the reflected glory of his association with Keenan Prince, who'd given him a high-five after the team came onto the court. Of course, the guy owed Cal— a limo and some courtside seats were the least he could do.

Settled next to some high-end Hollywood stars, Cal, Gabe and the other boys had nothing between them and the action but a couple of sports photographers seated cross-legged on the floor in front of them. Hannah and Christie were seated one row back. At regular intervals, a waiter came by to take their drink and food orders. Each time the crowd-cam zeroed in on the Lakers bench, the giant, eight-sided video monitors suspended high above the court flashed the boys' wide grins from one end of the arena to the other—nine preadolescent fans who looked like they'd died and gone to heaven. The boys had been warned to keep their butts in the chairs and their feet off the hardwood so they wouldn't trip up players or refs, but by the rapt looks on their faces as the action rumbled up and down the court, it was a small price to pay for their middle-of-the-thrills perch, with its attendant smells of sweat, rubber and Gatorade. Nine sets of parents were going to have to peel boys down off the ceiling with spatulas tonight.

Hannah's gift of a soccer ball, autographed or not, was looking more pitiful by the minute.

Never a big fan of any sport where players earned more than the gross domestic product of some small nations, Hannah was trying hard to focus on the game. Better that than have her gaze keep drifting to that tiny bulge under Christie's pink knit sheath. The harder she tried to ignore it, though, the more her traitorous eyes seemed to gravitate there.

So what's the big deal? Did you think they weren't having sex? Or that after five years married to someone else, Cal would suddenly realize he'd made a terrible mistake and come crawling back, begging forgiveness?

God forbid. If it weren't for that beautiful boy in front of her, clear evidence that her DNA once had done the two-step with Calvin Nicks's, Hannah would find it hard to believe she could ever have been married to the guy, much less in love with him. He was a stranger to her now, for all intents and purposes, a "what-the-hell-were-you-thinking?" reminder of youthful bad judgment. A rotten memory she would have buried long ago had it not been for this amazing kid they'd produced together.

Still, there was something wrenching about the notion that Gabe was going to have a baby brother or sister totally unrelated to her. As her thirtieth birthday drew nigh, Hannah had resigned herself to the likelihood that she'd had the only child she was ever going to have. It wasn't just the demands of her work that made motherhood problematic. She wouldn't willingly raise a child without a father, and since all her post-Cal relationships had been even more fraught and fleeting than her marriage, she had few illusions about the prospects of venturing down that road again.

So it wasn't like her gut had suddenly come up with some brilliant flash of insight when it told her something was amiss that evening. Her whole life was pretty much a flawed operation. And yet, it wasn't nearly as messy or treacherous as it was about to become.

25

Compton, South Central Los Angeles

Russo hovered over the paramedics working on his young partner. It was all he could do to hold himself aside, fists clenched, and not try to second-guess their every move. He had to let them do what they were trained to do. He refused to contemplate the possibility that their emergency arts might not be enough.

His ears were ringing, half-deaf from the gunfire that had taken down Billy Chen and the gangbanger, but if his hearing was wonky, the rest of his senses were on hyper-alert. He smelled the burnt, metallic tang of gunpowder and the police flares that cut through the cloying scent of night jasmine. Above that, more insistent and unsettling, he was picking up the coppery smell of blood—the blood of the dead banger who'd fallen off the roof, but Billy Chen's blood, too, on Billy, on the road, and on himself.

He stared at bloodied hands that had cradled his partner's head and at the stains on his jacket and pants. It was only the kid's second week on the homicide beat. Russo was his training officer. He was supposed to watch over his probie. He wasn't supposed to let this happen.

Pulling a handkerchief from his pocket, Russo wiped his palms, forcing himself to look away from the paramedics and take in the scene. In the absence of working streetlights, the roadway was dark, but emergency flares illuminated the critical elements: the gang-banger slumped over against the chain-link fence, handcuffed but unquestionably dead. Milling uniforms. Faces peering around window curtains, worried-looking and curious. More detectives from the sheriff's department homicide bureau on Rickenbacker Road. They'd shown up sometime in the last few minutes, no doubt ordered out as soon as the "officer down" call went out.

"Russo!"

He turned to see Lieutenant Lou Halloran climbing out of the dark gray Chevy Caprice he always drove. It was the oldest car in the bureau. Halloran's rank gave him first dibs on any unit he wanted but he always left the newer Tauruses and Crown Vics to his detectives, habitually fair with the detectives who worked under him. Or maybe, Russo thought, it was just that the big old boat was a better fit for Lou Halloran's lumbering frame. The lieutenant was six-four, broad as a house. He'd played college ball but that was a long time ago, and even a body as naturally graceful as Halloran's develops a paunch when its owner becomes a desk jockey. But if he'd put on a few pounds and acquired a few gray hairs, nothing in the lieutenant's demeanor suggested he'd lost the edge that had made him one of L.A.'s best cops for the past quarter century.

As Halloran signed himself onto the scene in the incident log that one of the uniforms had started, Russo went to wave him over, but remembering his bloodstained sleeves, he rammed his hands in his pockets and nodded instead. Halloran approached, worry shadowing his eyes. His coffee-colored face was deeply etched from years of dealing with too much violence, too much heartbreak on these

South-Central streets where he himself had grown up. His dark, intelligent eyes reflected the laser focus the man brought to combating the malicious forces that tore apart neighborhoods and the families in them, ordinary people for the most part, just trying to keep things together and live in peace.

Families, Russo thought. *Billy Chen has a family. Four-year-old twin girls.*

He had a strong urge to hit something. He kicked a stone instead, then took a slow, deep breath. There would be no losing it, not in front of strangers and fellow cops. It did nobody any good, least of all Billy. But that said, he was personally going to take down whoever was responsible for this bloody cock-up.

As the lieutenant moved alongside him, Russo noticed again how dwarfed he always felt next to the guy. It wasn't just height. Russo was just a hair under six feet, not exactly a midget, and as solidly built as his father and grandfather, Sicilian bricklayers both. His sense of smallness stemmed from the fact that Lou Halloran had been his training officer back in the day when he was a green patrol rookie. Halloran had laid the groundwork for everything Russo knew about being a cop, teaching him how to read people and read a situation, when to go in hard and when to take it slow. He'd taught Russo to cut fools no slack and show slackers no mercy. Russo still lived by those precepts but no matter how long he was on the job, he knew he'd never match Lou Halloran for street smarts or experience.

"How's he doing?" Halloran asked.

Russo turned back to the paramedics, who'd lifted Billy Chen onto a stretcher. One was securing restraints while the other taped down an IV line. All Russo could see of his partner was a pair of argyle socks ending in those dorky brown wingtips Chen always wore—that, and the shredded remains of his bloodied white shirt flapping off the gurney.

"He's lost a lot of blood."

"One of the chopper pilots was hit, too, did you know?"

"Yeah, I heard. Mike Tillman was at the controls. I heard him holler that his co-pilot had taken one, but my attention was focused on the shooter and then on Billy. By the time the dust settled and I looked up, the chopper had already headed out. Any word on how the other pilot's doing?"

"Okay, I think. Apparently he got a new part creased in his hair but he was lucky."

A metallic click echoed in the roadway. The paramedics had released the brake and were hustling the gurney toward the open back of the ambulance, one of them holding aloft a plastic IV bag. Billy's eyes were closed, his skin pasty-looking. A heavy white bandage covered his sternum. He hadn't been as lucky as the chopper pilot.

"They won't know the full extent of the damage 'til they get him into the E.R.," Russo told the lieutenant, "but taking one like that…"

His voice trailed off as his insides ratcheted tighter. There was no need to say more. Every cop knew there was nothing worse than being gut-shot, the bullet ripping through the labyrinth of the intestinal tract. Multiple entrance and exit wounds left the victim bleeding internally, leaking bile and infectious crap that took its agonizing time to bring death, sometimes days or weeks after the patient appeared to have survived the shooting.

"He wasn't wearing a vest?"

Russo looked up sharply, but Halloran's expression displayed no anger, only regret. Russo's head gave a guilty shake. He wasn't either. The lieutenant always encouraged his detectives to wear Kevlar, especially in neighborhoods where every banger was looking to earn a little street cred by taking a potshot at a cop. It was advice rarely heeded but there was no point in flogging that horse now. Russo was quite capable of flogging himself for not making Billy put one on—and would, too, he suspected, for the rest of his days.

As the stretcher slid into the ambulance, he made to follow, but Halloran held him back. "They're going to take care of him, John. There's nothing you can do right now."

"I'm his training officer," Russo said grimly.

"I know. We'll head over to the hospital soon as we're done here. Muller and Lopez will take over the crime scene." The lieutenant cocked his head at two of their colleagues from Rickenbacker Road who were even now snapping pictures and taking notes. "I need you to walk me through exactly what happened."

The ambulance pulled away, sirens launching into a scream. Russo took another step forward, on automatic pilot by now, but Halloran cut him off in his tracks with a voice like a knife. "Pull it together, Detective. There's work to do."

As the flashing lights disappeared around the corner, Russo nodded reluctantly. "Yeah, you're right. I've still got that kid in the car."

For the first time, Halloran seemed to notice the young teenager sitting in the back seat of the tan Taurus. The kid's eyes were wide, fearful. "That's the brother of the vic from over on Palmer?"

"Yeah. His name's Tristan Shipley. The dead kid's his older brother, Damon. I want Tristan there to take a look at the guy on the fence, make sure he actually was the guy that shot his brother."

"No, not you. Like I said, Muller and Lopez will take over. One of them will run your car back. You'll ride with me."

"This is my case."

"Not anymore it isn't."

"How do you figure?"

"You're off it. Off everything, for the time being. Look, John, we got two cops down, Billy and the chopper pilot. And on top of that, we got two young black men dead here, one of them at police hands."

"This creep shot Chen and the kid over on Palmer."

"Yeah, that's probably true. If so, I'm sure it'll be deemed a righteous shoot."

"For crying out loud, Lou! Damned straight it was a righteous shoot. There's no call to take me off—"

"Yes, there is and you know it." Halloran passed a hand over his grizzled head. "Goddammit, anyway. Why did you move in before SWAT got here?"

"We didn't. We thought the suspect was a couple of blocks away. We were holding back, waiting for them to show, when all of a sudden all hell broke loose. It might have been the chopper that flushed him out, I'm not sure. I told Tillman to hold his position but—"

"Was he hot-dogging?"

Russo threw up his hands. "I don't know! I know the chopper was real low at one point, but I don't know if he dropped down before or after this guy started shooting."

The lieutenant exhaled heavily. "Well, it'll come out in the investigation, but I'll tell you right now, it's only more fuel on the fire. Sheriff Ortiz is going to be one unhappy camper when this hits the fan."

"But we didn't—"

"Don't matter. It's an officer-involved shooting now. There's gotta be a full investigation. You know the drill."

Russo stared at him for a moment, then his shoulders dropped. "Yeah, I guess." It was standard operating procedure. The police weren't there to mete out street justice. "You know," he said quietly, "I've never shot anyone before, Lou."

The lieutenant nodded. "Yeah, I know. Neither have I."

Like cops in every major American city, Russo had drawn his gun many times in the line of duty—to warn, to subdue, to protect—but before tonight, he'd never actually fired at anything but a shooting range paper target. On the street, the threat was usually enough.

When an officer did injure or kill someone, however, there was always a chance, no matter how righteous the shoot, that the suspect or his family would file a lawsuit seeking damages for injury or wrongful death.

Relations between police and minority communities were particularly problematic in Los Angeles. The LAPD and the sheriff's department worked side by side in a sprawling jurisdictional jigsaw puzzle of interlocking cities, suburbs and unincorporated areas, all of them with different policing arrangements. Most communities contracted with the L.A. county sheriff for their police services. So far, the sheriff's department had escaped the kind of negative publicity that dogged the LAPD, but there was no room for complacency, no margin for error in officer-involved shootings. The OIS investigation had to be done by the book.

"Give me your car keys," Halloran said. "Muller can take care of the kid and ID your gangbanger over there. He'll bring the kid in for a full interview. Is he a minor?"

Russo nodded. "Just turned seventeen. Apparently his mother works nights at a restaurant over on Rosecrans."

"Right. I'll get the details and send an officer to notify her about her older son and bring her along to be with the other one. After you give Muller and Lopez the low-down, you can ride with me to King-Drew and we'll see how Chen's doing. I've already sent a department rep to notify his wife and run her over to the hospital."

"I should've been the one to tell her," Russo said grimly. "He's gotta be okay, Lou. He's got two little kids."

"You can talk to her at the hospital. She'll need to hear from you what happened."

Russo exhaled heavily. "Jeez, did it have to be King-Drew?" If Billy's wounds didn't kill him, the scandal-plagued hospital probably would.

"It's the closest E.R. We'll get him transferred soon as he's stabilized, but nobody wants him taking a cross-town ride right now."

"I suppose."

"We've gotta take care of business here, though. I need the crime scene guys to do a gunshot residue test on your hands. And John? When we get to the hospital, we're going to get a tech to draw your blood."

"My blood? What the hell…" And then it dawned on him. "Oh, man! To test for alcohol and drugs. You seriously think I'm working out here stoned, Lou?" There was a time when that might have been true, but those days were behind him. Halloran knew that.

"I know you're not."

"I haven't touched a drink or anything else in nearly two years."

"That's why we get the test done. To prove it. That way, there's no criminal or civil liabilities later."

"Right. Nice. Way to watch the department's butt, Lieutenant."

"It's *your* butt he's watching out for, Detective," a voice behind him said.

Russo looked back over his shoulder to see that Detective Finn Brophy had shown up out of nowhere. He had a habit of doing that, kind of the way cockroaches did.

"What are you doing here, Brophy?"

"He's handling the OIS investigation," Halloran said.

Russo opened his mouth to protest, but then closed it again. There was no secret about how Finn Brophy felt about John Russo. Of course, Brophy disapproved of lots of people on the job—blacks, Latinos, gays, women. Anyone, in short, who wasn't a good ol' hetero white cracker like him. He reserved a special brand of venom for Russo, though, probably because Russo had slept with his ex-wife.

Was that why Brophy decided to make life a living hell for Billy Chen when the kid had come over to Homicide? Russo wondered.

Probably not. Brophy didn't need a reason to be a jerk. A couple of days earlier, after one smirking "chop-chop" crack too many out of him, Russo had accidentally-on-purpose upended Brophy's chair, sending him sprawling in front of a packed squad room. He had nothing to lose by humiliating the guy since Brophy already hated his guts. Up to now, Russo had never had any reason to worry about Brophy's craving for payback. Despite his own missteps—and there'd been plenty back when he was drinking—Russo was still one of the senior detectives in the department with a solve rate second to no one.

"So," Brophy said, surveying the scene, "I hear young Charlie Chan got himself some high velocity acupuncture. Jeez, Johnnie, you really screwed up here, didn't you, boyo?"

"Hey, Brophy?"

"What?"

"Bite me," Russo said.

He could almost feel paranoid about the fact that it was Brophy who'd been assigned to his OIS, except he knew that officer-involved shooting investigations were handed out on a strict rotational basis. Every detective in the bureau hated them, squeezed as they inevitably found themselves between angry communities and the media on one hand and nervous departmental brass and politicians on the other. It was a thankless task, but standing policy said the homicide bureau handled them, and every detective had to step up when his number was called.

At the moment, however, Brophy looked like he was enjoying himself immensely. He extended his beefy hand, palm up. "Now, you wanna hand over those keys like the lieutenant ordered?"

Russo reached into his trouser pocket, pulled out the keys to the Taurus and tossed them over. Brophy fumbled and nearly dropped them.

"There's one more thing," he said, scowling.

"What's that?" Russo asked.

Brophy extended his hand once more. "You're gonna have to give up your gun."

26

Staples Center, Los Angeles

The packed, brilliantly lit arena rumbled with the cheering voices and stomping feet of nearly twenty thousand fans as Lakers center Keenan Prince and his teammates thundered up and down the court.

New Yorkers loved baseball enough to keep both the Yankees and the Mets in cleats; a Chicagoan's heart beat faster when the Bears ran pigskin into the end zone; but Los Angeles was a basketball town, first and foremost, and the Lakers' top players were second only to Hollywood royalty in the west coast peerage system. When the team made the NBA playoffs, as it very often did, every other vehicle on the jammed freeways sprouted a flapping purple and gold pennant. When a Laker went down with an injury, the entire city ached. When a flamboyant star like Keenan Prince got into trouble, no one was indifferent.

Despite Hannah's general unease and the struggle she was having not kicking the legs of the chair in front of her out from under her ex, she was having a great time watching Gabe and his friends enjoy themselves. When the eight-sided Jumbotron over the basketball court sent up a digital fireworks display at one point that spelled out Happy Birthday, Gabe!, the kids erupted in a tumult. The cheer echoed throughout the arena as the crowd-cam zeroed in on the birthday boy and broadcast his beaming face around the arena. At half time, during the Laker Girls' sizzling cheerleading routine, one of them flicked her pompoms playfully at Gabe, and his face went a deep, adorable shade of pink as he struggled to maintain his ten-year-old cool. When Keenan Prince came back out on the court for the second half of the game and high-fived Gabe, Hannah could have kissed the man for making her little boy feel so special, no matter how much she loathed his off-court antics.

Christie had remembered to bring a camera, of course, and was getting digital pictures of all the fun. "Not a problem," she said when Hannah bemoaned leaving hers behind in the rush to get over to Mulholland Drive. "I'll e-mail the good ones to you."

"Thanks," Hannah said, trying really hard not to sound grudging. She crossed her legs, only to uncross them again and drape her hand casually over the stain she suddenly noticed on one knee of her pants.

"I probably wouldn't have remembered mine," Christie said, "but I still had it in my bag from last Saturday's soccer game. Gabie scored the winning goal, did he tell you?"

Hannah nodded. She'd been out of town on the Beckham security job when Gabe e-mailed her about it. So what else was new? Christie went to all Gabe's games, she took pictures, she brought after-game snacks—hell, she probably even coached the team in her spare time.

"Maybe you could send me some of those shots, too?"

"Sure." Christie switched the digital camera's screen over to view mode. "I haven't downloaded them yet. Take a look and tell me which ones you'd like."

Hannah took the camera and began flipping through shots of

more domestic bliss than she might be able to stomach were it not for the fact that Gabe was in most of them. "Nice camera. Takes a good picture."

"It was a Christmas present. I'm really pleased with it. Mostly I like the big viewing screen. Makes it easier to see what you're shooting and what you've got. And for such a little thing, it has a really powerful zoom. Helps with those action shots at Gabie's soccer games."

Hannah nodded. "These are good."

"I'll just send them all to you and you can keep whichever ones you like."

"If you think of it, thanks." Internally, Hannah winced. Why did she end up having to thank this woman so much?

She handed back the camera and turned her attention once more to the action on the floor, wondering how soon she could claim that nonexistent business meeting in order to make her escape. The game was winding down with the Lakers way ahead, so there were unlikely to be any surprises there—not that she cared. And she certainly wasn't going to get any one-on-one time with Gabe when it was over. Better to beat the rush to the exits and avoid awkwardness later, when the boys would be itching to get down to the team's locker room.

"I have to head out shortly," she told Christie.

"You're sure you can't come back to the house? We've got birthday cake."

"I know, but I've got that business thing I mentioned earlier, and…"

"I'm a dolt. I should have served the cake before we left the house."

"And spoil their appetites for all the nice greasy burgers and nachos and fries the waiters have been bringing them here?"

Christie smiled ruefully. "Gross, isn't it?"

"Hey, they love it."

"They would. They don't have to worry about it settling on their butts."

"There you go. Anyway, my mom's going to have a cake for him when I take him down to her place on Saturday. My sister and her kids will be there, too, so he'll get a whole 'nother party. Not as memorable as this, of course," she added, waving a hand around the arena and—

"Hannah?" Christie asked. "What is it?"

Hannah was looking up, frozen to the spot. Her gaze had landed on the big eight-sided Jumbotron screen above the floor. The arena cameras had been panning over the crowd, filling time during a lull on the basketball court. As it passed over the skybox levels, Hannah's heart felt as if it had literally stopped.

"I...I..."

"Are you all right?"

"It's just—I saw someone..."

The crowd-cam had moved on from the face that had startled her, but then it paused in its circuit of the arena to focus on a particularly colorful group of fans. They were not only wearing Lakers purple-and-gold jerseys, but they'd also painted their faces to match. A couple of them had even dyed their hair purple. They were nothing if not dedicated, these Laker fans.

"Christie, those crazy people on the screen—can you see where they're sitting?" Hannah craned her neck left and right, then swiveled to check out the seats behind them, trying to find those purple- and gold-painted faces in the swaying rainbow colors of the sellout crowd. She continued to scan every corner of the arena until Christie nudged her elbow.

"There! I see them." She pointed across the arena. "They're up there in the nosebleed seats."

Hannah followed the direction of her finger. Realizing they were on-camera, the über-fans had started dancing in their seats. The crowd was going wild. Nothing like beer at sports events to fuel the nutcases.

"You know those people?" Christie asked.

"No," Hannah said distractedly. She panned her own gaze down and over to the right, back to the skyboxes where the crowd-cam had been focused before it rose and zeroed in on the lunatic fringe higher up. The Jumbotron, meantime, returned its attention to the players and the action resuming on the court. "I thought I spotted someone just before those painted doofuses came on-screen."

"What does he—she?—look like?"

"He. White hair. Wiry guy, somewhere in his forties. I think he was wearing a black leather jacket. He was in one of the skyboxes."

"Hard to make anyone out in such a huge crowd," Christie said, scanning faces across the way. "Hold on, is that him?"

"Where?"

"Up there, in the box over the Toyota sign?"

Hannah looked at the executive boxes strung like high-priced pearls around the middle rim of the arena. Three tiers of skyboxes fronted catered suites leased by wealthy fans or by corporations who used them to wine and dine clients. Following the line of Christie's outstretched manicure, she spotted a white head of hair. The man was seated with another man and a woman. "That's the guy," she said, nodding.

"Who is he?"

"Can I borrow your camera?"

"Sure." Christie rummaged in her soft leather sac purse. "Here. Let me switch it on for you."

Hannah took the camera she handed over. "Where's the zoom control?"

"Right here."

Hannah panned the camera until the view screen picked up the skybox across the way, and then she zoomed in on the white-haired man. As Christie had said, it was a terrific little camera. She could really use one like it in her line of work, Hannah thought, although knowing Cal and Christie's budget—or lack thereof—it probably cost a fortune.

"Son of a bitch," she muttered under her breath. At least, she thought she'd muttered. Of course, her luck being what it was, the noise level in the arena chose that precise moment to drop.

Cal turned, frowning. "Children present, Hannah. You wanna watch that mouth?"

She was tempted to do something childish and huffy, but she refused to be baited. "Sorry."

Turning her attention back to the camera screen, she found she'd lost the white-haired man. She squinted at the line of skyboxes until she'd picked out his box once more. He and the people he was with had gotten to their feet and were walking up the steps, back into the suite behind their tiered seats. Like a lot of people around the arena, it looked as if they were making moves to leave. When the game was all but decided like this, a lot of fans tried to get a jump on the after-game scramble for the exits.

Hannah gave Christie back her camera and leaned forward, tapping Gabe on the shoulder. "Hey, sweetie, you know what? I have to hit the road."

"You do?"

"Yeah, 'fraid so. I've got a meeting. But I'll be at your game on Saturday, and then we'll head down to the OC for a little more celebrating with Nana and Aunt Nora and the gang. That work for you?"

Gabe nodded. "Yeah, that's cool."

"Okay, then. Happy birthday, my guy."

Hannah reached around his shoulders and hugged him tightly, planting a kiss on his cheek. Gabriel hung on to her until he realized his friends were watching—that "pathetic absent parent" curiosity once more, Hannah thought ruefully. She released him and ruffled his dark hair.

She turned to Christie. "You sure you'll be okay to go back in the limo with the guys?"

"Absolutely," Christie said.

"Okay, well, anyway…thanks for everything." Hannah got to her feet.

Cal glanced back at her. "You're leaving?"

"Yup, gotta fly. I'll pick Gabe up at his game on Saturday."

"Whatever. See ya." He turned his attention back to the Lakers.

Christie pulled in her feet to let Hannah slip by her to reach the aisle. "I'll make sure Gabie has his overnight bag with him when he goes to the game on Saturday," she said.

Hannah thanked her. Again.

Then, with one last glance up at the skybox across the way, she started for the exit, only to stop in her tracks at the sound of Gabe calling after her. "Hey, Mom!"

She turned. "What, sweetie?"

"Thanks for the Beckham stuff. It's really cool."

Hannah smiled. What a great kid.

27

King-Drew Hospital, South Central Los Angeles

It was like emergency rooms the world over—chaotic and over-crowded, infected with panic, desperation and dread. Maybe more than most. As the primary county-run facility in that part of the L.A. megalopolis, King-Drew's E.R. drew more than its share of nonemergency cases among the working poor, people who were ailing and uninsured with nowhere else to turn. But situated in the heart of South-Central, with its endemic high crime rates, the hospital also gathered to itself an inordinate number of victims of violence. It was all the more reason to be scandalized by its record of negligence and incompetence. Nowhere was a first-rate critical care facility more desperately needed.

It was only one of many reasons that Russo hated being there now.

He peered through the window of the treatment room where an attending physician and a couple of nurses were working on Billy Chen. The linoleum tile floor was littered with bloody bandages and swabs. When Russo and Halloran had arrived twenty minutes earlier, the treatment room had been in a state of frenzy. Chen had gone into arrest for the second time since arriving at the hospital. After a few tense minutes and a couple of hits with the paddles, the medics had gotten a heart rhythm back.

"You okay, John?"

Russo turned to the lieutenant. Halloran had just come back inside after leaving to take a call on his cell phone. "Yeah, I'm fine," Russo said.

"You don't look it."

"Well, I've had better nights, that's a fact. On the other hand, Chen's sucks a whole lot more, wouldn't you say?"

"Why haven't they taken him into surgery yet?"

"Damned if I know. I'm about ready to wheel him up there myself."

"I guess they want him stabilized first."

Russo grimaced. "I think I heard a nurse say they were waiting for another surgeon to show up. Apparently they're short-handed and it's been a busy night."

"Like it isn't busy here every night." Halloran shook his head. "Sweet mother of God! When is somebody going to fix this damn place?"

Russo and the lieutenant turned to the window again, standing shoulder to shoulder, a silent honor guard for Billy Chen. Russo hoped he looked more held together than he felt. His body was crashing from the adrenaline superdose that had kicked in during the firefight in Compton. The urge was strong to crawl into a hole somewhere and hibernate for about a year. And then, there was his reaction to being in a hospital E.R. It was the first time since Sarah—

"That call I just got," Halloran said.

"Yeah?"

"It was about the gun they took off the dead banger in Compton. Ballistics got a hit on it."

"Already? That was fast."

"Dontcha love computer databases? And since this one's an OIS, I told Brophy to pull out all the stops."

"Yeah, right. Guy's having a whale of a time," Russo said. The homicide bureau might resent being saddled with responsibility for officer-involved shooting investigations, but Brophy would be thrilled at the chance to poke a hole in the rep of John Russo, maybe get him thrown off the job altogether. Better still, locked up for life.

"Turns out ballistics from the gun match a murder that went down in Long Island a couple of years back," Halloran said.

"Long Island? Like in New York?"

"Yup. Drug case. Mob turf war, it seems. They think it might have been a contract killing."

"They arrest anyone on that one?"

"Nope. Shooter went to ground."

"You're saying that mope we took down in Compton is a contract killer from back east?" Russo snorted. "I don't think so."

"No, you're right. He's been ID'd as James Michael Morris, aka 'G Rider Jimmy.' He was in our gang database, I'm told. Hung with a Crips subset called the Alvarado Angels."

"So the kid he killed—Damon Shipley—that was a gang hit?"

Halloran shrugged. "Sounds like. Shipley's mother swears he didn't run with the gangs, but that's mom. They're always the last to know what their precious offspring are really up to."

"So the gun this G Rider Jimmy used—bought off the street, you figure?"

"Probably. Whoever did the job back east wouldn't have wanted to hold on to it. Getting caught with it would've meant a direct ride to Sing Sing. Would've been smarter to throw it off a bridge but some of these mugs are frugal little buggers. Guy probably sold it to a street broker who recycled it out of the area."

"Wouldn't be the first time." Russo felt a tap on his shoulder.

"Detective?"

He turned to a uniformed sheriff's deputy who'd just shown up with a pretty young Asian woman. Russo's heart sank. He recognized her from a picture on Billy Chen's desk back in the squad room. "Mrs. Chen," he said.

She nodded. "Andrea. Call me Andrea, please."

"Andrea. I'm John Russo, Billy's partner."

She smiled faintly. "Detective Russo. Billy's spoken very highly of you."

She reached out a hand, then seemed to change her mind. She stepped forward and Russo instinctively put his arms around her. She was trembling. As her fists wrapped themselves in his blue cotton shirt, Russo was thankful he'd ditched his sport coat, stained with her husband's blood. Andrea Chen was tiny, the top of her smooth black hair just touching his chin. It was baby-soft and smelled like flowers.

"It's going to be okay," Russo murmured.

Stupid thing to say. He didn't believe it for a second, but it was instinct to try to shield her from the ugly truth, even if just for a few moments. It would be obvious soon enough. And as she stepped back from him and nodded, her face told him she knew he was lying.

"This is Lieutenant Halloran," Russo added.

"How do you do, Lieutenant?" Her tiny hand disappeared inside Halloran's huge mitt. "Thank you for sending a car for me."

"It was no problem. You came by yourself?"

"Yes. We don't really know anyone where we're living. We just moved into a new house in Riverside. My mother's been staying with us, helping get things set up. She stayed behind to take care of the kids. We have two little girls, twins. They're just four and they were asleep. It didn't seem like a good idea to wake them."

"Is there anyone else I can call for you?" Halloran asked.

"Thanks, but I called my brother on the way over. He lives in Monterey Park. He should be here shortly. His name is Edward. Edward Woo. He and Billy have been friends since high school. That's where Billy and I met, too."

"I'll make sure someone brings him in as soon as he gets here," Halloran said.

Andrea Chen nodded. Then, finally, reluctantly, as if she'd been forestalling the moment of truth, she turned to the scene inside the treatment room, and her face crumpled. Russo put a hand on her shoulder. She pressed her lips together for a moment, then asked, "What are they saying? How is he? The officers who came for me weren't able to tell me exactly what happened."

"We were looking for a gang member who'd shot and killed another guy," Russo said. "The shooter had hidden out on a rooftop and he ambushed us. Billy got hit in the abdomen." He nodded at the team working on her young husband. "They're going to take him up to surgery to repair the damage, but they want to make sure he's stable first."

"Let me see if we can get a doctor or nurse out here to bring you up to speed," Lieutenant Halloran said.

"I don't want to bother them while they're busy."

"No, I know, but they'll want to know you're here." Halloran tapped on the window glass. One of the nurses glanced over, then touched the attending doctor on the arm. He followed the direction of her cocked thumb, nodded and held up one latex-gloved finger. It was covered in blood.

"Oh, God," Andrea breathed.

Russo wanted to put his arm around her shoulder, but it was a little too late to play the big hero now, and there was no protecting her from this anyway. The one he should have protected was her husband.

Andrea's brother arrived just as the doctor emerged from the treatment room. Woo had apparently found his own way in and made a beeline for his sister. Russo and Halloran hung back to let the two of them speak privately with the attending physician. They already knew what the doctor would be saying. That Billy's wounds were extremely grave. That there were always grounds to hope, but that even if Billy survived surgery—hell, *made* it to surgery—there would be further dangers ahead. When it was all spelled out, the doctor led the two family members into the room to be at Billy's side.

Halloran turned to Russo. "You should take off," he said.

"No way."

"I'll call you if anything changes."

"Forget it, Lou. I'm not going anywhere."

Halloran nodded. "Yeah, okay. I guess I'd do the same."

"Course you would."

"While we're waiting, though, I'm going to see about getting that blood drawn from you like we discussed back at the scene. For your own protection," the lieutenant added.

Russo knew Halloran was watching his back. It wasn't the first time. After Sarah and the baby died and he went off the rails so badly, it was Halloran who finally pulled him back in line. He'd gotten Russo into a program, then gone to bat with the departmental brass who wanted to kick Russo out to the curb. Halloran knew he'd been flying straight ever since and would never let him down again, but the lieutenant was also a by-the-book cop, and the book said an alcohol and drug test was mandatory after an officer-involved shooting.

It was still galling, and just reinforced Russo's fear that he would never lose the stigma of his behavior during those lost months when he'd messed up so badly. He could barely remember most of it, and yet he'd have to keep proving for the rest of his days that he wasn't that stoned, obnoxious screw-up who'd lurched from one disaster to another for eighteen ugly months.

A few minutes later, Russo was in a cubicle down the hall, watching his blood flow red into a test tube, when he heard the commotion outside. There were multiple cases in the E.R. that night, but somehow Russo knew, even before Halloran walked through the curtain to tell him, that young Billy Chen, his trainee and his partner, had coded for the last time.

28

Thursday, January 27, 2005
The Oval Office, The White House, Washington, D.C.

The presentation of ambassadorial credentials was an archaic and formalized ceremony rooted in pre-Biblical history. In ancient times, when monarchs sent emissaries to speak on their behalf to other monarchs, the protection of these envoys was guaranteed— sort of a gentleman's agreement never to shoot the messenger, even if you weren't wild about the message sometimes. It was the only way, in those days before telegram, telephone, e-mail or fax, to guarantee that kings didn't launch their armies into bloody wars on the basis of stupid misunderstandings.

Technology had simplified direct communication between heads of state but the posting of permanent emissaries in national capitals still served its purpose. In Washington, for example, ambassadors kept a finger on the pulse of the administration, warning their own governments when America came down with a bellicose condition that might prove infectious. On a day-to-day basis, they were also Johnny-on-the-spot, a gnat in the ear of the lumbering American elephant, entreating it to please not step on others as it went about its business.

The arrival of an ambassador was always accompanied by a certain amount of pomp and circumstance, but few embassies could outdo Saudi Arabia's when it came to celebrating a newly arrived envoy. It was going to be a long, tedious day, Richard Stern thought wearily. After this formal ceremony, there was a White House reception in the East Room where the Saudi Ambassador would be presented to the entire diplomatic corps. That evening there would be a gala dinner at the opulent Saudi Embassy in north-west Washington.

The assistant national security advisor had his back to the wall near one of the French doors that opened onto the balcony off the Oval Office. The winter sun was sinking fast and snow was swirling outside the windows, but inside, soft ambient lighting and a crackling fire in the hearth cast a warm glow on the scene as Ambassador Mohammed Alsaqri bent slightly at the waist. He was directly in front of the president, who was standing before his broad wooden desk.

"I have the honor, sir," Alsaqri said, "to present to you my credentials as the official representative of King Abdullah."

He handed the president a soft, black, leather-bound folder. Alsaqri was himself a half brother to the Saudi king, a prince in his own right. The irony was not lost on Stern that all this fuss and attention should be bestowed on the representative of one of the most feudal, undemocratic nations on the planet. But for all the administration's fine public pronouncements about promoting freedom abroad, it was a very elastic policy, easily stretched where important strategic allies were concerned.

The president took the folder, opened it, glanced briefly at the calligraphied contents, then closed it again. "Excellency, I'm very pleased to accept these credentials and to welcome you to Washington as the representative of your king and your people. I look forward to working closely with you in the ongoing spirit of close friendship and co-operation that exists between our two great nations."

Solemnly, he shook hands with the dapper, gray-haired ambassador. Still holding hands, the two men turned shoulder to shoulder to face the cameras recording the event for the media and for posterity. The secretary of state was off to one side, beaming like a proud mother hen. She often stood in for the president when ambassadors presented their credentials, but when it came to allies as important as Saudi Arabia and an ambassador like Prince Mohammed Alsaqri, on whom such high hopes rested, only America's head of state would do.

When the cameras were done flashing, the president handed the leather-bound folder to an aide. Then, grinning, he turned back to Alsaqri and slapped him on the back. "Well, now that we got that formal stuff out of the way, Mohammed, I think it's time to party down. What do you say?"

The prince's stiff posture also vanished. "Yes, indeed, Mr. President. Let me first, if I may, introduce my children who are here with me today?"

As Alsaqri presented two sons and a daughter who'd accompanied him to the White House that afternoon along with several members of his embassy, Stern felt Evan Myers sidle up next to him. "He brought his kids, but no wife?" the deputy chief of staff murmured.

"Which wife? He's got three of them," Stern said. "Or four, maybe. I've lost count. And something like fifteen kids. Most of them have studied in the States. These three just happen to be living here at the moment."

"I gather you know the prince fairly well?"

Stern shrugged. "We've had dealings over the years."

"Must have, for you to come out of your hidey hole. After five years, Dick, I think I can count on one hand the number of times you've actually lifted your head out of there. So, all I want to know is this—is Alsaqri your creature? Or are you his?"

Stern frowned, but the question was surely rhetorical. Myers should know by now that it was pointless to expect him to elaborate on his relationship with the ambassador or anything else. Mohammed Alsaqri might be a prince, but Stern was the king of compartmentalization. He sucked up information like a Shop-Vac but he volunteered nothing to anyone without a demonstrable need-to-know.

"Did you see today's *New York Times* piece on the prince?" Myers asked.

"What did it say?"

"It was pretty high on him. They think he might be the last, best hope for a balanced Middle East policy. Apparently he's well respected by all sides over there—radicals like Syria and Iran. The Palestinians. Reformers inside the Saudi kingdom who think it might be time for that place to progress politically—maybe up to the nineteenth or twentieth century, at least, if not the twenty-first. I gather even the Israelis are willing to talk to him—and he to them, incredibly enough. That's pretty rare. Sounds like he does everything but walk on water."

"Prince Alsaqri is an extremely able diplomat."

"Can he handle the Muslim fundamentalists, though? I hear bin Laden's put a price on his head."

"Alsaqri won't buckle to that bearded yak herder. The prince is a very good friend of the United States."

They turned back to Alsaqri and the president, who were arm in arm, heading out the door to the reception. Myers went to follow, but when he noticed Stern hanging back, he paused. "Are you coming?"

Frankly, Stern would rather poke hot needles in his eyes than attend a diplomatic reception. He hated the champagne-lubricated small talk at these damn things, but he had to admit, they served their purpose. He was very good at extracting useful gossip, especially from those who reacted to his forbidding reticence by prattling on. It required only that he guide the direction of their prattle for them to eventually let slip some useful nut of intelligence that he could add to his vast store.

Stern exhaled wearily. "Duty calls, I suppose. Let's get this over with."

29

Friday, January 28, 2005
The Golden Dragon Restaurant, Los Angeles

Sheriff's department headquarters was in Monterey Park, one of many cities-within-a-city that made up the greater Los Angeles area. As far as Hannah was concerned, it couldn't be a sweeter location. With a population sixty percent Chinese-American, Monterey Park had the best *dim sum* restaurants, bar none, in the western hemisphere. Of course, that was just her opinion, but she'd sampled enough of them, both before and after her time in the department, to have an extremely well-informed take on the subject.

A lunch date with Val Underwood, longtime friend and mentor, was her latest excuse to pig out on primo spring rolls and barbecued pork buns. It was Underwood, a detective at the time, who'd been the first to see Hannah's potential back in the day when she was working dispatch to put Cal through law school, and Underwood who put wheels in motion to get her enrolled in the police academy. These days, Val was head of the sheriff's department's homeland security unit, liaising with federal agencies to beef up the city's response to terrorist threats.

Hannah nodded to a waiter approaching with yet another selection of *dim sum*. The Golden Dragon was packed, as always, with a capacity crowd of hungry locals and cops. The large, open room seated something like two hundred patrons, and every last seat was taken. There was barely enough room between tables for the waiters to maneuver their trolleys laden with an ever-changing selection of delicacies.

The place was a riot of red-flocked wallpaper and gleaming, gold-toned bas-relief dragon sculptures cavorting across the walls. It smelled of hot oil, garlic, ginger and soy. Starched white linens, several layers thick, overlaid each table. As each group of diners rose and staggered off, sated and dopey, busboys swarmed in, whisking away dirty dishes, snapping soiled cloths off tables to reveal the next gleaming linen layer beneath. Then, condiments and fresh place settings laid down, a new group of patrons was ushered in from the line that snaked patiently from the restaurant's tiny lobby out the front door and into the parking lot. The whole process took about thirty seconds, Hannah calculated.

She and Val had been lucky enough to snag a corner table that let them actually hear each other in the midst of the lunchtime clamor, a raucous mix of Mandarin and Cantonese, English and laughter.

As the waiter she'd spotted rolled his trolley up to their table, she pointed to a plate of soft, fluffy, beautiful barbecued pork buns.

"Good lord, kid, have you no shame?" Underwood leaned back in her chair with a groan. "I'm set to explode here. Look at this wreckage." She waved a hand over a table stacked with empty plates and steamer baskets, the remains of the six or seven courses they'd already demolished.

"Call it dessert," Hannah said. She watched as the waiter cut two juicy, meat-stuffed buns in quarters with a pair of kitchen snips.

"Get real. I haven't eaten dessert since I last gave birth. That was in 1988. It was the last time I could justify having no waistline."

"Get outta here. You're looking fabulous, girl."

"You're very kind, I'm sure, but fabulous I never looked. Decently groomed, I like to think. Moderately cute on a good day, back when I was a spring chicken like you."

"Spring chicken? Ha. Not anymore." Hannah's chopsticks speared a piece of bun. "I can't believe I'm turning thirty."

"Please. I haven't seen thirty for a couple of decades. I can barely remember that far back."

Hannah rubbed together the thumb and finger of her free hand, the one not busy with chopsticks and the sticky, succulent buns. "See this? It's the world's tiniest violin."

"Cute. Anyway, I'm not complaining," Underwood said. "The girls are doing great, they managed to survive adolescence, and Ray and I haven't killed each other yet. All in all, nothing to whine about."

"There you go," Hannah said.

Underwood had two daughters, twenty-one and twenty-three, one in college, one in med school. Her husband of twenty-five years was a high school principal and gourmet cook. Steadfastly loyal, Ray Underwood doted on all three of his girls. Val, Hannah decided, had married the last good man in L.A.

Her eyes closed in ecstasy as the warm bun fairly melted in her mouth. "You really should try one of these."

"Nope. I'm done."

Hannah opened her eyes and glanced at her watch. "Sorry, are you in a rush to get back?"

"No, I'm still good. I've got a meeting at two with a couple of officials from the Saudi consulate, but I'm ready for it."

"There a problem?"

Underwood shrugged. "Not really. Some Saudi students at UCLA think they're being targeted for harassment by cops and rednecks."

"You get involved in that kind of thing? Sounds like small potatoes next to the other stuff on your plate, keeping the city safe from terrorists and suicide bombers and all."

"Well, it's something we have to keep an eye on. You never know whether these little problems might blow up—not literally, hopefully. Mind you, some people see a radical in every Arab exchange student—a potential terrorist just waiting for the chance to blow up Disneyland. Takes a certain amount of delicacy to deal with the consulates, too. I'd delegate, but I don't have anyone with the chops to handle these folks. I *would* have," Underwood added, "if you'd come back to the department and work for me like I keep asking. I've got the budget, I just can't find the people I need."

"I don't know. There are days when I'm tempted, but—"

"But mercenary work pays better?"

"Ouch!"

"Sorry. I'm just grumpy. I'm understaffed and I could really use you."

"It's tempting, Val, but I've kind of gotten used to freelancing. God knows, there's not a lot of security in it, and some jobs are boring as hell, but I like the variety."

"And the money."

Hannah grimaced. "It's not quite as lucrative since that fiasco in Iraq, but I do okay. Although at this point," she added, "my original reason for doing this is pretty much a lost cause."

"You've given up on getting Gabe back?"

Hannah exhaled heavily. "I'm just trying to be realistic. Realistically, I have to resign myself to the fact that it's probably not gonna happen. He's settled, he's happy, he's doing well in that school they've got him in. How can I throw a wrench in everything now?"

"It's not right. You're his mother."

"Yeah, but that's exactly why I want what's best for him. And much as I hate to admit it, Christie's turned out to be a pretty decent person. Not your stereotypical wicked stepmother. Oh, by the way, guess what? She's preggers. Gabe's going to have a little brother or sister."

"Ow! That hurts. You okay about it?"

"No, but it's none of my business and there's not a damn thing I can do about it anyway. No reason why Cal shouldn't have other kids with her. God knows, it's not like I want him back."

"Still, it's gotta feel a little weird."

"Yeah, it does. But," Hannah added, spearing another piece of barbecued pork bun, "I can always drown my sorrows in *dim sum*. Are you sure you won't have some of this?"

"No, you just go ahead. Don't mind me. I'll just sit over here and drool. Nobody will notice. At my age, they think it's just senility."

"Yeah, senile like a fox. I want to be you when I grow up. As it is, I could despise you for your life, but then who'd be my friend?"

Underwood laughed. "Oh, poor, pitiful you. Anyway, you just want me around to do your grunt work."

Hannah brightened. "Hey, that's what I'm talkin' about. You'll do it?"

The older woman sighed. "I suppose." She held out her hand. "Give me the number."

Hannah put down her chopsticks and rummaged in her jeans pocket for the piece of paper on which she'd scribbled the license plate number and other details of the car.

The basketball game two nights earlier had had only minutes left to play when she'd spotted the white-haired man in the skybox across the floor. By the time she calculated its exact location and then took her leave of Gabe and the rest of the birthday party, she barely had time to make it around to that section of the arena before the sellout crowd began to leave ahead of the final buzzer. A security guard had blocked her path when she tried to go up to the restricted skybox level, so she stationed herself behind a pillar near the descending escalators and prayed her quarry didn't decide to make a circuit of the floor on his level before descending to the ground level exits. If she missed him there, the odds were slim to none that she'd ever pick up his trail again.

"So who is this guy really?" Underwood asked as Hannah handed over the details of the BMW in which he'd driven off.

"I don't know his name—that's the problem. I ran into him two years ago on that job in Iraq when that kid got killed. He was the shooter."

"That would be the job where you guys were taking a stolen car across the border when all hell broke loose?"

"It was 'liberated', not stolen. I told you, the owner was one of Saddam's ugly, kleptomaniac sons. He was dead at that point, so it wasn't like he was going to miss it, and the car was slated to be turned into junk anyway."

"Hmm…"

"Anyway, this guy I spotted at the Staples Center? He's the one who killed Oz Nuñez, I'm almost certain."

"*Almost* certain."

"Ninety percent. Things were pretty hairy when that disaster at the border went down, but I wouldn't forget that face and those cold blue eyes, believe me."

"So your killer was American."

"He sure as hell wasn't an Arab. Beyond that, I haven't got a clue. That's why I want to take a closer look at this guy. Check him out, make sure it really is him. I tailed him on foot to the parking lot the other night, but there was no way to get back to my car in time to follow him out of there."

"And if I come up with a name and a home address? You're going to do exactly what with it?"

"A little surveillance, that's all. If it is him, try to figure out what he's up to now."

"Do I look like I was born yesterday, little girl? I know you. If this *is* the guy who killed your friend, there's no way you're going to walk away. And there's probably no way you can pursue him legally, you know that. Aside from anything else, your friend's killing didn't happen on U.S. soil, so there's the jurisdictional problem. Plus, you guys were driving a 'liberated' vehicle at the time. This guy might argue that he was engaged in a legitimate police action to recover it and bring you guys in. So what options does that leave? You think you're Rambo? You're just gonna take him out on the streets of L.A.? I don't think so."

"No, I know that, Val. I'm not stupid. In the first place, I've got a kid. I'm not about to get sent away on a murder rap. And in the second place, I wouldn't do that to you, not after you're going out of your way to help me out on this."

Underwood shook her head. "This is wrong on so many levels. We're not supposed to be running plates on nonpolice business, you know that."

"Yeah, but I also know everybody does it anyway. Look, Val, I promise, I just want to check the guy out. If he is who I think he is, then what are the odds he's suddenly turned into a saint? And what's he doing here? Maybe he's into drugs or gun-running or something. Who knows? Maybe he's a terrorist. If so, I'll pass the information on and you can take a look at him yourself."

"I don't know."

"Please, Val, just get me the plate information. I have to follow up. Oz Nuñez was a really good guy, a husband and a father. I owe him at least this."

Underwood studied Hannah for a moment, and then, with a resigned sigh, she nodded.

30

Monday, January 30, 2005
Pico Hills Cemetery, Los Angeles

The whole business of death and dying seemed incongruous in the City of Angels. By day, at least. Nighttime was another story, Russo thought, but funerals rarely took place at night.

By day, L.A. was always sunny. Vast parts of the city were so damn picture perfect that sometimes you had to wonder if somebody had declared ugly a crime. Palm trees swayed in ocean breezes, lining boulevards that seemed populated by nothing but the gorgeous, the tanned and the toned. Southern California was the kind of place where Disney could invent a pristine Main Street, U.S.A. that had never existed in the real world yet still evoked nostalgia in millions of visitors—like they'd actually grown up on a street like that. Dying in a place so chirpy seemed like bad form. Funerals were positively surreal.

Russo studied the drawn, somber faces around Billy Chen's gravesite. These were not the Botoxed beautiful people. These were just hardworking, ordinary folks—Asian, black, white, Hispanic—

trying to get by and raise their families, only to be bitch-slapped by the shock of sudden, ugly death.

The burnished mahogany casket, gleaming in the warm afternoon sun, rested on black canvas straps stretched taut across an open pit. Off to one side, a sheet of bright green felt discreetly covered the dirt that would fill the hole once everyone had departed. The cloying scent of a dozen floral tributes was overpowering. It was a wonder anybody could stand to be around a single posy after something like this.

Russo felt exhausted and wired taut at the same time. He hadn't slept more than an hour at a stretch since his partner's death. Neither, he sensed, had Andrea Chen. The young widow's tearstained face was ashen and strained. Billy had turned thirty-one just three days before he was gunned down in Compton. His wife, Russo had learned since that godawful night in the King-Drew E.R., had just found out she was pregnant—maybe carrying the son Billy had been hoping for to balance out their family, an ally for him in a household of females. Had Billy known about the baby before he died? Russo had no idea.

As the priest droned on about there being a season for everything—a time to reap, a time to sow, etc. etc.—Russo bristled. What a crock. How could death as premature as this fit into any grand scheme of things? He'd been raised Roman Catholic and so, it seemed, had his late partner. These days, though, religion was a mystery to Russo, and not the sacred kind, either. The irritating kind. When he'd lost his wife and child, he'd found no comfort in its rituals. If anything, the prayers and platitudes offered up during their joint funeral service had only fed his rage. If he'd made uneasy peace with some of the demons that haunted him since Sarah and Juliana died, God was still on his hit list. Only his fury with himself exceeded his wrath at the deity.

He glanced over at Andrea Chen. At least she would be spared that kind of self-loathing. The innocent have no need to reproach themselves.

Although Russo had turned his back on the faith of his forebears, the Chens had apparently been active members of the parish in Monterey Park where they'd lived before their recent move to a bigger house in Riverside. Their family church was nowhere near large enough for the funeral of a police officer killed in the line of duty, however, so Billy's memorial had been held at the newly-built Cathedral of Our Lady of the Angels in downtown L.A. Police forces from one end of the country to the other sent representatives to honor a fallen fellow officer. Members of the L.A. County Sheriff's Department and LAPD, both deputies and support staff, turned out in force. The mayor, the sheriff, a city council member and Russo himself spoke at the service presided over by the local archbishop, as did two members of Billy's large extended family. Afterwards, a full-dress honor guard complete with pipes, drums and sixty motorcycle police outriders accompanied the casket to its final resting place in the Pico Hills Memorial Park and Cemetery.

Russo was one of six pallbearers.

"Billy was so pleased to be training with you," Andrea had said when she called to ask him. "He said you were the best detective in the department."

"I don't know about that, but I was proud to work with him. He was a good man and a very good police officer."

"He said you were tough but fair. And you know," she added, her voice catching, "Chinese tradition says the blessings of the deceased are bestowed on his pallbearers. Billy would want that for you."

Standing next to the grave, Russo's brain balked at the idea. He didn't deserve blessings from Billy Chen or anyone else. It was sure no blessing for the kid to have drawn him as a training officer.

According to Lieutenant Halloran, preliminary results of the investigation into the disaster in Compton suggested the helicopter had played a role that night, flushing out the shooter too soon, before SWAT backup was in position. What Halloran didn't know was how much Mike Tillman, the chopper pilot, hated Russo's guts.

Tillman and Finn Brophy, the detective in charge of Russo's officer-involved shooting investigation, were best friends. Finn Brophy and his wife, also a cop, had been separated the night he walked in on Russo and her going at it in the bedroom at someone's Christmas party. It had been about a year after Sarah and the baby died, a time when Russo was running right off the rails. For the life of him, he couldn't remember why, much less how, he'd ended up in that bedroom. Now, he couldn't shake the guilty feeling that if it hadn't been for his stupidity and for Tillman's ongoing pissy mood over the cuckolding of his buddy, Billy Chen might still be alive today.

The gravesite was situated on one of the highest hilltops in the rolling cemetery. "Better *feng shui*," Andrea had said when she called about the funeral arrangements. "Billy and his folks are ABC—American-born Chinese—but his grandmother was born over in China. She's kind of a weird mix of her missionary school upbringing and the old traditions, so the service will be a Catholic mass, but we had to make sure the grave was on a hill to catch good spirits. Oh, and it can't be facing west, either, because that's supposed to be the direction of hell. Go figure."

Now, as the service wound down, a police honor guard moved into position to fire a three-round volley of blanks to honor a fallen comrade. As they cocked and raised their weapons skyward, Russo's eye caught a movement in a copse of trees in a depression below the hilltop. A figure stood half-hidden behind a live oak about fifty yards down the hill. It was a woman, African-American, heavyset and on the upside of forty, dressed in a dark blue skirt and flowing flowered jacket. Her hair was cropped short and big silver hoops dangled at her ears. She could easily have melded into the large, diverse group at the gravesite, but for some reason, she was holding herself apart. Still, there was no doubt in Russo's mind that she'd come here expressly for this service. The guns fired and she winced. So did half the people there, but even accounting for the loud crack of the rifles, she seemed very nervous.

He was curious, but he lost sight of her as the salute ended, smoke and cordite wafting on the breeze. The crowd began to break up and withdraw, drifting downhill toward the long line of cars parked on the verges of the roadway that meandered through the cemetery.

"You heading over to the reception?"

Russo turned to Lou Halloran, who'd moved up beside him. "Yeah. You?"

The lieutenant nodded. "For a while. You need a lift over there?"

"No, I've got my car."

"You're okay to drive?"

"Lou—"

"That's not what I meant."

"Oh, that's right. 'Cause you've got blood work that says I'm sober, don't you?"

"Would you just chill? I don't need blood work. I just meant this is tough for you."

"Tougher for Billy's wife and family."

Both men looked back to where Andrea Chen and other members of the family were talking with the priest. He handed her a rose from one of the sprays covering the casket and she began to weep.

Halloran nodded. "That's a fact."

The two men walked off a way to give the family more privacy.

"Look," Russo said, "I know we've gotta go through the hoops on this OIS investigation, Lou, and I know I can't go back on the street till it wraps."

"It shouldn't be long. Prelims are done and testimony's been collected. I've got a meeting with the sheriff's office later this week to go over what we're going to release in the public report."

"Are we taking a lot of flak?"

"No more than usual, at least as far as the community's concerned. This 'G Rider Jimmy' character took three bullets, one from your gun, two from other cops at the scene, but the fact that he shot Chen and that boy and was a known gang member takes a lot of heat off the department. There were a couple of procedural mistakes, but they won't necessarily come down to you. We've got at least two uniforms, plus the kid you were talking to about his brother's shooting, all testifying they heard you tell the chopper to hold back until SWAT got there."

"I should've made Chen wear his vest."

"Yeah, and you need to wear yours, too. But the fact remains, this creep was a bad-ass piece of work with a long rap sheet. Turns out there's a couple of other shootings he might have had a hand in over the past year. My biggest regret is that nobody took him out of commission long before this."

Russo nodded. "Well, it's good if there's no political fallout, I guess. I need to get back to work, Lou, and sooner rather than later."

"You will. Like I said, this should wrap up in short order. Meantime—"

"I could do paperwork. Maybe take a look at some old cases."

Halloran shook his head. "You should take some time, John. You've talked to the department shrink, I hear."

Russo scowled.

"Yeah, I know, but it's part of the drill," Halloran said. "Better than keeping things bottled up. And a break's a good thing, too.

Have you had a vacation in the last three years? 'Cause I'm here to tell you, bud, you look like hell."

"Thanks. I don't want a holiday. I want to be busy."

"So get busy. Find yourself a hobby. Man, if there was ever a guy who needed to take up gardening or golf or something…" Halloran cracked a smile. "Maybe you should try a yoga class. Great way to meet babes, I hear."

"Right. That'll happen."

"Look, just take the rest of the week, okay? Next week, we'll see where things stand."

A soft buzz sounded. The lieutenant reached into his coat pocket and withdrew his cell phone, glancing at the display. "I've gotta take this," he said, cutting off any further argument. He flipped open his phone and started down the hill. "Halloran."

Russo hung back, feeling awkward. Most of the cops he knew were already in their cars and heading off. The Chen family was having a last quiet moment with Billy's casket. There was sure as hell no place for him there. Reluctantly, he started down the hill. He had completely forgotten about the woman behind the trees until she stepped out and planted herself in his path.

"Excuse me. Are you Detective Russo?"

"I am."

"I need to talk to you."

"Have we met?"

"No, but I overheard that big man call you John. The paper said the lead detective's name was John Russo—last week's papers, I mean, after the trouble in Compton."

Russo glanced around, but there was no one within earshot. "Ma'am, this is my partner's funeral."

She had the grace to hesitate. "I know. And I'm very, very sorry about that officer's passing."

"So—"

"I called the sheriff's department. They said you were on administrative leave. They wouldn't give me another number to call. I didn't know how else to get in touch with you."

Russo frowned. "But you knew I'd be here today. Are you a reporter?" She didn't look like one, but why else would a stranger be in such an all-fired rush to talk to him unless she was out to raise a stink about the shooting?

"I'm Lillian Shipley."

"Shipley?"

"It was my son Damon that Jimmy Morris murdered last week. The night your partner was killed."

"The gangbanger they called 'G Rider Jimmy'?"

She scowled. "Those gangs and their stupid nicknames. Think it makes them sound so bad. They wreck everything, and nobody stops them."

"I'm very sorry for your loss, Mrs. Shipley, but there wasn't much point in you coming all the way out here today. They must have told you when you called the department that I'm not working your son's case anymore."

She nodded. "They said when a police officer shoots somebody, there has to be an investigation."

"There you go. Your son's case was taken over by another detective. His name is Frank Muller. He's a good man. If you want, I—"

"I've already spoken to Muller," Lillian Shipley said, "and to Lopez, his partner. They aren't listening to what I'm telling them."

"Well, there's nothing I can do for you. I'm out of the loop."

"I just buried my first-born child, Detective!" Her eyes were bright, but her anger was obviously as strong as her grief. "He and his brother had gone out that night to pick up a pizza. A pizza! I'd left them supper in the oven, but they're boys, you know?" Mrs.

Shipley's voice wavered as a tear ran down her cheek. "The pizza places won't deliver in our neighborhood, so they had to walk over to get it. My boy died because he wanted a pizza? That can't be right."

Russo put a hand on her arm. "I really am sorry for your loss, Mrs. Shipley," he said again. Useless words, but what else—

She flicked his hand away. "I don't want your pity, Detective! I want you to find out why my son was killed!"

Russo looked up the hill. Andrea and the rest of Billy Chen's family were making moves to leave. "Look, this is not—"

"And I would think," Lillian Shipley added, her voice more insistent—and louder, "that you would want to know why your partner died."

Russo took her firmly by the elbow, brooking no resistance now. He had to get her out of the family's path. "This is his funeral," he hissed. "It's no place for this."

"Well, I'm very sorry, but I don't know where the right place is," she whispered right back at him. "I took three buses to get here, Detective, and I am damned if I will be hustled off like I was when I tried to talk to those other cops. My family just had a funeral, too, you know. Not like this, mind. Nobody played bagpipes for my boy. But somebody damn well needs to listen and I'm not leaving till that happens."

Russo had her back in the copse of trees and they were more or less hidden from sight. He watched and waited until the Chens had passed by. When the family was back at the limos and cars at the bottom of the hill, he turned once more to Damon Shipley's mother.

"All right, look," he said, "I could use a coffee. How about if we go somewhere and get a quick cup? I warn you, I don't have long. I need to get over to the reception for my partner. Will that work for you?"

It was only then that he realized she'd been practically holding her breath. Lips pressed together, she pulled a tissue from her jacket pocket, wiped her eyes and nodded.

* * *

"Kids don't always do what they're told, Mrs. Shipley."

Russo and Damon Shipley's mother had found a corner booth at a Denny's Restaurant about a half mile from the cemetery. The lunchtime crowd had long since thinned out and they had the place almost entirely to themselves. Russo offered to buy her lunch, but she was obviously too nervous to eat. So was he, for that matter, though for different reasons. They stuck to coffee. A waitress brought it right over, then returned to cleaning tables across the empty dining room.

"I know they don't," Shipley said wearily. "Almost grown or not, I always made my boys stay in after dark or I'd give them what for. It's real hard when the days are so short. They get to feeling cooped up. Next thing you know, they decide they want a pizza." She sighed. "It shouldn't be dangerous to go for pizza, should it?"

"No, ma'am, it should not."

"It's not like that all the time, you know. Our neighborhood's not such a bad place before dark."

"I know," Russo said.

"Lot of people take pride in their homes. One of my neighbors has a rose garden you wouldn't believe. More than sixty different kinds. Most of us go to church every Sunday. Rest of the week we're workin' our butts off, tryin' to make a better life for our kids. You watch the TV news, though, only thing you learn about Compton is robberies and drive-by shootings."

Russo grimaced. "Yup. If it bleeds, it leads. Believe me, I'm no fan either."

"It's disgusting. They try to make out like we're animals or something, always at each other's throats." Her voice caught. "You think anyone wants their child to die in the street like a dog?"

"No, of course not."

"Course not. We want what everybody wants for their kids. I've been working fifteen years at Mount of Olives Academy so my boys could go there instead of to the public school. Even with scholarships, it's expensive, but at least there's enough books and computers and whatnot."

Mount of Olives was a private academy offering classes from pre-K right through high school. It was a smaller, safer alternative to the overcrowded, underfunded L.A. Unified schools. No surprise a conscientious parent would want that for her kids, Russo thought. Still, something from the night of the shooting niggled at his memory. Whatever the detail was, though, it hung annoyingly out of reach.

"Your son Damon was nineteen?"

"That's right."

"Was he still at Mount of Olives?"

She shook her head. "No. My younger son, Tristan—the one you talked to the night Damon was killed—he's a sophomore, but Damon graduated last June. Or almost did. He had trouble with math and missed it first time round. He took a remedial class last fall, though. Real intensive. And you know what? He passed. I was proud of him. He just sent in his college applications couple of weeks back. Was hoping for USC, but he thought his grades might not be good enough. Figured he had a shot at one of the smaller UC schools, though. Didn't matter to me. Long as he went. That was his ticket out of Compton, I told him. It's what I told both my boys. You study hard, you can go anywhere, do anything. You don't wanna be hanging with these raggedy kids think they're so tough. Nowhere fast is where they're goin'."

Mrs. Shipley gripped her coffee cup like she wanted to throttle the life out of it. "That's what makes me so mad, Detective."

"How do you mean?"

"They're saying my son's murder was some kind of gang thing. Settling scores or turf war or some such nonsense. But it's a lie."

"Could it have been your younger son Jimmy Morris was after that night?"

"No. My sons had nothin' to do with the gangs, neither of them—not Damon, not Tristan. When you talked to Tristan the night his brother died, he told you they didn't."

"Yes, ma'am, he did. But he also knew exactly where this G Rider Jimmy was hiding out. How would he know that if neither boy had anything to do with the gangs? Because," he added, "we know for a fact Morris was a member of the Alvarado Crips."

"Oh, for heaven's sake, Detective! My boys have known Jimmy Morris all their lives. They used to build tracks for their Hot Wheels in that shed behind the Morrises' house. A while back, though, Jimmy fell in with bad characters. After I heard he'd been arrested that first time, I forbid my boys to go over there or have anything more to do with him."

Russo studied her. Was she protesting too much? Like he said, kids didn't always do what they were told. Maybe she suspected they'd slipped out behind her back while she was at—that was it! "Mrs. Shipley, I was told you were working the night of the shooting."

"So it was my fault?"

"No, ma'am. It's just that my lieutenant said that night he'd sent a car to pick you up from a restaurant over on Rosecrans where you worked."

"Ah, I see. So you think I'm lyin' about Mount of Olives."

"I'm just trying to figure—"

"I'm poor, Detective, I'm not stupid. It's like I told you, I work as an aide at Mount of Olives. Have done for fifteen years now. But I took an evening shift at the restaurant to earn extra money. Been there since mid-November. I was helping Damon buy a car."

"So you were working two jobs."

"Not the first time, believe me."

"I hear you. You wanted to get him a car for college?"

"Not just that. He had a job over in Culver City. It was a good job, but it took him over an hour each way on the bus, so I told him I'd help him buy a car—just a used one, nothing fancy. We were going to go out next weekend and try to find something. His hours were weird and he was gettin' back from work later and later, but he really liked the work. He was hopin' it might turn into a career."

"What kind of work was it?"

"A movie. They just started shooting last month, but they were in what they call 'preproduction' all last summer and fall. One of his teachers helped him get the job last summer. It was with this rich producer who'd come to Damon's school a couple of years ago. This past June, he went to Mount of Olives and offered to take on an underprivileged youth for the summer, give him a sort of apprenticeship, pay him a salary, like that. Damon got the job, and it worked out so well they kept him on. Even let him work around his class schedule so he could get that math credit. I think it's part of the reason Damon did so well on the math. He was happy, you know? He really didn't want to let Mr. Farran down."

"Farran? That's the name of the producer?"

She nodded.

"First name?"

"I'm not sure, to tell you the truth. He's a foreigner, an Arab from one of those countries with all the oil, but apparently he went to school here in the States. Damon said he had more money than God, but he was a real nice guy."

"Did you meet this Mr. Farran?"

"No, I never did. He sent some beautiful flowers when Damon passed, though. And," she added, wringing a paper napkin, "he

called. He said he was real sorry that he was going to miss the funeral 'cause he had to be out of town for some family thing, but…"
She hesitated.

"What is it?"

"He wanted to pay for Damon's funeral."

"Did you accept?"

"I thanked him, but it didn't seem right, so I said 'no thank you.'
Only then, when I talked to the man at the funeral home, he said
it was all taken care of. They did a beautiful job and all, but I feel
kind of funny about it, you know?"

"It sounds like this guy can afford the gesture," Russo said, although the suspicious side of him couldn't help wondering if the
philanthropic Mr. Farran wasn't just a little too good to be true.
"What kind of work was Damon doing for him?"

"He was just a gofer at first but then he got a promotion. Mr. Farran was only a few years older than my boy, I think. Damon said he
graduated from film school at USC. That's what got Damon thinking about trying to go there. Anyway, when the movie started shooting, Mr. Farran made Damon his assistant."

"Wow, assistant to the producer. Pretty neat. Sounds like a dream
come true."

"That's what I'm sayin'. There was no reason for Damon to get
mixed up with the gangs. It's why it makes me so mad they keep
saying that's why he was killed."

"When I talked to Damon's brother that night, he said Jimmy
Morris just came up and fired for no reason."

Lillian Shipley winced, but she nodded. "Tristan told me he
thought Jimmy was looking for Damon that night. When they ran
into him on the street, Jimmy said, 'good, you saved me some steps,
man.' Then he just shot my Damon in the head."

"Tristan didn't tell me that part, about what Jimmy said."

"He was scared to death, Detective. He thought Jimmy was gonna kill him that night, too. But after he shot Damon, Tristan said, Jimmy just turned on his heel and walked away, cool as a cucumber." A tear ran down her cheek. "It's evil. Just pure evil."

Russo sat back, frowning. What she was describing was an execution, a shooting with the hallmarks of a contract killing more than a gang thing. Gangbangers tended to travel in packs, like hyenas, but Jimmy Morris seemed to have acted on his own. And gangbangers were also notorious braggarts. G Rider Jimmy hadn't lived long enough after murdering Damon Shipley to broadcast his achievement in the graffiti that police gang units analyzed like ancient hieroglyphics, but someone in the Crips' chain of command should have had a notion the shooting was about to go down. As far as Russo knew, however, the street was as mystified as anyone else about the motive for Damon Shipley's murder. Up until now, he'd been operating on the assumption that it was either a turf war or a simple street robbery gone bad, the Shipley boys being in the wrong place at the wrong time. But Tristan Shipley's account of Jimmy's last words before the shooting put a whole different spin on things.

"What do you think it was about, Mrs. Shipley?"

"I don't think Jimmy Morris had any reason to kill Damon, not on his own. They weren't friends anymore, but my boys hadn't done anything to cross him either. Not Jimmy nor his homies, neither."

"You think Jimmy was working on someone else's behalf?"

"Maybe."

"Why?"

"Because my neighbor's daughter hangs with those boys. She said one of the other boys saw Jimmy talkin' to some stranger a couple of weeks ago—guy drivin' a real fancy car, not the kind you see in our neighborhood."

"And that's it?"

She said nothing for a moment. "No," she said quietly. "There was something else. Damon skipped work last week. Two days running, he wouldn't get out of bed. Said he wasn't feeling good, but I know my boys, and believe me, I know when they're fibbin'. At first, I thought maybe he got fired, but then, I got the feeling he was plain scared to go in."

"Did you ask him what was going on?"

"I tried to, but he was…I don't know…just strange. All fidgety and nervous. Finally, I got mad, and I said whatever it was, he couldn't just hide under the bedclothes all day. That's when he told me."

"Told you what?"

"That those were bad people, and he wasn't goin' back there."

"Bad people? Well, maybe, Mrs. Shipley. They don't call those Hollywood types sharks for nothing, believe me, but still—"

"No, Detective, not just sharks. Not just sleazy or fake or sneaky or nothin' like that. I mean bad, scary people. Dangerous. Real, real dangerous. I don't know what Damon saw or heard or found out over on that film set. All I know is my boy was terrified to go back there. And then he was killed."

31

The Silver Lake Neighborhood of Los Angeles

Hannah was sitting at her dining room table, laptop open, trying to concentrate on paying bills that had stacked up while she was away on the Beckham job. Her checking account balance was healthy for the moment but it wouldn't stay that way long if she didn't get another job in short order. She worked her way through the pile of bills, ripping open envelopes, tossing them aside and laying the invoices on the table beside her. Then, signing into an online banking session, she moved down the list, settling up electric, gas, phone and a raft of other bills.

She was going to have to start dialing for dollars, touching base with some of her private security contractor buddies. Her skills must be in demand somewhere. As much as she hated the idea of going back on the road so soon after the Beckham gig, a short-term overseas job would do her finances a world of good. The big bucks were in the hot zones. One contract there was worth a half dozen celebrity babysitting jobs.

Maybe a call to Brandywine, she thought. Surely they'd be ready to forgive her by now, two years after Al Zawra. Even if she wasn't ready to forgive herself.

Oz.

Was it really Oz Nuñez's killer she'd spotted at the Staples Center the other night? She'd been so sure at the time, but the more she thought about it, the unlikelier it seemed. What would he be doing in L.A.?

But dammit, Hannah thought, it *was* him. During the firefight at the Jordanian border, she'd only flashed intermittently on his face, lit up, strobelike, in the hail of gunfire. It had been a wild and adrenaline-charged few minutes, admittedly, but it was still enough to sear the man's image into her brain for all time—that white hair, those Arctic blue eyes. She didn't know why he was here now, but he was. The only question: what was she going to do about it?

She exhaled heavily. *One thing at a time, kid. Pay the bills, then call Val Underwood, see if she's come up with anything.*

Her gaze shifted back and forth between the computer screen and her pile of invoices, her bank account shriveling a little with every entered amount. A job. She needed a job. She'd done good work on Brandywine's dime, regardless of what went down after they'd finished rescuing the old woman and her granddaughter from Al Zawra. From what Hannah had heard via the grapevine, Brandywine was still active on the ground in Iraq and had contracts running elsewhere in the Middle East as well. It wasn't like Arabic speakers were a dime a dozen.

So, call them. A little groveling never killed anyone.

She hit the Pay button at the bottom of the screen, printed a receipt, then signed out of the banking session. She was cleaning up the paper mess when the phone rang a few minutes later.

"Speak of the devil," she said when she heard the voice on the other end of the line. "I was just about to call you."

"Impatient little monster, aren't you?" Val Underwood said.

"Hey, nothing ever got accomplished by sitting around waiting for the phone to ring."

"Hmm…that's true, but I'm not sure you're going to be so happy when you hear what I found out."

"Uh-oh. That doesn't sound good. Who is he?"

"Your man from the Staples Center? I have no idea."

"The info didn't pan out?"

"Oh, I found out who owned the car he was driving but it's not going to help you much."

"How so?"

"The car's registered to a VIP by the name of Farran Alsaqri. That name ring a bell?"

Hannah frowned. "No, I don't—oh, wait. Alsaqri? Isn't that the name of the new Saudi ambassador?"

"Bingo. Give the lady the big, plush bunny. That would be Prince Mohammed Alsaqri, half brother to the king and the Saudis' new ambassador to Washington."

"So this other Alsaqri…?"

"Farran. The ambassador's son."

"His kid would have diplomatic status, no? And so, dip plates on his car? That BMW at the Staples Center had regular plates."

"Uh-huh. The car you saw is registered to a company owned by the ambassador's son. Farran Alsaqri's twenty-eight. He attended prep school back east, then came to L.A. to study at USC. He was here on September 11, 2001, and he was one of a couple dozen Saudi VIPs who were quietly spirited out of the country over the next couple of days."

"When every other plane in the country was still grounded."

"Yup. Some people in Washington were very anxious that certain good friends of theirs not get caught up in the blame game when the entire country was baying for blood."

"Well, most of the 9/11 hijackers *were* Saudis," Hannah pointed out.

"Yeah, I know. Don't even get me started on why we cater to that medieval regime over there. Anyway, Alsaqri the elder obviously had friends in high places long before he was appointed ambassador to Washington 'cause there was no question his kids would be at the top of the list of people hustled out of town."

"But this Farran came back, obviously."

"Yeah, he lost his year at USC, but the next fall, he was quietly allowed to return. He was a film major. After he graduated, he set up his own production company. Apparently he has ambitions to become the Saudi Spielberg."

"So the BMW I saw my guy drive off in the other night belongs to his film company?" Hannah frowned. "The White Fox can't be Farran Alsaqri."

"The who?"

"That's what I call Oz Nuñez's killer—the White Fox. The guy's got to be late forties, early fifties, I'm thinking. Too old to have been a college student on 9/11."

"Not only that, but Farran wasn't at the Staples Center last Wednesday night—although it turns out he does have a skybox," Underwood added. "Apparently he's a big Lakers fan."

"How do you know he wasn't there? My guy was with a younger couple. Maybe the other guy was Farran Alsaqri."

"Nope. He left for D.C. on Wednesday morning, according to the consulate. I double-checked airport passenger manifests, just to be sure. His father presented his credentials at the White House on Thursday. Farran was at the ceremony, along with another brother and a half sister who live back east. There's pictures to prove it. He didn't return to L.A. until Sunday night."

Hannah frowned. "Okay, but this is something, anyway. We still don't have a name for the White Fox, but maybe he works for this

Farran Alsaqri, which would explain why he was driving that car. Have you got an address for his studio?"

"Hey, slow down there, Mario Andretti. Did you get it that Alsaqri senior's a major VIP? A friggin' prince, for crying out loud? My contacts at the Saudi consulate were practically throwing fits at the idea we would dare to cast our peasant eyes on his son. I had to make up some nonsense about unpaid parking tickets Farran's employees were racking up with the company car, and then I promised the consulate I'd see they were torn up."

"Yeah, but Val, aren't you curious what Oz Nuñez's killer is doing here, working for this wannabe Saudi Spielberg?"

"Alleged killer. Maybe it's not the same guy."

"It's the same guy. I know it is. Look," Hannah added when Underwood started to protest, "a little surveillance, that's all I'm going to do. I'll check the guy out, try to find out who he is and what he's up to here. I'll stay away from the little prince, I promise."

"You'd better, Hannah. I mean it. The consulate's already feeling aggrieved these days. I don't need them going over my head, complaining about harassment to the sheriff or to Washington."

"I read you, loud and clear. So, the name of Farran's company?"

Underwood sighed. "Skylight Productions. Offices are in Culver City." She gave Hannah an address and phone number.

"Thanks, Val. I really appreciate this."

"You're welcome, I'm sure. But, Hannah?" Underwood added. "Don't make me regret this, okay?"

"Cross my heart."

32

Wednesday, February 2, 2005
Laguna Beach, California

Russo had to do some digging to find the full name of Damon Shipley's "Mr. Farran," the movie-mogul heart-of-gold philanthropist who took a kid from the 'hood and made him his personal assistant. It wasn't easy, given that Russo was supposed to be off the job until his OIS investigation wrapped. But if Finn Brophy had taken the service weapon he'd used the night he shot G Rider Jimmy, Russo still had his badge. That, plus the blessing of Lillian Shipley, was all he needed to get time with the headmaster at Mount of Olives Academy and the teacher who'd hooked up Damon Shipley with the producer offering a job and a potential ticket out of Compton.

Once Russo had the full name "Farran Alsaqri," it was a simple enough matter to use his home computer to tap into the sheriff's department system for an address and to check for priors on the guy. Of course, nothing was ever truly simple. Farran Alsaqri, it turned out, was the son of an ambassador, which made him all but bulletproof when it came to American justice. That wasn't going to stop Russo from checking out the guy to try to learn what Damon Shipley might have seen or heard that scared the bejeezus out of him, according to his mother. But if Alsaqri was up to no good, doing anything about it could be a little tricky.

When Russo took a run over to the Culver City offices of Skylight Productions, he was told that Alsaqri was out of town on location for the next several days, working on a movie he was producing and directing. Fortunately, not far out of town. The film shoot was in Laguna Beach, just an hour's drive south of downtown.

Movies were southern California's bread and butter. In a time of runaway production, when films and TV series were being shot in countries with better tax incentives or cheaper production costs, local communities were fighting back, cutting filmmakers a lot of slack to get them to stick around. Traffic and commerce might be disrupted for days on end while a director, cast and crew put a movie in the can, but better that, municipal officials decided, than watch Toronto stand in for Chicago or Prague for old New York, with those cities reaping the spin-off economic benefits.

On that day, it seemed, Laguna Beach was standing in for Marseilles. Russo located the Skylight Productions crew shooting at the town's main beach. According to an assistant producer he waylaid at the edge of the action, Alsaqri was shooting a caper flick about a jewel heist on the French Riviera.

"We've got a second unit over in the south of France getting some establishing shots," the woman said, "but the rest of the script's being shot here in Laguna and on a rented sound stage in Burbank."

She turned away for a moment to speak to a young gofer. Like everyone else standing around on the set, they were both bundled up in ski jackets, scarves and sheepskin boots. The sun was brilliant but the temperature was hovering around sixty with a cold breeze off the water, and southern Californians were a thin-skinned bunch.

Russo had on a windbreaker, but he found himself wishing he'd thrown on a sweater under it, as well, instead of just an open-necked denim shirt.

"So which one is Alsaqri?" he asked when the woman turned back to him.

"That's Farran over there, talking to the cinematographer."

She pointed to a good-looking young man in a backward-facing ball cap, black leather jacket and jeans. He was speaking to a couple of camera operators. Alsaqri wore rimless glasses and the careless ease of someone who has never, ever had to worry about where his next rent check was coming from. Or maybe, Russo thought, it was just his own research and working-class roots coloring his take on the guy. To be honest, he could pass Alsaqri on the street and not look twice.

He started toward the director, but the woman put a restraining hand on his arm. "They're just getting ready to shoot," she said. "You can't bother him now."

"Did I mention I'm a police officer?"

"Yeah, you did, but this setup's costing thousands of dollars an hour and we're going to lose the light soon. You think you can wait a little bit? It shouldn't take long. They've already done a couple of takes. Farran'll probably wrap it after this one. He's not the type to do a scene twenty times over."

"Sounds like a pretty frugal guy, for somebody so rich."

"From what I've seen, he doesn't waste money, his or his investors'. He's just starting his career and he's careful of his professional rep."

"His rep?"

The woman shrugged. "A lot of people would like to write him off as a playboy dilettante. I know I did, before I started working with him."

"But not anymore?"

"Nope. I think he's the real deal."

Russo turned back to study the director once more. Alsaqri had moved over to a man and woman standing on the boardwalk, apart from the crew. The couple—actors, it seemed—shed their warm coats and handed them off to aides. She had on a bikini underneath, he was dressed in expensive sportswear—the gentleman thief, maybe? Somebody stepped up and artfully tousled the woman's long red hair, while another guy with makeup brushes took a swipe at both actors' noses and foreheads.

"I can have someone bring you a chair and some coffee while you wait," the assistant producer told Russo.

"No, thanks, that's okay," Russo said, wondering if the cameras would pick up the goose bumps on the poor, shivering actress—not to mention those bumps in her teeny-tiny bikini top. "I'll just hang out over here and watch."

"Great. I'll tell Farran you're here and see if he can talk to you while the crew sets up for the next shot."

Russo nodded. He glanced around. A tiled chess table and a couple of benches stood near a children's play structure, offering a good view of the boardwalk. He parked himself on the tabletop as the woman approached her boss, tapping him on the shoulder. Alsaqri listened, frowned, then followed the direction of her cocked thumb, back to where Russo was sitting. If he was fazed by having an L.A. cop show up out of the blue on his movie set, he didn't show it. The director just nodded to him, then turned back to the task at hand.

Russo thought he recognized the two actors from some movie or TV show he'd seen, but he wasn't sure. They weren't big box-office stars, for sure, just part of the army of hopefuls that cycled through Hollywood's endlessly spinning turnstile. Like most L.A. natives, Russo was used to seeing movie people in action, but it always surprised him how many worker bees flitted around a set. It wasn't obvious what most of their jobs were, but no one seemed to question their need to be there.

While the cast and crew moved into position and waited for the director's signal to get underway, Russo turned to check out the park off the boardwalk and the sidewalks beyond. Most of the beach area had been cordoned off for the movie shoot. The few people on the sand were apparently extras, also wearing bathing suits under warm track suits and jackets. It wasn't like they'd displaced anyone. It was a southern California truism that nobody but movie people and tourists were at the beach in winter, and even the tourists had more sense than to romp around half naked on a day like this, no matter how much colder it might be back home in the snow belt.

In spite of the nip in the air, though, the arrival of a film crew in town had drawn a fairly large crowd of curious onlookers. Three beefy guys in black windbreakers emblazoned on the back with the word SECURITY walked up and down the rope line, chatting up a few pretty young things who giggled and flirted back with the guards and with any crew member whose attention they could snag.

All but one, Russo realized, his gaze coming to rest on a tallish woman who seemed to be holding herself well back from the action on the ropes. A black beret partially covered her dark hair and large sunglasses hid a good part of her face. She was attractive but a far cry from the chirpy blond whippet-girls southern California favored. Dressed in jeans, sneakers, black turtleneck and long leather coat, she was having none of the security guards and their pickup lines. Every time one of them planted his beefy frame in front of her, she shifted position irritably, her unsmiling attention locked on the film crew.

Russo frowned. He knew no one who lived in Laguna Beach, yet something about that woman seemed familiar. The context was all wrong though. He'd seen her before, but for the life of him, he couldn't think where their paths might have crossed.

As she ducked farther back behind a couple of elderly dog walkers, Russo realized it wasn't the whole crew she was fixated on, just one guy. When the white-haired man turned to face the rowdy onlookers behind the ropes, she slipped back even farther behind a couple of football jocks. As much as she seemed to be checking him out, clearly she didn't want the guy to spot her.

The man, dark shades obscuring his own eyes, called over one of the security guards. He obviously delivered a dressing-down because the rent-a-cop straightened his spine, nodded sharply, then returned to the rope and whispered something to the other guards. With a nervous glance back at the white-haired guy, they snapped to, cut the kibitzing and went back to walking the line.

All right then, Russo thought. The older guy was obviously in charge of the muscle here. And that grim-faced woman? What was the deal with her?

A bell clanged and someone called for quiet. The security guards made damping-down motions with their hands and the crowd obediently went silent. By the time Alsaqri called "Action!", the only sound to be heard was the pounding of the surf.

Russo watched the actors do the scene, but aside from some mock-heated body language suggesting an argument, he couldn't make out their lines. The big boom mikes were obviously picking up the dialogue just fine, though, because after the one short take, Alsaqri removed his earphones and called "Cut and print!"

As the actors scrambled back into coats and sweats, the crew went into action, shifting cameras, video monitors, microphones and other gear, setting up for the next shot. All the actors, including the extras on the beach, scampered across the park and past the rope lines, heading for trailers lined up along the roadway. Parking meters on the street had been covered with canvas hoods and tempo-rary No Parking signs, the city reserving the prime beachfront spaces for the film company's trailers and RVs.

Turning back to the boardwalk, Russo spotted Alsaqri walking toward him. He got to his feet.

"Janet said you wanted to talk to me, Officer…"

"Detective," Russo said, extending his hand, "John Russo. I'm with the Los Angeles Sheriff's Department Homicide Bureau."

"Detective. I'm Farran," the director said. They shook hands. "How can I help you?"

"I'm looking into the murder of Damon Shipley," Russo said.

Alsaqri nodded soberly. "I thought that's what this might be about. Please," he said, indicating the benches, "have a seat. The crew is setting up for another shot before we lose the light, but I have a few minutes, and I'm certainly glad to answer any questions you have. I'm not sure what I can say that will help, but I'm truly sorry about what happened to Damon."

The two men settled into the benches on either side of the tiled chess table.

"Damon's mother told me you called with condolences but weren't able to make it to his funeral?"

"That's right. I was sorry I couldn't go but I had to go out of town. Family business. My father's an ambassador. He was presenting his credentials the day of Damon's funeral and I was obliged to be in Washington."

"Mrs. Shipley said you paid the funeral costs?"

Alsaqri looked uncomfortable. "I did. I had offered to when I spoke to her. She declined, but I understood from things Damon had told me that finances were tight in his home. I gather Damon's father was killed in an industrial accident when he and his brother were little. Damon told me his mother worked very hard to provide for her sons. Helping her out with the funeral expenses seemed like a small thing."

"Mr. Alsaqri—"

"Farran, please. Mr. Alsaqri is my father."

"Did you feel guilty about Damon's murder, Farran?"

"Guilty? Why would I feel guilty?"

Russo shrugged.

"I felt very sad about it. Damon was a good kid, and he really seemed to take to this business." Alsaqri waved a hand back at the movie crew.

"What made you hire him?"

"I met him when he was a high school freshman. I was in film school. A group of friends and I made a documentary on his school for one of our classes. We were looking at programs for kids from poor neighborhoods. Mount of Olives Academy offers scholarships and a safe environment. A lot of their students have gone on to four-year colleges and made the jump out of poverty, thanks to that school. I was pretty impressed by what they were accomplishing. When I started my own film company, I called the headmaster at Mount of Olives and told him I'd be willing to offer a paid internship to a deserving young person. When I asked him if he could recommend anyone, he reminded me about Damon. We'd featured both Shipley brothers in our film, so of course I remembered Damon."

"What did you have Damon doing?"

"At first he shadowed different people, learning about their jobs. It was just going to be a summer internship, but when fall came, I decided to make Damon my assistant while we shot this film. He helped keep me organized, took notes, did some fact-checking for me, that sort of thing." Alsaqri shook his head. "He was a bright kid. I was talking to one of my professors at USC not long before Damon died, putting in the good word for him."

"Any thoughts on who would have wanted to murder him?"

Alsaqri sat back on the bench, looking puzzled. "I thought the police shot the guy who killed him. Are you saying they got the wrong guy?"

"No, he was Damon's killer all right. But my question was, who would have wanted Damon Shipley dead?"

"I understand the question, Detective, I just don't understand why you're asking it. I thought it was a gang thing—a robbery or a case of mistaken identity. Pretty awful, considering that the Shipley boys weren't into that scene. It sounded to me like those poor guys were just in the wrong place at the wrong time."

"And yet Damon's brother walked away without a scratch," Russo said. "From the way Tristan described Damon's murder, it sounds more like an execution. Why would that be, do you think?"

"Good God, I have no idea."

"Could someone here have hired that gangbanger to kill Damon?"

"You tell me."

"Damon's mother said he didn't go to work the last couple of days before he was killed."

Alsaqri crossed his arms and rested his chin in one palm, studying Russo. "That's true," he conceded. "I was surprised and, frankly, a little disappointed."

"Disappointed?"

"I expected better. I knew he was trying to buy a used car, so the first day he didn't show up, I thought maybe he must have finally gotten it and then had a breakdown or something. But when he didn't come in the second day, I called his house to see if everything was okay."

"And? Did you talk to him?"

"I did. And…" Alsaqri hesitated.

"What?" Russo pressed.

"Well, basically, he blew me off."

"What did he say?"

"He said he was busy and he didn't think he was going to be able to work for me anymore."

"But you said he loved the work, wanted to make a career of it. That's what his mother said, too. You didn't think it odd he went cold all of a sudden like that?"

"Of course I did. It made no sense at all. I tried to talk to him about what was going on, but he completely shut down on me. In the end, I had people waiting on a meeting, so I just told him to think about it and then I rang off. I decided if he didn't come back in by the end of that week, I'd take a run over to Compton on the weekend, try to find out what the hell was going on. Only then," Alsaqri added, "on Thursday morning, we got word that Damon had been murdered."

"Who told you?"

"I think I first heard about it on the news driving into work, and then, of course, some detectives showed up at our offices later that day. I was pretty shocked, I can tell you. I heard there was a police officer killed that night, too."

Russo said nothing, but his face or his posture must have spoken for him.

"I'm very sorry about that officer, too, Detective."

Russo nodded. "So you never did follow up on why Damon flaked out on you?"

"Well, I called his mother, of course, but at that point, there didn't seem to be any point in reproaching her for what he'd done. My inconvenience wasn't really the point, was it?"

"No, I guess not."

"I asked one of my people to make some discreet inquiries, see if there was any further information. The whole thing just seemed too awful to believe. My guy made some calls, but he said it seemed to be a random act of gang violence, pure and simple." Alsaqri shook his head. "What a bloody, stupid waste."

"Who was it you had looking into the murder?"

"My head of security, George Kenner."

Russo looked around, but the guy he'd spotted reaming out the rent-a-cops earlier was nowhere to be seen now. "Kenner? Would that by chance be the white-haired guy who runs your rope detail over there?"

Alsaqri nodded. "Among other things."

"This guy's an ex-cop?"

He didn't believe that for a minute, but the movie biz was where a lot of former L.A. cops landed after retirement, so maybe... Alsaqri's hesitation, however, told him his doubts about this Kenner character were well-founded.

"No," the director said finally. "George came to me on the recommendation of...hmm...how should I phrase this?"

"Straight up works for me."

"Let's put it this way, Detective. My father, as I said, is a diplomat. I'm really not into the world he lives in. My mother was Italian, actually. She died when I was a teenager but I spent more time in Italy and the States while growing up than I ever did in Saudi. However, because I am my father's son, I'm stuck with a certain amount of baggage, including certain demands of a security nature."

"And this George Kenner is part of that baggage?"

"I'm afraid so. Don't get me wrong. He's all right, I suppose. A little lugubrious for my taste, but as long as he doesn't crowd me too closely, I keep him on to keep my father happy."

"Got it. He comes on the recommendation of someone your father deals with on security matters in Washington, that it?"

"Yeah, basically. We don't broadcast the fact, but that's about it."

Made sense, Russo supposed. But it still didn't answer the question of what could have frightened Damon Shipley so much that he'd walk away from a job he could only have dreamed of before Farran Alsaqri came along like some magic lamp genie.

"Mr. Alsaqri—"

"Farran."

"Farran," Russo amended, "I can see your people are dancing around here, trying to get your attention, so I won't keep you any longer for now. But I do have one last question. It's a little awkward—"

"Well, as you yourself said, Detective, you might as well just give it to me straight up."

"You mind telling me where you come down on Islamic terrorists?"

Farran burst out laughing.

"You think this is a funny subject?" Russo asked.

"No, no, of course not. Forgive me. But if you're asking me if I'm a closet terrorist and that's got something to do with why Damon Shipley was killed, then I can only say, you're way off the mark. I'd make a terrible radical fundamentalist. I'm far too westernized. I like wine, women, basketball, hip-hop and the movies way too much. That demented compatriot of mine, Osama bin Laden would probably take my head off—literally—if he ever got his skinny, fanatic hands on me."

Farran got to his feet, still chuckling. But then, he paused, sobering.

"That said, Detective, I really am sorry that Damon and that police officer died. If there were anything I could do to bring their killer to justice, rest assured I would—except it sounds like the police already got their man when they killed that gangbanger in Compton." Farran shrugged. "Roll credits, end of story."

33

Laguna Beach, California

It didn't look like the movie bunch was going anywhere soon. With the White Fox overseeing the security crew holding back looky-loos, Hannah was gambling he was locked down for the duration, as well.

Someone called for quiet on the set, and the cast and crew readied themselves for another scene. She decided not to push her luck and run the risk of him recognizing her. Better to take a walk, see if she couldn't spot the BMW she'd seen at the Staples Center. She needed to be able to track this guy back to his lair. After a visit to her favorite electronics shop, she'd come prepared to do just that. She could only hope the Beemer was his regular ride. If it wasn't, or if the White Fox had driven to the shoot with someone else that day, she was hosed, but she'd deal with that problem if and when.

That afternoon, however, the surveillance gods decided to smile on her. She found the Beemer just around the corner on Forest, a narrow avenue of trendy shops, restaurants and the galleries that gave Laguna Beach its artsy cachet. The expired meter and the ticket on the car's windshield told Hannah all she needed to know about the White Fox's respect for law and order.

Parking spots on Forest Avenue were diagonal rather than parallel to the sidewalk, which meant the Beemer's butt end was poking out into the roadway, making it a little tricky to get at the rear passenger-side wheel well, where she'd decided the White Fox was least likely to spot the GPS tracking device she planned to plant on the car. She got another break when a big, black Hummer pulled into the parking spot next to the BMW. As a short, balding, middle-aged guy clambered out of the driver's seat, Hannah tried not to think Freudian thoughts about big monster vehicles compensating for littleness elsewhere. This little guy with his gargantuan ride was her lucky charm. Why pick on him?

After he dropped a handful of quarters into the meter and sauntered up the street and around the corner, Hannah sidled into the space between the Hummer and the BMW, where she was well concealed by the gigantic SUV. Reaching into the pocket of her leather coat, she pulled out the tiny transmitter she'd bought at the electronics store. A casual look around told her the few pedestrians on the sidewalks were window-shopping. Leaning on the Beemer's rear fender, casually checking her watch as if she were waiting for someone, she reached behind with her free right hand, letting the swing of her coat conceal it while she positioned the device inside the wheel well. The tracker's attached magnet clamped onto the metal. Once she'd jiggled it to satisfy herself it wasn't going anywhere, she took one more ostentatious look around, then pulled out her cell phone and headed back onto the sidewalk, miming a call to that mythical misplaced friend.

She was almost back at the corner where Forest Avenue meets Pacific Coast Highway and the beach across the way when she felt a hand clamp onto her elbow and heard a low voice murmur in her ear. "Care to explain what that little charade was all about?"

Heart sinking, Hannah braked. She yanked her elbow away, but when she turned, she found herself facing not the White Fox, as she'd feared, but a medium-tall, Mediterranean-looking guy—dark, neatly-cut hair and dark eyes to match. Late thirties, guessing by the few silver strands at his temples. Dressed casually in a bomber jacket, denim shirt and tan Dockers. Too alert-looking to be a vacationing snowbird or beach bum. He was the textbook illustration of a plainclothes cop. Not good, Hannah thought.

"I beg your pardon?" she said.

The man glanced up and down the street, then leaned in closer. "I'm guessing," he said, "that you don't want the owner of that BMW knowing you just tagged it with a GPS device."

"I have no idea what you're talking about. I was supposed to meet a friend here and—"

"Yeah, yeah, right. I caught that act, but you know what? I'm not buying it. Maybe you should go across the street, talk to the people on that movie set you were casing, see if they can offer a few lessons. 'Cause I'm here to tell you, lady, that performance isn't going to win any Academy Awards."

"Who the hell are you?"

"You first."

"Take a hike, buddy." Hannah started to move away from him but he was on her like white on rice.

"Fine," he said, "be like that. How about I tell that white-haired dude what I saw?" He poked a finger in his cheek. "Oh, wait. Gee! Could it be that's *his* car you bugged?"

Hannah stopped and turned once more, hoping he couldn't hear her heart pounding. It was reverberating like cannon fire in her own ears. She couldn't let this idiot, cop or not, throw her off the trail now that she'd found Oz's killer. "What do you want?"

He studied her, frowning. "I've been trying to figure it out ever since I first spotted you. Have we met somewhere?"

"Oh, please. You've gotta have a better line than that."

"Yeah, it's pathetic, that's a fact. Fits the bill, though. I'm damned if I can think why you look so familiar."

Hannah studied him for a moment. Now that he mentioned it…

"Look, I don't know about you," he said, "but I've been standing in the wind off the water over there for over an hour and I'm freezing my butt off here. What do you say we duck in here and grab a cup of coffee?" He nodded to a café behind them on the avenue. "It's not like your guy's going anywhere—at least, not without you knowing exactly where, thanks to that little goodie you planted in his wheel well."

Hannah debated, but like he said, the White Fox probably wasn't going anywhere for the moment. "Fine. Coffee. But we sit where I can keep an eye on the car."

"You got it."

"So—name, rank and serial number," Hannah said, after the waiter took their coffee orders. They were seated next to the café's big front windows. She had her back to the wall and a clear line of sight to the BMW.

"Sorry?"

"You're a cop, right?"

"That obvious, huh?"

"Totally."

"Fair enough. John Russo. Detective, Homicide Bureau."

She frowned. "L.A. Sheriff's Department?"

"Yeah, how'd you know?"

"What are you doing down here, so far off your turf?"

"Hey, come on, it's your turn to answer a question," Russo said. "How'd you know I was with the LASD?"

"I know your name. I worked dispatch there a million years ago."

"Aha. And you are…?"

"Hannah Nicks."

"Nicks? Like Calvin Nicks, ex-ADA turned asshole lawyer to rich bad boys?"

She rolled her eyes. "He's my ex."

"My deepest sympath—hey, hang on. Now I remember. You're the undercover cop whose house got blown up by some mobster. He was trying to keep you from testifying against him. Drug and murder-for-hire case, right?"

She nodded. "With a bunch of other charges added on after he bombed my place."

"So the intimidation didn't work?"

"Nope. He got something like three consecutive life sentences."

"You go, girl. Are you still on the job?"

"Nope. I quit not long after that case."

"So what are you doing now?"

Hannah glanced out the window, but the Beemer was still there. "Private security work. Some domestic, some overseas stuff."

"And this?" he asked, cocking a thumb at the car. "You're tailing this guy for a client?"

"Sort of."

"Seems to me it's an either/or thing. You are or you're not."

"It's a little complicated."

"Complicated how?"

The waiter showed up with their coffee just then, giving Hannah a chance to consider how much to say. She watched surreptitiously as Russo opened a couple of creamers and sugar packets and stirred the contents into his coffee. He had strong-looking hands with broad, blunt-tipped fingers. She found herself mesmerized by his ropy wrists, tiny hairs caught in the winter sunlight that was streaming in through the café's big windows.

"So, you were saying?" Russo prompted. "Your client on this surveillance gig? It's complicated how…?"

She looked up, startled, and feeling her face go warm as he watched her, waiting. How hard up was she? Put her in close proximity to a little testosterone and she turned into a basket case.

She dodged his gaze, busying herself with the coffee and creamers. "I guess the client is me."

"And why are you tailing this guy?"

She sighed. She didn't have to tell him. On the other hand, he was a cop, and he knew about working with a partner in a dangerous environment. "I spotted him last week up in L.A., completely by accident. I tracked him down through the license plate on his car. This is the first chance I've had to get a close look at him, make sure he's really who I thought he was."

"And who's that?"

"The guy who killed my partner two years ago."

Russo had been looking vaguely bemused up to now, but his expression went dead serious in an instant. "This guy's a cop-killer?"

"No," Hannah admitted. "It happened after I'd left the force. I was in Iraq two years ago, right after the fall of Saddam. I'd gone in on a mission to rescue some civilians, and ended up working another freelance job to rescue a kidnapped doctor from Boston. I did the job with a young guy who was fresh out of the marines. The mission was successful, but then, a couple of days later, we were attacked by one of the kidnappers and he killed my partner."

"That white-haired guy's not Iraqi, is he?"

She frowned and shook her head. "No, that's it, I'm pretty sure he's not. I don't know what his story is, but when I spotted him the other night, I knew I sure as hell wasn't going to rest until I found out."

She felt her eyes tearing up and turned away hurriedly, watching as a young mom with a stroller stopped on the sidewalk outside. The toddler in the carriage was crying. He looked about two years old. His mother cuddled and kissed him, then pulled out a plastic container of Cheerios that she tipped into the grooved tray in front of him. One last, glistening tear rolled down his chubby cheeks as he turned his attention to the cereal treat. In spite of herself—the stress and frustration of being so close to Oz Nuñez's killer, and yet not having the slightest clue how she was going to deal with him—Hannah smiled, remembering Gabe at the age of that toddler in the stroller. That part of his life and hers had gone by way too fast; she wanted a rerun.

The waiter returned to top up their cups. Russo stirred his coffee distractedly, frowning, saying nothing. Hannah couldn't read him. Did he think she was lying? That she was some movie groupie/stalker type?

"What about you?" she asked. "What are you doing down here?"

Russo put down his spoon and looked out the window. The young mom and baby had moved on and Forest Avenue was quiet. A late January afternoon in Laguna Beach was the best time to enjoy the pretty little town, with its shady streets and picturesque views. In summertime, southern California's beach communities were overcrowded and perpetually traffic-jammed, but in winter, the locals remembered why they lived there.

Russo finally looked back at her. "I'm here for the same reason as you, actually. I'm following up on the murder of my partner."

It was Hannah's turn to be taken aback. "What happened?"

"We were in a shoot-out in Compton a couple of weeks ago. We were investigating another murder. The police chopper accidentally flushed out the suspect, he opened fire on us, and things went south fast."

"I read about that. Shooter was a gang member? And he ended up dead, too?"

Russo nodded.

"I'm really sorry about your partner," Hannah said. "But I don't get it. The papers said it was the banger who shot the sheriff's detective who died that night. So, what are you doing here?"

"Like you said, it's complicated."

"There must have been an OIS investigation, no?"

"Yeah, it's still ongoing, matter of fact."

"So you're off-duty."

"Right again."

"That means I'm not the only sketchy operator here."

"I think I resemble that remark. Look," Russo said, "are you hungry? 'Cause something coming out of that kitchen smells pretty good, and from what that movie director over there told me—"

"You talked to him?"

"Yeah, I did. And he said they were trying to get as much footage as possible in the can before they lost the light, which tells me they're probably good over there for another hour or so. You want to have something to eat, maybe compare notes?"

Hannah glanced back at the BMW, but he was probably right. It wasn't going anywhere for a while. And as much as she liked to work independently, she instinctively trusted this Russo, especially now that she knew he was fighting the same guilt demons she was. Or maybe, she thought, it was just that she spent so much time alone....

"Why not?" she said.

34

Thursday, February 3, 2005
Sheriff's Department Homicide Bureau, Los Angeles

Russo was back at his desk on Rickenbacker Road for the first time since the Compton shoot-out. The big, L-shaped homicide squad room was chock-a-block with double rows of desks arranged face-to-face so that detectives could sit opposite their partners. Billy Chen's space had been cleared of his personal possessions and it looked unnaturally tidy amidst the clutter of laptops, cups and coffee-stained papers that covered every other surface in the room.

Russo's OIS investigation had pretty much wrapped and Lieutenant Halloran was scheduled to meet with the sheriff later that day to go over the draft report. Russo had read it. No matter how much Finn Brophy might personally want to see him fry, he was a loyal cop who wouldn't undermine the department by washing dirty linen in public. The report was par for the course—mistakes were made, but the officers in question were in hot pursuit of an armed and dangerous suspect who'd already committed one murder earlier that evening. Given the circumstances, their response had been appropriate.

The operation was a success, even though the patient died.

Barring any unforeseen complications, Halloran said, Russo would back on street rotation as of the following Monday. There was no word yet on who his new partner would be back. Older detectives who'd known him in his dark period were giving him wide berth, no doubt wondering if this incident would prompt another meltdown. Junior guys who might have been eager to learn from someone with Russo's track record for clearing cases were probably thinking twice about it now. Nothing clung like the stink of personal disaster.

While he waited to learn how things would shake out, Russo sat at his desk in the near-empty squad room, catching up on paperwork and doing some personal research on the side. He was logged onto the department's computer database, looking up Farran Alsaqri and his security chief, George Kenner.

He found seven George Kenners with California driver's licenses. Before he could check criminal records to see if the Kenner he was interested in had any priors, he sifted through DMV files to check photographs. He found the guy Hannah Nicks called the White Fox in the third record he examined. No question it was him. As she said when she told Russo about running into him in Iraq two years earlier, the guy's mug was unforgettable. According to the DMV record, Kenner was five-ten, a hundred and sixty-five pounds, and had been born in 1954, which made him fifty-one. His listed address was in Brentwood. Security work must pay well, Russo thought.

Security work. That was Nicks's current line of work, too.

Russo had already taken a look at her DMV record as well. When he saw her date of birth, he decided she was the oldest thirty-year-old he'd ever met. It wasn't so much her physical appearance. Her driver's license picture was one of the few he'd ever seen that didn't look like a mug shot of a serial killer, but that was no great surprise.

Russo doubted she was capable of taking a bad picture, with those warm brown eyes and that face like a Botticelli angel. But in the photo, as in person, she was sober and wary-looking, like someone expecting the knives to come out any minute. He could relate to that.

This George Kenner, though—he was a bit of a mystery. His California Department of Motor Vehicles record was only a few months old. Prior to its recent issuance, there was no trace of him. Nicks had run into him overseas in 2003. Farran Alsaqri, the film director Russo had interviewed, had said Kenner was parachuted into his present position because of Farran's father's security connections in Washington. That being the case, it was probably no surprise the guy seemed to have no past. "George Kenner," Russo would bet, had not been born with that name.

He pulled out his cell phone and ticked through his contact list until he came to the phone number Nicks had given him the day before in Laguna Beach.

She picked up on the second ring. "Hello?"

"It's Russo. Where are you?"

"Burbank. Sitting in a Burger King parking lot across the street from what looks like a warehouse. Kenner's been inside with Alsaqri all morning. A bunch of the people who were on the shoot in Laguna yesterday are in there with them."

"One of Alsaqri's assistants told me yesterday that they were shooting the indoor scenes on a rented sound stage in Burbank."

"That's it, then," Nicks said. "It's a bummer because the place is small. No way I can slip inside to keep an eye on the White Fox. I've got a clear view of the car, though, and it hasn't gone anywhere. I'm just hoping he's not sneaking out any back doors."

"Your bug still working okay?"

"Yup."

"Did you tail him home last night?"

"I did."

"His DMV record says he lives in Brentwood."

"Alsaqri's got a big house there. It looks like Kenner's got a guest cottage on the property."

"Shades of OJ and Kato Kaelin," Russo said.

"Were you able to find anything on Kenner or Alsaqri?"

"Not really. Kenner's DMV record only goes back a few months, and there's nothing on him in any other files I checked. I don't know where he was before he showed up here, but he's got no priors in state or out that I can find. Alsaqri was picked up for DUI a couple of years ago. That was when he was still a student, before his old man was appointed ambassador to Washington, but somebody must have pulled some strings anyway, because no charges were ever filed."

"Nice to have friends in high places."

"I'm just waiting to talk to the detectives working Damon Shipley's and my partner's murder, see if they've found out anything else that might link back to that movie bunch."

"Shipley's the kid who was working for Farran Alsaqri?"

"Yup."

"I'm gonna—hang on," Nicks said suddenly. "I've got another call coming in. I'd better take it."

"No problem."

"Let me know if you find out anything else?"

"Better idea," Russo said, "you let *me* know. I mean it. Don't be winging it out there."

She grunted. It didn't sound like assent to him.

"Gotta go," she said.

"Check in with me later," Russo warned. But he was talking to dead air.

35

Burbank, California

It was Val Underwood on the phone. "Tell me again what you saw at the Staples Center," she said, after Hannah explained how she was sitting outside the sound stage where Farran Alsaqri was shooting his flick.

"Why? What's going on?"

"Just humor me. You said you saw your White Fox with a couple?"

"That's right. The guy was short, balding, maybe a few years younger than Kenner."

"Kenner?"

"George Kenner. That's the White Fox's name," Hannah said. "At least, the name he's going by these days. Mind you, if that's this scuzzbucket's real name, I'll eat my flak jacket."

"And you found his name out how?"

"Reliable source. Ever run into a sheriff's department detective named Russo?"

"Yeah, sure. John Russo, homicide. He's a good guy."

"Is he a good cop?"

"One of the best. Most of the time, anyway."

"Most of the time? What does that mean?"

"He went through a rough patch a couple of years back."

"How so?"

Underwood sighed. "His wife and baby died."

"Oh, God." Hannah felt the bottom drop out of her stomach. She'd spent only an hour or so with Russo the day before, but he'd struck her as one of the straighter shooters she'd run into in a while. She found herself almost trusting the guy, which was saying a lot considering the fact that ever since Cal, she'd been walking around feeling like a third-degree burn victim where men were concerned. And no matter what Russo was about, nobody should ever, ever have to lose a child.

"What happened?" she asked Val.

"Circumstances were kind of murky. I think both deaths were finally ruled accidental, but apparently it could have been a murder-suicide. The whole thing was such a tragedy, I think the coroner cut the family a little slack, especially since Russo's on the job. Not that the coroner's ruling did anything to lighten the load of guilt the poor guy's carried around ever since."

"How did they die?"

"The baby suffocated. She was just a couple of months old. I think the coroner's report concluded that Russo's wife had been nursing her in bed, maybe fell asleep and rolled over on her."

"And his wife?"

"Drug overdose. Tranquilizers or something. That might have had something to do with why the baby died."

"She passed out while she was nursing the baby?"

"Maybe. The timeline was a little unclear. She might have overdosed after she realized the baby was dead."

"You said it could've been a murder-suicide. Does that mean there's a chance she deliberately suffocated the baby?"

"I wasn't working with Russo at the time, and I've never talked to him about it, but from what I heard, she might have been suffering from postpartum depression. It's possible she snapped and killed the baby, but they say it was a tough call, so the coroner came down on the side of accidental death."

"And Russo? Where was he when all this happened?"

"Working, of course. Why else do so many cop marriages end up as train wrecks? It was around the time of the Malibu Strangler. You were off the job by then, so I don't know if you remember what it was like."

"Oh, yeah. The whole city was up in arms."

"Was it ever. Russo was one of the lead detectives, so of course he was working around the clock. His wife hadn't been living in L.A. very long, so it wasn't like she had family or friends around for support. Poor thing was all alone with a new baby and—well, you know how that can be. Anyway, it was Russo who found them. The baby was dead, like I say. His wife was still alive, barely, when he found her, but she was DOA by the time the ambulance got to the E.R. John buried them, then went into a tailspin. It just about wrecked his career."

Hannah shook her head. "Poor guy. Nothing more toxic than guilt."

"You got that right."

"But he's okay now?"

"From what I hear. He and Lou Halloran are real tight. Halloran got him into a program, finally helped him straighten up and fly right."

"Russo was in that firefight in Compton a couple of weeks ago, did you know?"

Underwood sighed. "Yeah, I heard. Bummer. He needed that like a hole in the head. I hear he comes out okay in the OIS report though. Anyway," she said, "you and he crossed paths on this White Fox business? How did that happen?"

"I ran into him after I located Kenner." Hannah decided not to tell Val about the tracking device Russo had caught her planting on Kenner's car. "I'd followed up that license plate info you gave me. Kenner works for Farran Alsaqri. They were on a film shoot down in Laguna Beach, and that's where Russo and I met up. He was chasing down some leads, too."

"Russo was? I'd have thought he was on administrative leave after the Compton thing."

"He is, but it turns out there's a link between the Compton business and Farran Alsaqri. Russo and his partner had been called out on a murder investigation that night, and the murdered kid, it turns out, also worked for Farran."

"Get outta here. And your White Fox?"

"He's Alsaqri's bodyguard. Farran told Russo that the guy came to him by way of his father's diplomatic security contacts in Washington."

"Weirder and weirder."

"What's going on, Val? Why were you asking about what I saw at the Staples Center the other night?"

"You really need to come and work for me, you know," Underwood said. "I so need another pair of hands and eyes I can trust. There's this massive federal machine I'm supposed to be liaising with. It's a nightmare. Their definition of information sharing is for me to tell them everything I know and for them to reciprocate with precisely nothing. Plus, with a couple of notable exceptions, the people they've got on the ground here are not exactly the brightest crayons in the box. L.A.'s a Tier 2 threat in their grand scheme of things, well behind New York and D.C. Even San Francisco and Chicago get more money and manpower. Those cities get the cream, we get skim milk. I don't even want to think about what it must be like dealing with the clowns the feds must have in Minneapolis or New Orleans."

"So if some terrorist wanted to launch a full-scale attack, those would be the places to put it together, huh?"

"For sure. I'm telling you, kiddo, I could really use your BS detector to help me navigate this swamp."

"Yeah, yeah." Hannah could hear a faint drumming sound in the background. "You're doing that tapping thing with your pencil again, Val. What's going on?"

"I pulled the security tapes from the night you were at the Staples Center. I got curious about who was using Farran Alsaqri's skybox the night you spotted your White Fox, since we know the little prince himself was out of town attending his father's presentation of credentials ceremony. We managed to zero in on his box and I got a good look at that couple who were with your guy. I recognized the man, and I'd sure like to know what he, of all people, was doing there."

"Who is he?"

"You wouldn't believe it if I told you."

"You know what, Val? At this point, I've lost the capacity to be surprised by anything," Hannah said. "Try me."

36

Old Executive Office Building, Washington, D.C.

Dick Stern stood at his window. Snowflakes like swan feathers were wafting down, turning the late afternoon capital into a fairyland scene of sparkling streets, wedding cake buildings and pristine white lawns. The deputy national security advisor was unmoved. He clenched the phone receiver like some small animal he was intent on strangling. Stern was not happy. Not happy at all.

"When I agreed to bring you in from the cold—"

"The cold?" On the other end of the line, George Kenner snorted. "That godforsaken desert hellhole I was stuck in?"

"You had adequate hardship pay, as I recall. I didn't hear you complaining about that burgeoning Swiss bank account of yours."

"I earn my fee, Mr. Stern."

"That's debatable."

"And after seventeen years of loyal service, I think it was time for a less punishing assignment, don't you? I'm not that young warrior you recruited. Neither of us is."

"And the world isn't what it was then, either, may I remind you, but I've kept you on anyway. You've had a good long run." A run that could end at any time, Stern thought.

In 1988, Stern had been a covert CIA operative in Afghanistan supplying the *mujaheddin* resistance to that country's Soviet invaders. One day, when his Afghan clients reported capturing a Russian civilian, Stern prevailed upon them to hand the man over. The Russian, Stern discovered as he proceeded to debrief the prisoner, spoke near perfect, idiomatic American English, the kind perfected in the infamous "charm school" where the KGB trained its agents. It took weeks of intense interrogation, but eventually the captured Russian broke. His name was Gennady Kirnikov and he was a KGB captain. No surprise there. All that remained was for Stern to capitalize on the opportunity presented by having this Cold War enemy land in his lap.

Kirnikov had already spent three years bogged down in that Afghan hellhole where so many of his compatriots were dying miserable deaths. He was primed to be turned, Stern decided, if the man could "escape" and return to his masters in Moscow. Kirnikov wasn't stupid. Working as a CIA double agent inside the KGB would profit him financially and, more important, provide some insurance against a possible shift in fortunes for the USSR.

It didn't take a genius to see that the Afghan misadventure was turning into the Soviet Union's final death knell. Sure enough, a year later, beaten and humiliated, the Russians slunk away from Afghanistan. That year, as well, the Berlin Wall fell. The Soviet bloc crumbled soon after, and by the early nineties, Lenin's great experiment was over.

But when the Soviet Union died and the Cold War ended with America the victor, Kirnikov's usefulness as a double agent was in question. Since the man had good language skills and was ruthless in the field, however, Stern decided he could make use of him elsewhere. When Stern himself left the CIA and moved on to more deeply buried functions with the U.S. intelligence community, he retained control of Kirnikov. The Russian had turned into a most useful asset, Stern's own personal pit bull. Reborn as Canadian mercenary "George Kenner," Kirnikov had gone on to carry out a series of unsavory missions abroad, ops known only to his master and a very select few in Washington intelligence circles.

"I brought you to the States on the understanding you were to keep a low profile," Stern told him. "That's what Ambassador Alsaqri wanted, and as they say, whatever Lola wants, Lola gets."

Stern had long ago pegged Prince Mohammed Alsaqri as someone to cultivate, a figure of potentially enormous influence within his oil-rich kingdom. Saudi Arabia had $600 billion deposited in U.S. banks and massive investments here as well, all financed by this country's insatiable hunger for those vast oil reserves. It was pathetic, Stern thought, that America actually paid the Saudis to hold its economy hostage, but by now the desert kingdom was far too critical to U.S. economic health to be taken for granted. If part of keeping Saudi Arabia happy was keeping Prince Alsaqri happy, then Stern would make it happen.

The prince's appointment as his country's next ambassador to Washington had been announced a few months earlier. Immediately, his children in the U.S. were assigned Secret Service bodyguards. It was an unusual step but one that was warranted for this most valued of partners. Out in Los Angeles, however, young Farran rebelled.

"Cheap-suited heavies," Farran called the bodyguards. He didn't want them dogging his every step, even if his father saw the value in it. The ambassador prevailed upon his old friend Dick Stern to make different arrangements for Farran. Since Kirnikov/Kenner was also agitating to be allowed to leave the field and move to the States, Stern decided to kill two birds with one stone.

"Protecting Farran and keeping your head down was what I stipulated as a condition of arranging your immigration visa," Stern reminded him.

"I can see him as we speak," Kenner said. "He seems to be in very good health."

"Why am I getting reports that people are asking questions about you?"

"What people?"

The man sounded smug, Stern thought irritably, like he didn't realize the precariousness of his situation. Stern had set him up in that cushy post and he could rip it away just as easily. Kenner might know where the bodies were buried—literally—but he was hardly Stern's only asset, and he could be un-recruited just as quickly as he'd been recruited. Permanently un-recruited. The man was delusional if he thought he was in a position to be cocky.

"Never mind *what* people," Stern said sharply. "These things get back to me. What the hell have you been doing out there?"

"Babysitting your princeling, nothing more, I assure you."

"So why is the Los Angeles Sheriff's Department making inquiries about you?"

"The sheriff's—? Oh, yes, the detective. He came out to Farran's film set on the beach the other day."

"What did he want?"

Kenner snorted. "This princeling's not just some Saudi playboy with Hollywood wet dreams, you know. It turns out he's a liberal do-gooder. Thinks he's going to save the world, one ghetto kid at a time."

"What are you talking about?"

"Farran hired a black kid from the inner city. Made him his personal assistant. But you know how they say you can't teach an old dog new tricks? Turns out the young ones are not so trainable, either. Once a gangbanger, always a gangbanger."

"What happened?"

"The kid got himself gunned down by a rival on his home turf. The police tracked down the shooter, but by the time the dust settled, both the killer and a cop were dead."

"Great, a cop killing. How did your name come into all this?"

"The detective, as I said, came to talk to Farran about the murdered boy. I suppose Farran must have told him I handled his security."

"They don't think you had anything to do with it, do they?"

"What motive would I have to kill some ghetto punk?"

"Did this detective talk to you, too?"

"Briefly. I ran into him as the crew was breaking down the set."

"And...?" Stern pressed.

"And nothing. I told him the boy had been employed as a junior assistant. None too reliable, as it turned out, but what would you expect? By the time we heard he'd been murdered, he'd already stopped showing up for work."

"And that's it?"

"That's it," Kenner said.

"I want to know immediately if anything more develops, do you understand?"

"Absolutely."

Stern hung up the phone without bothering to say goodbye. Then he stood, frowning at the placid winter scene outside his window. The Russian was an accomplished liar. It was only one of the reasons he'd proven so useful all these years. But Stern had a finely tuned threat detector and it was humming loudly now.

Before he made any decisions, he would make a few more inquiries. Then, he would consider his options. It might just be time to finally pull the plug on "George Kenner."

Kenner gritted his teeth at the sound of dead air in his earpiece. But then, as he snapped his cell phone shut, an image of his aged mother suddenly came to mind—strange, since she'd been dead for over thirty years. Raised on a collective farm on the Ukrainian steppes, she used to have a saying: *"Today a rooster, tomorrow a feather duster."*

Few roosters strutted as proudly as Dick Stern. Tomorrow would see those tail feathers plucked but good.

He tucked the cell phone away in his pocket and glanced across the vast Burbank sound stage. Farran was talking to the actors while the crew set up a shot. The Saudi princeling was dressed in torn jeans, a burgundy sweatshirt that was already faded when he bought it at one of those West L.A. grunge boutiques he favored, and a pair of three-hundred-dollar sneakers—an obscenely rich boy masquerading as one of the guys.

Farran worked long hours, allowing himself few distractions besides his adoring girlfriend, a blonde he'd met at USC, and his Lakers basketball games. The blonde ran a poor third to the movie business and the Lakers. The young mogul's perpetual distraction had worked to Kenner's decided advantage.

Farran employed a business manager for his film production company, a doughy, bespectacled woman named Wanda. Three weeks earlier, Wanda's mother had taken an unfortunate tumble down the long front staircase of her Boston town house. She had ended up with a badly broken leg, but she'd been lucky not to have killed herself, everyone agreed. How regrettable that she hadn't noticed the slick, clear silica spray that an associate of Kenner had applied to the top step. The old woman thought she'd hit a patch of ice. Luckily, she was expected to make a full recovery. In the meantime, Farran had given Wanda time off at full pay to care for her mother, just as Kenner had calculated he would. The little prince was nothing if not generous with his employees.

Farran was a modern young man in every way, certainly not

given to superstition. If he were, he might have seen it as a bad omen that another, more tragic misfortune had befallen one of his staffers hard on the heels of Wanda's mother's accident.

The murder of Damon Shipley happened the following week. That, too, had been the handiwork, indirectly at least, of Kenner and his deep-pocketed associates, who knew just how to find an inner-city cutout to do their dirty work. Kenner's associates had a veritable army of Crips, Bloods and other gangbangers on their speed dials. America's underclass was the superpower's Achilles' heel, ready to be exploited by those who knew what they were doing. Senseless killings committed by gang members were so common that the police had little incentive to spend much time investigating them or looking too deeply into their true motives.

Of course, Kenner hadn't planned on taking out Damon Shipley. That part of the operation had been a bit of ad hoc damage control. It was the brat's own fault for snooping where he had no business.

Kenner had thought he had all the bases covered when he got Wanda out of the way. Normally, the office manager was the only one to occasionally use Farran's personal computer, transferring funds from his bank to the film company's production accounts and watching for e-mails that suppliers sometimes erroneously sent to Farran instead of to her. Farran rarely spent much time on the machine. Once a film started shooting, he was too preoccupied even to check his e-mail, but Wanda could be counted on to keep him organized. Kenner, however, had need of Farran's computer, and he didn't need Wanda becoming suspicious of the tracks he planned to lay down there.

His plans were proceeding well until the day before filming was to begin on Farran's latest project. That day, cast and crew were at Farran's Culver City offices. Some plot detail was needed for a scene he planned to shoot later that week. Farran asked Damon Shipley to get online and research jewelers in Marseilles.

The director was working with the lead actors and a dialogue coach in a boardroom down the hall when Damon started surfing the Net in Farran's office. When the boy didn't return after an hour, Kenner started to worry. It shouldn't have taken him that long to get the information. Farran didn't need his assistant while the dialogue coach was there, and Damon would have known that, but Kenner didn't like the idea of the kid spending so much time fooling around on the computer—not when he himself had already started planting a trail of evidence on it that painted Farran Alsaqri as an Al Qaeda sleeper, a terrorist-in-waiting.

After the dust settled, it would seem that the young Saudi's film business had been nothing but a cover, a way to justify his presence in L.A. as he awaited orders to launch a bloody suicide attack. If everything went according to plan, the apparent suicide bombing that Kenner would orchestrate would result in hundreds of deaths right in the beating heart of the city.

The information on Farran's computer—e-mails, a Web sites-visited history, financial records—was only part of the extensive digital and physical evidence of the young prince's supposed treachery that had been planted by Kenner in anticipation of the big event. A bright kid like Damon Shipley, stumbling onto the computer evidence, would have found the cyber trail frightening enough without knowing anything of the guns, C-4 explosive and other equipment Kenner was laying in. All of it was accompanied by a paper trail that led straight back to the son of the Saudi ambassador.

Kenner hadn't thought it possible for a kid with skin as dark as Damon's to visibly blanch, but when he slipped down the hall that day to peek into Farran's office, the boy's face left no doubt that he'd stumbled across at least some of the planted trail. Startled, the boy said nothing, not even when Kenner subtly pumped him about what he'd been up to in the office all that time. Damon just hurried back to Farran and the others and said nothing. His nervousness, however, spoke volumes, and Kenner knew the kid would have to be eliminated.

He was taking no chances, not when the plan was so close to realization. He kept an eye on the boy for the rest of the day and ordered up round-the-clock surveillance on him when he left the building. They bugged the kid's house and phone, and even tailed his mother and younger brother. Damon never did return to work, although the only thing the listening devices heard him tell his mother was that he wasn't going back because Farran and his associates were bad people. That mother of his was a tough customer, though. Kenner knew it was only a matter of time before she got her son to spill his guts. Damon Shipley had to go, but in a way that no one would connect back to Farran—at least not before Farran, too, was as dead as the victims of the "suicide bombing" that would be the Saudi princeling's final production.

37

Friday, February 4, 2005
Los Angeles Sheriff's Department Homicide Bureau

Russo was at his desk, tidying, catching up on the kind of paperwork he usually avoided as he prepared to return to active duty rotation the following Monday. The squad room was quiet, only one pair of detectives on hand, running telephone leads on a case from the previous night's shift. The teams on ups position on this evening's roster were out getting food. They could have stayed home, waiting to be called in, but Friday nights were always busy, so it made more sense to hang out in the squad room until the dead sheet came down the pipeline. On-call detectives ate when they could, not when they were hungry. Once a "body found" call came in, there was no telling when they'd have another opportunity.

Russo's fervent hope was that Lou Halloran would decide they were short-handed and send Russo out on a case that night, not wait for the following week. Russo didn't even have a new partner yet, but he wanted to be working. It was the best way to avoid thinking—about guilt, about loneliness, about having a drink or smoking a joint to dull the gnawing in his gut. A gnawing that had nothing to do with hunger and everything to do with regret.

Three long days until Monday…

He was just debating going into Halloran's office to shoot the breeze, drop some hints about speeding things up, when his cell phone rang. When he heard the voice on the other end, another kind of thrumming bit into him.

"Hannah," he said. "What's up? Where are you?"

"Sitting in my car outside Farran Alsaqri's house in Brentwood."

Russo pictured her in that silly little gray Prius. Pictured those dark curls he'd had an urge to touch the other day in Laguna Beach, just to see if they felt as soft as they looked. Thought about deep brown eyes a guy could lose himself in. What a putz.

"Sorry," she said. "Is this a bad time?"

"No, I'm just twiddling my thumbs here, trying to look busy."

"I heard your OIS wrapped."

"Where'd you hear that?"

"A friend. Val Underwood," she added. "Sorry, I'm not trying to be mysterious. I don't mean to pry into your business."

"It's okay. It's public record. Or will be, for the most part, anyway. So, how's Val? I haven't seen her since she was named chief of liaising with paranoid spooks."

"She's fine."

"She a friend of yours?"

"The best. I had lunch with her yesterday. I mentioned I'd run into you and that you were nice enough not to blow my cover when you caught me planting that bug on Kenner's car."

Russo felt his face go warm, and he glanced around, hoping no one was noticing. Nicks thought he was nice. Foolish woman.

"Actually," she added, "I didn't tell her about the GPS device. No point in compromising the entire department."

"Val's good people," Russo said. "So, is your White Fox still there with Farran Alsaqri?"

"Yeah. I can see him through the gate. I don't think he strays too far from the boy director. Kenner just came out of the guest house. He and Farran are hanging by Farran's Mercedes. I think they're waiting for Farran's girlfriend. She was outside watching for them when they first got back from the studio. I got the impression they were supposed to be going somewhere and she was getting antsy."

"You going to tail them?"

"Maybe. I was debating whether I should try to get inside Kenner's cottage, take a look around."

Russo pushed back on his rolling chair. "Nicks, you do realize I'm a cop, right?"

"Yeah, and you know I'm not a thief. I figure I can use you as a character reference if I get arrested."

"Dream on, girl."

"There's a Lakers game tonight," she said.

"Yeah?"

"Yeah, my son and his dad are going."

Thunk. She had a family. Russo felt more than a little disappointed to hear it. Sure brought a guy's daydreams down to earth. He glanced up. Lou Halloran had just come in the door. The lieutenant walked over to the detectives working the phones across the room. Maybe he could corner Halloran, have that talk about coming back to work before Monday.

"So anyway," Nicks said, "I'm thinking these guys are going to the basketball game. That Staples Center skybox where I saw Kenner last week? Turns out it's Farran's season box. Given your interest in these guys, I was wondering…"

"Wondering what?"

"Well, I haven't got a ticket, and all the Laker games are sold out these days. There's always the scalpers, I suppose, but I'd just as soon not part with a couple of hundred bucks of my hard-earned money."

Russo caught the lieutenant's eye and he got to his feet. "Yeah, those scalpers sure earn their rep. Look—"

"I was wondering if you'd consider meeting me at the Staples Center and badging me inside."

Russo sat back down. "You want me to what?"

"Show your shield and walk me through the gate. You could say I was your partner and we're working a case. Or a witness, and we're trying to ID a suspect. If you're not busy."

Across the squad room, Halloran's cell phone rang. Flipping it open, the lieutenant headed back out the door, nodding distractedly to Russo as he passed.

Russo considered his options. He could sit at his desk all night, enduring awkward but scrupulously polite comments from busier detectives, who were treating him these days much as they had after Sarah and the baby died—like he had some vaguely communicable plague. He could hang out with an attractive but apparently unavailable woman who was obsessed, like some damn fool female Don Quixote, with a hopeless mission to avenge her lost partner. Or he could go back to his empty apartment. (Calling the place "home" would be a gross misnomer.) That last option struck him as the most masochistic of all.

What did people with actual lives do on a Friday night? Damned if he could remember.

"I'll meet you at the Staples Center in an hour," he told Nicks.

38

Staples Center, Los Angeles

Kenner followed Farran and his girlfriend, Irene, through the Staples Center VIP entrance. At the base of the escalators, they showed the passes that allowed season-long access to Farran's suite on the middle of the three skybox levels.

Thanks to the deputy national security advisor, Kenner also carried ID that allowed him and his charges to bypass security screenings. He had a permit for the gun he carried, so he would have had no concerns on that score, but the other items he'd brought along that evening would not have passed muster so easily. Dick Stern would be mortified to learn that his security arrangements allowed this stuff to get through unnoticed.

Irene and Farran, arm in arm, started up the escalator. Kenner hiked up his shoulder bag and stepped on behind them. Irene looked over her shoulder and grinned at him. She had blue eyes the size of Dresden china plates and lips like spring roses.

"George? Are you planning to move into the place?"

"Sorry?"

"That bag. It looks like you're taking up residence."

The soft Italian leather tote bag was one that had originally belonged to Farran, but he'd given it to Kenner a couple of months ago when his bodyguard needed something for a weekend trip to Aspen, where Farran had planned to get in a little skiing.

"Just some reading I'm catching up on," Kenner said. "I'm not a big fan of basketball."

"Ah, I see," she said, prettily tossing her long blond hair. "Well, it looks like you brought half a library. You must be a fast reader."

"You had me fooled, George," Farran said. "I never pegged you for a reader."

"You'd be surprised to know some of my interests, Mr. Farran."

"I'll have to put you to work reading those scripts people send me. You must be bored to tears hanging around the set all day long."

"Not at all. I find it endlessly fascinating."

They stepped off the escalator, rode up one more level, then headed down the hall toward Farran's skybox suite. Despite the sellout crowd, there were very few people on this level. Thick carpets muffled noise from the basketball court, and soft lights and furnished alcoves made the place feel more like a luxury hotel than a sports arena.

As Kenner opened the door to Farran's skybox, the noise of the crowd drifted in from the open side of the suite overlooking the basketball court. Savory smells of roast beef wafted out to greet them. When he spotted someone inside the box, Kenner held out his arm to prevent Farran and Irene from entering until he had checked it out. His free hand instinctively went to the gun under his jacket.

A man in a waiter's white coat stood at the buffet that ran along one full side of the suite, his back to them. A spread of appetizers, breads, meat, salads and desserts, enough food to feed an orphanage, was arrayed on the buffet. The young Hispanic man turned at the sound of the opening door, and Kenner noted a long, gleaming carving knife in his hand. A platter before him held a small roast surrounded by greens and tiny red tomatoes.

"Good evening, lady…gentlemen," the waiter said, smiling. "Welcome."

"I'll take that, thank you," Kenner said, stepping up and taking the carving knife from his hand.

"But I need it to carve the meat," the waiter protested.

"I don't think so." Kenner waved his charges in.

Farran walked by the waiter without acknowledging him, but when Irene unleashed her high-wattage smile, the fellow blushed. Kenner set the leather bag down on the floor beside an upholstered armchair. The suite held a couple of deep chairs, a sofa and a coffee table. A long bar at the far end overlooked the arena, while tall stools arranged along the bar allowed guests to eat comfortably while they watched the game. Beyond the bar area was a tiered bank of private seats, twenty-four in all. Farran often treated a gang of friends to his box at the Staples Center, but this time out, after working all week, dealing with the pressures of his job, cast and crew, he'd decided to bring just his girlfriend and bodyguard.

Actually, ditching the coterie of hangers-on had been Kenner's suggestion, the better to implement his plan, but Farran, exhausted, had quickly latched onto the idea of a little solitude and made it his own. How very accommodating of him, Kenner thought.

"I'll carve the roast," Kenner told the waiter. He reached into his pocket, pulled out a twenty and handed it over. "You can go. I'll call if Mr. Farran needs anything else."

"Yes, sir. Thank you very much, sir," the waiter said, bowing as he backed toward the door. "There's a buzzer on the wall here. Just push it and I'll get whatever you need."

Testing the keenness of the blade, Kenner watched the waiter open the door and scoot out into the hall. As the door closed silently behind him, Kenner turned back to the suite. Irene was in front of the minifridge, checking out the contents.

"Farran? Honey?" she called. "What would you like to drink?"

He was already on one of the bar stools, watching the arena, where the game was just about to get underway. "I'll take a beer," he said without looking back.

Not a very good Muslim, Kenner thought, not for the first time. Not that he cared. In fact, at the moment, it made his job easier. "I'll get it," he told the girl. "What can I get for you?"

"Hmm…" She was rummaging in the fridge. "Ah, good!" She pulled out a split of Dom Perignon. "Would you mind?" she asked sweetly, holding up the champagne.

"With pleasure," Kenner said. "Something to eat?"

"Not right now, thanks. Honey?" she called to Farran. "Do you want me to fix a plate for you?"

"I'll get something later," he said.

Kenner took the champagne and Irene went over and perched on a stool beside Farran, draping an arm around his shoulder. Watching the basketball players bound onto the court below as their names were called, the director absentmindedly stroked her back. Kenner watched as his hand settled on her lovely, blue-jeaned butt.

Turning back to the minibar, Kenner withdrew a bottle of Heineken. After popping the cork on the Dom Perignon and uncapping the beer, he took a champagne flute and a beer stein from over the bar. Then, he paused and glanced back at the couple, but they were absorbed in the Lakers and themselves. Kenner fingered a vial in his pocket, debating whether this was the right moment. Not yet, he decided. There was no rush. Better to wait until everyone was well relaxed and engrossed in the game. Still, he exchanged the beer stein for a smaller glass so that Farran would be ready for a refill that much sooner. Kenner filled the glasses and walked them over.

Farran nodded.

"Thank you," Irene said. "Are you going to have something, George?"

Kenner shook his head. "Better not. Driving, you know."

"Very conscientious of you," Irene said. "Lucky us, hey, honey?" The couple tapped their glasses together, turning back to the court.

Kenner nearly smiled. Drink up, children. Enjoy what little time you have left.

As some pop singer came onto the hardwood court, microphone in hand, and proceeded to massacre "The Star Spangled Banner," most of the audience got to its feet.

Listening to the lyrics of the national anthem, Kenner glanced back at the bag he'd parked in the corner, and he allowed himself a small smile. The rockets' red glare, indeed. And bombs bursting in air? How apt. How very, very apt.

39

Hannah was pacing the floor in front of the Staples Center VIP entrance, trying to ignore the glances of the security guards manning the doors. The looks they were giving her had started out innocent enough, but they seemed to be degenerating. One guy offered himself rather rudely as an alternate to the date who'd apparently stood her up. She considered offering him an alternate way of looking at the world—from flat on his back and through two black eyes.

She glanced at her watch. When they'd spoken on the phone, Russo had said he'd meet her there in an hour. It was twenty minutes past that, but he wasn't the only tardy arrival. The roads into the neighborhood around the Staples Center were heavily congested. Angelenos were forever arriving late to events, victims of the city's perpetually gridlocked freeway system. Friday was the worst rush hour night of the week.

Hannah had tailed the Mercedes driven by Kenner all the way from Brentwood, watching Farran and his girlfriend canoodle in the back seat. On arrival at the Staples Center, the Benz had entered a parking lot reserved for VIPs. By the time Hannah found a spot in one of the gargantuan lots reserved for the common rabble and then made it over to the building, the White Fox and company were nowhere to be seen.

She glanced at her watch once more. She was just debating whether to call Russo to check on his progress when she heard a shout and a hurtling body coming from behind nearly knocked her off her feet.

"Boo!"

Regaining her balance, she turned into the skinny-armed bear hug of her mischievous son. "Gabe! You little monster, you nearly gave me a heart attack." But she was laughing as she wrapped her own arms around him. "Let me give you a big smooch."

Since he was allowing her to hold him and even kiss him, Hannah knew Gabe's friends couldn't possibly be within a couple of light years of the Staples Center tonight. Finally, though, he wriggled away.

"What are you doing here?" he asked.

"Working. I was hoping I might run into you."

Gabe looked around. "You're working? Who you guarding?"

"Nobody. Just doing some fact-finding. Where's your dad?"

"He's coming."

Gabe pointed back toward the parking structure across a narrow roadway, the same VIP lot that Farran's Mercedes had entered. Cal was just crossing over the road, a frown creasing his handsome face.

"I saw you as soon as we came out of the garage," Gabe told her. "I wanted to sneak up and surprise you."

"Well, you got me good."

"Hannah? What are you doing here?" Cal came up alongside them. "Been stood up?"

"Cute," Hannah said.

"Mom's on an investigation," Gabe told his father.

"Really? What are you investigating?"

Hannah shrugged. "Can't say. Client confidentiality. You know how that is. Where's Christie tonight?"

"Home," Cal said. "She's pretty tired from the pregnancy these days, especially with getting up so early for her news shift down at the station. I'm trying to get her to quit. It's not like we need the money."

"Tell her I said hi," Hannah said. She turned back to her son. "That cute little tush of yours warming the Laker bench tonight?"

"Nah," Gabe said. "We're sitting way up in a skybox with one of Dad's clients."

"Hey, plenty of people would love to watch a game from a skybox," Cal said.

"That's true," Hannah agreed. She was tempted to ask which depraved, grateful client was wining and dining Cal tonight, but she'd sworn to herself she wouldn't snipe at him in front of their son.

"I'd still rather be down on the floor," Gabe said. Then, looking past Hannah, he did a double take. His adorable forehead puckered. "Mom? Do you know that man over there?"

Hannah turned. John Russo had apparently just come around the corner of the building, but he was hanging back. He looked as if he were trying to decide whether to stay or flee.

"Hey, you made it," she said.

"Yeah, sorry I'm late," he said, approaching. "There was an accident on the 5 freeway."

"No problem. I think the game's just about to get underway. Gabe, this is Detective Russo from the L.A. Sheriff's Department. My son, Gabriel," she added to Russo.

Russo held out his hand. Gabe shook it, eyeing the detective curiously.

"And this is his dad," Hannah added, waving a desultory hand in Cal's direction.

As Russo looked up, his face underwent a subtle transformation, while Cal looked bemused. "Detective Russo and I have met," he said, thrusting out his own hand.

Russo hesitated a second before taking it. "Counselor."

Cal looked from Russo to Hannah and back again, apparently enjoying some private joke. Hannah had no idea what it was about, but it was all very annoying.

"You guys should probably head in or you'll miss the game," she told Gabe, ignoring her ex for fear her noble personal resolutions would go by the board.

"Your mom's right," Cal said. "She and Detective Russo have their extremely important investigation to get on with." He said it like it amounted to a search for a lost cat.

"Are you still coming to my game tomorrow, Mom?"

"Absolutely," she said.

"Great," Gabe said. "Bye, Detective."

"Bye, Gabe. Nice to meet you." Russo's smile faded as he nodded curtly at Hannah's ex.

As her son and his father headed into the building, Hannah watched them go. Then she stood for a moment, eyes closed, waiting for her frustration to depart as well.

"You okay?"

She opened her eyes. "Yeah, I guess. Sorry about that."

"Nothing to be sorry about."

"You and Cal have met before?"

Russo nodded. "In the courtroom. He was defending someone I'd arrested. A murder case."

"Figures. From his smug look, I'm guessing he got the guy off?"

"Yup. Unfortunately, I helped him do it."

"What happened?"

"Oh, I was pretty much decimated on the stand. Let's say it

wasn't my finest hour. Or my finest week," Russo added. "Or month or year, for that matter."

The silence hung between them like a curtain. "Was that after your wife and baby died?"

He seemed taken aback. "You know about that?"

"Val told me you went through a rough time. I'm so sorry."

"Val was being way too generous," Russo said. "I was an obnoxious jerk after it happened—and that was on a really good day. I let down a lot of people. Maybe worst of all, I let down the job. That guy your ex was defending, for example? No way he would have gotten off if I'd done my job right."

"Well, Cal has a talent for bringing out the worst in a lot of people, I find."

"When you mentioned your son on the phone…"

"Yeah?"

Russo colored. "I guess I thought you were remarried. I didn't realize you and Nicks had a child."

"Yup, we do. Believe me, it's the only reason I'm still walking around with his name."

"Gabe seems like a real nice kid. A little older than I expected, though. What were you, like, twelve when you had him?"

She laughed. "Oh, yeah. Practically a baby myself. And he is a great kid. So terrific, in fact, that it's hard to believe he's related to Cal."

"You're obviously doing a great job with him."

Again, one of those awkward silences.

Russo grimaced. "I just said something wrong, didn't I?"

"No. It's just that I can't really take the credit for Gabe. I'm not raising him, except on weekends and alternate holidays. He lives with Cal and his wife. Not my choice, believe me, but there it is. I'm just stumbling along, trying to make the best of a bad situation."

"Oh. Sorry."

She sighed. "Yup. Well, there you go. You're sorry, I'm sorry, we're both sorry about a lot of things. Now, what do you say you talk us through the door here and we find out what Farran and the White Fox are up to?"

"Check."

They started toward the entrance, but after a couple of steps, Russo stopped. "Umm…hey, Hannah?"

"What?"

"Before we drop the subject, can I ask one more thing?"

"What's that?"

"Are you remarried…or…anything? Engaged? Committed? Anything like that?"

"Who wants to know?"

He shrugged. "Inquiring minds. For the record, that's all."

She pressed her lips together, determined not to smile. "Well, then, for the record," she said, "no, I'm not married or engaged. Committed? Yeah, I probably *should* be committed. I can think of a few people who'd attest to that. But no, not that either. Okay?"

"Okay."

"Good. Now, you want to talk us in here?"

Russo was feeling inexplicably cheerful as they left the security guards behind and headed for the stands inside the arena. Hannah had suggested they enter on the ground level from the same side where she'd sat the previous week so she could relocate Farran's box.

"I brought some binocs," she said, pulling a miniature pair out of an inside pocket in the padded down vest she was wearing over a black turtleneck and jeans. As she withdrew the binoculars, Russo noted a shoulder holster under the vest.

"Have you got a carry permit for that?"

"Of course. But why do you think I wanted your help getting in here? I could probably have bluffed my way past those clowns at the door, but I didn't think I'd make it past the security scanners without having to submit to a search. Things might have gotten a little complicated."

"I feel so used."

"Cry me a river. Come on, it's down this way. We were sitting beside the Lakers bench."

"Right on the floor? Well connected, aren't we?"

"Not me. This was Cal and his bosom buddy Keenan Prince's doing."

"Oh, right, I forgot about that. Your boy does have a stellar client list."

"Please. Cal hasn't been 'my boy' since he *was* a boy. I refuse to claim ownership."

As they walked down a hall toward the seating area, someone approached to see their tickets, but Russo flashed his badge again and they were waved through. Inside, they stood at a railing, looking over the court. The Lakers bench was just a few rows in front of them. Hannah's gaze rose and she scouted the skybox levels overhead.

"Val called me back today," she said as she searched for Farran's box. "She pulled the security tapes from the night I saw Kenner here. Farran was in D.C. that day. His father was presenting his credentials at the White House. Kenner, it turns out, was in Farran's box with a guy from the Russian consulate and his wife."

"A Russian?"

"Yup. And what's weirder? A friend of Val's in the FBI's L.A. office said this Russian, who's supposed to be a trade attaché, is actually an intelligence officer. A spy, basically. The FBI's been watching him because he's real cozy with the local Russian *mafiya*— who," she added, "are not my favorite people."

"Why's that?"

"Because it was a wannabe Russian drug czar who blew up my house four years ago. That's when I lost custody of Gabe."

"I worked a case last year where it transpired that some Russian organized crime figures in West Hollywood were linked to a string of murders carried out by Crips brothers they'd recruited to—" Russo smacked his forehead. "Son of a bitch!"

Hannah looked over, startled. "What?"

"The gangbanger who murdered my partner and Damon Shipley? Farran's personal assistant? He was a member of the Crips."

"You told me Damon was afraid to go back to work with Farran because something scared him there. Maybe it wasn't Farran. Maybe it was something Kenner was up to that scared him off." She went back to scanning the skyboxes. "Man, that makes a whole lot of sense."

"Can you see which box it was?"

"It was somewhere up around that Toyota sign."

"Which level?"

"The middle one, I think. Wait, there! I saw a white head, I'm sure of it. In the box over the 'toy' in Toyota. See it?"

"I don't—yeah, okay, got him. He just went back up inside the suite. I see Farran and his girlfriend at the bar."

Nicks was still peering through the binoculars. Suddenly, she cried out.

"What's wrong?" Russo asked.

"Oh, hell, Russo, I see Gabe. He's in the skybox right above Farran's. I don't like this."

"It's okay. They're just watching the game."

Hannah shook her head. "I'm not so sure. Something doesn't feel right here. Come on. Let's get up to that level."

40

"Ready for a refill?" Kenner held up the champagne and Irene extended her flute.

"Mmm, please."

"Mr. Farran? How about you?"

"Is there a bigger glass back there? Or if not, just give me the bottle."

"Let me check."

Kenner took Farran's glass. Back at the minibar he pulled down a beer stein just as a roar went up from the crowd. Farran and the girl had their backs to him, absorbed in the basketball game, and they took no notice as Kenner withdrew the vial from his jacket pocket. Thumbing off the lid, he put a few drops of the clear, colorless liquid into the stein, then emptied the other half of Farran's Heineken into it. Recapping the vial and returning it to his pocket, he carried the stein over to the bar and handed it to the young mogul.

"This is the last half of that bottle of Heineken I opened. Drink up and I'll grab another out of the fridge. You wouldn't want to mix vintages," he added, winking.

"Yeah, right," Farran said, downing it in a couple of swigs. He wiped his mouth and handed the stein back to Kenner. "Never mind the glass. The bottle's okay. Maybe something other than the Heineken this time."

"Not a good vintage, honey?" Irene asked.

Farran shrugged. "I don't know. Tastes a little bitter. Probably just me. Is there a Coors or something in there, George?"

"Let me check." Kenner returned to the minifridge and rummaged around for an American beer. When he turned around again, Farran was getting to his feet.

Irene touched his arm. "What's the matter, babe?"

"I'm going to sit where I can put my feet up. This bar stool is killing my back."

"Poor baby. I'll come with you."

Kenner frowned. He'd really rather they stayed put here in the suite, but there was no point in worrying about it. He could make this work no matter where Farran collapsed. He uncapped a Coors and passed it over to Irene, who took it with her as she followed Farran into the top row of the box's tiered seats.

The drug had had no effect on Farran as yet, but it would soon enough. It was a potent solution of potassium chloride. A moment of excitement was all the drug needed to do its work—a goal scored, a free throw successfully landed. Farran, fanatic that he was, would do his part, excitement throwing his metabolism into overdrive, his pulse rate soaring precipitously. Then, just as suddenly, his heart would seize up and stop beating. Permanently.

It was unlikely, given the general level of frenzy in the arena, that any of the other twenty thousand fans would even notice anything untoward—with the exception of Farran's girlfriend, and Kenner, of course. The drug he'd used to dose Farran was nearly undetectable at autopsy, but Kenner had no worries on that score anyway. Once he remote-detonated the explosives he'd brought up to the suite, there would be little or nothing of Farran Alsaqri left to autopsy.

As for the girl, Kenner had originally planned to spike her drink as well, but the waiter's carving knife had suggested another plan. Improvisation was, after all, the assassin's prerogative. With two different metabolisms in play, there was no calculating whether the drug would kick in at precisely the same time in both targets. When Farran collapsed, however, the girl would be sufficiently preoccupied with him that she wouldn't notice Kenner coming upon her. He'd decided to use his palm blade. The specialized assassin's tool was tailor-made for close kills, swift, silent and deadly.

The basketball game continued down on the floor, lanky players pounding up and down the hardwood, but Farran, exhausted after his long week, seemed to be having trouble working up much of a lather over it. No matter, Kenner thought. Sooner or later something would happen down there to make the princeling's heart go "pitty-pat, pitty-pat, boom!"

He moved back into the suite, keeping one eye on the couple as he began withdrawing supplies from the Italian leather bag he'd carried in—a vest of the sort favored by suicide bombers in the Middle East, its many pockets packed tight with C-4 and nails, the explosive charges wired together and connected to a detonator. There were several extra packages of the moldable C-4, which Kenner readied for packing around the pillars holding the cantilevered section of the skybox and any other load-bearing surfaces he could conveniently locate. He'd also carried in a thick packet of fanatic Islamic and anti-American tracts, including copies of communiqués from Osama bin Laden and a couple of Iraqi insurgent leaders downloaded from the Internet onto Farran's personal computer and printed off at his office. When the skybox exploded, the damning papers would shred and scatter like confetti. Some eager-beaver FBI or Homeland Security type would spend days puzzling them back together, Kenner thought, bemused. Then, it would be an easy enough matter to tie the printouts back to the idiosyncrasies of Farran's office printer.

The fundamentalist rants, together with other evidence Kenner had salted around Farran's home, office and laptop, would leave no doubt that the son of the progressive new Saudi ambassador to Washington was just another Muslim fanatic bent on the annihilation of as many Americans as possible. The people of the United States and their leaders would turn angrily against the ambassador and his country. Saudi Arabia, in turn, would give up trying to appease these demanding, greedy Americans once and for all and begin allying themselves and their vast resources with others. The end of American global domination was at hand.

And Kenner? After seventeen long years pretending to be a traitor to his homeland, all the while working actively on its behalf — playing that arrogant bastard, Dick Stern, for a fool—he was going to pull off this one final operation. After that, "George Kenner" would exist no more. Gennady Kirnikov was going home.

Hannah and Russo rode the escalators to the second skybox level, mounting the steps at a brisk clip, squeezing past stragglers still entering the building. At the middle of the three skybox levels, they barged into a suite opposite Farran Alsaqri's.

"Hey!" someone shouted, as Hannah flew past the suite's startled occupants.

Russo, hard on her heels, held up his oh-so-useful police shield. Hannah ran down to the front of the box's tiered seats, nudging aside a couple of women, ignoring their indignation as she raised her binoculars. She was searching for Kenner, but the first face she landed on was her son's. Gabe was leaning on the railing directly over Farran's box, his rapt attention on the game.

"Oh, God," she murmured.

She lowered her sights and zeroed in on the skybox below him. Farran and his girlfriend had moved down and were sitting in the seats with their feet up on the chair backs in front of them.

"I see Farran and the girl, Russo." She felt him move up beside her.

"Can you see Kenner?"

"No, I don't…wait, there's his white head. He's back in the suite. What's he—"

A sudden tumult erupted in the arena. Startled, Hannah glanced down to the court floor. Keenan Prince had just scored a basket and was high-fiving his fellow Lakers. When she turned her attention back to the box, Farran and the girl, like everyone else in the sold-out crowd, were on their feet, arms outstretched victoriously.

And then, Farran was down.

"Russo!"

"I see it."

It looked as if Farran had dropped to his knees, and then he crumpled over the back of the seat in front of him. The girl was struggling to pull him upright.

Hannah looked left and right. "Was it a rifle?"

Russo leaned out over the railing, checking out the ranks of spectators above and below them. "I can't see a shooter."

A woman in the seat nearest Hannah shrieked. "Oh, my gawd! A shooter? Let me out, let me out!"

Hannah shoved her back into her seat. "Nobody's shooting at you, idiot."

She handed Russo the binoculars and whipped her cell phone out of her pocket. She had to get Gabe out of there. But when she looked at the screen, her heart fell. No reception.

"Hannah!"

She looked back across the arena. The White Fox had emerged from the skybox suite and was heading down to where Farran's girlfriend was still trying to lift him up. He might have been going to help, but there was something in his arms, black and bulky. A blanket…?

"What's he carrying?" Hannah asked.

"Damned if I—oh, hell." Russo turned to the people on his side of the aisle and pointed to the nearest guy. "You, get out in the hall, find a fire alarm and pull it."

"I'm not going to—"

"Now! I'm a cop and that's an order!"

The man nodded and ran up the steps.

"The rest of you," Russo said, "round up every cop or security guard you can find. Tell them a sheriff's detective said to get this building evacuated, fast!"

The others in the box scrambled out of their seats. As the woman who'd screamed tried to squeeze past, Hannah grabbed her by her sweater and handed over her cell phone. "See this number I've pulled up?" she said. "I want you to go outside and dial it until you get an answer. A live body, not a message machine. Tell the guy who picks up that Hannah said to get Gabriel out of the arena right away. Do you understand? Dammit, woman, answer me!"

The woman nodded. "All right, all right, I'll do it. Sheesh!"

She took the phone and Hannah let her pass. It was a long shot, but Cal had a different carrier than she did, and he'd definitely been using his phone in here the night of Gabe's birthday party. She could only pray that if the woman moved outside, she'd be out of the dead zone affecting Hannah's own service.

She raised the binoculars once more. Farran's girlfriend was frantic by now, screaming at Kenner. He laid down his load—it was almost certainly a suicide bomber's vest—then put one hand on the struggling girl's shoulder. His other hand pressed into her neck, and as it did, Hannah saw a glint of metal between his fingers.

"Russo, did you see that?"

"Yeah," he said grimly. A series of alarm whoops suddenly sounded and Russo had to yell to be heard over it. "He's got a palm blade. I'd say he just severed her spinal cord."

Kenner seemed startled by the alarm but he was a cool customer just the same. Keeping his hand on the girl's neck, he lowered her into her seat. As she slumped, an automated recording came over the PA system with evacuation instructions. Kenner then pulled Farran upright and settled him into the seat beside the girl.

Hannah unholstered her gun, gripped it with two hands, planted her feet and took aim.

Russo put a hand on her arm. "Forget it! It's no good with a handgun. We're out of range. You'll just hit an innocent bystander."

She hesitated, then nodded. "Let's go." They clambered up the steps and into the suite. "He won't detonate the bomb as long as he's in the building himself."

"You don't know that," Russo said.

"Yeah, I do." At the hall door, she grabbed Russo's arm and pointed across the way. "He's no suicide bomber. Look. He's planting the vest beside Farran. It's Farran who's meant to take the blame for this. The White Fox is a killer, but he's also a survivor—a bloody coward. I saw how he operates when I was in Iraq. He'll escape in the confusion, and then he'll set off the bomb from a distance."

"Then we'd better get to him first."

They moved into the hallway, where fans were streaming out of the skyboxes. A few were hurrying toward stairs and escalators, but most treating it like a joke or an annoyance, slouching resentfully ahead of prodding security guards. Shouts and laughter competed with the whooping alarm and the recorded loop of evacuation instructions.

"What a zoo," Hannah yelled. "Our only hope is to corner him on this level. Once he's outside, we'll never find him."

Russo pulled out his cell phone and glanced at the screen. "I've got a signal."

She grimaced. "I've really gotta change phone companies."

Russo hit speed dial. "I'm calling for backup. Meantime, you go that way, I'll go this. The building's a circle. We'll close in on him from both sides."

Hannah nodded, turned and started running.

Kenner was busy packing C-4 around the suite's pillars. That done, he stepped back down into the tiered seats and packed more there, staying out of the line of sight of the skyboxes around him, which were rapidly emptying, in any case.

He had to move fast. He'd hoped to have the luxury of setting this up at a more leisurely pace, letting anyone who happened to glance over at the slumped young couple presume they'd dozed off after too many trips to the minibar. Farran's death was bloodless and the girl's very nearly was, so efficiently had Kenner shut down her autonomous nervous system with a well-placed thrust of his palm blade just below her brain stem.

This fire alarm was disrupting his plans. Probably some kid had pulled it, but he had to presume the worst. He hadn't survived all these years by taking things for granted. Better to cut and run, even if there were loose ends.

The explosive-packed vest, for example. He would have preferred to put it on Farran's body. The forensics people really should find pieces of the young princeling on the inside of the thing and not just the outside. Otherwise, they might start asking awkward questions, and the next thing you knew, the conspiracy theorists would be having a free-for-all.

Too bad. It couldn't be helped. Anyway, he'd double-banked such a damning trail of evidence that no reasonable mind would doubt that the bombing of the Staples Center had been the work of Farran Al-saqri. Once detonated, the force of the explosives Kenner left behind would be enough to bring down most of that side of the building. Not as dramatic as 9/11, but one worked with what one had at hand.

Down on the court, players were milling around while referees, coaches and other officials conferred, trying to determine what was going on. The building was slowly beginning to drain of spectators, which was not at all convenient, from Kenner's perspective. In order for this gesture to have maximum impact, there had to be mass casualties. It was time for him to go.

He took one last look at his erstwhile employer. "Poor Mr. Farran. You won't grow up to be the Saudi Spielberg after all."

He bounded up the steps, back into the suite and out the door, leaving behind Farran's Italian leather bag. The bomb's remote detonator was in his hand. As the door to the suite whooshed shut behind him, Kenner joined the stream of exiting fans. Arriving firefighters might start checking the building, looking for people left behind, but the odds were slim that anyone would find Farran's and Irene's bodies before Kenner detonated the bomb.

A female security guard was directing traffic in the hall, standing on an upended beer crate, windmilling her arms like a Hong Kong traffic cop. "People! Head for the stairs! The escalators are backing up. You'll make better time on the staircases."

Kenner nodded obediently and moved along past the escalators. He felt like a cork bobbing in a flowing river of humanity, but his mission demanded that he get ahead of the wave and leave as many victims behind him as possible, so he stepped up the pace.

He was almost to the stairs when a woman's voice called out his name. "Kenner!"

He was startled, but he kept moving forward, never glancing around.

"George Kenner, or whatever the hell your real name is! Stop right there!"

Kenner's hand moved toward his weapon, but the crack of gunfire stopped him in his tracks. Glancing left and right, he found himself standing in a crowd that had hit the decks or was ducking and running for cover. He turned. Only two people remained upright in the immediate vicinity, Kenner and a dark-haired young woman. She stood about thirty feet ahead of him, just back of a spot where bits of tile and dust were falling from the ceiling. Her pistol was trained on Kenner now, and her double grip and spread-legged stance, one leg angled back, was classic police academy.

"That was a warning shot, Kenner. The next one goes through your heart, and I won't miss, believe me."

Her bravado was admirable. "Madam," Kenner said, "you seem to know me, but I don't think I've had the pleasure."

"Pleasure? I've had no pleasure at all where you're concerned. Taking you down tonight will be a nice change."

"Have we met?"

She nodded. "The road outside Al Zawra, two years ago. You'd kidnapped an American doctor, Amy Fitzgerald. I was one of the people who rescued her."

"Oh, my goodness. The madwoman in the burqa."

"At your service."

"But you are misinformed about her kidnapping, Miss...?"

"Hannah Nicks. You'll remember the name from here on in, I guarantee, especially after I testify against you. You're going down on several murder counts, starting with Farran Alsaqri and his girlfriend. You left them in that skybox along with a suicide bomber's vest."

"Really. Any other nasty deeds I'm supposed to be responsible for?" Kenner was much closer to the stairwell than she was. All he needed was a distraction.

"Your friend from the Russian consulate used his *mafiya* cronies to order up a hit on Damon Shipley. They made out the poor kid's murder to be just another gangbangers' turf war."

"Fascinating theory."

"And then there's Oz Nuñez," the woman said.

"I have no idea who that is." Kenner was watching the stairwell out of the corner of his eye. People from the upper skybox tier, unaware of what was transpiring on the middle level, were continuing to make their way down. The woman was behind the wall of the stairwell, out of their line of sight.

"Oswaldo Nuñez," she said. "He was a young security contractor in Iraq. It was he and I who yanked Amy Fitzgerald."

"I did not kidnap Dr. Fitzgerald," Kenner said. "I was merely trying to spirit her out of town on behalf of Sheikh Salahuddin and his injured men."

"You ambushed Nuñez and me afterwards on the Jordanian border. You shot my partner and he died of his wounds."

Just then, a little boy paused on the stairwell landing. It took a child, apparently, to wonder why one man was standing still while everyone else in the building was heading for the exits. The boy poked his head into the hall.

"Mom?"

"Gabe, no!" she yelled—too late.

Kenner grabbed him.

Russo was coming around the circular hallway from the opposite direction when he heard Hannah's yell. He ducked behind a pillar when he saw Kenner and Nicks standing face to face. Kenner had her son clamped by the neck in the viselike grip of his right arm. The boy's father was nowhere to be seen.

Kenner raised one closed fist. "I have the bomb detonator here in my hand. It's spring loaded. If I let it go, the trigger is released."

"Gabe, it's going to be all right," Nicks said. "Let him go, Kenner."

"I can't do that. Drop your weapon."

"Not a chance."

"Drop your weapon or I'll break his neck here and now."

"The place is crawling with cops. There's not a chance you can walk away from this. It's over."

She was right, Russo thought. The only reason she'd beaten him here was that he'd slowed to call for backup. But if Kenner really was holding a spring-release trigger on the detonator, it was going to be tricky to take him out without him dropping it and setting off the bomb.

"It's not over until I say it is," Kenner said. "This bomb must detonate."

"Then you'll have to go up with the place."

Kenner was silent for a moment. "Then so be it."

His shoulders rose with his resigned sigh. As they dropped again, Russo made eye contact with Nicks. She seemed to come to a decision.

"Kenner, all those people who ran out when I fired my gun," she said. "They'll have called 9-1-1 by now. This hallway will be swarming with SWAT units any second. Let my son go, and you and I can duck into one of the skyboxes. You can even barricade the door if you want. We can talk. I'll help you negotiate a deal. You don't have to die here."

Gabriel, Kenner's arm still around his neck, stood very still as the man considered.

"I have a better idea," Kenner said. "The boy will come with us. We're going back to Farran's box."

"You don't need him."

"Oh, yes, I think I do, if for no other reason than to make sure you behave yourself. Now, drop your weapon and let's go."

Nicks bent her knees and laid her gun on the thick carpet. Kenner cocked his head, signaling her to precede him and the boy back along the hall. Russo ducked out of sight. He thought he understood what Nicks was thinking. It was just a matter of whether he would have the time he needed to set it up—time, and the right weaponry.

"Are you all right, sweetie?" Hannah asked Gabe as they entered Farran's skybox.

He nodded—not an easy thing to do with a killer gripping his windpipe.

"That's my guy." She looked back up at Kenner. "Would you let him go now?"

"Not yet."

"What do I have to do?"

"There's a vest down in the seats, next to Farran and the girl," he said. "Go and get it."

She nodded. The bodies of the director and his girlfriend were propped against one another in their seats. A small bloodstain on the back of the girl's blue cashmere sweater was the only indication they weren't sleeping. Hannah was grateful for small mercies. Gabe was a smart kid. He'd know what was what here, but all the same...

Her gaze traveled across the arena to the skyboxes on the opposite side. They were empty by now, but with any luck at all, they wouldn't be for long. Russo would know what he had to do. Her job was to keep the White Fox's attention away from that side of the building.

"Hurry up!" Kenner snapped.

The canvas vest, studded with nails, its pockets stuffed with packets of an oily, claylike material, was tucked into the armrest between the two bodies. She wrestled the thing loose and carried it back into the suite. Kenner backed himself up against the buffet, dragging Gabe along with him. Hannah laid the vest down on the low coffee table.

"Push these armchairs in front of the door," Kenner said.

"Couldn't we just lock it?"

"There is no lock."

"Right you are," Hannah said. She started tugging on one of the upholstered chairs, inching it across the room.

"Speed it up," Kenner said.

"A little help would be nice."

"You can manage. You're not such a weakling. You seem to forget, I've seen you in action."

"Touché." Hannah moved faster—a little. It took her a few minutes to get the chairs piled and wedged against the door according to his instructions. Finally, she straightened. "Now let him go, Kenner."

"The vest. Put it on."

"Let my son go."

"Not yet. Put it on."

"Why are you doing this?"

"I have my reasons."

"You're not American, are you?"

"No, I'm not."

"Your English is perfect but I don't think it's your first language, is it?"

"No. Put on the vest."

"I'm just curious." She moved around the coffee table and settled on the sofa. Pulling the heavy vest toward her, she started undoing the buckles. "What's the harm in telling me where you're from?"

Kenner pushed off from the buffet and moved back into the middle of the room. "I'm from a great nation with a noble history and a long memory. We don't appreciate being treated like a backwater. We never have."

"I can understand that."

"We have vast resources and the skills to develop them. And unlike you spoiled Americans, we also know how to survive hardship. We've done it many times, but we always emerge triumphant. We've had some reversals of late, but we're on our way to becoming a great power again. Allied with other countries as rich in resources as we are, we'll be a force to be reckoned with. America's short reign as the only superpower is fast coming to an end."

Hannah nodded. "Ah, I see. You're Russian."

"Very good, Ms. Nicks."

Gabe squirmed.

"Could you loosen your grip on him?" Hannah asked. "Maybe let him come over here and sit next to me? Much as I hate to admit it, it looks like we're not going anywhere. You've got the detonator, so that makes you man of the hour."

"I'll release him when you've put on the vest."

"Don't do it, Mom!"

"It's okay, sweetie."

"Leave my mom alone!"

Gabe struggled. Kenner squeezed his windpipe until the boy began to gasp.

"Your mother, young man, should have left *me* alone."

Hannah jumped to her feet. "Stop it!"

"Put on the damn vest!"

"I'm doing it, just leave him alone!" She grabbed it off the table and struggled to flip the thing around, putting first one arm and then the other through the armholes.

"Do it up!"

Gabe's face had gone red and his beautiful blue eyes were brimming. Hannah fumbled with the long straps and buckles.

"Let him go, goddammit!" she cried, tears running down her cheeks. She threw her arms out to the sides. "There! It's done!"

Kenner loosened his grip a little. "Sit down," he ordered.

Hannah dropped onto the sofa.

"In just a moment," Kenner said, "the boy and I are going to leave. There's a telephone over on the side table beside you."

Hannah glanced over. Sure enough, there was.

"It's just an internal line, but I'm sure the operator can patch us through to the police. You'll tell them to have a helicopter waiting for me."

"Where do you want it to take you?"

"Not your concern. If you do as I say, then when I get outside, I'll let the boy go."

"What about my mom?" Gabe croaked.

Kenner shook his head. "I'm afraid your mom has caused me far too much grief. Now, I need her to stay here and serve as an object lesson."

"What does that mean?" Gabe asked.

Kenner bent down and murmured in his ear. "It means, sonny, that like every good captain, Mom is going down with the ship."

"It's okay, Gabe," Hannah said. "You just get out of here, okay?"

"Make the call," Kenner told her.

At that moment, Hannah's heart soared. A bead of red laser light had appeared on Kenner's right temple. Russo must have gotten the SWAT unit set up in one of the skyboxes across the way.

"I'll make the call," Hannah said, "but can I give my son one last kiss first?"

Kenner shook his head. The sniper's targeting beam lit his white hair like a Christmas light against snow. But if he turned now, he would surely spot the sniper, and the game would be up.

"I put on your damn vest, Kenner! You said you'd release him when I did. For God's sake, didn't you ever have a mother?"

"Oh, low blow." Kenner shook his head, bemused. He glanced down at Gabe. "Fine. Give your mother a kiss and say goodbye. Then, she's going to make the call, and you and I will be on our way."

Hannah stepped around the coffee table toward the hall door so that when Kenner turned, his guard up against any sudden moves on her part, his back was to the arena. She stood in front of the chairs piled in front of the door, arms out to her sides.

"See? Nothing up my sleeve."

Kenner nudged Gabe toward her.

It all happened in a split second. As her brain registered the flash of the sniper's muzzle on the far side of the arena, she shoved her son to the floor, then leapt at Kenner's hand holding the bomb's remote. Cupping her hands around his, Hannah squeezed tight, and she and Kenner crumpled together in a heap on the carpet.

And then, it was over. He was dead. She wasn't.

41

Monday, February 7, 2005
The Golden Dragon Restaurant, Los Angeles

Hannah couldn't get over how many people were Lakers fans. Everywhere she went, people recognized her as the woman who'd faced down the Staples Center bomber. Even the owner of her favorite *dim sum* restaurant was grateful she and Russo had saved the home of the city's basketball heroes.

"Oh, Miss Hannah, so good to see you!" Mrs. Lee said the following Monday when Hannah showed up for lunch at the Golden Dragon with Russo and Val Underwood. She pumped Hannah's hand, then turned, beaming, to Russo.

"And you are Detective Russo! You are very welcome! You and Miss Hannah, you come to Golden Dragon, you sit at lucky table number eight. Your money no good here! My family big Laker fans! Also big fans of you!"

Russo grinned. "Thank you very much. I appreciate that. I'll take all the lucky tables I can get, but I'd better pay for my lunches or I'll be in big trouble with the sheriff."

Mrs. Lee laughed. She was about four foot eight, and she had to stretch to pat him on the back. "Detective Russo very lucky for business, too!" she said, grinning at Hannah.

After they were seated at lucky table eight, had had their picture taken with Mrs. Lee and her staff, received congratulations and thanks from a few other patrons, and then finally started to dig into the restaurant's rolling trolleys of delight, Underwood turned to Russo.

"Speaking of lucky," she said, "how lucky was it that Kenner didn't actually have a spring-loaded switch on that bomb remote? Otherwise, that sniper shot might have taken out half the Staples Center, along with poor Hannah and Gabe."

"Yeah, I had a nervous few minutes worrying about that," Russo admitted. "When the SWAT team showed up with the high-powered rifles and scopes, we tried like hell to get a close look at the switch in his hand, but no dice."

"I hear they left the call up to you, in the end," Val said.

Russo nodded. "Yeah, but Hannah really had Kenner pegged."

"How's that?"

"She told me when we spotted Kenner in Farran's skybox that for all his ruthlessness, the guy was a coward. He wasn't going to take a chance on getting blown up by his own bomb. He intended to be blocks away before he set it off, so the odds were it was a conventional switch."

"After all," Hannah said, "what if Kenner had accidentally tripped on that ego of his?"

She cradled her teacup between her palms, frowning at the leaves in the bottom.

"Hannah?" Russo asked. "Are you okay?"

"Yeah. I was just thinking about Oz Nuñez. I'm glad we got the guy who murdered him, but it still doesn't change the fact that if it hadn't been for me, Oz would never have died in the first place."

Russo nodded. "I know. I feel the same way about Billy Chen. If I'd handled things differently, he'd still be alive."

"Listen, you guys," Underwood said, "I know you're grieving for your partners, but this Kenner/Kirnikov guy caused a whole world of hurt to a lot of innocent people and their families—Oz and Billy, Damon Shipley, Farran Alsaqri and his girlfriend, and God knows how many others. He would've killed a lot more people at the Staples Center the other night, too, if you two hadn't stopped him in his tracks."

"I wonder if he really expected to make it out of there once he knew he'd been made," Russo said.

"He'd escaped tight spots before. Probably thought he was invincible." Hannah shrugged. "Or maybe he was just getting old and losing his edge."

"He obviously had people in the Russian consulate watching his back," Russo said.

"The night of Gabe's birthday party when I first spotted the White Fox," Hannah said, "he and that spy from the consulate must have been scouting the Staples Center as a possible bomb site."

Underwood speared an egg roll with her chopsticks. "Poor Farran Alsaqri. Who knew being a Lakers fan would turn out to be a deadly obsession? And speaking of that guy from the consulate," she added, "he's been declared *persona non grata* and is winging his way back to Moscow as we speak."

"I hear people are asking tough questions in Congress about how a thug like Kenner got an immigration visa," Hannah said. "Somebody in the administration's going to have to fall on their sword over this one."

Russo nodded. "Good. They should. How's Gabe?"

"He's going to be okay. His larynx was bruised, but there's no permanent damage. Nothing physical, anyway. Emotionally, I'm not sure. I'm going to have to keep a close eye on that."

"Pretty scary stuff for a ten-year-old," Russo said.

"Yeah, but he was still ready to take on Kenner to protect his mom. What a guy. Oh, by the way," Hannah added, grimacing, "did you hear where Cal was while my son was being taken hostage?"

Russo shook his head.

"He'd left Gabe with his clients in the skybox while he ran to get the cell phone he said he'd left in the car. Only it turns out he'd actually gone courtside to chat up a Laker Girl. Then, when the fire alarm went off, the guards wouldn't let him back upstairs."

"It showed up on the security tapes," Underwood said. "There's good ol' Cal, canoodling with some redhead."

"Whoops. Busted," Russo said.

Val helped herself to some rice. "What a schmuck!"

Just then, somebody's cell phone rang. Half the people in the restaurant scrambled for pockets and purses. Russo won the lottery. He glanced at the screen on his phone. "Sorry," he said, getting to his feet, "I'd better take this."

Hannah watched him walk to the door, wishing he'd just turn around and walk back. Stupid. She barely knew the guy. Maybe that was going to change, but maybe not, too. She had to earn a living, and when she wasn't preoccupied with that, she was trying to spend more time with Gabe. And Russo, for his part, was a homicide detective. Their time was never their own. A guy like that needed a woman who was a lot more flexible than she could be—and a guy like that wouldn't have to look very hard to find one, either.

She turned back, only to find Underwood grinning at her. "What?"

"So?" Underwood's eyebrows danced.

"So what?"

"How's it going?" Underwood smacked her arm. "Don't go all coy on me, girl. With Russo, of course."

"This is the first time I've seen him since the Staples Center! I was tied up with Gabe all weekend."

"Oh, yeah, right, I believe that. I can see how he's looking at you. Besides which," Underwood added, "if you haven't seen him, how did he know to meet you here for lunch today?"

"Well, maybe there have been a few phone conversations," Hannah conceded.

"How very Jane-Austen-meets-the-twenty-first-century. So what does that make me? Your chaperone?"

"He said he hadn't seen you in ages, so I invited him to come along."

"Yeah, right. Well, you go, girl."

"I have no idea if I'm going anywhere at all." Hannah shook her head. "I don't think I'm ready to start something right now, Val."

"Hey! You know how you always say I got the last good guy in L.A.? I'm here to tell you, girlfriend, there's at least one more, and he's been sitting next to you for the past half hour, devouring spring rolls and you. And look at it this way," Underwood added, lowering her voice to a whisper as they caught sight of Russo coming back in the door, "he's gotta be a better role model for Gabe than Cal is."

"That's true." Hannah watched the role model settle back in his chair. A pretty appealing model he was, too. "Everything okay?"

Russo nodded. "That was my lieutenant. I'm supposed to go in later this afternoon, meet my new partner."

"Anyone you know?"

"Nope. Some new guy. Halloran wants me to train him up." He shook his head. "Something about getting back on the horse."

"Well, for my books," Hannah said, "that's one lucky trainee."

Russo smiled, while Val Underwood sat back in her chair, looking very smug. As another trolley approached, Underwood tapped Russo on the arm.

"Order up some barbecued pork buns," she told him, grinning. "I happen to know they're Hannah's favorite."

Russo seemed pleased to comply.